Myron W. Wepper

August 20, 1977

731 McRoberts St.,
Mason, Mich.

The Tooth Merchant

Books by C. L. Sulzberger

THE Tooth Merchant

A NOVEL BY

C. L. SULZBERGER

Quadrangle Books

Library of Congress Catalogue Card Number: 72-88881
International Standard Book Number: 0-8129-0268-8
DESIGNED BY VINCENT TORRE

For Marina
whose love and tolerance
and understanding
transcend anything in fiction

"Dentists of the world, unite!"

PAREGORICUS

*None of the characters
and all of the events
described in this Cold War episode
are real*

The Tooth Merchant

CHAPTER

I

THE foulest brothels in Europe, and I know them all, are on Abanoz Street in the Pera district of Istanbul and there I was sleeping one late summer morning in 1952 beside a Turkish whore named Iffet with a cunt as broad as the mercy of Allah when suddenly there was a scream at the door followed by a thump on the stairs. "Aaaaaaiiiiieeee, the American fleet," moaned Iffet, hauling the flyblown sheet about her head as the police burst in.

We Armenians have a poem which says "From my soul I wish to wash off the dust" and this perhaps is what I may have felt when I rolled over and stared with my unbruised left eye at the three intruders, just barely able to squeeze below the lintel, large men with big bellies and thick necks, wearing military uniform, one with a gendarme's insigne.

"Sasounian," said the first. "Kevork Sasounian?"

"Who wants to know and why?"

"Birinci Buro," grunted the reply. "Come with us."

I knew the Birinci or First Bureau of the police and regretted it. The First Bureau dealt with espionage and it was not gentle. During the War, when my parents were threatened with forced labor under the Varlik law that sought to wipe out Jews and Christians, I had saved my family by performing favors for the First Bureau. It valued the fact that I, the son of a linguistics teacher, spoke seventeen languages, frequented the Levantine underworld, and was reputed to be without scruple. The last, of course, is not the truth.

"The war's been over seven years," I growled, "thanks to the timely intervention of the glorious Turkish army. And the Varlik's dead. I want no more of you."

Bang came the gendarme's billy. A karpuz-shaped knob suddenly began to sprout on my shaven head.

Karpuz is what the Turks call watermelon.

We Armenians call it tzemerouk.

Iffet, which means chastity, moaned again, pulling the rest of the sheet around her immense and glabrous body. I stumbled naked on to the unvarnished floor, gathered up my clothes, and stated with huge sincerity:

"May your truncheon take root in your orifice and become a cactus." Bam, bam went the billy, accurately aimed at the fast-growing karpuz-tzemerouk.

Two of them bent my right arm, forcing me to stoop, while the third carved a passage through the happy crowd of youngsters and old women gathered like a shrewdness of apes amid the garbage just outside. There was a stink of dead fish. They shoved me along the cobbles to an army car. Above the bubbling uproar Iffet hollered: "Where are my twenty lira, dirty dogs?"

We screeched down Balo Sokagi, Ball Street, and pulled up at a gloomy, granolithic building near the waterfront. I was led between the sentries, shoved past a sergeant who seemed to be expecting us, joined by a trim young captain, marched through a parvis, and halted before an office with no name on the door. The captain knocked respectfully; we entered.

A woman secretary nodded and pointed to another room. There, two wooden-like colonels, one of whom I knew from my experience with the Birinci Buro, were planted before a great desk. Behind it lolled a plump dark civilian. Above, hanging on the wall, were stilted photographs of Kemal Ataturk and Ismet Inönü, heroes to Turks but not to Armenians.

"Naci Perkel," announced the civilian in elegant accents, rising unexpectedly and waving me to a chair. To my astonishment he signalled the captain and my guards to leave, offered me a Yenice cigarette, raised his eyebrows at the colonels and continued: "You know these two gentlemen already, I am told. As for me, it should not be a secret that I am Chief of Milli Emniyet, the National Security Service. And you," he said, calling me Gentleman George in English, "I am most interested to encounter you, the Armenian Lexicon." Kevork is Armenian for George.

"Yes," I replied, "as a very young woman my mother wrote a thesaurus. Before she came home to be raped by a Turkish soldier." There was a distinct silence. I added, "I assure you there is no Turkish blood in my veins."

It may surprise that one of our noble Armenian race, blessed with the brain of philosophers and the body of heroes, educated in fine schools and endowed with gifts for drawing, music and what is said to be an exceptional ear for foreign tongues, should discover himself in such woeful circumstances. However, since I was taught the value of sex at the age of ten by a one-armed German housemaid with a gimp in her left leg who also introduced me to shoplifting, my life has been richer than most. My father used to say: "Kevork, if this continues you will go to jail some day." He did not, as did my mother, know that I had already spent one summer holiday in reform school or Erziehungsheim, as they call it in Germany. Maybe we Armenians are born unlucky.

Nevertheless, to say I was puzzled by my present circumstances is the least of it. I tried to look as self-possessed as possible for a man with a two-day hangover, a three-day growth of beard, a blacked eye from a bar-fight, a club-bump on the noggin, no necktie, and a sordid mixture of ashes, raki stains, and vestigial vomit decorating a jacket which at best was neither clean nor tailor-made.

"I want your help, Sasounian," continued Naci Bey with suave courtesy. "And what is more, I mean to have it." The colonels regarded me silently, their eyes mirroring no heaven.

"Why me?" I inquired. "And why you? What have I done? There is nothing that concerns the authorities. Peccadilloes and tracasseries, perhaps," I admitted, proudly exhibiting my rich vocabulary even in the unspeakable Turkish language, "but peccadilloes unworthy of either your distinguished attentions or those of the Birinci Buro."

Naci said nothing. Colonel Number One stolidly reached to a coign of the desk for his well-waxed briefcase. He extracted a paper folder bearing an official stamp and what looked like a series of initials in Arabic, an alphabet Turkish officials are no longer supposed to use.

Impassively, the colonel called out in amphorous tones: "Selling heroin to United States sailors. Complaint from Washington on basis of report from special Treasury agent Violet. 1945. April. Gold smuggling to Marseilles. Arrested by French Sureté. Released on turning state's evidence. 1951, suspected smuggling Rumanian refugee girls into Istanbul en route for Sultan's harem in Oman. 1950. Involvement in Zionist underground. Handed over Bulgarian Jews to Syrian government representatives at Aleppo . . . for a fee. Mixed in Baluchistan slave trade . . . Breaking and entering . . . Disorderly conduct . . . Suspected rape . . . Forgery. Five charges . . . And so forth, Naci Bey. Do you want more?"

Naci Bey focused his basilisk eyes. "Would you wish these charges to be raised formally?" he wondered. "The police of this tolerant city tell me that if your recent escapades are brought to court it will be possible to resurrect every incident in this file. That would qualify you for forty years' hard labor."

Colonel Number Two added in a feral voice: "Kevork, we were kind to your parents during that misunderstanding on the Varlik. We were kind because of your willingness to cooperate in the national interest.

"But, while you know we harbor no prejudice against Armenans (sniff), it is well for you to realize that we are aware of your father's activities in the bazaar. That fifteen-year-old Tartar virgin he furnished the American naval attaché. Not what we call antique business.

"Would you wish your father to go off to Anatolia again? He is no longer young. And the pay was never good."

I shrugged my shoulders, nodded, and remarked: "As the proverb says, he who is born on a goose-feather bed will all his life a wanderer be. We had geese in the village of our grandparents. All right. What do you want me to do?"

Naci lifted the ivory telephone at his elbow and ordered four unsweetened coffees, a sign of disciplined habits in view of the Turkish love for sugar. The coffees must have been ready because the woman secretary immediately brought them in on a small brass tray.

Then the first colonel arose, marched to the wall facing the window and pulled down a large-scale roller map. It was marked TOP SECRET (NATO COSMIC) and, in red, overprinted, ÇOK GIZLI. For me, as an Armenian, the map was easy to identify because it embraced our homeland on the Soviet-Turkish border as well as Russia's Caucasus republics.

"What you are now about to hear," said Naci Bey, "is so highly classified that any leakage would be considered treason. The punishment for treason makes other measures mentioned by the colonel seem like a piece of baklava."

He leaned across the desk, reached for a memorandum pad, and held it in an unusually smooth, pale hand. His face was bland, expressionless, like that of a poker player with four knaves.

"I am advised, Sasounian, by the files of Birinci Buro, that you are a remarkable linguist, a genius of a sort, Armenian and Turkish, of course. But also, without accent, Russian, Georgian, the Azerbaijani, Kurdish, Adzharian and Abkhazian dialects. English, French, German, Arabic, Persian, Albanian. Greek, both classical and demotic. Italian. I suppose there may be others. Azerbaijani and Kurdish are scarcely languages to be included in the seventeen with which you're credited."

Even both colonels looked impressed.

The head of Milli Emniyet continued: "You are a bum and unsuccessful crook. Yet you are surely the world's most brilliant bum and most flamboyantly unsuccessful crook. I am astonished that a man with your brains now finds himself in so lamentable a situation. Your father once was a philologist?"

"Full professor, University of Tübingen."

"Today he is a pettifogger. And—I mean no offense but let us speak the truth—his only son is, shall we say. . . ."

"A chicaner?"

"However, you are reputed to be endowed amazingly in some strange ways: courageous, unreliable, lazy, with a lyceum education and wholly without morals.

"You were discharged from Robert College faculty for interfering with the boys?"

"Turkish civilization brews Turkish habits, Excellency," I observed.

Naci Bey ignored this, saying: "You will permit me to add that

[7

nothing in your record shows you to be an unusually patriotic citizen of the Republic.

"I confess to a certain understanding of your view, even if I don't approve it. You Armenians are not without grounds for complaint. Therefore I think it wise to emphasize," and emphasized, tapping the folder listing my alleged misdeeds, "that possibly this record should persuade you to some degree of Turkish chauvinism—dictated by your head if not your heart. Your head, from all accounts, is excellent." He focused on the watermelon with a thanatoid expression.

"What we want," he continued, "is so incredibly important that we have determined to insure your permanent cooperation—at least so long as your father, your mother, and your two sisters are alive and here.

"You will recognize that no discourtesy is intended when I remind you, albeit bluntly, that your family is considered hostage for your good behavior while you are abroad. We shall protect them very, very well until you are back home."

"Abroad? Back home?"

"Abroad," Naci Bey repeated.

"You are not, I presume, a military expert," he added, "despite the help with which you once obliged these gentlemen (nodding at the colonels). Nor do I imagine you even realize Turkey is now a member of the NATO alliance led by the United States. Therefore, I suggest you listen most carefully to the following.

"In September, 1949—more than four years after the Americans —the Russians exploded their first atomic bomb. We are told Moscow is now experimenting with a thermonuclear weapon, and will be ready to detonate it in about a year."

"What's that?" I asked with mild curiosity.

"A thermonuclear device is so deadly that its relationship to an atomic bomb is approximately that of an atomic bomb to TNT. Can you grasp the significance?"

I looked blank.

"Even I do not comprehend the terms myself," said Naci Bey. "But NATO wants to know if Russia is really preparing to test what experts call a 'dry' device. Because this test would bypass and outmode American experiments with a 'wet' device.

8]

"The Americans are developing a brand new set of weapons based on the fusion of two minerals called tritium and duterium. But the Russians are said to be leapfrogging them by producing a superbomb based only on uranium.

"This is entirely possible because uranium is easily available to Moscow. There are rich deposits in Czechoslovakia at Jachimov, which are operated entirely by Soviet officials with Soviet security forces. Everything is under the direction of Comrade Beria, who, as the most powerful member of Stalin's Politburo, controls the police, the secret services, and the growing atomic weapons industry."

Naci Bey arose and said, "And now we come to your assignment." He strode over to the wall-map, took a pointer from the colonel's hand, and indicated an area.

"This is Lake Sevan," he said. "In the Armenian Soviet Socialist Republic as I undoubtedly need not add. And here," he continued, moving the pointer slightly southward, "is the Razdan or Sanga river, flowing toward Erivan.

"We have reports that Beria has built an underground factory there. To produce fissionable materials from uranium.

"This project could be of fatal importance to Turkey and Turkey's allies. Your job is to learn all you can about it and to inform us. Details will be given later.

"In any case, let me tell you what we believe. We think six subterranean caverns have been scooped from hillsides in the Razdan valley north of Erivan. Near the villages of Kanagiri, Akhti, Giumush, and Sanchigay. We will familiarize you with these names—in the next few days.

"We hear that some half million cubic meters of hard rock had to be blasted and removed from the basalt massif on the left bank of the Razdan to make space for installations. It should therefore be possible to confirm if something serious is taking place.

"To produce fissionable material, immense amounts of electric power are needed. The Razdan is a logical site. Despite its nearness to our border.

"Since 1932 a series of hydroelectric stations have been constructed in the area. A high voltage network has been built up; estimated minimal power 300,000 kilowatts.

[9

"Until four years ago this network supplied energy for almost all the Armenian republic's industry. However, we now hear the bulk of this power is being channeled into the new atomic project. Regular industry is rationed on a makeshift basis linked to local stations while other hydroelectric plants are developed.

"One thing to keep an eye on is housing, permanent or otherwise. Available billeting facilities have been very limited in the past. They were strained to handle returning Armenian refugees from America—and Turkey," he added with the hint of an ineffable smile.

"To explain the sudden influx of personnel, the Russians are said to be advertising a series of expeditions, hydrological surveys, and cinematic enterprises."

At this point Naci pileoled his left ear and quite deliberately regarded the wax on his little finger. He continued:

"We must confirm whether these reports are indeed exact. That is primordial. It will not be easy to pick up information despite the project's massive scale. The Razdan valley between the Alagez and Kanakiri mountains has been declared prohibited. Both uniformed and secret representatives of Beria's security apparatus maintain constant watch.

"This is the most urgent of the tasks we require of you. But once you have made an initial investigation we have more in mind. You will receive subsequent instructions from designated agents.

"For the present, find out if a deadly power complex to make weapons of mass-destruction has been established on our frontier. The location may seem an unnecessary risk for the Russians. But Beria, we understand, insisted. He wished to avoid delays involved in building sufficiently large thermal stations planned for Siberia.

"That region is strategically safer and harder for NATO to investigate. Stalin didn't like such a vast undertaking near our border—especially since President Truman promised U.S. military support for Turkey. But time was the decisive factor. Apart from time, more overriding elements favored Armenia.

"The railway system from the main Soviet European network through Tbilisi and southward is convenient. Uranium ore from Saxony, in the Soviet zone of Germany, and from Jachimov, is already being shipped to the Razdan region. And Soviet mineralogists have discovered uranium deposits north of Tbilisi—here," he demonstrated with the pointer, "in Ossetia, and here, in Svanetia, the northwest corner of Georgia.

"These ores are being processed and sent where you are going. Furthermore, enormous masses of machinery have been transferred from East Germany to the same area and are now being installed by Russian and East German experts.

"So you see what we want. The precise signs to watch for will be explained by our scientific counsellors. And by those of our allies. But it must be obvious that immense developments of this sort cannot be wholly and indefinitely hidden. This is indicated by reports already received."

"Why do you need me to check them?" I inquired sceptically.

"The trouble is that aerial reconnaissance is inadequate," said Naci Bey. "The Russians are experts at camouflage. And they have strengthened their anti-aircraft defenses to an appalling degree.

"It is not an indiscretion to tell you, since Moscow knows it, that we have lost four planes in the border region during recent weeks. What we want is a resourceful, well-briefed, adaptable man on the scene itself. You, my dear Sasounian, are that man."

I swallowed hard and rubbed my unshaven chin, feeling the bubo beneath the whiskers covering my tonsil. "And if I am not that man? What you want, Naci Bey, is an avatar."

"Should you succeed, this file will be destroyed. And you will be generously rewarded. Or your family, in case of accident. Should you fail . . ." He shrugged and aimed the pointer at my dossier lying open on his desk.

"Ah well," I said. "You Turks have always been hard masters. Your ancestor, the Hittite King of Carcamesh, had a favorite saying: 'There was a man. He was five years in jail. When they told him, tomorrow we let you out, he strangled himself.'"

CHAPTER

II

EVERYONE knows a Greek is brighter than a Turk, a Jew is brighter than a Greek, and an Armenian is brighter than a Jew, but only an expert such as myself knows that a Dönme is even brighter than an Armenian.

The Dönme is the Turkish Jew who was converted to Islam so many generations ago and whose habits are so furtive that no one is now sure whether he is a Moslem secretly practicing Judaism or a Jew publicly practicing Mohammedanism.

To my shrewd eye it was evident that Ahmed Emin Bey, in whose care I was placed for briefing, was indeed a Dönme although naturally he couldn't admit as much: an earnest little man with insect eyes, large ears, the nose of a fishhook, whose tightly held lips were roofed by a toothbrush mustache.

I never did know his last name so I had no chance to confirm my suspicions about his origin, suspicions that certainly ran contrary to the habits of Milli Emniyet which, when it was not blackmailing idiots like me into the dirtier branches of espionage, preferred to hire only fullblooded Sunni Turks.

Under Ahmed Emin's supervision I was installed in a small villa close to Rumeli Hissar on a verdant height above the fast-running Bosphorus. My physical wants were tended by a massive, perspiring peasant woman with a fine sense of smell; you could smell her for miles. Her odor was so pungent and her beam was so broad that my prick was never tempted to penetrate her secret despite the enforced abstinence of its condition.

The gate to our establishment was both chained and padlocked; the surrounding walls were high; the gardener had marked off the lawn with a bilboquet; and from my upstairs bedroom I could occasionally spot, under the brachiate trees, unmistakeable gendarmes seeking, in mufti, to masquerade as human beings.

Ahmed Emin Bey saw to it that I was decently clothed (by no means easy for a man of my stature), cleaned, barbered, fed, poked about by medical specialists, and educated in the various arts of forging false papers, coding and decoding, demolitions, silent close combat, and other basic culture.

I was also given intense map-reading and terrain study instruction on the Soviet border area and the trans-Caucasus. Language experts tested my accents in different tongues. And I was painstakingly lectured on current economic, political, social and athletic events in the southern Soviet Republics and autonomous regions so that I should be able to acquit myself in superficial interrogations concerning local personalities.

An unctuous tailor, with a miniature anadem pinned to his lapel, brought me a badly cut suit of gray, striped cloth, and told me it was made in Georgia at the factory in Tbilisi. "Here," he said, "good Russian material. Trouser bottoms that an elephant could walk in." When I had been completely dressed in well-worn articles of Soviet manufacture, topped by a visored cap, the tailor stood back, regarding me with satisfaction:

"There. How handsome. Six feet two inches. It was difficult to find the proper fit for you, my eagle. I am not supposed to guess where you are bound for. But their hearts will flutter, those plump little doves."

"Stop the chatter," commanded Ahmed Emin who had been watching this performance.

One day I was taken to the office where Perkel had first received me and there introduced to a tall Englishman wearing a gray suit with turned-up cuffs at the sleeves. A monocle was fixed into his mazarine right eye and his hair was slightly curled. Nevertheless, his bearing and fierce mustache were obviously military and he followed the Scottish tradition of leaving unshaven the hair below his cheekbones.

"This is Mr. Smith," said Ahmed Emin Bey. "He will tell you something about Soviet security methods and what you should watch out for." It was clear that Mr. Smith was an Allied Intelligence officer.

Mr. Smith said that in an area of vital importance it was entirely possible that some of the top Soviet counter-espionage leadership might be near the vicinity. He therefore produced blown-up photographs of several of these men and added details about personal characteristics. I was instructed to commit what I could to memory:

Semen Denisovich Ignatiev, appointed last year as head of the MGB and controller of all secret police as well as espionage and disinformation abroad. Mr. Smith was certain that any Razdan installation required Ignatiev's personal attentions. Sergei Nikiforovich Kruglov, boss of the MVD. His talents as an operator of slave labor camps were vital to the new atomic installations in the U.S.S.R. and also the uranium mines in Czechoslovakia and occupied East Germany. Kruglov had organized the secret killer outfit, SMERSH: a well-decorated man in cavalry boots with wide mouth, cleft chin and unusually white skin.

I was told about the Army Intelligence Service, the GRU, under General Mikhail Alekseivich Shalin. They were trying to stave off Beria's efforts to subordinate them to the police.

Mr. Smith explained: "Normally it would be unlikely for the GRU to become involved in administering or even maintaining security for this kind of project. However, there have been reports that it is trying now to muscle in on MGB territory. Until now GRU has carefully avoided internal politics. We are therefore most interested to get any clues on this."

He then brought from his attaché case another set of photographs, also enlarged, one of which was stamped, "SS." "Sovershennoe Sekretno," said Mr. Smith. "Top Secret. These officers are also most important but are very little known," he said. "Keep an eye out for them. They are the aides. No top Russian in this business goes anywhere alone. They are guarded by the Ninth Guards Directorate of the MGB and each has a special witness assigned to him in case of subsequent investigation. I suggest you study these with special concentration."

After Mr. Smith had left, Ahmed Emin diligently tested me on recognition of the Soviet officials, using projector slides and showing them in civilian clothes amid groups. He supervised a primary course on the shape and size of atomic manufacturing installations. These were demonstrated with American slides stamped "A.E.C." One of his assistants refreshed my rather limited expertise in forging.

I was given a crash course in explosives, mine detecting and astral navigation, and then an army sergeant demonstrated how to traverse defended positions, in this case forbidden frontiers. A bulky man built like a neckless gnu, showed me how to roll lengthwise over ploughed strips of land and thus minimize tracks, how to walk backward, weight on the toes, in order to leave a trail leading in the wrong direction, how to test with a twig or strong reed for the presence of trip wires, how to prod with a sliver of metal for mines and hidden pitfalls.

After three weeks I received a final examination from the Milli Emniyet physician who pronounced me fit, handed me a bottle of finely ground pepper with which to put off border dogs should I be forced to flee them, and also offered a tiny plastic phial, explaining that I should tape this under my armpit before leaving Turkey. Were I picked up and were I to recognize the situation as hopeless—which in the former event would be more than likely —I could slip this into my mouth and, if there appeared to be no other way out, I might escape torture by crushing it between my teeth. Death would be instantaneous. Ahmed Emin, who was present during the colloquy, added: "Inshallah, this is a precaution you will never need."

For an Armenian, from the oldest Christian nation, to depend on Allah, I thought! I remembered the words of our great hero, Mher: "May you always be thirsty and wander hungry! May you be without children, without heirs! May you call upon death and not find it till the time when Christ comes to give judgment upon you!" I said to myself: "Ahmed Emin, may Allah be unable to protect you against that curse."

Little did I then know that my flamboyant period as a Turkish spy, blackmailed into unwilling servitude, would lead me to the threshold of sorcery, to four continents, that it would produce a miraculous discovery, contribute to Great Stalin's death, to the threatened burning of Cairo, to a chance to alter the course of guerrilla warfare in Cyprus, and almost change the science of twentieth-century military planning, conventional and otherwise, by posing the problem directly to President Eisenhower. Moreover, it would occasion the greatest mass murder since Genghis Khan and Hitler—although this crime hitherto has never been revealed. But neither Christ nor Allah could, in the end, protect me from our Armenian hero's malediction.

On a late September afternoon in Ankara I was taken to the railway station by Colonel Refik of the Milli Emniyet, a short, thin, dapper man with taut features, a mouth cruelly downturned at the corners and sheltered behind a neatly trimmed mustache. His oiled black hair grew thickly back from a low forehead and his eyes were like coals, heavy, dull-gleaming.

Hot afternoons have I seen in Jidda, in Alexandria, in Naples, in Tangiers and in our own steaming marshes off the Adana coast but this one was as memorable for its torridity as for the extraordinary events which followed.

I had flown with Colonel Refik from Istanbul through leaden clouds lumbering like whales above the Anatolian plateau. He was dressed in neat civilian clothes. I wore a U.S. sack suit, provided by my new official tailor, and carried a valise holding my two false identities—a double-double: Soviet garb, a tiny Latvian pocket camera, inkpads, stamps, a small Russian device resembling a rudimentary Geiger counter, and other equipment; also a passport and several cards and letters establishing me as Joseph Dynamo, American.

Refik explained that he would be travelling with, but apart from, me and that I was to impersonate Dynamo, pretending to speak only English, until delivered at Sarikamish, my last Turkish destination. I was to proclaim myself a U.S. archaeologist with permission to search for Kurdish and Armenian ruins in the vicinity of Lake Van, starting from Ardahan. Just before crossing the border into the U.S.S.R. I would abandon these papers and the valise with my American clothes near the border, first cutting myself and dabbing them with blood. Mr. Smith, Refik said, wished to insure that Moscow knew of America's all-pervasive interest.

The Ankara station is a formidable monument to the willful Ataturk's determination: a long, dun-colored cement structure, ugly but well proportioned. Despite oppressive heat which melted the tarred street outside the main entrance, idlers strayed by the platform to watch the departures of the regular night train to Istanbul and that which went eastward to Erzurum, in old Armenia, where we were bound. Prosperous businessmen gathered in the depot restaurant with friends and families. Shoeblacks and gnarled, bent porters slouched about looking for custom. Officious employees of the state transport system strutted in their faded, cheap uniforms. Everyone sweated.

Obeying Refik's instructions, I went directly to Wagon Lit 5, compartment 11, carrying my suitcase, my ticket and two magazines, a *Saturday Evening Post* four months old and a recent issue of *The Undertaker's Journal*. Refik himself was berthed at the other end of the same car.

There were not many passengers for Erzurum. Even before the train lurched out in a series of sluggish jerks I wandered to the restaurant car and began eating a large meal of kebab and beer.

Turkish beer is excellent. They must have stolen the secret from our ancient Armenian kingdom. We Armenians were drinking beer centuries before the first Turks rode down upon us behind the horse-tailed standards of their pashas, cutting raw meat from beneath their saddles and gulping fermented mare's milk out of leathern bottles.

As I ate, I stared glumly into the evening, trying to forget that Refik sat across the aisle. At last it had begun to rain. Great drops splashed against the windows. A rainbow was forming about vestigial rays of the declining sun. I could see a siege of storks solemnly pecking for frogs in the swamp puddles. They flew off as we bucketed by, lifting their legs carefully like the undercarriages of aircraft fighting to gain initial altitude.

In the iridal distance Ankara's first lights flickered along the slopes leading up to the Hittite citadel. The locomotive chuffed around a slow curve and I was alone in Anatolia. The crescent moon rose with its customary bright attendant star.

I thought to myself. This is a fine life, I thought. Spying for the enemy against the enemy. Why am I such a fool, I thought? Could I not have used my education? Was adventure ever important? How had I slipped into the dungheap of my life? At 35 one should have a future, a future far more promising than my own. Linguistics phenomenon. Seventeen languages. And to what purpose? To say shit seventeen different ways.

At that moment a sleazy merchant named Agaoglu whom I had once met in Izmir, where he kept a catamite in his cellar, waddled to the chair opposite me, reeking of garlic. "How are you, effendi," he inquired with that unctuous smirk so often reserved for Armenians whom one would really prefer to do in. I felt as antisocial as a flea, arose, replying with deliberate American accents: "I do not understand. Pardon me." I paid my bill, beamed, bowed, departed.

For fifteen minutes I read *The Undertaker's Journal*. Then, lying among the bedbugs on my blanket, I dozed off in my underwear to the sleep only a man in supreme physical condition and possessing no conscience whatsoever can embrace on a Turkish train.

CHAPTER

III

Any Armenian coming to Erzurum, a city banned to us by the brutal Turks, cannot escape a flash of nostalgic pride. Once this great fortress featured our kingdom when it ran between the Black Sea and the Mediterranean and we were a nation courted from Rome to China.

But now it is a grim, hostile town that seems ready to fall in upon itself. Perhaps this is an architectural mood induced by its endless history of earthquakes.

On Refik's instructions, I took a ramshackle taxi from the station to a cafe on the outskirts where I ate a miserable breakfast of tea and yoghurt speckled with drowned flies.

As heat welled across the rugged plain, the colonel arrived in a khaki German command car, driven by a shaven-headed corporal, and I piled in, placing my suitcase in front.

It was a long, dreary ride across rudimentary roads, through flaming huge clouds of dust, past farmers in buskins, baggy pants and proletarian caps, taking grain to primitive querns, and by black-swathed women ignorant of the official ban on Islamic veils. When the road rose toward the Caucasus, we entered woodlands that soon turned to deciduous forest dotted with terebinth and teil.

At one point Refik signalled the chauffeur to stop. He beckoned and led me to a limpid spring bubbling among mossy rocks. First he, then I, plumped down on our chests to suck up handfuls of water. It was cold and strongly gaseous, bubbling over our dusty faces.

When we reached Sarikamish, near our old Armenian mountain citadel of Kars, Refik halted the command car before a sentry, asked the way to headquarters and explained to an inquiring lieutenant: "I wish the Colonel's office itself. We are travelling on a special mission from General Baransel. Third Army. Erzurum." He flashed an impressive-looking movement order.

Colonel Mahmut Kayaalp, commanding officer of the garrison, had just finished lunch when we arrived. Grumpily, his tight cavalry collar unbuttoned from a perspiring throat, he sat in the wardroom off the mess and read with care a letter handed him in a sealed envelope by Refik. A heavy, strong man, clearly bothered by the high temperature, he kept fingering the wet circle of his neck. At last he looked up, scrutinizing me with sharp, dark eyes. His skin was the color of tobacco juice.

"I shall take care of this man," Kayaalp told Refik. "I shall communicate with General Baransel. You need concern yourself no more, Colonel."

Refik stood to attention, saluted, and stomped out the door. An orderly showed me to a dark little room in the nearby barracks, posted a guard and ordered me not to attempt to leave. Supper, some kind of stinking, oleaginous gallimaufry, was brought by a private carrying a wooden tray. That evening I heard the officers of the mess shouting and singing as the gibbous moon rose over the mountains to the East.

It was one o'clock in the morning when I felt myself roughly shaken. The unshaded light burned brightly and I saw the orderly leaning over my cot. Beside him was another man, a civilian.

"Get dressed," said the orderly. "Colonel Kayaalp waits." As I stumbled out of bed, naked, the civilian handed me, one by one, the articles of clothing from my valise, and checked them off on a list. He was evidently a Circassian. We Armenians know these things at a glance.

When I was ready, even sporting my Tbilisi cap, the Circassian took my American clothes and papers and wrapped them in an old copy of *Ulus*. The orderly then placed the bundle under his arm and the three of us went to a courtyard office that was brightly lit and protected by sentries with bayonetted rifles. Inside sat Kayaalp, attired in buttoned uniform jacket and neatly shaven. Beside him stood a saturnine young captain.

"Very well," said the colonel, dismissing the orderly and the Circassian. "You may sit down." Suddenly he became friendly and informal. He offered me a glass of tea from the tray beside him and spiked it with a shot of kanyak. He and the captain remained silent while I drank. Then Kayaalp made a gesture. The captain opened a cardboard folder. "Here," he said. "This is the most essential document."

He produced a Soviet passport stamped with *Nationality, Armenian,* and made out in the name of David Avetikyan, 35, of Erivan. My picture and signature, magnificently forged, gave it a most valid appearance. He gave me an inkpad and rubber stamp. "The ink is Soviet ink," said the captain. "The stamp is an original MGB stamp. We took the papers from a Muscovite agent."

"Who will not be needing them any more," Kayaalp commented.

The captain lifted a fibre suitcase from the GUM store in Erivan. Inside everything was of Russian origin: my Geiger counter, two frayed shirts, underwear, razor, Russian soap, toothpaste, copies of *Ogonyok,* a nightshirt, a wallet with 730 rubles in various denominations, a worn leather frame containing a photograph of Mount Ararat and of two barely distinguishable old people. "Your parents," he said. "You have been fully briefed on them."

There was also a cheap icon of St. George killing the Emperor Diocletian. "It is not that your real name is Kevork," said Kayaalp with a sudden smile. "But that I know that all Armenians admire George. And since Diocletian had him tortured to death, this is their revenge. I suppose we Turks are Diocletian."

The captain observed: "The more Communist these Soviet Armenians are, the more Christian they proclaim themselves." He handed me a wad of faded newsprint in Armenian. It was exceptionally heavy.

"Open it," ordered the colonel. I unwrapped thirty gold pieces, old Persian coins, the size and weight of a Louis d'or, with Arabic writing. "That is your emergency fund. You will find even Communists are human. Venality is a human trait. I suggest you keep these here," he added, pulling out of his table drawer a metal tube that looked like a thick aluminum cigar casing. "This is a charger. You should shove it up your asshole. In no time you will find there isn't any inconvenience.

"One more thing," Kayaalp added, nodding eastward, "when you are there, tell your controls to listen regularly every evening at ten-thirty to the Ankara Radio broadcast. Whenever Nezi Manyas sings 'I Can't Give You Anything But Love, Baby' (he pronounced this like a French peasant with malformation of the jaw), "it means a message for you. A message will be transmitted thereafter each hour on the half-hour for a period of one full day. They should make arrangements to note this down.

"And now," he said, rising, "I see no further reason to detain you. Captain Orbay will conduct you to the take-off point. Needless to say, if you are caught no one will even admit to your existence. You are an unperson. Avetikyan does not exist except as a Soviet statistic. And Sasounian died in hospital of tertiary syphilis after he was picked up in an Istanbul red-light raid."

I remember Fouché's motto: It is no good killing a man unless you also destroy his reputation. I also remembered Perkel's reference to my family as hostages. I said nothing. I merely shook the colonel's broad, hard hand and followed the captain into the night.

At the compound entrance idled an ungainly Borgward half-track. The captain lumbered aboard, motioned me to the seat beside him and insured that my new suitcase and the package of American clothes and documents were at my feet. Then, with a horrendous grinding of gears, we bounced away.

The Borgward felt like a cement mixer. Each time we hit a stone in the dirt road, it shook and rattled, sometimes flaking sparks from its rear tractor treads. Dogs barked; roosters crowed at the descending moon behind us. Soon we were beyond the last sullowed hovels outside town, and then the captain swerved us suddenly off the road.

He explained: "You are now going eastward past Kars. This trail bypasses Başgedikler. Long before I drop you it will be morning. But no one will see us. This is an uninhabited region. It used to be Armenian. There are no Armenians any more.

"When we are there I shall leave you to reconnoiter the terrain from these heights. You have been instructed on the geography and know precisely where you start from. Here" (dropping a flat object in my left hand) "is a Russian compass. The kind sailors use. It can point you to Leninakhan. You must avoid the roads, southeast past Aragaz to Erivan."

We rumbled on. Neither of us spoke. The sun slid through the predawn opacity and shot up over the trans-Caucasus and far-Caucasus ranges. On a steep hillside under the trees, the Borgward jerked to a stop. "Now I say goodbye," said the captain, handing me the bundle and my border-crossing tools (pepper and probe), and waiting as I lifted the suitcase and climbed over the vehicle's steep side.

He neither wished me luck, nor shook my hand. He merely turned the halftrack in a clearing, laboriously punching it backward and forward amid the underbrush, and then headed it westward down the trail.

The silence was oppressive as I climbed the scree up to the crest and seated myself beneath a pine.

CHAPTER

IV

I must have fallen asleep and woke up late during the gradual seasons of the night, chilled by the mountain air. The stirring of frogs and the flittering of birds and crickets vexed the surrounding quiet.

I looked into the flat valley and thought of that awful poem I once taught snot-nosed Robert College bastards: "This is my own, my native land."

Then I shouldered my belongings and edged nervously down the slopes as the first hint of light filtered across the Armenian flats.

In a small pile under a eucalyptus I deposited my American possessions. I had liberally splashed them with blood from a gash on the wrist so that the American, Mr. Dynamo, might be satisfactorily accounted for. So much for Colonel Refik and Mr. Smith. Walking with economy, I picked my way to the border.

The crossing was even easier than the Milli Emniyet experts had predicted. On the Soviet side I could see a ploughed strip of land more than two hundred meters wide, nubbled whenever searchlights, sited at watchtowers half a mile apart, swept the area in nervous arcs. Well-tended fencing of barbed wire spiked the actual frontier and, by the moving beams, I watched two soldiers disinterestedly trudge into the distance.

I cut a thick twig, trimmed it, poked beneath the fence for

trip wires, and then carefully slid underneath, dragging my suit-case behind. I timed this operation carefully while the border patrol continued to amble in the other direction toward one of the wooden towers, and I probed cautiously ahead of me for mines, while simultaneously inching rapidly forward. I rolled, when pos-sible, and I kept covering my tracks. Just to make sure, I shook out the pepper to confuse inquisitive dogs.

By the time dawn's first pink rays were mounting the peak of Mount Aragaz across the way I had crawled half a mile into a cornfield of the Soviet Republic of Armenia.

I confess it was a disappointment; this was no land of lentisk and asphodel, arbutus and euphorbia, blessed with nightingales singing in the medlars and wooded mountains tenanted by peris and kobolds. It was hot and dusty. The only sound was the rustle of corn and the only smell was that of marl spread among the stalks.

I slipped out to the dirt road bisecting the rows of grain and waved to a farmer riding in a cart drawn by three trotting don-keys. As I hailed him for a lift, I realized that, for the first time, I was speaking my national tongue in its proper home. Armenian is composed of rich, lithe, heavy and dark-tinted words and it gave me pleasure to roll them through my lips. I felt a vernal surge of life gush through my veins.

There is no other language save for English which contains so many of our rustling poetic sounds: henna, gentian, cinna-bar, lilac, jasper, sofa, muscadel, saffron; mostly signifying agree-able things. Ah, I thought to myself as the little donkeys hauled me toward destiny, had the people of Armenia known what a hero was now among them they would have planted my way with flowers.

We clattered past orchards, past vineyards, past old shepherds bearing crooks, until we reached the village of Asatan, where I left my driver and bought a bus ticket to Leninakhan. Upon arriving in that ungainly but unexpectedly large town I walked, as I had been instructed, to the public bath, checked my clothing and bag, sat naked on a bench inside the steaming hot-room, and held my old copy of *Ogonyok*—upside down.

Several of the inhabitants regarded me with interest, noting my large thighs, small waist, the breadth of my shoulders, with their muscled arms, steely wrists and spatulate fingers, my black eyes and hair, the proud large nose set athwart my bold face and the impressive testimony to my manhood. As the sweat began to trickle down my neck and chest and legs I could see them whispering to each other, inquiring whence this magnificent compatriot had arrived.

Before long an obese young man with maculate chops squatted beside me, saying: "You look comfortable, Comrade."

"One pays for comfort in fear, Comrade," I replied.

"The more lavish the comfort, the more lavish the fear," said he.

"It is good to follow those who know," said I.

"Bissama Allah oua Alard Stalin," said he. "In heaven Allah, on earth Stalin."

I watched the strength of his bow-legged shadow as it clumsily followed him around the corner to our clothes and then I noticed that he was circumcised, obviously not a Jew, but archetypal of his race. How strange for the Turks, who surely had but few surviving agents in Russia, to select an Arab as my very first contact.

My new and lavishly frightened friend led me to the railway station restaurant, ordered pilaff, insisted on paying and, in the late afternoon, took me to a truck, loaded with bags of apples, that was to bear me to his controller in Erivan. He introduced me to the driver, handed him a five ruble note and murmured: "Here is your passenger." All night we rumbled southward. We were halted for our papers only once.

Erivan is a big city set in a bowl that seems to cherish all the ferocious heat whirled down to it by eddying winds. Even at night the oxygen is burned out. I gasped like an aquarium fish in dirty water. No one was yet abroad as we rumbled toward the market place through wide streets, some of them lined with cherry trees.

After sunrise I walked with my suitcase to the central Lenin Square, when a wiry, furtive figure appeared at the opposite end and scuttled like a crab across the enormous space. I was not surprised to note that he was sucking at an orange held in his left hand.

"Can you tell me," he asked, "if this is the way to the cei works?"

"The cement of life is hardened with tears," I answered.

"Come," said he. "My name is Spartacus."

I soon discovered that Spartacus was an energetic, exceptionally friendly little man. He had a peculiar, ferocious hairdo like that of an African chief, and immense feet, encased in sandals. His eyes, I saw, when he took me home for breakfast of tea and dvorog, were flat and unbelievably sad.

He lived in one room of a jerrybuilt wooden house set in an unsalubrious alley just behind a stone-built façade of apartments running along a magnificent avenue from the square. On the avenue Erivan looked like an impressive capital; but in the capillary lanes that fed the modern arterial system it seemed a Turkish village, with rusted pumps over the community wells, spreading fruit trees, and grape vines running pleasantly up the balconies of tumbledown shacks.

At the entrance to Spartacus' house a woman with her long hair bound in a clean white cloth was stuffing cherries into glass preserve bottles. She nodded as we climbed the ladder to his room.

"I have been briefed," he said, ladling out the clotted white dvorog from a jar. "I know your assignment and I will help. But I do not think you will find what you are looking for. There are many tales and many tale-bearers. There is more disinformation than there is information." I thought to myself of what the Englishman had told me of Ignatiev's role.

After breakfasting, Spartacus locked my belongings in his little room and then proceeded to guide me around the noble capital with its Potemkin fronts. We walked past shops half-filled with shoddy goods, past queues of patient women waiting by butcher stalls, and fruiterers notable for the paucity of their products.

It was, nevertheless, evident that we Armenians had gained existence if not freedom by exchanging a Turkish for a Russian master. Although Spartacus made few comments, his pale, taut face betrayed the nature of his secret thoughts. I suspected he was an "illegal," infiltrated by the Turks. As for myself, I felt hope and energy seep from my body. I who had been a tiger in the Turkish jungle was becoming in this Soviet cage but a sleek tabby cat.

Spartacus confided that his real name was Varashak. He boasted, as we trudged through the heat, that Soviet Armenia was but one-tenth of our ancient territory; one day we should get it all back.

"How?" I inquired, "by spying for the Turks?" He looked glutted with remorse. "You, who are new, have no right to talk in such a way," he said. "All Armenians have been buggered by fate. Some by Turkish fate. Some by Russian fate. Say no more, Comrade David."

For a moment I forgot he was talking to me. Spartacus drew himself up and stared me straight in the eye with none of the shiftiness of a pariah.

We wandered down a broad boulevard where numerous derricks hoisted the girders for massive new buildings. He took me to inspect a magnificent collection of our manuscripts and early books, quite worthy of the oldest Christian state: fifth and ninth century parchments and illustrated treatises on mathematics, medicine, philosophy and music, all in the lovely alphabet of our learned Mesrop Mashtots; miniatures painted with the throat hairs of three-month-old kittens bound in the quill of a squab, colored with the blue paint of crushed insects and the red paint of crushed worms, with gold affixed to the vellum by garlic juice.

From a height on the city's rim we looked westward over the Razdan river toward St. Rhipsime church and ancient Echmiadzin in whose cathedral rests the piece of Noah's Ark found on the snow-clad Ararat peak towering just across the border behind in Turkey.

Spartacus began to boast of what we Armenians had done and what we again would do when, with Turkish aid, we had shaken the Russian yoke and, with Russian aid, we had shattered the surly Turk.

A strangely synergistic doctrine: he seemed to be heartened by the blatant and insistent reaffirmation of the obviously untrue.

I regarded him quizzically, thinking: that cannot be what has brought him to this tawdry trade. And then, like the poet, I thought: what would become of us Armenians without the barbarians who rule us and have ruled us for five centuries or more. Surely barbarians are a kind of solution.

Finally we bought bread, sausage, and two bottles of sour beer so we could dine at home and listen to the late shortwave broadcast of Ankara Radio to which Spartacus methodically tuned for occasional instructions transmitted in simplified triad codes. He carefully placed the receiver beside his head under a blanket so no eavesdropping neighbor might accuse him of tuning in on the detested Turk.

There was no hint of a message. That night, as we slept side by side in his tight and hot little trundle bed, I dreamed the catatonic dream that I was a mouse and wondered, when I awakened in the morning, whether I was really a mouse dreaming the catastrophic dream that I was me.

The following morning we took off on our inspection trip. The alley where Spartacus lived was already abustle. Children played pingpong on a table under a beech tree. A boy stood before a circle of admiring friends singing while they clapped in time. Old men in caps were picking grapes and cherries, now beginning to wither on the branches. A policeman sat at the exit to the main thoroughfare, munching a piece of unleavened lavash bread.

It all seemed pleasantly peaceful. I lost my doubts about this gentle Soviet system. Again I wondered how a man like Spartacus could risk his life for the unspeakable Turks with their policy of "Armenia without Armenians." I thought of the sadness lying behind my companion's eyes.

Spartacus read my mind. "It isn't the money," he said. "Money, money. An exaggerated commodity. After all, what is money good for but caprices and doctors?" I nodded, considering my own circumstances.

As we strode down the sidewalk, past a queue at the doorway of a gastronome, I remembered the song taught me by an Armenian from California: "Who knows, who knows, where we go, When we kick the bucket. Tell him who pretends he knows, That he should fuck it, fuck it."

One advantage of being a driver in a Soviet cement combine is transportation. Spartacus found his truck immediately among the hodgepodge vehicles parked under the bridge that leads across the river in the direction of Echmiadzin. "Get in," he commanded gently. He handed me a document, adding that no one would

circumference to test for what might easily have been a camouflaged deception.

This required care. I had been warned by my instructor that Geiger counters could register even more strongly in the vicinity of a granite building than in that of a sheltered and more remote nuclear pile. But obviously the installation contained neither granite nor uranium; the light scarcely blinked above the norm allowed for atmospheric radio-active disturbances.

I scrutinized the guards and the procession of capped workers, some marching, arms swinging in cadence, others pushing barrows in and out. But no face even remotely resembled the MGB, MVD, and GRU rogue's gallery I had so assiduously committed to memory.

Finally we drove on. At one point I started muttering to Spartacus as the light began to flicker. Then, to my dismay, I realized that as he had thrown his left hand across the steering wheel to navigate a deep rut, the radium dial on his watch had elicited the probe's response.

Ultimately it became apparent, as the rising plateau curled eastward and opened more than a mile high on placid Lake Sevan, that just as Spartacus had foreseen on our very first morning, the tale contained no truth. Indeed, as he had said, it represented more disinformation than information.

I am not sure whether I was pleased or displeased to discover my mission had no justified purpose. It would have fattened my vanity to flense the cover from a vital Soviet secret. Yet it was comforting to think I might soon go home and achieve the release of my relatives held hostage by the Birinci Buro.

A chill high cirrostratus haze shadowed the turquoise lake surface. Spartacus halted the truck at the base of a peninsula jutting into the water and on which were sited two ruined cruciform churches. A wrinkled woman in a roadside shed was vending boiled trout in a colander. We ate off filthy plates a pair of fish au bleu which stared at us through contumelious pale eyes.

That night Spartacus abruptly signalled to me as he huddled beside the radio in his modest room. I placed my head beside his under the blanket. We formed a symbiosis of fear. His African pompadour tickled my ear and he was already scribbling madly in a lined pocket notebook. "Yildizlar parliyor," said the announcer from Ankara, and again: "Yildizlar parliyor, the stars are shining."

"My signal," hissed Spartacus when a barely intelligible couplet from the poet Yahya Kemal Beyath was read with strangely slow and artificial emphasis. Spartacus took it down painstakingly, shut off the receiver when it began to howl feline music, and then seated himself by his single bare table to decode the triads which composed the message.

I waited. "The key," he murmured to himself, "is doghru." He kept on mumbling "doghru" and printing out three-letter series. At the end he said, slightly puzzled, "Kevork? You must be Kevork.

"Clearly David is Kevork. Kevork must go Tbilisi when survey ended. Contact Teimo. Contact Teimo. He has news."

"Who is Teimo?" I inquired. Spartacus told me. I drank a huge potion of brandy: Armenian nepenthe! I needed it; destiny was thrusting me deeper into trouble.

CHAPTER

V

THE bus ride to Tbilisi was droll. On one side of me sat an Azerbaijani peasant carrying an antique blunderbuss which he insisted on jamming into my ribs. On the other side of me sat an embarrassed, nervous goat whose elderly mistress crouched next to him. I am not sure which of my neighbors smelled worse.

To my regret, as I am not by nature patient, it had taken several days for Spartacus to arrange my departure and to notify his Tbilisi colleague, Teimo, that I would be coming. Spartacus explained there was unusual tension in Armenia. An American had apparently been murdered on the border and the Turks were blaming the Russians.

"Was his name Dynamo?" I asked casually. Spartacus was startled. He stared at me as if I were a wizard.

When I finally climbed aboard the wheezing, overcrowded bus I found it filled with Armenians, Georgians, and a few Azerbaijanis, but, escaping the surly sullenness of slavdom, not one single Russian. We retraced the road to Sevan, rocking along from bump to bump on the quite inadequate surface, and from that lovely lake we began to climb the high pass leading across the combs to Tbilisi.

Slowly, the engine grunting and steaming, we labored up the slopes, stopping every few minutes to cool the motor. At each stop a group of young Georgian girls piled out to pluck wild flowers from green fields wholly untenanted save for occasional flocks of sheep. My own goat never moved so I remained a prisoner.

We emerged from the pass into a green valley with purling streams issuing out of the wooded heights. This valley at its end disgorged into a fertile plain, containing many orchards and vineyards. Old shepherds with crooks and white lambskin hats tended their animals. Occasionally a little cart drawn by a troika of asses rattled past.

The greenness faded as we entered the western part of Azerbaijan, a dry, barren, brown hill country much like Turkish Anatolia. I have always been fascinated, as I travel about, to see how much the various provinces of the old Ottoman empire resemble each other in geology and nature.

Here and there Moslem cemeteries mirrored the past with their huge, slanting grave slabs. Youngsters stood beside the highway selling apricots and cherries. Most women wore black and some of the older men wore pantaloons and turbans.

I was delighted and appalled by the free and easy hurluberlu of conversational interchange aboard our merry vehicle and, I may add, I was worried that the communal indiscretion might get us in trouble. This could conceivably not have bothered my fellow-passengers but with my set of false papers I was not happy at the prospect. I kept looking about to decide which of the travellers might be an MGB agent but, on examining them with care, the thought was too ridiculous.

There was no single lingua franca although everybody, even the Azerbaijanis, seemed to speak either Armenian or Georgian. The general topic was raised by a pert youngster in the front row, sporting what looked like an imitation jockey's cap. "Have you heard the latest on the Armenian Radio?" he inquired in Armenian.

Then, without waiting for an answer, he continued: "Riddle. How can an elephant rupture himself? Answer. By raising the agricultural question. Ha, ha, ha. Hee, hee, hee."

Everyone knows the Armenian Radio is the Soviet circuit for political jokes. I was horrified when a girl who looked as if she might be a university student continued in Georgian: "What is the difference between capitalism and communism? Capitalism is the exploitation of man by man and communism is the opposite."

There was a roar of laughter and a magnified muttering as this was translated into Armenian. "I am a housepainter," said a large swarthy man, "and therefore I know something about painting. Let me tell you what I have learned. Naturalists paint what they see. Impressionists paint what they feel. And Socialist-Realists paint what they hear."

"Is that so," demanded a stern woman with her gray hair done in a tight bun to keep it free of dust. "Well, did you know the Politburo once ordered all elephants to be shot because they had been destroying crops—in one of our southern provinces I suppose. A rabbit ran by the secretary in charge and was caught and brought before him.

"The rabbit was trembling. 'What's the matter?' he was asked. 'I am frightened because the Politburo has ordered that all elephants should be slaughtered.'

" 'But why should you worry? You are not an elephant.' "

" 'I know,' said the rabbit. 'But how can I prove it?' "

I could no longer restrain myself. "You know what we Armenians say? Last summer that joke took first prize in a joke competition. And do you know what first prize was? It was ten years in jail."

At this point everyone fell silent, except the goat. He bleated.

Finally we came ricketing, racketing down to the Kura valley and there before us, sprawled like a long ribbon, lay Tbilisi. At the terminal where we drew up and disgorged I noticed an absolutely immense man, about six-and-a-half feet tall, weighing at least a seventh of a ton, with clipped blond hair and upturned mustache, not a bit Georgian in appearance. I knew from his description that this was Teimo, my contact.

From a distance he looked like a Prussian but from close up like an imbecile. Spartacus had sneeringly described him to me as a man who boasted of his revolutionary past (before he turned sour) but who had never been a revolutionist, merely one who hung around revolutions. I hoped he was more talented and devoted to his trade of espionage. As soon as he spotted me I made the recognition signal (nose scratching, earlobe pulling, folding a copy of an Armenian menu). He came heavily up, wreathed in his own bluster.

Teimo (T'eimuraz Tchenkelli, as I discovered during the weeks I stayed in Tbilisi) was as unusual as his appearance. I suspect he was a fruit; at least he never showed the slightest interest in any woman during all that time, that is to say any woman save his mother.

She was an excellent cook who adored stuffing his huge frame with complicated dishes which he devoured with unrestrained enthusiasm. But when I remarked that I would not take amiss the opportunity to meet some of Georgia's renowned beauties, he simply grunted.

Thanks to my great appeal and Armenian ingenuity I was able to circumvent this obstacle. Before long I discovered that the whores or semi-professionals of Tbilisi clustered in small evening gaggles near the railway station or by the trees beside the antique Intourist hotel where they waited for randy commissars or foreigners with valuta. To any eye less practiced than my own they looked more like steamfitters than prostitutes but they did the job. And, before I had departed, I managed to squeeze, sniff, twiddle, and screw several handsome Georgian girls, some of whom were almost amateurs.

I asked Teimo how he had obtained the combination of light blond hair and gigantism in this land of dark and aquiline human architecture. "My grandmother was Circassian," he boasted, which was scarcely an answer. I suspect his mother once cooked too hot a stew for a German Feldwebel during World War I.

For reasons beyond my comprehension, Teimo was the only accredited Turkish agent in the Caucasus, apart from Spartacus and a man in Batumi whom I never met. This puzzled me because he appeared to have no consanguinity or other link with Turkeydom nor even the remotest ideological awareness of anything whatsoever. His heroes appeared to be Josef Stalin and Charlie Chaplin, neither of whom could be considered in Ankara's pay.

"Ah, Charlie," he would say: "incomparable, incomparable." At one time, Teimo had worked for the Intourist travel agency and was assigned to meet a group of tourists including a certain Mrs. Dorothy Chaplin. Assuming she was the actor's wife he brought a bouquet of flowers to the railway station and, once he had identified her, bowed deeply and inquired: "How is Mr. Charlie Chaplin?"

"How should I know?" came the answer from an elderly, disagreeable, Canadian hag. He promptly resigned and returned to a career made up exclusively of Mama's home cooking and Turkish espionage.

Teimo hated all religion. He boasted that his grandfather had been jailed by the Czar for riding a plough horse into church. He also detested the Russians and venerated Stalin as a Georgian. He had a curious theory that the Turks were pro-Stalin because both they and the Georgians disliked Russians and Jews.

As I was to discover, however, he was by no means an idiot when it came to his profession. "Teimo is my code name because Teimo is my real name," he explained in his glottal voice. "Nobody would think me stupid enough to hide behind the truth."

His transmitting station—the only one available for the Turks this side of their Moscow embassy—was a compact American set which had somehow been smuggled in to him and which was light enough to be carried about with ease by such a huge, powerful man.

Mrs. Tchenkelli, his mother, supported herself by black market laundering on an extensive scale. Teimo delivered this in boxes, baskets, and bags as he drove about the city in a peculiar truck he had manufactured by cutting the rear body of a ZIS limousine away from the front with a blowtorch and welding a platform to the exposed portion of chassis.

When he had messages to send, which was seldom, he chose to deliver washing at hours that accorded with a time schedule he knew Turkish receivers at Kars, Sarikamish, Trabzon, Erzerum, and Ankara would be tuned in on. By transmitting rarely, briefly, and from continually different sites around Tbilisi, and by carrying the set in laundry containers, he had managed to avoid detection.

Teimo lived in one large, dark room of a decaying house across the street from the synagogue, and here I was established during my long and frustrating stay. He shared with other tenants a wash basin and shower at the end of the dingy hall and an outside toilet in the backyard which always, as I soon learned, creaked and swayed ominously when he squeezed his immense bulk inside.

He also had rights to the extraordinarily simple kitchen facilities but these he eschewed, preferring occasional cups of tea or coffee outside and the delicious and interminable meals prepared at her home by his adoring mother.

The one luxury Teimo allowed himself in his modest quarters was an old-fashioned phonograph with a large, horn magnifier to which he had attached a record player capable of handling modern disks. His collection of these was astonishing, considering the lack of facilities in the Soviet Union.

In addition to the Russian classics like Tchaikovsky and the Georgian classics like Paliashvili his collection contained many American works which he had acquired from foreign visitors during his Intourist days, including the songs of Frank Sinatra and Nat King Cole. It was, moreover, useful to keep the horn blaring at night when Ankara might signal him (as it rarely did). His housemates were so impressed by his titanic bulk that they rarely grumbled about the noise.

I learned early that Teimo cherished an abiding detestation for the congregation which met regularly in the little synagogue. Since he was clearly not Slavic and could therefore not have inherited the usual Russian bias, I wondered if this too might not be an unacknowledged sign of Prussian antecedents.

He would stare gloomily from his window at the courtyard where well-dressed Jewish children played while their fathers and mothers lined up at the shed where a ritual butcher slaughtered chickens they brought fluttering to his attentions. Teimo resented the aura of tidiness, cleanliness, and comparative prosperity reflected by this small society and muttered aloud as he glared ferociously from the ledge: "Yids. Contemptible Yids. Why does Grandfather Stalin tolerate those Yids?"

These complaints perplexed me. I could not understand why Teimo hated the unfortunate Jews since he was at least half-Georgian, a gracious, unbigoted race. I could not understand why he thought Stalin tolerated Jews since it was known to one and all that the dictator was purging them right and left. And I could not understand why he liked and admired Grandfather Stalin so much (as many Georgians did).

I came to realize that Georgians, when drunk, sometimes confided a satisfaction that one of their own should now be taking revenge on the Russians for past sins, ruling that great people and making them suffer what others in the past had suffered from them.

But how this prejudice could be reconciled with the deadly dangerous profession of anti-Stalinist secret agent was something I never comprehended. Perhaps, unlike Spartacus, it was a question of money, the capitalistic instinct that penetrates so many Georgians. Espionage may not be the most respectable work, but it is relatively well paid and rarely strenuous.

Teimo always smelled like a cabbage factory and suffered constant indigestion at both ends. He had hung a dirty blanket from a rope across the middle of his room, thus generously allowing me a modicum of privacy. He slept in a wide, sagging bed which wheezed in counterpoint to his nocturnal snores. I was allotted a broken-down sofa. To say this was the happiest of times would be an exaggeration.

I generally ate at least once each day at Mrs. Tchenkelli's. She was a fantastic cook, knew all the complicated, oily, well-seasoned, calid Georgian dishes which are so like our own Armenian cuisine and she also managed to find quantities of glorious red wine, the best type that was generally unavailable in Georgia but reserved for exportation to Moscow and abroad. Nothing gave her more pleasure than to watch Teimo stuff incredible quantities of these delights into his broad maw and slosh it down with gulps of Mukuzani.

The first time I met her she was visibly unimpressed, inspecting my girth of six-foot-two and 195 pounds, then turning with despair to Teimo towering beside me and saying with asperity: "We shall have to fatten him up" (as if for some evil cannibalistic purpose). She herself had hips wide enough to drive a truck through, and a firm globular belly which rose upward from between them, embraced two pumpkin-sized breasts, and disappeared into a panoply of chins.

There was little I could do to amuse myself once I had given my brief and wholly negative message to Teimo who transmitted it from a hillside stop on his laundry route. He received prompt confirmation that it had been received and only the categorical order that I must await further instruction.

Although my Armenian, Georgian, and Russian are impeccable

and although I had every reason to rely upon the false documents with which the Birinci Buro, Spartacus and finally Teimo had supplied me, I felt it more discreet to minimize my contacts with normal Tbilisi life.

Teimo himself was of little social use. He required no company but his mother's. I, however, yearning for divertissement, went alone one evening to the opera, then producing "Daisi" by the incomparable Paliashvili. Teimo had refused to come, explaining that he had seen the work seventeen times which even I acknowledged was sufficient.

It was agreeable to watch and hear, a romance taking place in a mountain village, filled with pleasant Georgian patriotism, dancing and sentimentality. The dances were performed by capering men in orange or black leggings and jackets, with black or white headcloths, most of them wearing daggers and belts of silver cartridges slung across their chests. The girls who swung happily with them wore long dresses, medieval coifs and veils draped swaying behind.

One of these girls was particularly lithe and sparkling with long black eyes and long black hair. I fixed my most admiring and dedicated stare upon her hoping, since I was sitting in the second row, that she would recognize me again.

When the performance ended I waited in the little park through which the actors' entrance disgorged and eventually she slipped out, a shawl around her shoulders, a saucy red toque upon her delicate head. My cock became inquisitive.

She was in a great hurry, peering neither left nor right, and I followed furtively as she rushed through the still night, ignoring the crowds of strollers who honored the fact that this was a Saturday and tomorrow would be workless.

There are no taxicabs and rare buses in Tbilisi so I was easily able to keep her in sight as she limbered lightly along to the square, high-domed Cathedral of Sioni. Late as it was, a few decrepit hags sat on the stone pavement outside gossiping with a solitary lame beggar. Inside, about fifty people, most of them women and most of them old, stood before the altar while the choir, invisible behind a screen, sang beautifully.

My charming soubrette crossed herself, slid beside a row of crones, and began to form the syllables of prayer on silent lips. I realized it must be a holiday which was why the midnight service was being performed.

Candles flickered, throwing shadows up to the clerestory; there was a faint smell of incense; a lady in a booth beside the entrance sold small cubes of bread for communion, the symbol of a cross stamped in the crust.

Bearded priests bearing tapers surrounded a little bishop with white beard, high golden miter and gorgeous yellow silk robes as he emerged from behind the rood screen. After him came a red-robed officiant with long black hair, swinging a censer while the bishop chanted and held a lighted candle in each hand. There was a rotting smell as of corpses draped in floral wreaths.

Just before the service ended—and I knew when the moment came because the Georgian rite is so much like our own—I tiptoed to the portal and, as my friend appeared, shaking her toque, I murmured: "Mademoiselle (ah, what a splendid word!) may I have the privilege of escorting you safely through these dark streets, wherever you are going?"

She started, eyed me askance, obviously recognized me from the theater audience and then giggled. "Why not?" This was easier than I had reckoned; Georgian girls are famous for the valorous way they guard their chastity. Then, as we walked and walked, she spoke nervously in Russian, and told me she was not Georgian but Ukrainian.

Later I discovered she was Jewish, from Kharkov, although she did not boast about it and had converted to orthodoxy. Her father had disappeared during the war and her mother had fled to Novosibirsk and married an Armenian from Tbilisi.

After forty-five minutes of trudging we arrived before an old-fashioned building whose front leaned outward over the Kura beneath a steep escarpment. "May I come up?" I asked. "Why not?" Again she laughed nervously. "Should you hunger for bread we will slaughter a nightingale."

We climbed a creaking staircase and I could see the tender strength of her legs unfold from her skirt. At the top she fumbled with a key. I heard her whisper in the dark as the door swung open. There was a stirring and, against the faint glow from the window, I watched another girl gather a blanket about her and disappear into the room next door.

"Come," said my friend, taking me by the hand. "My name is Raja." She led me to a tumbled bed still warm with the other's woman-fragrance. I tasted her soft broad lips. That night, by our presence we made her house a garden. It was the season of the last lurid cis-Caucasian roses and she had thrust a huge bouquet into a pot, filling the air with heavy attar. "Breathe deeply," she whispered. "The rose is a guest for only a few swift days and they are almost past." How Georgian my Ukrainian Jewess had become!

Raja had the supple back of a rabbit, a mouth like honeycomb, breasts like over-ripe peaches, dark fragrant hair and the torso-torsion only a Russian ballerina can develop. "I knew you would be an athlete," she murmured, "from your appearance. But not so ingenious and inventive, Armenian."

"My name is David," I murmured in her ear, "and the Armenian David died while drinking at a stream." "Drink," she whispered. After a time I whispered back: "I shall not escape. I shall be lost here."

"I suppose that's from an Armenian epic," said she. "Just like my stepfather. All you Armenians quote Armenian epics." As a matter of fact she was right.

In the morning I was awakened by Raja bringing glasses of tea with misshapen lumps of beet sugar. She wore felt slippers, nothing else: long, lean body; long, lank legs; long eyes, mouth, ears; long, low-hanging night-colored hair; and a curled triangle at the base of her flat belly.

"It is Sunday," she said as I sipped my tea. "Isn't there somewhere we might go?"

Only Teimo, alas, had both car and driver's license. After a lingering embrace we dressed and I escorted her to our dingy apartment.

A deep caterwauling noise echoed down the stairwell. When we entered we found Teimo seated beside the phonograph horn, his cavernous back toward us, his head buried in pudding-shaped hands. He turned around, a beam on his beefy face. "Bix Beiderbecke," he said with evident satisfaction. "American trumpeter."

Raja seemed frightened when he clasped her slender fingers in his own sweaty palm. I explained that we would like him to take us on a motor tour, hoping his mother had no delivery work to interfere.

"Gladly," he said without gladness. "But Nezi Manyas sang that song while you were away. I have a message for you. A message came in last night from your employer."

"Who is your employer, David Avetikovich?" Raja asked inquisitively, using the patronymic.

I cited from Melik, our hero: "Oh Lord, how shall I escape? He leaped to the left; he leaped to the right. He flew to the wall. He prayed: Lord, give me strength to leap over the wall."

My literary sorrow was wasted since neither Raja nor Teimo understood. "It can wait," I said. "That is your affair," he answered. Raja paid no further attention. She was staring at Teimo as if he were some grotesque in a museum wax collection; perhaps he was.

We followed him down to the truncated ZIS and he wedged himself behind the wheel, Raja squashed between us. At the end of the street there was a commission shop selling champagne. Teimo pointed proudly: "It comes from the Tbilisi factory. Only Tbilisi, Moscow, and Kiev have champagne factories."

"It tastes like factory wine," I commented with appropriately acid tones. "Of course," said Teimo, "I cannot drink too much because I am a sportsman."

Raja regarded his massive build and asked: "What is your sport?" "Chess," he answered. "The sportsmen of Georgia have scored big successes in U.S.S.R. competitions. Nonna Gaprindashvili, the world chess champion, lives in Tbilisi."

My idea had been to have Teimo drive us to the country and then lose him in a large plate of shashlik while the two of us found solace around a bend. Now, in view of my message, such opportunities promised to be all too few, but Teimo regrettably relished his reincarnation as an Intourist guide.

He started us off on the cliff above Raja's house, overlooking Tbilisi and the Kura gorge, using the courtyard of the Metekhi church-fortress as a podium for his lecture. Across the way, he explained, those ruins were the Shuritsikhe fort, now called Nakivali, built by a Persian leader famous for his envy of another Persian leader. Shuritsikhe means envy.

He led us to the Art Museum and insisted on showing off the

icon and sculpture collection, item by item, pausing interminably over the scattered fragments of the enamel portrait of Our Lady of Khakhul. He postured before lumbering oxcarts, four thousand years old. He took pains to explain how beautiful the fat, tough-looking Queen Tamara was in medieval frescoes.

I longed for Bix Beiderbecke. Raja became increasingly impatient. Finally, when we were all set to start our tour, Teimo insisted we first lunch in a dreary cellar restaurant where the murals by Pirosmani, unrefined as they were to my Armenian taste, exceeded the cuisine.

Finally, prompted by the lubricious Raja, I did persuade Teimo to stop munching his muscular shashlik, jimmy us into the truck and set up the river toward Mtskheta and the handsome church of Jwari which, despite our guide's expatiation, seemed to me built in pure Armenian style. When we got to the hilltop upon which Jwari is set, overlooking the Aragvi and Kura rivers where they join their snowy waters, Teimo puffed his chest, deflated his enormous belly, leaned forward like an uncertain diver, pointed below and began to recite:

> "Where Kura and Aragvi flow
>   Together in tumultuous race."

He then added with ineffable satisfaction: " 'Mtsyri.' Lermontov. Russian poet."

To my astonishment Raja continued in her musical voice:

> "Now through the evening twilight rose
>   The rune of monks who pray for souls."

"By the mother of Tovma Terzian," I said. "How on earth did you possibly learn that poem, much less remember it?"

"One receives an education in the Union of Soviet Socialist Republics," she replied. I could not tell if she was being sarcastic.

We drove on to Gori which is Stalin's birthplace.

Fortunately the engine of our awkward truck was sufficiently antiquated and the axles so ungreased that their combined noise discouraged further intellectual exhortations from Teimo. We sat in silence, I furious that all the time wasted in Tbilisi might have been better spent exploring Jwari's hillsides, Raja rather delighted with herself for showing off a knowledge of "Mtsyri."

Gori lies on another river, the Liakhvi, in a broad valley with distant peaks. I could not help but wonder why this sunlit, blooming, open landscape should have produced so closed and furtive a character as Stalin's, impressions I had already read about and would soon be confirming for myself.

Maybe it was only because it was a fine autumn Sunday or maybe it was because there was so little else to do, but there were large crowds wandering along Stalin Avenue and Stalin Square where a large bronze statue of Stalin looked down toward Stalin Museum and the marble shed in front containing the minute cottage in which Stalin was born to a shoemaker's wife.

Immediately Teimo became the practiced Intourist envoy. Dragging the unenthusiastic Raja up the broad museum stairway atop which stood Stalin, he began his lecture as we entered the very first room of dreary photographic displays, intonating: "Comrade Josef Vissarionovich was the son of Vissarion Ivanovich Djugashvili, the only son and third child; the other two died. His father wanted him to be a cobbler but his mother wished him to have an education. So he went to the Gori Religious Seminary and proved to be an excellent pupil. He was a choirboy."

I found it intriguing to contemplate our modern Ivan the Terrible singing alto in a clerical smock. Perspiring with the mental effort, Teimo continued, with evident pride in his own profession: "As an illegal young conspirator of the Bolshevik wing of the Social-Democratic party, Comrade Josef Vissarionovich worked in the underground and as a secret agent. He was a great secret agent."

CHAPTER

VI

RAJA shrugged her delicately sculptured clavicle when we left her near her house and I refused to come along. There was no Sunday performance of "Daisi." She wanted me to compensate for a fruitless day but I had to hasten back for my message. As we rattled toward Teimo's sordid quarters, he sneered: "That girl, she is a Jewess, a Russian Jewess. The worst of both worlds. I can smell them."

"You're full of cranberries. Raja is Armenian," I lied, knowing perfectly well that what he really had against her was the fact she was a woman.

The message, which Teimo had inserted between his Shostakovich and Sinatra disks, was brief and noncommittal. It acknowledged receipt of my negative report from Erivan, originally encoded by Spartacus and transmitted by Teimo from his laundry truck after my arrival in Tbilisi. Then it instructed me to go to Kutaisi, the former Georgian capital, and on to Sukhumi.

I was to check the report of uranium shipments by railroad through those cities. Thereafter I should use my judgment. If I discovered urgent news, I was advised to return to Tbilisi and Teimo's transmitter. Otherwise I could find my way southward to Turkey along the Black Sea coast. Teimo had deciphered the triads and printed all this out in astonishingly minuscule handwriting. I wondered how that hamlike fist could make such tiny letters.

I never again saw Raja of the sullen mouth and flexible pelvis. Instead, that very night, I followed Teimo as he lugged the rectangular laundry box containing his radio down the groaning stairs, and as he shoved it into the ridiculous but useful truck. We drove across the Kura bridge and up a steeply winding road while he boasted that Tbilisi was about to build an enormous tourist restaurant on the cliff above the river.

"To drink factory-made champagne?" I inquired. "Of course," he answered with evident satisfaction.

When we reached the summit he explained that his modest apparatus sent clearer signals from heights. We parked under a copse growing beside a narrow lane and he turned, jamming his great bulk into the compartment carrying the transmitter. I stood nervously by a tree, keeping watch. In no time I heard the delicate tap-tap-taps and the susurrous wheeze of his radio. Taps, silence, wheeze, silence. He seemed to be listening with great attention through his headphones, and scribbled on a pad by the light of his pocket torch.

Teimo was crisply efficient. Within five minutes he had reboxed the set, muttered that the contact was excellent, turned the truck and headed back to the city. He didn't seem in the least worried about the chances of interception by the MGB or GRU. "They don't have time to triangulate and find the transmission point," he said confidently, pointing to his chronometric wrist watch. This was of East German manufacture and, he bragged, never varied more than one second in a month.

"Fine," I commented. "But how soon can you decode my new instructions and tell me what they're all about?"

"Oh, that's no trouble. You are supposed to leave tomorrow."

The journey to Kutaisi is dreary. I had to take the later train because it was necessary for Teimo to alter my documents before I could qualify for lodgings further along. He gave me some more rubles and walked with me to the station, explaining that he did not wish the truck to be further involved in my adventures. As I joined the ticket queue, clutching my crummy suitcase, he strode off with no farewell. I noticed he had that astonishingly light step of muscular dancers and fat fairies.

The only other passenger in my hard compartment was a garrulous horticulturist from Sochi named Nikolai Globa. Nikolai, who had been a bomber pilot, had a flat, osteal face with square jaw and upturned nose. His body was short and his head was shaped like a cannonball. I suspect this suited its contents.

"Ah, you Armenians," he said. "What do you know of war? It was thanks only to the heroic Russians of Sochi that we kept the fascists out. They bombed us. But we bombed them back. I myself, Nikolai Fyodorovich, flew 237 missions, I was shot down three times but always on the territory of our beloved motherland."

I noticed that Nikolai used every possible cliche. He had careful pride in his stilted vocabulary. "Have you a fair sex?" he inquired, meaning was I married. "Do you like tiny tots?"

He filled me with needless information about his hometown. He boasted: "It never rains in Sochi which has the best and most salubrious climate in the world." Pocketypocketypock went the train as the old steam engine puffed us into the uplands. "Sochi is the narrowest city in the world. It is ninety miles long. It is named for a Circassian tribe, Sha-che. It is part of the Krasnodar territory of the Russian republic and its time is the same as Moscow's."

"Do you speak Circassian?" I asked him in Circassian. He didn't understand, but that didn't stop him.

"We have tea plantations and palm trees and orange orchards and magnolias," Nikolai continued, the horticulturist taking over. "We even have sequoia trees imported from California in the United States of America. We have more different types of flowers per square meter than any other place in the world. We are the only region in the Soviet Union where olive trees can grow, thanks to our benevolent climate. We have the Matsesta mineral water which is good for the kidneys, the liver, the heart, the lungs, the bladder, the urinary tract, the testicles."

I looked at him. "There's nothing wrong with my testicles," I said. "Besides, if you knew Circassian you would know that Matsesta means fire. Fire is not good for the urinary tract."

"Were you aware," Nikolai continued, unperturbed, "that the cypress tree was not known in Italy or Greece until Columbus and Magellan brought it back from America?"

I asked him what kind of plane he flew during the war. He certainly looked more like a bomber pilot than a gentle flower-lover. "Ilyushin-4s," he said, slightly put out by the interruption. "And, at the end, American B-25s. But they were no good.

"The Americans always gave us inferior material. The sugar they sent us wasn't sweet. Even then they were preparing to do us in. But, thanks to the all-seeing wisdom of Comrade Stalin, we have fooled them. Besides, we are better fighters. And we have more natural beauties than America."

"That is reasonable Socialist logic," I stated, looking straight into his puzzled eyes.

Kutaisi is a drab town even though it brags it is Georgia's second city and real capital and boasts that the wines from the sweeping aquarelle plateaus around it are unequalled. Once it was the citadel of Imeretia until the Turkish bashibazooks marched in and ravaged it. Now, as Nikolai explained, it makes trucks. I thought about sending one to T'eimuraz.

Because we arrived at night things were simplified for my assignment. I bedded down on a bench in the terminal waiting room together with dozens of others expecting trains to Tbilisi, Batumi, and Sukhumi. When I opened my fibre suitcase to take out a kolbasa sausage and black bread, I also extracted the Geiger counter, wrapped in the Tbilisi edition of *Pravda*. Stooping, I slipped it under my shirt.

After I finished gnawing my sandwich I laid my belongings on the bench where a charming old babushka with all the right wrinkles promised to look after it. I gave her my benison, then went in search of a kiosk where I might buy a sour beer and find my way to the yards. It was surprising how easy this proved to be.

The kiosk was open, tended by a vulpine boy. All other representatives of the efficient Soviet state were in various conditions of stupor, some from fatigue and some from alcohol. The station stank of cabbage-farts, vodka, and coarse makhorka tobacco. The tracks outside just smelled faintly of coal.

I wandered slowly and apparently aimlessly up and down the lines of freight cars, some of them shepherded by soughing locomotives. I could hear the baaing and mooing of incarcerated livestock. The mere fact that none of the cars were under guard indicated they could not contain a cargo of radiation, even before I confirmed this with my counter. The registering light didn't flicker, except once when I stumbled over a drunken fireman, sprawled beside his tender. "My God," I thought, "how this system fosters fecklessness, sloth, and lassitude."

I had completed my surreptitious survey and even managed an uncomfortable nap, leaning against the bony shoulder of my small babushka friend, when the train for Samtredi and Sukhumi lurched in from a siding. Slowly we staggered off toward the Ryonyi and Inguri rivers, through Adzharia and into the Abkhazian Autonomous Soviet Socialist Republic.

To the east I could see snow-covered mountains glistening in the sun. To the west were fields of grain, vineyards, and villages rich in rooting pigs and skinny dwarf cows, hemmed in by picket fences. I noticed an unusually large proportion of old people, all of them dressed in black. We rumbled further northwestward through a flat, green, swampy plain leading across the ancient land of Colchis to Poti, through citrus and tea plantations. Finally we arrived at the flat border of the sea.

It was early afternoon when we reached Sukhumi, an hour that scarcely favored my own special brand of research. I strolled toward the waterfront and quickly discovered a cafe where I filled myself with beer and where the proprietor, a friendly fellow with handlebar mustachios, agreed to look after my suitcase until I returned. Naturally I had full confidence in his reliability: he was an Armenian.

I wandered out along a lengthy mole on which were built a restaurant and coffee stands. It was rimmed by fishermen dangling handlines, catching little minnows and gossiping while the slate-colored sea lapped unctuously at their feet. It was astonishingly warm considering the season. At one table outside the restaurant five young deaf-mutes drank tea and gabbled with gesticulating fingers. At the outer end of the pier twenty gaffers in rumpled jackets, high-buttoned shirts and visored caps, argued around an earnest game of dominoes.

Of a sudden there was jabbering excitement. One of the fishermen had caught a curious, bloated, etiolated specimen that must have weighed two kilos and had a sickening malignant growth on its side. The poor creature couldn't even flop when it was hauled from the water and spread, gasping, on the wooden pier. There was a clamor of congratulations for the lucky angler; even the deaf-mutes came around to clap him on the back and wiggle their fingers like flexible sea-worms.

Sukhumi proved to be a sleepy town with a shorefront park, featuring oleanders, and a line of low houses near the water. Greek-and-Turkish looking men ambled by the quays haggling with vendors of seeds and nuts and fingering their strings of prayer beads, all of them wearing visored caps and all of them needing a shave.

At one jetty a splendid looking white ship was moored. It bore the name "Gruzia" which is what the Russians call Sakartvelo, as Georgians know their own country in their own language. I was more than puzzled, however, to see a Marseilles registry painted on the bows and life-preservers and also to see stippled in English at the stern: "Keep clear of the propellers." However, all the brass signs affixed on the decks and visible from the wharf were in cyrillic-lettered Russian. Just one more sign of craziness in this crazy land of Potemkin villages, I thought.

Further along the seafront I watched teams of girls on graticulated earthen courts being given rigidly tough coaching at volleyball. Instructors stationed on high stands above the net banged balls down at them. Their chief tutor meanwhile exhorted the girls in a ceaseless rodomontade. Small groups of soldiers wandered past, still wearing their summer uniforms: khaki tunics, brimmed forage hats, and light boots.

It was lovely and peaceful looking out over the palms and cypresses through the soft air and across the calm, gray-blue sea toward distant hillgirt capes to the south. Music sounded not too brazenly on the public radio. It was all so like the Marmora coast near Istanbul—and yet so different.

As the sun slid into the Euxine depths I headed back toward the main square. Just before turning away from the harbor I noticed a group of doleful tourists, Bulgarian or Rumanian from their appearance, filing along the pier to the "Gruzia." A handful of sailors from the crew descended the gangway, their eyes fixed in the direction of a flourish of seedy local strumpets, gathered to entertain them. Regarding the oily sludge, lapping the beach below, I was astonished to see a Turkish newspaper, *Cumhuriyet*, flopping gently like a dead jellyfish.

Hungry for any news, no matter how old, that did not emanate from the stifled Soviet press, I descended and removed the soggy paper. I straightened it along a flat stone and saw a blazing headline: "Earthquake Disaster." Fascinated, I read on . . . "horrible temblor along Anatolian fault . . . entire area shaken . . . at least fifty thousand homeless in Hinis region . . . everyone in Bingöl killed . . ."

Bingöl was the village where, Naci Perkel had told me, my entire family, my father, my mother and my two sisters, were interned until I returned to Turkey from the Soviet Union. They were the hostages for my good behavior; and now they were gone.

If you are not yourself Armenian you cannot truly comprehend what such news means. We are a family people. Our blood is richer than that of others, thickened and rendered more vital by centuries of suffering. I stumbled to the cafe where my suitcase was and ordered a zubrovka, thinking what young Mher told the original David of Sasoun (ah, how right Raja was when she spoke of our affection for the ancient poets). I drank and pondered his words, so often related by my foolish father:

> "My son, how can I help you?
> You have had enough of wandering, my son.
> Enough of wandering.
> Your place is at the Bird Rock,
> Go up to the Bird Rock."

I called the Armenian proprietor and ordered a whole bottle of zubrovka. He sat at the rickety table and watched me gulp it down in silence. When it was empty he in turn quoted to me:

> "Drunkenness took David and carried him off.
> David was drunk, he hung his head on his breast."

How wise the heroic poets were. The proprietor said not a word. He merely summoned his wife and together they supported my tottering bulk to a pile of jute sacks in one corner of the garden behind the coffee house. There, sobbing quietly in my stupor, I spent the night.

Next morning I suddenly realized that while I had lost my family and any meaning for which to live, I had not really ever had a meaning. Besides, the Turks had lost their hold on me.

My new friends gave me eggs and tea and assured me they would protect my belongings. Knowing with the empathy all Armenians share that something awful had befallen me, they urged me to walk in solitary grief.

I headed in the direction of the railway station, realizing for the first time that there was no longer any reason for me to survey it. I was in an unfree country, to be sure, but I was suddenly a free man. I was no longer subject to blackmail, no longer menaced. My heart beat stronger in its sadness.

I looked at the shops across from the jerrybuilt hotel constructed years ago to encourage visitors who didn't come. There were few and appallingly expensive trinkets such as fake Georgian drinking horns rimmed with imitation silver. In the window of one store flapped a tattered admonishment in three languages:

"The sun should be taken in moderate doses, beginning with no more than five minutes . . . only the robust may stay in the sun for two hours at a time. Sun-bathing on an empty stomach or within less than 1–2 hours after meals is not recommended . . . It is not advisable to bathe more than once a day.

"Rowing is one of the most healthful of pastimes. One should bear in mind, however, that it is dangerous to take a boat out to sea in rough weather, to dive from a boat, to approach ships or intersect their course. You are requested to keep within 500 metres of the shore."

What appalling mollycoddles, I thought. Also, looking around at the shabby early morning strollers, I wondered if any tourist had ever actually come to this glum provincial capital and read this sign. Then I recalled the stolid Bulgarians and Rumanians filing from the "Gruzia" and assumed they would obey.

Across the main plaza and beyond the pompous façade of buildings erected by the Abkhazians to grace their capital, a steep hill rose behind the city. I started up a street leading in the direction of the heights. Rather to my surprise I came to what looked like a zoo, an area bordered by an iron fence inside which I saw a few apes brooding in cages. A queue of schoolchildren waited at the entrance. One of them, a bold little girl, asked: "Are you going to the monkey farm?" "Why not," I said, quoting Raja.

The monkey farm proved to be a center for scientific experiments. Baboons, apes, chimpanzees and rarer species were segregated in areas divided by deep ditches or wiring. Uniformed attendants, male and female, nursed, fed, innoculated or bandaged them as required in the name of man's inhumanity to missing links.

There were tiers of cages and several large compounds in between, isolated by dry moats and walls, in which various clans and families of our cousins were leaping about, squittering or huddling in groups to pick nits from each other. Some of the adult creatures, having been subjected to experiments, sat mournfully in corners feeling sorry for themselves, resting their little hands on swaddled bandages about their middles and regarding the world with properly injured looks.

As I stood before a cluster of baboons displaying their red and purple behinds, a pleasant woman in dirty white hospital dress, looking half like a nurse and half like a butcher, asked me if I had particular interest in monkeys. I expressed keen concern and she guided me enthusiastically about, explaining how many diseases these creatures were deliberately infected with and how surgeons neatly cut them up before transferring their attentions to the human species.

After two hours I decided this was scarcely the mental lift I needed and turned to wander out beneath arbors of budding trees when I saw a woman of chryselephantine beauty. She was gazing intently and with undisguised sympathy at a family of baby apes merrily romping over their mother, a sad-faced creature who sat, stroking her retractile pudenda. Her chest was swathed in bloodstained bandages.

The woman stood by the wire netting, clasping a rolled-up newspaper whose print was wholly obscured. One could not even decipher what language it was in. She was tall, which is rare enough in the U.S.S.R., and willowy, with slender, lithe legs, which is even rarer; she had luxuriant golden hair artfully put up, encircled by a single black ribbon, and she was wearing a dress of machine-made trim. Its drabness could not conceal that she was a woman, magnificently made.

Her forehead was high, her eyes blue and deepset, her face well-sculptured with smooth brow and angular cheekbones. Her nose was delicate, straight, and extended in a perfect line to fiercely sensitive nostrils; her mirable mouth was broad and warm, and her chin was prominent, but well-chiselled. Had she not been smiling generously, uninhibitedly, and in a quite unFlorentine way, she might have been a Botticelli maiden.

I went up to her in a correctly earnest way and asked: "Comrade, is that by any chance the Baku edition of *Pravda?*" She seemed puzzled.

Then, ignoring the paper and looking me straight in the eye, she said, "Why, no. But if you wish, you may look at it."

Lamely, like a cheap flirt in the Oteli Londra garden above Istanbul's Golden Horn, I thanked her, picked up the paper, which was from Sochi and in Russian, and pretended to peruse it. She again gazed at the monkeys.

Suddenly something caught my eye, a terse item on the foreign news page: Turkey. More tremors. Yawning gap swallows houses. 1,400 dead now counted at Gonen alone. Bingöl holocaust.

Perhaps mnemonic shock was reflected on my face. I heard her ask, "Is anything wrong?" I showed her the article. "There has been a terrible earthquake at my home," I said.

"Are you Turkish?" she inquired with a suspicion of hostility.

"No, Armenian. Originally from Anatolia. But I found freedom in Erivan. The trouble is my people stayed behind. My mother and my father, they must be dead. See this picture of the corpses? I pulled out from my pocket the rumpled *Cumhuriyet*. "There! My father's fork-shaped white beard."

A sympathetic look embraced her features. With tenderness she murmured: "I am so sorry, Comrade. I too am of the region. My father was Circassian, my mother Greek."

I could say nothing. For the first time in my life I had no wish to mask my thoughts in false words.

She took my hand. "Are you a stranger here?" she asked. I nodded.

"Come, let me show you around. This is a moment when a man needs a woman with whom to talk."

I had a strange foreboding, an intuition that destiny was opening another door, that great new vistas would soon be exposed to me by this offspring of two famous ancient peoples. I needed not just a woman but this particular woman. But not for a moment could I suspect the extent of her magic, nor that through her influence upon me, the actual course of history was dislodged.

Together we strolled into dusty streets, on crumbling side-walks, along cobbled alleys. After a time she said: "My name is Rima Azen. My husband is Abkhazian. We live north, where the mountains begin. My husband administers the trout hatchery of our Abkhazian Autonomous Republic. It is a peaceful life. We have no children. My husband likes to say the trout are our children."

I said: "Children are fish only before they're babies." She blushed.

We came to an old-fashioned, single-story building. Rima suggested we enter. I found myself amidst a hodepodge of stuffed animals, agricultural production charts, huge, silver-rimmed Georgian drinking horns, and photographs of centenarians in long Caucasian coats dancing like light-footed elves.

"This is our museum," Rima explained. "Those Abkhazians live longer than anyone. Shamyl, my husband, says it is because they drink so much, even though they are or were Moslems. The doctors say it is because they take quantities of sour milk. I think it is because they chose the right grandparents. And a healthy place to live. Come, let me show you."

We found a shabby taxi, like the stuffed dolmüz cars Turks share with other people. The driver took us up a hill to the entrance of a park, dropping the other passengers en route.

When we got out Rima led the way along dirt paths beneath clusters of pines and deciduous trees. Everywhere oleander and rhododendron flowered in this strange subtropical autumn. The air was soft and fragrant.

When we reached the summit of the hill, a splendid view opened up. Rima pointed south at a cape sloping gently toward the tranquil sea.

"There is Dioscuria," she said.

"Where? What? I see nothing."

"Because it is underwater. Dioscuria was a fine marble city, built by two brothers who came to Poti, in Colchis, with an old Greek galley looking for gold."

"You mean Jason? And the Argonauts? Of course. And Dioscuria? Twins. You must mean Castor and Pollux."

"Castor and Polydeuces. Yes. But you speak Greek? You knew what Dioscuria meant?"

"Yes. I speak Greek. Modern Greek and ancient Greek."

"How?" she asked in demotic. "Why?"

"Because I speak seventeen languages."

Her own Greek was peculiar. Its accent was thick and the construction awkwardly archaic. "Is your family from the Crimea?" I inquired. "I mean originally?"

She seemed embarrassed. "I do not really think so. My mother says it comes from here. We come right from Colchis, over there, south of Dioscuria. That is what my mother told me. And her mother told her. Our family has been here since always."

"Since always? You mean since classical times? Before the Russians? Before the Turks? Before the Persians?" I fixed her with a soothing and seductive look.

"Yes, and before the Georgians. Even before the Abkhazians. Since the days of the Dioscuri, of the twins. Since Dioscuria."

I was bewildered. Not even lovely women can beguile Armenians into idiocy. "That is impossible," I said. "There are no such families. Do you speak any Hellenic Greek?"

To my amazement she said, in what might have been an accent of more early Doric purity than anything I had been taught in lycee or in university: "Ames, esmen aristoi. Ames Ellines esmen. Entha d'afigdimen. Entha kai paramenomen. We are the aristocrats. We are Hellenes. Where we have come, we shall stay."

Then she added: "Perhaps some day you will believe me. This is our family secret. We tell very few people. Everyone thinks we are mad. Even Shamyl. He laughs. But he boasts about it to his drinking friends."

"And why do you tell all this to me?"

"That is easy. You are the first man to ever show an interest. You listen when I speak."

"Are there other Greeks around here?" I asked.

"Oh, plenty. There are still a few Hesychasts, the mystic brethren, in the monastery. There are large Greek and Armenian colonies in Sukhumi. And all the way to Novi Aphen. But these are new Greeks. Some came from the Crimea. And some came from Smyrna, after the Turkish massacres."

"Yes. The Turks helped build the Armenian colony too. By the same pleasant formula."

Rima looked at me. There was a hint of misery in her eyes.

Finally she spoke: "Perhaps that is what brings Armenians and Greeks together. They make many marriages. And the few priests left do not object, even if they pray differently and in different languages. Not many people pray here any more. At all."

"Do you pray?"

"Yes, sometimes. But I pray to different gods."

That sounded strange. I did not pursue the point. I doubted if the gods she spoke of were Karl Marx and Vladimir Ilyitch Lenin. Her deities were likely to be a more earthy and chtonian variety.

"Where are you going?" she inquired suddenly. The idea hadn't occurred to me. I didn't know. I had no mission any more. I was a free man, a freedom bought by the blood of my nearest kin. No one was hostage to me nor was I hostage to anyone. My only mission, indeed, was to get out of the Soviet Union; and, if possible, to avoid Turkey.

"I cannot tell you. Life is uncertain. It doesn't matter. My mother had a friend at Gagra. Gagra is not far, I think?"

"No," said Rima. "You can come with me. It's on the way to my home. I can leave you at a crossroad where you may find a bus or farmer's cart."

"Your husband? Shamyl? He is waiting for you?"

"No. I came here to bring Shamyl to a meeting on norms between agriculturists and ministers of our Autonomous Republic. He will be here for days. Someone will bring him home. After the drinking." She added this with a sad smile, and then led me down the pebbled path.

Near the waterfront, drawn up by a cafe that seemed to specialize in beer, ice-cream, and sidewalk shoeshines, stood a battered tank truck. It looked as if it carried gasoline to factories and garages but Rima explained it was used to transport trout. She pointed out a thermometer gauge, fixed into the rear above a large tap, and explained the water temperature had to be maintained at constant levels, depending on the age and type of fish. Now it was empty.

She opened the door on the righthand side and I climbed in while she went around to the driver's seat. She didn't look efficient; she was perhaps too womanly; but she drove well.

We rattled and bumped along the narrow road northward from

Sukhumi past flat green fields leading up to the Caucasian foot-hills, tenanted by little cows which Rima assured me were "very productive."

We went through Novi Aphen. To my surprise, people were still swimming off the sandy beach. "It is our warmest town," she explained. Above, on a steep hill, was the bleak fortress from which the Abkhazians fought the Turks. Nearby, on a plot given them by the Czar when he took Abkhazia, towered the Orthodox basilica built by monks of Pantaleion at Mount Athos.

Finally we came to the gray, swirling Mtchishta river. Rima mused: "It is late; why should you go on? Come, we have room. There are many beds. We have a dormitory at the hatchery where anglers stay in summer. It is not summer any more."

I didn't hesitate. There was no real reason to continue onward. The earthquake had severed the umbilical cord that bound me so menacingly to the Turks. At least, by going with Rima, I might have time to reflect on my future.

We turned right and followed the Mtchishta along a series of pools and rapids. It occurred to me to inquire how it happened that a woman, half Greek and half Circassian, should be a golden, blue-eyed blonde.

"You are not the first to ask," she smiled.

"There are red-headed Circassians, you know. As for the Greek side, we have always been blonde my mother says. She claims it is from the Achaians. They were light-haired men from the north. I don't know. I suspect there were Khevsours and Russians in my family past. Maybe even Turks."

The tank-truck swung around a sharp curve to a fork and followed the river course to a cluster of ugly low buildings. We descended and I carried my suitcase into a one-story house. The door was unlocked. Rima guided me directly to the kitchen.

"Let me put on supper," she said. "Then I will show you the hatchery. You can take your suitcase to leave where you will sleep. There is no one here. Shamyl needs no helpers until the summer anglers come. Or when we prepare a shipment. I look after things when he is gone."

I watched while she cut pieces of fat bacon from a vermiculated carcass hanging in a wooden cupboard. She poured broad beans into her hands. Then she ladled out pickled cabbage, put the entire mixture in a pot, set it on a wood stove which she lit, stirred the stew, seasoned it, and left it simmering over a slow fire. She took my hand and guided me outside.

First she slid a key from a dress pocket, unlocked the door of a large shed, and told me to leave my belongings on one of the dozen cots that lay before us, naked without mattresses. "I shall give you blankets later," she explained, and took me out to see the fish.

There was a series of flat, rectangular pans cut out of the loam and connected by intricate open conduits in the earth through which a small arm of the Mtchishta had been diverted. Each rearing tank contained thousands of trout, ranging in size from the tiniest minnows, fresh from incubation, up through fingerlings to catchable fish. The pans were screened off from each other at the conduit mouths. There were larger ponds and a water recirculation system.

As we walked past, a swirl disturbed the surface when sensitive trout felt the pressure of our footsteps and scurried for safety. In one pan, filled with fine, fourteen-inch fario, I saw four or five albescent salmon, almost a yard long, basking in the shallows near the intake, their dorsal fins protruding slightly from the water.

"Yes," Rima explained. "They really are salmon. Not many people besides Shamyl know they are native to this area. He has tagged some of the fish. Several come back a year or two later to breed. All the way up the Mtchishta."

Rima flung handfuls of feed into the pans of greedy fish, depositing the various buckets containing food under wooden benches, and then conducted me from the fish farm itself to the shores of the river where a wooden platform had been erected, protruding over a milky-blue pool. It was evidently very deep and issued from a catchment that tumbled into the torrent below a mountain cliff. "This is where the anglers go," said Rima. "We give them worms and they are allowed to catch what they can. It is not very exciting, I think."

She pointed at the cliffside rising perpendicularly for hundreds of feet. Occasional scrub pines grew right out of the wall. "There is a cave in there. A huge cave. An enormous, long, winding cave.

Very few people know of it and even fewer can find the entrance leading up. It is called Bzoum Ya-Khuapè."

I almost leapt into the stream. Bzoum Ya-Khuapè means the Bird Rock in Circassian. "Your place is at the Bird Rock," said the poem.

We Armenians believe in self-determination. We are not blindly led by fate. And yet I now knew, deep inside my marrow, that I was being guided toward a new destiny by some suprahuman force. And that this last descendant of the fleeing Argonauts had been designated as the instrument of this force.

Rima continued talking. "Hundreds of years ago," she was saying, "when Queen Tamara captured Abkhazia and placed it under Georgia, a Circassian robber chieftain lived there with his men. They were good robbers. They stole from the rich and gave to the poor. Often I go up there and sit, looking out toward the sea, thinking about these things. Those times were romantic. Maybe, after supper, I shall show you. I have lanterns. Now come. We shall eat."

"The Bird Rock," I kept repeating to myself. "Go up to the Bird Rock."

The stew was bubbling in the pot. It smelled magnificent. Rima poured red wine from a large earthenware jug with a wooden stopper. It was good wine, heavy and sweet. We ate and drank a great deal. When I proposed we should make love, she said, "Of course."

She took me to the next room. We tumbled on a broad, soft, unmade bed below a shabby icon of St. George killing the Emperor Diocletian disguised as a dragon. She made love remarkably well. Her body, stripped of its factory dress, was even whiter, more soft and infinitely more feminine than my experienced eye expected. Her breasts were huge, like Persian melons. Her waist was slender and her thighs were strong. Her navel winked with mischief.

"Ah," she sighed into my mouth at last. "David you were designed for me." And then again, later, gasping: "Millions of fish. Millions," she whispered.

"Dioscuri," I said. "Thus. The twin-backed beast."

"Otototoi," she murmured in classical accents. "My Apollo."

Again we made love. Who was the poet who spoke of infinite variety?

As we lay in each other's arms, resting at last beneath the benevolent ferocity of St. George, I asked how Shamyl, either a bad Moslem and a good Communist or vice versa, could bear to exact his connubial rights in the name of Christian hagiography.

"The situation does not often arise," she said, "and when it does, he is usually too drunk to care. He is a bad Communist as well as a bad Moslem. Only Armenians and Greeks can keep their inner thoughts while worshipping at strange altars."

I have learned through the years to take what comes and to ask no questions; I have learned to regret nothing. Were I to start, one lifetime would not suffice to regret the mistakes I have committed. I thought of the hideous and evil women I had known in sordid places, and of the chirping little innocents I had deflowered in my pedagogic days at Roumeli Hissar.

Now all these stains were washed away. For a moment I was what I might have been. For this, more than anything, I thanked Rima. She was asleep. I put my face inside the tent of her tender hair and cherished her in my arms.

It was black darkness when she awakened me. I saw her, leaning on an elbow looking down. Moonlight silhouetted her face and neck from behind.

"Come," she said. "We must leave. Something dangerous could happen. But I shall not let you go far.

"Come with me. To the strangest place you have ever seen. Come, take everything along."

I dressed while she lit the light and made tea in a samovar upon a chest of drawers, and I watched her drawing on her dress, a home-knitted cardigan sweater, and heavy, laced boots. She bundled her astonishing hair into an overflowing lump and tucked it under a shawl.

Then she took a torch, handed me two kerosene lanterns, a fistful of wooden matches, a flat loaf of bread and some goat's cheese; she led me to the dormitory to pick up my suitcase, seized three blankets from a pile in the corner, and beckoned me to follow.

"Just imagine," she said, "if the meeting ended early, if Shamyl came back unexpectedly. When drunk he can be very fierce. Abkhazian men are jealous and ferocious."

"Even alcoholics?" I asked.

"Above all alcoholics. Besides, sometimes other visitors arrive. It is known we have room. People in these parts expect hospitality."

I followed Rima's torch beam as we picked our way past the deep Mtchishta pool, along the path leading by the wooden anglers' platform and up a series of stepping stones to the waterfall. When we reached the cascade, Rima slipped behind an immense boulder.

For an instant I stood in the darkness, splattered by cold spray bouncing from the rocks. Then she returned, extended her hand, and I followed her down a dank passage, the cliff-face wall dripping on the left, a sheet of downward-sliding water thundering on the right. It was deafening.

At the end of the fall her torch turned left. A steep set of rough-hewn stairs mounted interminably, broken only by irregularly cut landings, along a zigzag passage that finally led into a large cavern entered by an angular iron saltire. Rima successively lit the kerosene lamps placed at spaced intervals. She showed me a mattress and heaped blankets.

Then she took me to the spelunk rim, sheltered by a tangled spinney of brush and pines sprouting from the cliff-face, and showed me how it opened directly into the sky. Far below, we could see dim lights in cottage windows and in the hatchery.

She stood on her toes, flung her arms tight around me, gave me an exhausting kiss, and murmured: "In the morning, when I can, I'll bring tea and sugar and bread." Then she was gone, leaving me in unexpectedly jejune loneliness.

CHAPTER

VII

BEFORE the vistas of my new existence opened up, I spent many days in the cavern over the rushing river. The winter winds passed through the woods and slipped stirring down to the pool, snapping off twigs, leaving behind faint uneasiness. The stirring invaded my calm; the sap expanded in the cracking trees. Shamyl had returned to the hatchery below but Rima had installed me within the Bird Rock and whenever she came, which was often, there was a new rustling. I would turn, to suddenly glimpse her figure moving far below or, at night, the twinkling of her torch. She brought me books, food, wine, blankets, fuel and a little stove as if to insure my permanent presence. Somehow she endowed me with new reality. We could find no words equal to the fact of being together.

One morning I worked furiously and built a fireplace of large rocks, and, tossing aside branches and dirt and boulders, I cleared a space. I spread pine needles about evenly, and I chopped saplings with the dull hatchet I found in the corner. All the while I imagined myself as that early Circassian robber who, taking from the rich to give to the poor, dwelled in this place during Queen Tamara's day. The afternoon was spent in anticipation.

That night drew around cold and clear; the wind swelled and, above, it was furious, whipping the clouds. When Rima came, I said soon this wind will rub against us as it does against the clouds; and I detected her shiver.

We lay on a pine needle carpet by the cavern entrance and stared up at the clouds. I could feel the blood running through her from head to foot and when she sat up I put my arm around her and started to take down her hair. Enormously sexual, she lay close, heart to heart, thigh to thigh, breast to breast, hand to hand, mouth to mouth, close as close but never quite one being. The night gleamed above and shone silver on the running Mtchishta.

Rima told me tales of the warring, clashing tribes that had fought among these hills and jagged peaks since the first dish-faced Scyths stole through the passes, with gleaming eyes that saw secret beauties no one else could see.

From these fastnesses the fighting Moslem Murid monks, forming behind their fanatical leaders, leaders never taken alive, slaughtered all intruders and dwelled in their mountain Aôul villages, without women or children, only warriors and eagles, singing their songs of death to the howling winds. And Agha Mohammed, the Persian Eunuch, whose troops marched northward here from Tbilisi, raping and murdering. His soldiers marked their triumphs by hamstringing one leg of each captured virgin.

Here in the gloomy clefts, storms had always battered with sudden spitting flames. Above us to the East was Kazbek where the haunted Prometheus, stealer of fire from the gods, lay tethered. All along the intervening aretes flew the great white bird of Solomon, regarding—like me—the past with one eye and seeking the future with the other.

I contemplated Rima and I thought of how love creeps in by stealth and by stealth slips away, just as Rima did, and of how wives are said to be young men's mistresses, middle-aged men's companions, and old men's nurses; and of how I never had a wife nor would I ever be old.

One morning I saw a timid little snake peep out from a crack in the rocks and taste the sunlight with his flicking tongue. I remembered Rima's telling me that the flat Moughan, dividing my Armenia from the Persians, had always been defended by hordes of deadly serpents writhing in sinister formations along the lower Arax river. Even Pompey, when he wished to march into the Caucasus, was afraid of the evil multitude and turned elsewhere.

It began to rain that night. I awoke, cold and lonely. There was a restlessness again, a noise beyond winter. First there was a hollow noise of the wind and then there was a shimmering noise as of flames; then a thudding of drops upon leaves and a dull thrumming at the cavern edge.

It rained harder and harder. The drops splashed into the cave and steamed from the dank pine needles. The smell pervaded everything, and it was fresh and at the same time mouldy which is a paradox.

That night Rima came to me softly, abruptly, and where there had been nothing but emptiness, there she was.

And once again she said: "I have a foreboding. Something terrible is in the air."

My mother's teachings came to me, from the Nazarene text: "Surely those who believe and those who Judaize, and Christians, and Sabians, whoever believeth in God and the last day and doth that which is right, they shall have their reward with their Lord; there shall come no fear on them, neither shall they be grieved."

There was a look of desperate sadness on Rima's face. Almost before she had finished kissing me she said, "He is in a black mood of suspicion. Shamyl. It is the last night for a long, long time. I cannot stay. But before I leave you I will confide my secret. Only you, you with your courage and ingenuity and knowledge and imagination; only you with your deviltry and refusal to believe in the impossible, can make something of it. And if it destroys you, what does it matter? Perhaps you will think of me when it does."

Then I knew there was an inner meaning in the words of David of Sasoun, which my father always quoted to me, the words of the White Devil.

Rima lit three kerosene lamps in the back of the cavern. She took a sharp, short stick from her sweater pocket, walked to the triangular illuminated space and scratched shallow furrows on the soft sweating loam. Then she put three gnarled, brown kernels into my hand and ordered me to cast them into the ridges. Wondering, I did so. "Watch," she said, staring with peculiar ferocity.

Suddenly first one, then another, then another tip of bright metal began to protrude from the earth and visibly to grow upward. Moments later, two ancient helmets and a foxskin cap thrust silently out of the dank floor.

I crossed myself. A spasm of terror shook me. "What magician's trick is this?" I whispered between gritted teeth. "Ssshhh," Rima murmured, placing her forefinger to her lips. And three men grew before our eyes. Fearfully, I intoned my father's words:

"The White Devil called out to Mher:
'Hey, human! Neither birds on the wing nor snakes on the belly
Fly hither or crawl hither.
How have you dared to come hither to me?' "

As if they understood and accepted my challenge, the three warriors turned as one, two of them aiming spears at my chest while the third, a little man with tattooed forehead and the fox-skin cap, carrying what appeared to be a wicker shield covered with hairy hide, drew back a slingshot in one compact, graceful motion. I stood still, sweat running down my forehead. Rima threw a pebble among the three. Instantly they turned against each other and began hacking with their primitive weapons.

Two wore corselets that appeared to be bronze. Loud clangs sounded as they dropped their spears to slash away with swords. The third, unable to cast aside his sling and seize the dagger beneath his shield arm, was instantly stabbed. He sank with a groan while the others hammered and cut until, one after the other, they fell, amid their wounds, with gouts of blood welling on to the loam.

"Eleleu, eleleu," they shouted in harsh screams.

"My God, they are Greek," I murmured unbelievingly, "ancient Hellenes."

"Yes," said Rima quietly, the glint in her eyes reflected by the lanterns. "These are the sons of Cadmus. You have sown the dragon's teeth."

In minutes, all three were dead.

"Now help me," Rima ordered. Like a sleepwalker in some frightful nightmare I helped her roll and push the bodies to a pit looming ten feet beyond the furthest lamp. The bodies were small, trimly built, and although well-muscled and armored in breastplates, quite easy for a man of my strength to move alone.

At the verge of the pit I could hear the ripple of a subterranean stream. I shoved each corpse over the edge and heard dull splashes. "This river flows into the Mtchishta," Rima said. "But it is almost blocked by rocks near the entrance. Nothing large can seep out into the open."

"But the men?" I asked. "The soldiers? The ghosts?"

"Those were no ghosts. They were flesh and blood. The underground stream is filled with huge blind pike and crayfish; they will eat the flesh. The bones will rot. And the arms and armor will rust upon the bottom.

"Come," she said, picking up one lantern, nodding at me to take the others, "and now I will tell you my secret, the greatest in the world." Shivering, I followed her through the long, constricted passage.

Rima's story is less easily believed than told.

Agenor, King of Phoenicia, ordered his son Cadmus to go in search of his daughter Europa after Zeus in the guise of a bull kidnapped her. Cadmus consulted the oracle which told him to follow a cow to its pasture and there build a city named Thebes. In a nearby cave he met an enormous serpent with fiery eyes, triple tongue, and an incalculable number of small sharp teeth set in three rows.

He fought the monster with javelin and spear, killing it, and immediately he was commanded by a disembodied voice to take and sow some of the teeth. When he did this, a crop of armed warriors rose, writhing, from the earth. At first they turned on Cadmus, but when he threw a stone among them they turned against each other. All but five were slaughtered; these survivors helped Cadmus establish Thebes.

In the thirteenth century B.C., Jason, pirate of Argos, organized an expedition to sail along the coast of Thrace, north through the straits into the Black Sea, and east toward the Scythian kingdom of Colchis, famous for its gold dust. This was collected by spreading sheep skins along the rapids of rivers rushing down from the deposits of the high Caucasus mountains where Prometheus had been pinioned.

Among the prizes Jason took along on the voyage of his galley, Argo, was an enormous sack of cowhide containing the remaining teeth of Cadmus' serpent. This was safeguarded by Daskylos, son of King Lykos and descendant of Cadmus, the only Theban among the fifty Argonauts. Each night he slept upon the nobby treasure. There were said to be hundreds of thousands of tiny, hard, light teeth in the sack.

When Jason landed in Colchis, King Aeetes agreed to give the Greeks his most famous golden fleece, that immense collection of sewn pelts, its wool rich in yellow dust, if only the Argonauts would sow their fabled dragon's teeth. In the grove of Ares, before Aeetes and his sorceress daughter, Medea, Jason ploughed a field and into it flung a handful of the awful seed.

Immediately a company of armed soldiers sprouted. They turned on Jason, seeking to kill their progenitor, as children always hope to slay their parents. But Medea, being a witch, knew the secret of the teeth. She hurled a stone among the warriors; and each attacked the other, shouting: "Meddle not with our civil war."

Amid the drinking and celebrating that followed, it became clear to Daskylos that Aeetes intended to seize the sack of teeth so he could use its army to overrun all opposing states. Daskylos consulted two of his shipmates, the wrestler Castor and Polydeuces the boxer, both Spartans and known as the Dioscuri, or twins.

Polydeuces had been angry with Jason ever since he forced him to box with Amycus, son of Poseidon, on the island of Bebrycos. Amycus had covered his fists with seaweed containing bronze spikes. Although the resentful Polydeuces did manage to kill his opponent, he and Castor later conspired to overthrow Jason. Daskylos then persuaded them to join him in fleeing the Argo.

On the night Aeetes celebrated Jason's betrothal to Medea, both the twins and Daskylos fled. They stole a small sailing vessel, slid it into the water beside the unconscious drunken guards, loaded it with the precious Cadmean sack and a dozen small fleeceskins of gold dust, and set off northward along the coast of Colchis. They reckoned this would deter any pursuers, for so small a party of mutineers would most logically return to Greece rather than risk further hazards.

The Dioscuri and Daskylos sailed three days from what is now called the Ryonyi river. Finally they put in at a low bluff pleasantly covered with meadows and pine trees. Here they decided to establish their own colony, and bribed a peaceful tribe of shepherds into helping build the city that became known as Dioscuria. It was agreed the twins should rule as joint kings. Daskylos, who married a tawny Scythian girl, was named to supervise the treasury and arsenal, whose priceless possession was the Theban sack.

Custody of the dragon's teeth became the hereditary privilege of Daskylos' family. The crop was never sown. Instead it was carefully protected for generations.

Centuries after the founding of Dioscuria, earthquakes threatened the area, and it was soon evident the city was doomed. The peninsula on which it had been built tipped more and more dangerously into the sea.

The custodian therefore dragged his great sack onto a cart with massive solid wheels, drawn by six white oxen, and lumbered along the shore in search of a new haven. While this procession rattled northward, an immense shock hit the coast; a tidal wave flung itself far inland; the peninsula broke off, and Dioscuria vanished under the sea. These are the ruins that, on a clear day, still can be seen, south of Sukhumi, reflecting below the waves.

Rima's mother was descended from the original Daskylos custodians, whose oxcart had borne the sack to the Mtchishta, and perhaps had later transferred it to the cavern itself. The traditional leather bag was frequently replaced by the treasurers of Dioscuria and, ultimately by two strongly woven cloth ones, prepared by successive generations.

That was the story of a secret weapon more frightening than any clandestine nuclear development in Armenia's Sanga valley. But what did it portend?

"Why me?" I asked Rima, puzzled. "Why have you shown all this to me and what do you expect me to do with it?"

"It is you who have made a woman of me. You, a man. Now I shall give you the power to become a god. It is yours," said Rima. "It is all I have to give you for the sake of our passion, which is eternal."

"Perhaps," I said. "But nothing in this sack is eternal. That we have just seen. Eternity chips away even at dragon's teeth."

I began to calculate. Rima spread a blanket upon the stone ledge that formed a table on the cliffside high above the Mtchishta falls.

question my movements as long as I was with him; he was well known.

Then, grinding the gear-box, we laboriously mounted the grade from the river side, and headed northward and northeastward along the road that led by the Razdan toward the famous Sevan lake. Behind us the white peak of Ararat gleamed.

"Noah," I said, "at least was drunk when he first saw our native land." Spartacus reached down and handed me a bottle of brandy. "It is Armenian," he observed.

The road to Sevan, unrolling above the valley, twists beside ugly villages of rough stone houses with corrugated iron roofs where refugee settlements have been clustered. These are set among dusty, hot fields with enormous poppies flaming amid the grass and grain. A plateau behind stretches toward the great lake, pride of our people, bordered on both sides by vistas of purple flowers and framed by the bare mountains ranging between brilliantly white Ararat and Aragaz.

As we lumbered along and I swigged brandy with a mixture of appreciation and chauvinistic pride, the truck grumbled and bumped, springless but sturdy, and we peered below to our left at the river, looking for factory sites, material dumps, large building construction. I took the small Geiger counter from the bundle I had made around it in my jacket and set it furtively upon my lap.

The apparatus, which was smaller than a cigar box, was the type which registered by a blinking light rather than by beeps or a dial and needle. Its detection focused primarily through a probe as large as a banana. However, it had been adjusted, either by the Russians who designed it or by allied technicians who modified it, so that it could pick up responses with remarkable sensitivity at distances of more than half a mile.

Slowly we rattled northward while I did my diligent best to keep the counter sufficiently balanced so that the lights would have full chance to register any milliroentgen variations. At the Razdan installation of the cement combine that employed Spartacus we drew up by the roadside, two hundred meters from the main mixing plant, and Spartacus went through the motions of changing a tire while I carefully aimed my apparatus in a gradual

Then, together, we carefully ladled out handfuls of the deadly seeds, examining them behind a rock which hid the lamplight from the hatchery below.

Each tooth was about the size and color of a large tobacco grain, almost flintlike in hardness, and astonishingly light, like the desiccated, age-browned, weather-worn incisors of some primeval proto-pike. Laboriously I counted out a thousand, placing them in a scrap of newspaper and hefting it in my hand. It seemed to me they weighed somewhat less than a pound.

At this rate, I calculated, half a million would come to something like five hundred pounds, a load I could handle myself, if need be. I had no idea if more than that amount of the original crop was there.

I asked Rima if she had ever sowed the dragon seed before. She hadn't; nor had her mother. But her grandmother had seen the rite and told her as a child. And there were also family tales of careless guardians in the past. One had consumed too much vodka and tipped a cluster into the underground stream. At first no one knew of this but the cavern floor became flooded and, on investigating, the custodian's wife discovered the river egress was choked up with bones, rotting pieces of flesh and writhing schools of swollen pike, blindly snapping at the feast. Apparently some of the teeth had fallen into earthy crevices and taken deadly human form, only to drown in darkness.

I asked if a tooth dropped in water would become vitalized. Rima didn't know but thought not. When I suggested we test this assumption by dropping a soldier-seed in water, she drew back in horror.

"No," she said, "that would violate the trust. Also it would be immoral, a ghastly sin, drowning an innocent."

"An innocent what? A tooth?"

"A—a creature. A potential life. A living thing."

At first dimly, then appallingly, I was able to understand and, to my surprise, accept her logic. Yet, if indeed the innocent took corporeal shape, would it be more cruel to cut short his life by drowning than by murder?

"You speak demotic Greek?" I asked.

"Naturally. I often spoke it with my mother."

"Well, you know the saying. You kill him as with cotton wool. Ton skotoses me to vamvaki. Either way it is a death. Death by drowning. Death by battle. Death by water or by sword. Or death by simply never being born. Perhaps it is always a warrior's fate to die in battle.

"But here you have an army of men dead because you never gave them a chance at life. You are a goddess who can turn seed into living fruit. You are the new Prometheus whose gift is more valuable than fire. And far more deadly. For in the end, these sad grains are doomed to die. But aren't we all?"

"Yes, but it is sinful to exercise this death-power. So I have been taught." She looked both saddened and afraid.

I began to reckon just what fighting strength I had at my disposal. I had already seen two hoplites, that ancient infantry, and one Thracian slingman with fur winter cap drawn over his ears. The hoplites bore heavy armor and must have been Hellenes because their bodies glistened with hog's lard and sesame oil.

I assumed, harking back to my teaching days, that there were also peltasts with shields, the light, fast troops; Ambraciot seers, lance-bearing horsemen with corselets (not much use without horses, certainly not equipped for jeeps). There must be targeteers and ordinary men at arms with wooden shields and spears; bowmen, hundreds of slingers and javelineers, perhaps the renowned Rhodians with their lead pellets in plaited slings, Cretans with leopard skin kilts as in the ancient friezes.

How would I know their officers? By the color of their helmet plumes, red or white feathers or black horsetail? Would it be by the devices on their shields: painted boars, gryphons? Or by special standards like the golden eagle introduced by Persia? No, not that. The Persians came so much later. My trio certainly seemed bronze-age warriors. Perhaps the most modern of their fellows had clattered in their chariots before the walls of Troy.

What would be the command language? Was the classical Greek I knew sufficient to understanding? At least I did not use the dreadful Erasmian pronunciation. And even if I could communicate with the Hellenes among them, how about the Thracians? The Rhodians?

My Albanian might get through to the Illyrians, provided I avoided all the words of Turkish or slavic root. "Flet Shqip?" I imagined myself inquiring of a buff-jacketed cavalry commander from the Acroceraunian range.

"Some day," I warned Rima excitedly, "I shall have to sow another experimental crop, a larger one, and let them cut each other down so that I can test my communications system. I must know if I am able to bridge the language gap of time. Anything else, I suppose, is manageable. Soldiers don't really have to know what they are fighting for. Only their weapons. And how to understand orders. And perhaps, after creating a phalanx, I may yet have months to train it in our modern ways."

I pondered the job of instructing a white-kilted Spartan in the dismantling of a Schmeisser gun and how much patience and forebearance it would take—before he stuck me with his seven-foot spear.

Back at the stone fireplace Rima was stirring a pot. The fragrance of thyme and steaming mutton wafted through the smoke.

"Come," she said. "You must eat if you are to make love properly."

How wonderfully material women are, I thought.

All night I lay restlessly in her arms and dreamed a tapestry of dreams: of Phasis and Anthenios and the Scythians in Colchis, scrubbing alluvial gold from sheepskins laid out in tubs at the river washings. Of Jason and the fifty Argonauts; Hercules with his studded club; Mopsus, the Lapith, who wore the crest of a starling and could speak with birds; Eurydamus the horse-breeder of Thessaly; the Dioscuri with swansdown cloaks and swan feathers on their helmets; Erginius, son of Poseidon, with a cloak sewn in tuna stripes.

My dreams raced through ranks of warriors in bronze-plated tunics with cheekpieces on their helmets and silver-riveted swords. Were I to harvest tellurians like these would they bring along their ivory-inlaid chariots? Could warhorses be reaped from Theban serpent's teeth?

There were thickset kings with crimson-leather helmets nodding tall plumes, with long swords and daggers by the woodwalls of their sconces; charioteers in leather greaves, their flowing hair bound in clubs; hoplites with crystal pommels on their stabbing swords and gold-inlaid daggers; and noblemen, bare to the hips, with jeweled tassels protruding from the tops of their war boots.

Hairy infantry, their casques strengthened with rolls of thick cowhide, their chests and backs oiled, sword belts around their waists, wore leather pants and clutched shields with painted snakes upon the hide.

Their upper lips were shaven, giving their chamfered beards an oddly wagging emphasis as they roared out battle-cries. And here and there the Cretan levies screamed behind zebra shields from their horsehead helmets, complete with manes and ears.

At market time, in the morning, I dreamed of assembling my levies and they slaughtered donkeys and bulls for the lumbering baggage train. The phalanx dipped its spears and swords into boar's blood and ram's blood and bull's blood and shifted into hollow square formation, carts and camp-followers within, the bowmen and long-range slingers forming in rows behind, horsemen springing to their barebacked steeds, barbarian mercenaries flogging their javelineers, trumpets sounding and battle hymns screaming forth. Leaping Thracian swordsmen danced to the pipes and Armenians, from far to the South of Colchis, wrapped sacks around the hooves of their baggage horses or sat around watching, sipping beer from wooden tubs through reeds.

"What a splendid array," I thought to myself, stroking Rima's long hair, hiding my face in its silk integument. "I shall set forth with my own army and pit it against today's mechanics." I thought of the Turks and their German-made motorized gimcrackery. If a Turk can drive a 1944 Panther tank, why not a Paphlagonian? And I saw myself as our massive Armenian hero, Mher:

"As yet but a young boy, To all in Sasoun he was a pattern of strength, with bearing like his father's, his eyes brightly shining. His face like an eagle's, his cheeks noble: His curls a flame; His stance and his arms of steel—beware, do not touch." Mher! David Avetikyan! Kevork Sasounian! Heroes and conquerors!

"You are a poet," Rima whispered, reading my mind.

"No, it is you who are the poet," I murmured back. "You make love like. . . ."

"Like a slut," she said with pride.

"Thanks be to God," I added. And again we made love sluttishly, and still again, seeking to surmount this multiple death that we controlled.

CHAPTER

VIII

ONE February dawn I awakened to a silence so intense that it broke all romantic oneirology. I peeped over the brim of my cave to see if the world had been drowned in snow. For days a strain echoed in my nerves and my subconscious, as if I were listening to the shriek of a distant owl. But today the owl had nested in a trumpet; both the quivering brass and its own nerve-wracking call were silenced.

Suddenly I knew what I should do. When Rima arrived that morning I had already arranged my affairs.

"I shall go to Moscow," I announced. "It is obvious a man of my ingenuity can find a way of making useful connections. I am lucky—for an unlucky man. And now I have something to offer. I can offer a huge army, unprejudiced by past teachings, obedient and ready to be trained for any purpose. I can offer—at a price—to sell this army to a country that lost 20,000,000 dead in World War II. What could be more logical? I shall make my fortune."

"But," Rima asked, "what if you fail? What if you don't make contact? Or if you are arrested first?"

"Not for you, proud-brave-boy, you weren't meant to go into black earth," I quoted. "We adventurers must adventure. And besides, I shall take with me only a tiny handful of my pocket army. The rest will remain hidden in your secret cave."

"How brilliant you are," said Rima admiringly. "And yet you

have so often told me your profession is that of pimp. Why do you say such dreadful things?"

"I like the life. Plenty of girls." She slapped my face.

I showed her how I had tied three teeth in each of the four knotted corners of my handkerchief. Then I put only my razor and toothbrush and soap in my pockets. I pulled on my jacket and cap, and thrust my internal Soviet documents into my shirt.

"I am leaving my other papers, my inkpad, and my few belongings in my suitcase," I told Rima. I did not tell her that, wrapped in a page of *Pravda*, I was also leaving my charger of gold coins; plus my geiger counter and phial of poison. "If I succeed I shall have to return here to complete the sale," I added. "And if I fail, I shall try to come back in order to escape. With you, I hope, I intend."

Later that morning, she told me Shamyl would be driving to the Adler hatchery near Sochi. He could drop me off within a few kilometers of the airport before veering east to pick up a new load of fingerlings. I was to pretend to be Rima's distant cousin who had arrived while journeying northward through Sochi. She gave me a large sheepskin coat for the septentrional Moscow climate. She had been secretly patching the pelts left behind by one of Shamyl's forgetful drinking companions.

It was very easy and natural. That afternoon I worked my way down the dank stairs and strolled toward the fish pans where Rima and Shamyl were scattering feed. Rima glanced up, feigned delight and surprise, hugged me, introduced me as her mother's kinsman, and invited me to lunch. Shamyl seemed pleased to have someone to break the conventual silence of his household. He pointed with pride to his finny charges and boasted:

"Silver trout. It is this beautiful fish, which incidentally is called royal, that inspired the German composer Franz Schubert to write a sparkling, fiery song. This trout is famous not only for its beauty but also for its taste. Come along."

He maneuvered me to the kitchen where Rima already had three fish sizzling in a pan above the wood stove. The place seemed neater and cozier. Outside, through the windows, I could see the pheasant-colored woods of the subCaucasian winter.

After lunch Shamyl, who had learned of my plans, offered to

drive me to the fork off the Sochi road, and assured me I could easily walk from there to the airfield.

I said farewell to Rima with a courteous, familial embrace, quite unsuited to a leman, but when I climbed into the truck I saw her looking longingly at me and I could read the elided message in her eyes. She was still waving as we bumped from the hatchery path to the road that swung sharply in bend after bend to the main highway.

"Do you know what we call curving roads like this?" inquired Shamyl. "We call them Mother-in-Law's tongues."

I asked him if he was descended from Shamyl, the Murid who led the Caucasus tribes in their guerrilla war against the Czars.

"No, he was from Ichkeria," he said. "I think his family was Chechen or Tcherkess. I am Abkhazian. My father used to brag that we are of the blood of Ali the Djinn whom the Turks called Bulut Kapan, the Cloud-Catcher. He was a great warrior."

Shamyl, a slight, wiry man, seemed to gain stature as he said this. He had the bowed legs of a horse-loving people and fine pointed features, blue eyes, reddish hair and a toothbrush-trimmed reddish mustache. I could easily imagine him in the saddle wearing karakul hat and long tunic.

And yet, as we bounced along in the truck, a horrid odor began permeating the cabin. It was as if Shamyl smelled of rotten fish meal, a strange and nasty stench. Then he turned toward me and the full blast of his breath hit me direct in the face. It was unimaginably foul, as if his liver had decayed, corrupting his entire body.

I suddenly realized that, regardless of his performance in bed, poor lusty Rima must have felt condemned so long as she remained fated to live beside that tainted man. I knew, despite my pride, it was not simply my magnificent Armenian countenance and hero's body that had brought her so quickly into my arms.

As we swayed along the road, empty water-tank rattling, Shamyl boasted about the rocks that loomed on the horizon. "We Abkhazians got our share of land late," he said, "because we were offering a horn of wine to a passing stranger. So by the time we came along nearly all was gone, and God had to give us the last bit which He had been reserving for Himself." He turned to me; I withered in the sour blast.

We passed through Gagra, a resort for bureaucrats, and I was impressed by the fine beach and great trees. Some enormously fat men and women were taking the winter sun, underdone puddings clearly from Bolshevism's elite new class. Policemen with automatic rifles discreetly stood by the swimming area gates and, looking inland, watched gangs of old ladies drafted to labor on the pitted road.

As we approached the turn-off toward Adler and the disbursing hatchery, Shamyl slowed down to let me off. A tenebrous cloud lumbered over the sun. One of those sudden storms which give the Black Sea its evil name began to drop leaden rain. Letting me out, Shamyl not only made no offer to detour for my sake, but drove off with but a curt if fetid farewell.

I trudged along, carrying my sodden sheepskin which was far too heavy for this climate in the first place, and I hunched my shoulders up around my neck. Gusty winds blew from the west, driving wet sheets across the tarred surface. When I looked down on my left, I saw runnels of spume sliding ferociously along the surface of the water.

Finally, sopping wet, I arrived at the little airport and was promptly stopped at the entrance by the MVD guard. Grumpily he checked my internal passport and waved me on. I presented myself at the ticket counter; the long queue was evidence that at least one plane would be going somewhere soon. I noticed a hubbub at the waiting room entrance. A massive black ZIS limousine disgorged two civilians and two security men of, I presumed from my Turkish briefings, the Ninth Guards Directorate. They were all whisked into the salle d'attente specially reserved for superior beings.

I had no trouble purchasing my ticket, and discovered that the Rostov-Moscow plane was indeed due to depart in less than half an hour. I wandered to the window and saw a trim Ilyushin drawn up on its tricycle carriage, its two propellers already spinning. The four ZIS passengers were sheltering near the door of the distinguished-travellers' room, surrounded by a gawk of yesmen.

Among them, his head busily nodding like a chicken's, was the round-faced Globa. Rain glistened on his half-formed features. I could hear his pontifical voice droning: "It never rains in Sochi which has the best and most salubrious climate in the world."

Familiar words, I thought, watching drops spatter off his bluntly turned-up nose.

We were summoned to embark, and as I pushed through the door, Nikolai espied my sorry figure. He hailed me with unexpected friendliness, muttering loudly into my ear: "I am here as representing the Union of Former Frontline Air Fighters in Sochi." Then, before I realized what was happening, he said: "Comrade General, an Armenian comrade who seems to be travelling with you. This is Comrade David Avetikyan. Comrade General and Academician Artem Ivanovich Mikoyan."

I recognized him immediately: the brother of Stalin's friend and colleague; of Anastas, the famous salesman and member of the Politburo. To say the least, I was startled. But I had a rush of confidence: my faith in sudden luck, the luck that had started at the Bird Rock, seemed to be running full tide. Destiny was drawing me forward in a great, rushing sweep.

The short, trim man before me was dark-haired and had a swarthy complexion with sad lines on each side of his fleshy long nose, and skeptical lines upon his forehead. Besides being known as Anastas' younger brother, he was renowned in his own right as an aviation engineer and designer of the great MIG fighters.

Mikoyan ignored my disreputable appearance. He shook hands pleasantly and said it was always good to meet another Armenian. He inquired where I was from. Erivan, I said, and added that I was born in Istanbul. "At least, Comrade," he said, "you have the fortune to live in our Republic. As for me, I was born in Georgia and live in Russia."

An MVD colonel in a long coat came up and saluted, almost clicking his heels. Mikoyan and the other civilian took leave of Globa and, tagged by two security guards, sauntered to the aircraft. I followed at a discreet distance. The policeman by the aircraft steps didn't even recheck my papers. Evidently mere introduction to a member of the ruling class was sufficient to waive routine precautions.

I climbed aboard and sat in the rear, beside a turnip-shaped shawled Tartar woman. She had a preposterously huge ass. I simply couldn't imagine what monstrous shoehorn had squeezed her into the constricted seat. She smelled of garlic.

We took off immediately—no brakes, flaps and lights check; not even testing the propellers as they do in all other countries including backward Turkey. An agreeable plump girl, in brown dress and head-scarf, seemed to be the stewardess, although she said nothing about seat belts. As we rose from the runway and fought our way upward through the storm, I noticed that Mikoyan, seated in the front row beside his companion, was puffing a papyrossi.

When we had bumped over the clouds to a plateau of spotless sunlight, I felt my hand relax the grip it always takes upon the armrest when a plane climbs, and I looked about. The cabin was packed. The stewardess didn't even have a seat. She passed around tea and vodka and biscuits. Up front, she served heaping portions of caviar and champagne to Mikoyan and his friend. I envied them the former.

Across the aisle from him, in twin seats, I saw a couple in European clothes. The bearded young man was infinitely pale. He resembled the corpse of a priest. Beside him sat a farouche-looking young woman with a tiny Asiatic slant to her cheekbones. Although I know nothing about women's wear, I did know that hers was not made in the Union of Soviet Socialist Republics. While I speculated about them, the young man passed out.

Passengers, crew members, stewardess, and co-pilot all vied to bring him around. The stewardess rushed up, held his head by the hair, and clapped an oxygen mask to his face. Various travellers brought out pills, brandy, and drops from their pockets and handbags. Mikoyan and his friend paid no attention.

Suddenly the young man revived. He rose, clutched the small round brandy bottle and before even his lady friend had an inkling of his intention, he reached desperately across the aisle to brain the illustrious aircraft engineer. I, watching from my seat in the rear, sensed his intention and hurled myself down the corridor to block his murderous attempt.

The bearded man's rage subsided instantly. He lay back in his chair, and vomited. Then, again, he fainted. This time he seemed dead.

"Comrade, I must thank you," said Mikoyan in Armenian, smiling nervously at me. "I cannot understand. I have never seen that individual before."

I nodded as if to say it was nothing really, a routine occurrence in my normal life.

The plane which had been heading well eastward of its proper course, started to descend in long, slow, gentle ovals. Suddenly it dropped; the wings creaked; we are scuppered, I thought. Then down we lurched through the clouds, and I caught a last glimpse of snow-clad peaks rimming the thick gray bank to the south. The stewardess cupped her hands and shouted: "Mineralny Voda. We are making an unscheduled stop at Mineralny Voda."

When we hit the runway, I could see a cluster of men and women in shabby white uniforms hovering near the modest airport building. We taxied up in silence. An ambulance drove toward us; the captain emerged from his cockpit and murmured something to the sick man's pretty companion. She kept shaking her head negatively.

Two male nurses and two armed policemen came aboard. Without even bothering to check his condition, the nurses plucked the young man up by the shoulders and led him, stumbling, from the plane. The woman reluctantly followed behind, sobbing angrily, and hollering in what I took to be Finnish accents: "He is crazy, poor dear. He should not travel. They say he can't fly. That his head is too bad. Think what two days on our great Soviet trains will do to him!"

"Indecorous. Uncultivated. Mad," said the indignant stewardess as she escorted the unwilling procession to the door. "A danger to society."

When she returned I asked who they were. "Finns from Helsinki. They have just become Soviet citizens. They live now in Karelia. She claims he is a priest. What kind of priest do they make in Finland? Hah!" She busied herself in smoothing Mikoyan's unruffled feathers.

The police ambulance inched to the airport and the pretty girl walked behind, defiantly shaking off a bosomy nurse and thick-necked sergeant. Our plane swung around and whirred to the end of the runway. I seized the opportunity to take the now-abandoned seat across from General Mikoyan. He looked up from a document he was reading, and grinned. "Many thanks again," he said. I smiled back.

"It is odd to see you in an Ilyushin, Comrade General."

"Oh well, the planes that interest me aren't this comfortable." Then he added, as if in afterthought: "I have just been taking a holiday on the coast. When I am on holiday I like to use regular transport."

A commendable idea, I reflected, and rare in the Stalinist empire.

"It is always heart-warming to see a fellow Armenian," he continued. He waved at the stewardess, ordering caviar and champagne for me. "Vodka would be preferable," I interjected. As the girl brought a tray, he went on: "What takes you to Moscow, Comrade Avetikyan?"

"I hope to make my fortune."

"That is a strange idea for a Marxist."

"Not so strange, Comrade General. Look at yourself. With your incomparable talent you made a fortune—for the state, that is. And also for yourself."

"I see your point. What is your own talent?"

"Teeth," I explained. "I am a tooth merchant."

"That is most peculiar, Comrade. How could even the finest dentist benefit society very much or benefit himself at all by merchandising teeth? Who needs molars? I know something about merchandising. My brother is said to be the greatest salesman in the entire Soviet Union."

"I venture I could prove to you—and your brother—that, if only given the chance, I could benefit our great country as much with teeth as your esteemed excellency has done with your unequalled MIG fighters. I need one single opportunity to demonstrate the truth of what I say."

"But why do you not apply through proper channels? Through the party? Through the ministries of the Armenian Republic? Surely that is the way?"

"I regret, Comrade Academician, I am more cynical. You as an Armenian must understand. Sometimes our glorious system eliminates the top and brings everything and everyone down to the lowest common denominator in order to start upward afresh. Of course, the bureaucrats, technocrats and a few intellectuals climb. They are the most needed. But they are a handful."

Mikoyan chewed his caviar reflectively and looked slyly at his friend. "No matter," he continued. "My assistant doesn't speak Armenian." While I inferred the "assistant" might be an MGB agent, he added: "And what you say is heresy. After all, there is no room at the top for Dashnaks."

I decided it was time to temper my originality. "Indeed no, Stalin the Avatar, the Beloved, the Leader be praised," I protested. "I only wished to explain how difficult it is even for the worthy to become part of the rising social yeast. It is especially difficult for someone in the little-known trade of tooth merchant."

"Did you not try the Party's medical and social sciences sector?" inquired Mikoyan.

"No," I replied. "You may find this hard to believe. But my special genius, if I may be so immodest, belongs to national defense. It is military. If only I could demonstrate to you?"

"Can you demonstrate on a plane?"

"No. Not even on a MIG. But if you could grant me only five minutes of your time in Moscow. In the proper place. Out of doors."

Mikoyan's curiosity was piqued. "Very well," he said, "you shall have five minutes as a reward for what you recently did for me. Where will you spend the night?"

"I have not yet any arrangement."

"Nu, nu, then you will come with me. I have an apartment in the Krasnopresnyenkii Raion. For an enterprising Armenian comrade I will make room tonight." He murmured something to his aide.

Puzzled, the latter regarded me cooly, and nodded.

After we touched down at Vnukovo, outside Moscow, staggering through snow to the airport—I in my pushtun coat like some gigantic Afghan marauder—Mikoyan's assistant marched along beside us.

Breezily, he shoved past the police and Aeroflot officials trying to delay the normal processes of arrival, and guided me to a long, heavy ZIS. General Mikoyan was already seated within. In front, next to the uniformed driver, sat an airforce captain.

"He has no baggage," said my escort. "He prefers to travel light."

[83

"Excellent," said Mikoyan. "And now I will uncover his mystery." Suddenly he looked straight into me with his glittering black eyes. "It had better be good," he warned with a suspicion of stoniness. "A man who boldly seeks fate had best have something truly bold to offer."

I nodded, said nothing, and watched the swirl of snow drift across our headlights as we whirred into Moscow.

CHAPTER

IX

THE old-fashioned building in which the aeronautical engineer lived was impressive even if its outlines were largely obscured by a moving screen of snow. A sullen doorman with atrabilious face appeared when our chauffeured ZIS drew up. Artem Ivanovich led me and his assistant, the putative policeman, to a creaky elevator, leaving the baggage for his driver to handle.

On the top floor he rang the pushbell of his flat. A thick-set Chuvash maid, grinning like a cretin, promptly opened the door. I took off my smelly sheepskin, the others doffed their coats, and Mikoyan ordered something to eat. "It is well into the night," he explained. "I think we can all profit from some bread, wine and shchi before your famous demonstration."

I looked around. The apex of communism lives well, I surmised. I could not tell how many rooms there were but I guessed at least six. The Academician explained that his family was still vacationing in Sochi. He had been summoned back for discussions with Gurevich, his design partner, on the newest model MIG.

The living room in which we supped had a high ceiling ornamented by carved plaster. I could tell from the temperature of the tsinandali that either there was a refrigerator in the kitchen, or the maid had frozen her little pinkies getting the bottle in from the window ledge. These double-tiered Russian windows are no **easy** thing to open.

There was a parquet floor, kept admirably waxed by the Chuvash. A hideous, machine-made Khirgiz carpet extended over it. On a table draped with a garish fake Bokhara was a record-player. The assistant, without being asked, put on an old-fashioned two-step. Mikoyan started to hum.

The assistant, who clearly knew every inch of his boss's domain, offered me the use of a bathroom. It was fitted out with German plumbing, still stamped with the Dresden manufacturer's name. War booty, I assumed.

I returned to find a yellow linen cloth on the round table. The Chuvash had also set it with porcelain, German silver, and crystal glasses perhaps looted from Prague. A great bowl of steaming cabbage soup was ladled out. As I started to slurp it into my avid belly, the assistant lifted his glass of limpid Georgian wine and proposed a toast: "To the Dear Father of the Soviet People."

We drank in silence. Across the way, looking sternly down upon us, was a full-length portrait of Generalissimo Stalin from boots to Marshal's hat, glittering with decorations. The assistant eyed these with undisguised admiration as he fingered the Order of Lenin on his own lapel.

I, however, was more interested by another feature of this prepossessing flat. In one corner, ensconced in a massive brass pot, stood an unhappy looking rubber tree.

Mikoyan followed my gaze. He explained: "It was a present from the horticulturists of Sochi where we often go. I think your friend Globa was responsible. Do you like it?"

I said I too was interested in horticulture, and had discussed the subject at length with Nikolai. I then excused myself and went over to the pot, and fingering the heavy green leaves, assured myself that the brass contained plenty of earth.

A broad clay container was neatly inserted into the hammered metal pot. Its diameter was about a meter and it was more than a meter deep. It thus provided several cubic feet of rich, well-tended soil for my experiment, and avoided my depending on the snow-covered ground outside, which must have been frozen down to considerable depth. "A fine plant," I said, "an excellent specimen. And admirably cared for."

"Now," said Artem Ivanovich, as we pushed back our chairs

and finished sipping our glasses of tea, "I think it is time for you to convince us that the exotic profession of tooth merchant can affect the destiny of our beloved motherland. Remember, you promised a demonstration."

I nodded. I reached carefully into my pocket where, while in the bathroom, I had placed one grainy kernel of my treasure from a knotted handkerchief corner. I reassured myself by fingering it. Then I turned to the others and said: "Kind Comrades, please stand away from the rubber tree just a bit. And Comrade Mikoyan, forgive me, but although it is unlikely that you should carry firearms, your assistant, perhaps, has a pistol? If so, would he be good enough to keep it at the ready?

"Have no fear of me," I added, seeing their look of alarm. "It is just a precaution. An emergency precaution. Clearly I mean no evil. And clearly I carry no weapons myself or I should not have made this suggestion. Is that not obvious?"

Mikoyan nodded. The assistant, who had produced a stubby German Walther from an invisible holster slung beneath his shoulder, said nothing. His face assumed the expression of an intelligent, wary halibut. Both stood motionless in anticipation.

I walked to the rubber tree, poked my forefinger deep into the moist dirt and dropped in the tooth. Then I patted soil over the indentation and stood back to watch.

I was worried. Just what sort of earth nourished a tooth? Would too little produce only a midget? Did I need well-dunged loam to nurture a soldier, or special chemical fertilizers to mature him? As I stepped back, the answer came.

There was a strange, straining noise. The brass container, designed for slow-growing vegetation not fast-growing men, creaked. But it held. Suddenly the smooth surface budged, and a bronze-edged spear point protruded. The rubber tree, tormented by pressure, shook and listed.

"My God," said Artem Ivanovich with entirely uncommunist sincerity. "Holy Saint Rhipsime!" His MVD assistant stood riveted in awe, pale blue eyes almost glazed in galvanic trance.

Something was thrusting upward through the compressed earth. The bursting jar cracked; the rubber tree collapsed backward. The clay shattered. And suddenly before us, in a syncope,

stood a well-built little soldier. A bronze helmet with leather
flaps protected his neck and cheeks. He wore a barded Corin-
thian breastplate and gleaming Chalcis sword. He carried a multi-
layered leather shield, and an ashen-shafted stabbing spear—the
battle array of an Athenian infantryman.

He opened first one eye, next the other, and then stared,
dazed. Before anyone could intervene, three bullets fired from the
Walther drilled his cuirass. It gave less protection than a woolen
vest. The MVD guard had shot him through the heart. The
ephemeron fell, bleeding. The brass bowl overturned. The crash
was deafening. Screaming, the Chuvash servant rushed toward us
down the hall. Mikoyan slammed the door, shouting "go to bed."
The general's guard stood stupidly, jaw hanging slack, gun
clenched in a mutton fist.

Mikoyan muttered: "Only my brother can tell us what to do.
This is beyond my competence." Regarding me with terror and
respect, he picked up the telephone to call him, the Deputy
Chairman of the Council, and Minister of Foreign Trade, most
famous of living Armenians.

The communication was terse. "Immediately," my host kept
repeating. "Immediately. It is more than life and death." Then the
three of us waited in silence. No one thought of touching the
corpse, the pot, the fallen rubber tree, or the mound of blood-
soaked earth.

The bell rang. Artem rushed to the door and clasped his brother
in his arms. They went immediately into another room, and
closed the door. I could hear a confusion of voices. I became
nervous, but the MVD assistant slouched, without speaking. He
was clearly in traumatic shock.

The two Mikoyans returned at last. Anastas Ivanovich was introduced; shaking my hand, he scarcely noticed me. His head was
turned askance; he was staring at the little Athenian's hairy corpse.
For a long time, he asked nothing. He merely stared, seeking to
reassure himself that Artem had not suddenly gone mad. Then he
turned and inquired:

"You have more of these—these so-called teeth?"

"Yes. I have a few with me. I have almost half a million hidden
in a secret place. All are potential soldiers in perfect condition,

and requiring only training and equipment. And for a price—
for I too am an Armenian trader, your comradely and most respectful excellency—I can make all this available to the esteemed
Soviet government."

"And if we are not interested?"

"I should doubt if the all-seeing vision of . . ."

"Yes," interrupted Mikoyan.

Ignoring me, the brothers resumed an agitated discussion in
Armenian. I inferred the Trade Commissioner was no longer
certain of Stalin's friendship. Anastas said that recently, when he
had called, he could not even get to speak to the great leader.
"That Mingrelian," he spat. Mingrelian, I considered. Beria, the
security boss, was the only member of that Georgian subtribe
anyone had ever heard of.

"I thought you and Beria were on good terms," Artem ex-
claimed.

"We were. But conspiracy is his nature. He is behind that doctors business; now he is closing in on Molotov and me."

"But this is crucial, so incredible. You have to insist."

"Perhaps," said Anastas Ivanovich. "Perhaps you are right. Perhaps this might mark a turning point." He glanced at his watch.
It was close to midnight. "Stalin is certainly at the Nearby Dacha
now. I shall call Poskrebyshev."

He disappeared to the rear of the flat. "Aleksandr Nikolayevich
Poskrebyshev," Artem explained. "Head of the personal secre-
tariat. At this hour he will be with the boss. Comrade Stalin is
like an owl. He is at his best from midnight until almost dawn."

The Minister returned. "Sasha thought I was quite crazy," he
said with satisfaction. "I told him I was the bearer of even more
important tidings than the atom bomb."

He looked disdainfully at the mess on the floor. "Artya, get rid
of that," he said. He pointed to the assistant. "Have his colleagues
dispose of the body. They are good at that sort of thing. The
archeological museum might be pleased to have the armor. Tell
them it was found on Soviet territory. In the Caucasus. That will
stir them up. Think of the bullet holes. Oh. And I shall see to it
that you receive another rubber tree."

Briskly he grabbed me by the arm. "Come," he commanded.

"There isn't much time." To his distaste I drew on the stinking sheepskin coat as we slipped out the door.

It was still snowing. We climbed into the large black limousine and the chauffeur turned along an empty boulevard. "To Kuntsevo," commanded Mikoyan. He then turned to me and said: "Stalin has many dachas but Kuntsevo, the Nearby Dacha, is where he likes to spend his time these days."

I nodded. Talkative by nature, I felt this moment too ominous for conversation. But Mikoyan, more obviously anxious, chattered like a bird.

First he praised the genius of his brother. Then he talked of the Armenians with pride and regret, with pride for their qualities, with regret for their history: he, the great survivor of purges, most guileful of our guileful race. He spoke of his son killed as a pilot during the Great Patriotic War. He warned of Poskrebyshev and what a fawning toady he was. A pompous toady, a former veterinarian, a nonentity.

Above all, he spoke of Stalin, seeking to caution me on my behavior, warning me not to be surprised by what I would find. Surprised, I thought! And how surprised will Stalin be?

Lavender curtains covered the rear and side windows. I peeped around the one beside me, peered through the slackening flakes, and saw a completely deserted city. There was not an automobile, not a truck, not a pedestrian, not a tram, not even one police agent. "Normally we go out in three cars at a time," Mikoyan explained nervously. "And always we take a different route. They tell us how. But this is different. There was not even time to tell the Chekists. We go by Pravitelstvyushchi Chaussée."

He started to admonish me, the man on whose fate his own entirely depended. "Watch his eyes. Watch the eyes of Josef Vissarionovich. If they seem to go flecked, be careful, be discreet. Stay silent when his eyes are flecked." And, a few seconds later: "Be careful never to reach abruptly into your pockets. He is suspicious. He is afraid of swift gestures. Of hidden things. And there may be other people, equally suspicious. People you don't see."

The road was lined with snow-blanketed trees. A gate appeared, breaking the bland linearity. The ZIS slowed as it approached.

Mikoyan saluted when the first guard, in tall Astrakhan shapka, waved us on. "There are three stops," said Mikoyan, "three fences." He looked again at his leather-banded wrist watch. "Surely he must have finished the movie by now," he remarked doubtfully. "The chief likes movies. Many films."

We rolled along in slow motion, snow crunching on gravel. We pulled up finally before a low, wooden-eaved entrance. In the shadows stood two armed guards in white-dusted karakul hats. At the door, his bald head framed by the light behind, waited an obsequious pudgy man.

"Well, Sasha," said Mikoyan. He didn't introduce me but I gathered it was Poskrebyshev. We flung our coats on a rack and the secretary led us in to Stalin's presence.

The first thing I heard was a voice, the voice of a very old man, a low, soft, gutteral quaver with a peculiarly lilting accent, Stalin's voice. "So, Mikoyan," it said. "Lavrenti Pavlovich tells me you have brought a dentist to interrupt our meditations. Some kind of travelling dentist." The neume of this menacing phrase endured for seconds.

I was appalled. Lavrenti Pavlovich, naturally, was Beria: the dreadful little toad smirking behind with rimless pince-nez. He seemed to wear a carapace of smug hostility. Artem's assistant clearly had broken out of his trance enough to report to his lord and master. Our mission was off to an inauspicious start.

"Not a dentist," I interjected before Mikoyan, still flabbergasted, could recover. "Respectfully, Comrade Stalin, I am a tooth merchant. I deal in indescribable secrets and weapons of death."

Beria regarded me with what, in another, might have seemed an intelligently humorous gaze. "You know, I presume, of my latest directive," he said looking at Mikoyan rather than at me. Mikoyan wilted. He seemed to know precisely what to dread. "My directive," Beria repeated.

" 'The secret services of the capitalist states are trying to smuggle their spies, wreckers and terrorists into the U.S.S.R. and other countries of the Socialist camp.' " I glared into the police boss's glittering eldritch lenses and said with a confidence I did not have: "I am no spy or wrecker, only a tooth merchant of benevolent and patriotic disposition."

The comfortable room we were in was warm and ugly. It contained plush furniture, lace curtains, heavy drapes and clumsy, fringe-shaded lamps. On a corner table an impressive phonograph stood, topped by an ashet of oranges.

Even here, in the home of the mightiest potentate, everything stank of cabbage. Cabbage soup, cabbage salad, cabbage belch, cabbage fart combined in a clinging insidious odor which penetrated even the oak plywood trimming.

I was less impressed than I expected to be. I had become so accustomed to enormous paintings, posters, and statues to a Generalissimo victorious in sweeping military great coat that I was taken aback by Stalin's smallness.

Like Mikoyan, Beria, the servile Poskrebyshev, and a porcine general named, I think, Vlassik, who kept bobbing in and out, Stalin was at most five foot six. They were all the same. God must have formed all Communist leaders from one mold, I thought. They dressed themselves and got themselves faces once they arrived on earth.

The Generalissimo was but a pendulous-nosed old man puffing on a hooked pipe, whose bowl seemed filled—oddly enough—with Turkish leaf tobacco. He was indeed short; standing, I could see the bald spot in his graying hair. His mustache was dirty; his double chin desiccated. His hands were ugly, with fat fingers; and one arm gave the impression of ill-adjusted awkwardness.

He was wearing a worn service tunic and soft leather Caucasus boots. He seemed to be suffering a chill, for a brown cashmere shawl was drapped loosely about his neck.

He spoke with a pronounced Georgian intonation and his language was often deliberately rough. From his thick syllables, I had a feeling that he had already drunk a good deal.

Despite the air of informality I soon discovered—from the way even intimates treated him—that Stalin's private life, like his public life, was paved with ceremony and roofed with superstition. The Marshal himself made plain that he looked down on everyone, regarding people not so much as fools, but as different shades of scoundrels, all eligible at his command for sudden death.

While I studied our host, Poskrebyshev obsequiously slid in and said: "Yo Sarionich?" The implied intimacy astonished me. "Yo Sarionich, Malenkov on the phone. He wants to know if you expect him. And should he bring Khrushchev, Bulganin, Molotov, Voroshilov?"

"No," said Stalin, looking around him with a deadly humorous glint. "Let this be a Caucasian night. Only Georgians and Armenians. You Mingrelians, Lavrenti Pavlovich, are Georgians after all, are you not? At least when we permit it?" He glanced inquiringly to Beria. I noticed his eyes were becoming lightly flecked.

He went to the record player and put on a Lezghinka dance. Then suddenly, holding his arms out at an angle, he started to shuffle like a graceless penguin. He hummed, slightly off key. He said to Mikoyan: "You see how much better than Armenian music this is?" And then, slowly, he began to stamp his feet.

Stalin was dancing. His narrow, sloping shoulders moved above his vegetable shape; jagged, yellow teeth appeared behind the full graying mustache. With his sparse, mousy hair, he looked like anybody's shambling grandpa—until you saw his eyes. By now they were heavily speckled with discoloration.

Beria in Georgian muttered that it was perhaps time to pay attention to the unknown guest.

"What kind of an idiot are you, Lavrenti Pavlovich?" Stalin screamed in talionic rage. "I say we will drink first. That doesn't mean you have to get drunk all over the place yourself."

He clapped his hands; the sound was not very loud. "Matryona Petrovna. Drink. Something to drink," he shouted, suddenly genial. An aged servant staggered in, dumpy, with a round honest face and the Russian potato nose. She was bearing a tray. On it beside small glasses and a carafe of rose-colored liquor were two bottles with amber contents and unfamiliar labels. She smiled, and her rectangular mouth was like a ventriloquist's.

"Does the Armenian comrade, the dentist, know pertsovka?" Stalin inquired, looking behind my eyes.

"Yes, Comrade Stalin, I know pertsovka. But what is in the amber bottles?"

"Aha," he said. "You ask many questions. That is Kolkhida. It is a sweet Georgian liqueur. It comes from Kholkis, where the Greeks stole gold in ancient days. I drink it often."

Quite a coincidence, I thought, and I shivered at the idea of quaffing such an obvious sugary fake. "Thank you, Comrade Stalin, but on reconsideration I shall take pertsovka." Vodka mixed with red pepper, I reckoned, was less treacherous than sweet liqueurs. But I looked at the labels. There, indeed, was Jason's Argonaut, sailing on a white background above the Samtrest label of the state manufacturer.

His eyes gleaming, Beria took a glass of the Kolkhida. Mikoyan too complied with this ghastly Georgian chauvinism. Gulp went Stalin; gulp went Beria; and gulp, as if shriven in an alcoholic's league, went Mikoyan. I, meanwhile, swallowed my pertsovka, smugly confident that its fiery content, no matter how hot, was less awful than the amber poison.

Stalin pulled his shawl closer about his neck. With the faint suspicion of a totter, he walked around the room, staring into the garden through the twin sheets of glass that customarily shield Russians from their winter-fright; only his, with the yellow-tinged panes, were also bullet-proof.

Through the slightly blurred window I saw a small fenced-in garden; lamps set among the surrounding trees were focused brightly on the center. I noticed that this had been kept fairly clear of snow, but I hoped it wasn't frozen in one solid block.

Beria lifted his glass to challenge Mikoyan and myself. Reluctantly we both accepted another drink. Old Batyushka Stalin joined in. "You are always pushing people to the booze, dung-face," he said gruffly to Beria. Beria answered in Russian, with a heavy Georgian accent, "It is only to keep you company, Josef Vissarionovich." Despite his unctuous manner there was arrogance in his voice.

"And you, Anastas Ivanovich, why is your gaze so shifty to-night?" asked the Generalissimo in Caucasian intonations. "Why don't you look us in the eyes as do honorable men? Have you something guilty on your conscience?"

He didn't wait for an answer. "Nu," he said. "Let us eat." Again he clapped his hands, again the surprisingly soft sound, and again an elderly woman servant silently bundled in.

It was a different woman. "Gamardjoba batona, Valechka," said Stalin. Ruched and wimpled, Valechka didn't look Georgian but seemed to understand the language. Certainly someone in that strange household knew the secrets of preparing a good Georgian meal.

Stalin, following the woman in black dress and plain white apron, led us into the next room. He sat down heavily at one of the four places set about a round table. Eagerly he surveyed the food: caviar, sturgeon, cabbage salad, butter, pickles, salmon eggs, vodka, pertsovka, bottles of kakhetinskoye wine, flat round Georgian bread, like our Armenian lavash.

"So," said Stalin, tucking his napkin under his collar with evident satisfaction and anticipation, "tonight we are just a Caucasian brotherhood, the Caucasian chalk circle." I was surprised; not wholly uncouth, I thought. He knew about Brecht. Intelligent, informed, if vicious. To my astonishment, suddenly as if reading my innermost thoughts, Stalin looked right at me, again peering behind my eyes.

"Maybe we are not intellectuals, we old Chekist fighters. But not everything in the world escapes us. Ech, Comrades?" he said, staring at the uneasy Mikoyan. "Even if we Georgians, unlike you Armenians, are not bourgeois intellectuals. Or," he added, sliding his hooded glance over Beria's oily face, "accused of being agents of the capitalist-imperialists, like certain Mingrelians have been."

Our host began to eat. It was obvious he enjoyed both the quality and quantity of his food and that neither were good for him. He picked bits of caviar from his teeth and swallowed them. He slurped the thick kharcho lamb soup of Gori. Munching the flat bread, he chewed hard on the sticky crust; many of his teeth were obviously false. He wiped his fingers on his napkin and rapidly stained it. He drank heavily, at last abandoning the ghastly Kolkhida for pertsovka, and then for the Georgian wine.

All the while he didn't sample a dish or a drink until after someone had tasted from the same platter or bottle. Was he afraid his closest friends or servants might poison him? I also noticed that Beria, although drinking more than anyone, only ate vegetables which he stuffed into his mouth with greasy fingers.

"So, you like our pertsovka," Stalin said to me. "My father started me on it when I was still a babe. First he would let me suck wine from the end of his finger, then, as a toddler, vodka;

finally pertsovka. My father taught me well. Now, just you ask Beria here, this pertsovka serves a purpose."

He held up a glass of the rose-colored liquid so the fire reflected against the ceiling light. "Ask Beria," he repeated. "One must blast the way for what comes afterward. Atomic blasts, ech?" he added, pleased with himself.

"Comrade Josef Vissarionovich," said Beria with what passed for a hearty chuckle, "you are a strong, strong man."

"All of us whose fathers fucked on the floor are strong-backed," said Stalin with a dodderer's unconvincing boast. "Is that why you devils won't let me retire now when I want? Because you see there is strength in me yet?"

Immensely proud of himself and well warmed by the intoxicating infusion of bad alcohol, he turned and said, "Twice I asked my Committee. And they voted no. Yet there are those who call me dictator." He had a neural subcutaneous twitch.

Our host was obviously pleased that four mountain tribesmen were gathered here in the bosom of slavdom, and gathered at the top. Tipsily he talked about Georgians and Armenians and their old Christian history. He even recalled that many years ago he and Mikoyan had studied at theological seminaries.

"Malenkov is not the only one who knows words of Latin," he prattled, "And Greek too. The language of priests."

He spoke of the Persian invasions, how the Czars built the Military Highway southward, about the early migrations of the Scythians, Avars, Lombards, Chechen-Ingushi. I could not help but think how he and Beria had had the Chechens rounded up and destroyed.

He began talking about Jews and abruptly he assumed a ridiculous Yiddish accent. "You look like Jews, you Armenians," he grumbled, scowling at Mikoyan. "It is fortunate that you only look like them. They even say you are smarter than Jews.

"Well, let me tell you this. Beria and I are Georgians—that is, he's a Mingrelian—and we know it takes will as well as wit to rule. It is we, the Georgians, who rule the Armenians and the Jews."

"And the Slavs," said Beria smugly. "And the Slavs," said Stalin, nodding. Mikoyan sat quietly, his expression masked, his mouth a rictus.

Stalin continued: "I will acknowledge one thing. The Armenians and Jews at least share a common sense of judgment. They never speak well of each other."

The housekeeper, Matryona Petrovna herself, began bringing in successive platters. On one was trout that, I thought, must have been flown up from the south, perhaps fattened by Shamyl. "Where is this from?" Stalin asked. "From the base," said the housekeeper curtly. The others seemed to understand.

"Podlinaya forelle, podlaya forelle," said Beria. "Genuine trout. Base trout." A heavy, strangely belletristic play on words. Tsinandali succeeded the kakhetinskoye wine; then, as we chewed on nuggets of mutton shashlik, dark red mukuzani.

Stalin had the disagreeable habit of exposing the yellowed, rotten bones of his teeth when, after munching bits of meat, he would reach into his mouth to extract the remnants. Then he would lay the masticated mouthfuls in a row around the rim of his plate and seem to wipe his fingers on his greasy mustache.

He began to talk in cynical aphorisms, many of which did not logically follow in sequence. "The science of politics and the art of ruling are very different matters, ech, Beria?" he remarked. "They say the Romans knew. Bread and circuses. And some Czars. The knout. The real truth is the crowd only obeys the logic of its passions and people go where they hanker to go. This is the secret of revolutionary government. Revolution and liberty are words which must be kept apart."

"For the sake of the state," said Beria, "I should advise our grandchildren to be born with very thick skins."

"Beria is adroit," Stalin interjected. "He understands where bodies lie. Or how to put them there. He knows the value of fear. He knows where he is going but not how to get there. He began like Azov the spy; he continued like Yezhov. I wonder if he will end like Yagoda."

Understandably the police boss turned pallid and started to sweat. I remembered that Yagoda, his predecessor, was slaughtered by our host. Of a sudden, the Vozhd took another swig of pepper vodka. He seemed to shake his gloom.

"My true companions," he said warmly, regarding our dark Caucasian faces with alcoholic torpor. "My companions in arms.

They come from the balls of mountain men. Ech?" This especially pleased Beria.

"Give us music, Anastas Ivanovich," Stalin mumbled. Mikoyan went to the next room and placed a new record on the player. While he was gone, Beria, winking grossly at all of us, put a red tomato in the napkin of the Foreign Trade Minister, and left it on his chair.

When Mikoyan returned, Stalin suddenly shouted: "Sit." Jumping with nervousness, Mikoyan sat. His expression told us that the tomato had burst. Stalin and Beria exploded in guffaws of laughter.

"Ah, the Prosecutor," Stalin chortled, looking with pleasure at the beaming Beria. "What humor. What wit." Mikoyan smiled a courtier's smile. There was no happiness in his eyes.

One o'clock passed; still the eating and above all the drinking continued. The Generalissimo began to talk about the West. The evening's movie apparently had been American. He was much struck by the masses of automobiles he had seen.

"Garbage," said Stalin. "All they create is garbage. We put our steel in guns and tanks and ploughs and tractors to be used. They put their steel in foolish cars they drive one year and then leave by the roadside. Everything they create is garbage—of a permanent sort. They want to dominate the world and all they have to offer is one enormous garbage-making machine."

An original approach to ideology, I thought. Mikoyan, on safe ground, seized the cue. I could almost hear the mathematics ticking in his statistically-minded brain. "Josef Vissarionovich," he said, "the capitalists don't produce capital, they transmute it, they transmogrify it. They lack intelligent direction from the top.

"Now take this case. There are about two and a half billion human beings on earth. And they each shit about a pound a day, when it is all averaged together. That means approximately a million and a quarter tons of shit a day or over four hundred and six million tons of shit a year.

"We here in Russia use this valuable product to fertilize our fields. But the Americans are garbage-minded. Everything they make they throw away. The shit of their society is indestructible. All they leave is wreckage. They shit steel. Industry is too good for them because they don't know how to use it. They lack direction."

Stalin was enormously impressed. His eyes faded as he stared alcoholically at Mikoyan. "Nu," he said. "Most profound. Most profound, Anastas Ivanovich."

"There are too many Americans," Beria interjected. "They clutter up the planet. Now that we have our atom bombs we must get ready for the inevitable. The bomb and the rocket.

"They drip in fat, the Americans, and they do nothing. When we have finished with them the world population will be back in size to what it was after World War II. And a good thing for everyone. Who wants to be cluttered up?"

Obviously this was very high-level intellectual discussion. Stalin nodded more and more, sometimes in approval, sometimes on the verge of sleep. "Remember what the priests told us, Anastas Ivanovich?" he asked Mikoyan. "Everything is blessed by the sign of the cross. And what was the cross? An instrument of torture. Should that be a symbol of good? Are the Americans to be known by the sign of the electric chair?"

Mikoyan was pleased by the opportunity presented and perhaps befuddled by the Kolkhida and the Georgian wine. "No, no, no," he protested. "Maybe for the Americans with their breakfast foods and advertising. But our blessed fatherland would never be famed for the Lubyanka and the firing squad. The old saints of whom they told us in the seminary, Josef Vissarionovich. They were promoted like Comsomols. They weren't holy; they just waited in queues for sainthood."

Stalin neither followed nor particularly endorsed this line of reasoning. Again his expression became bleak. "Saints, Comsomols," he said, turning to me. "Very well, Comrade dentist, what do you think of this?"

"They go together," I added imperturbably. "Communism is surely the best system made for angels although anarchy might have its points for them. Men? Men are different. They need leadership, I suppose. Ideology makes no allowances, no elbow room."

None of them understood what I was saying. Nor, indeed, was I sure I did myself. The conversation abated. Obviously it was time to move. Stalin carefully wiped his hands, first in his mustache, then on his soiled napkin.

We drew back our chairs. Mikoyan, as if following normal custom, almost pushed me to a lavatory in the hall. There were two toilets; and as we stood, discharging the poisonous liquid bursting our bladders, the Foreign Trade Minister whispered: "He is in a doubtful mood. Be careful."

We were washing our hands when Beria stumbled in. "That Koba," he spat out. I gathered Koba was Stalin's comradely name. "He is too alone. He gets depressed. He stays in those damned movies far too long. And then he wastes our time because he cannot sleep." He pissed furiously. Neither Mikoyan nor I dared say a word.

Beria left first. Mikoyan, while buttoning his fly, whispered in Armenian, "Remember the Arab proverb. Kiss the hand you dare not bribe and pray for its destruction. Lavrenti Pavlovich!"

When we returned to the airless, stifling sitting room Stalin was personally pouring Armenian cognac into four small, gold-rimmed glasses. He gestured to us to drink, gulped, shook his head slightly as if to clear it, and then spoke with less fatigue and more clarity. "Now comrades," he said, "now to our affairs.

"We will see what the Armenian dentist has to tell us. And we will see what reason his sponsor, Mikoyan, had to bring him to this Soviet womb. This had better be as good as they say, Prosecutor," he continued, looking at Beria. He reached into a stone jar, stuffed some tobacco into his curly-stemmed pipe, and fingered his deep metopic wrinkles.

"Not all who come here are permitted to tell about it afterwards. It is not wise to disappoint us."

Beria belched as if restraining a desire to vomit. Stalin produced a pad and pencil from the table beside the tobacco jar. Absently he began to doodle. Wolves. One after another he drew wolves. He looked at me with a heavy drunkard's face and his bloodshot eyes were now feelingless, blank as agate.

"So," he began. "Mikoyan tells me you have a weapon of unprecedented force and subtlety. He also says you will sell it. Not exactly the altruistic spirit of socialism. But then, we will see.

"Mikoyan says you are prepared to demonstrate. To validate your claim. He will stake his head on it. Mikoyan has a very elusive head. Your own neck looks but moderately solid. I should not like to see you fail."

He resumed doodling. Beria took on an aseptic appearance. An evil quality appeared on his fish-bellied, pince-nezed countenance. Stalin added:

"Of course you realize you must pass this test. No one will ever know the consequences of a failure. Including you." I could tell what he meant without even bothering to examine his shaded eyes. I nodded.

"Mikoyan insists the proof is overwhelmingly conclusive. That it is not simple legerdemain. Well, we shall see. We shall see. Now tell us about the weapon you say you are prepared to sell. Then perhaps you will also tell us the price." There was an ironic undertone to the last remark.

Succinctly, as if I were explaining the virtues of an efficient new tractor, I ticked off the advantages to Moscow of my proposal. First I took pains to stress that I had only a small sample with me. I emphasized that, should anything unforeseen occur to me, the bulk, hidden in a place of maximum security, would be impossible to locate and utilize.

Moreover, I lied, in case I met with accident, ironclad arrangements I had made with the NATO command would immediately go into effect and automatically transfer my secret to their hands.

Stalin scrutinized me coldly. He doodled. Round and round his pencil—absently—drew one looping figure after another. Now the doodles looked like nooses.

"In this age of instant crises, what I have is the perfect instant answer," I said. "We already have instant tea, instant coffee, instant television pictures, and the instant rush of rockets. But what I have to offer is the instant homunculus, the instant soldier. And I can sell in unbelievable quantities.

"The price is a hundred million dollars," I continued, "in gold. Deposited to a numbered Swiss bank account on a stipulated date. I shall meet your designated agent in Switzerland when he has received confirmation that, pursuant to my instructions, the merchandise has been delivered and proven satisfactory. The transaction shall be immediately completed. It seems to me this is a fair and efficient formula."

Mikoyan regarded my Armenian acumen with a hint of admiration. He clearly endorsed my exegesis. Beria was both hostile and impatient. Stalin's expression was a mask.

"This is a negotiation," he sneered. "I do not care for diplomatic negotiation. It obscures the facts. Sincere diplomacy is no more possible than dry water or wooden air." I ignored this menacing remark.

I said, nodding to Mikoyan, "we may have fools in Armenia but we take care not to export them. Let me go on.

"Now for the description. I can deliver either immediately or piecemeal, as desired, 500,000 fully trained soldiers, ready to obey any command and to fight in any cause. And I will prove this boast to your satisfaction or the deal is off. Is that not fair?

"I guarantee, moreover, that these warriors are prepared to die upon instruction. Death and victory are the same to them."

"There is no religion on the battlefield," said Stalin. I continued:

"I will prove to you that you can transport my army secretly and undetectably to any battlefield you may desire, and at any time. You only have to dispatch your officers with these men to insure their commands are carried out."

Stalin looked intrigued. Beria, his face contorting into an undisguised sneer, spat, "Impossible." Stalin said, "Conjecturable at best," and drew about his neck the shawl discarded during dinner.

"Or," I went on, "if you prefer, you can smuggle them in smaller strength; in platoons, battalions, regiments, or even divisions to any country in the world. I guarantee the ease with which this may be done.

"They will follow without question, unhesitatingly, the orders of the commanders you place in charge of them. You can use them as secret agents. Or as hardy frontline troops for the most arduous assignments. They can even serve as parachutists—every one of the half million—and without parachutes. They are tough, fearless men."

"Hmmm," mused Stalin. "The standing army everywhere and in all countries is intended for use not so much against the external as the internal enemy. Lenin. How would this truth apply?"

"No problem," I said. "You can, as it were, keep my army absolutely passive and immediately ready anywhere, at home or abroad.

"There is only one serious drawback, which can easily be surmounted by a system with such vast resources and such ability at human engineering. My men, to be effectively commanded, must receive their orders in Greek. Classical Greek.

"That is the Esperanto of my force, the Volapük. It is international, and contains elements speaking languages which even your best-trained GRU officers are unlikely to know."

A gleam flickered in Stalin's eyes. "Greek," he said. "That should not be difficult. How many Greek partisan refugees came over to us after the Markos revolution in 1949? Comrade Beria, make me a report on this. Tomorrow. No, today." He glanced at his watch. It was already long past two.

Again I emphasized: "Classical Greek. This is of profound importance. However, if you can find an adequate officer corps for my special force, you will be in position to storm any objective you may wish; and with the advantage of complete surprise."

"Good," said Stalin. "Surprise is even more important than artillery. Surprise is the key to strategic success. From Lao-Tse to Clausewitz. Mask your intentions. Then strike with surprise." He brushed his retting mustache to the left and to the right with the forefinger of his right hand, and he inquired: "Are these men armed? How are they equipped?"

"Comrade," I said. "You shall see for yourself when Your Excellency allows me to give my demonstration. Admittedly, there are minor problems; at present, my men are equipped only with what you might call commando weapons. But they are ready for silent combat, above all hand-to-hand."

"Aha, cold steel," said Beria with factitious approval.

"Bronze," I replied. I went on:

"And their uniforms you will wish, I should think, to modify slightly. Their present garb differs from those of conventional Red Army units. But I see no major difficulties; their new uniforms will depend, presumably, on the assignments selected for them."

"Presumably." Nothing could disguise the interest now flickering in Stalin's mind. "But what, should I decide to accept your offer," the leader insisted, "convinces you that such a force is ready to obey my orders as implicitly and explicitly as they do yours? You say unindoctrinated Greek troops will die for any cause, simply on instruction?"

"I guarantee this," I said. "Furthermore, I shall soon persuade you of the validity of this guarantee. True, my men know nothing of Kutuzov, Suvorov, Rurik, or of Dmitri Donskoi. I suspect," I admitted somewhat archly, "their background on Marxism-Leninism is insufficient."

"Marxism-Leninism-Stalinism" purred Mikoyan. The pleonasm seemed to oil his confidence.

"But their discipline is complete. It is total. Totalitarian. You may reckon on it to the end. And their only homeland is the battlefield on which they fight. Their cause is your cause, whatever it may be. Their nationality is war, and their life is death."

Stalin seemed deeply impressed. "These are men of my own liking," he commented. "Good Communists. Should what you say prove true, I can do something with these men. As for officers, we can find them. We can get enough Greeks, and can train them in the classics if need be.

"Beria, if this test satisfies me, I want another report—as soon as possible—on the potential of our Black Sea Greek population. Odessa. Yalta. All the Crimea. Yes, and Sukhumi-Batumi. Even Uzbekistan, the suspects. Also I want from the Frunze Academy a time estimate on how long it takes to instruct intelligent officers in classical Greek."

"With emphasis," I suggested, "only on basic military doctrine."

"And now I wish to hear more about this question of transportation and surprise," Stalin remarked.

"The ease and secrecy of transportation is a primordial factor."

"Your Excellency," I said. "Vozhd. Comrade, if I may venture. I am prepared to guarantee and prove to your satisfaction that you could move the entire force—if so you wish—in one night by a single tiny U-2 biplane.

"The only problem is transportation for the officer corps you must provide. My entire army takes up less space in long-range carriers than one single officer with personal equipment. I shall demonstrate how and why.

"Officer personnel and weapons. Ordnance. Rations. Logistics.

These can be planned for and adjusted to the type of operation you require. Battalion strength. Corps strength. Airborne or seaborne.

"Allow me to repeat that under proper conditions and for rudimentary commando knife-work, you can drop my men without parachutes on a target area and all, if you require, from one or two gliders. Furthermore, they are fully capable of seaborne operations. You can land a force of thousands on hostile shores by one submarine, although they may not be trained for this in full. Yet no one will suspect their presence until it is too late to react.

"There is another overwhelming advantage: If you are willing to use them for uncomplicated slaughter, whether seaborne, airborne, or submarineborne, my warriors require no sustenance. No food, no drink, no special clothing. Until they are launched in action. Think of the savings in money and in transportation. Think how planning can be simplified."

"Aha," said Stalin. "What you say has interest. War has its own grammar but not its own logic. I am prepared to see what you will offer. We socialists are men of open mind."

Mikoyan's face was eagerly illumined by my speech. At last he seemed to feel the risk he had taken by acting as my sponsor was justified. Beria, cold, cynical, obviously not prepared to venture an opinion of his own, looked guardedly at Stalin. Stalin doodled in silence, frowning at his pad.

"I must say, dentist," he growled loweringly. "There had better be no farce about this. Marx said history repeats itself, the first time as tragedy, the second as farce. For you, a failed experiment will prove more tragic than farcical."

He relit his pipe. I could smell the tobacco. He had switched to Virginia leaf. "Very well," he said. "Now for the test. Let us be practical before we theorize. How and where do you intend to convince me?"

I had already prepared myself. I said I needed space outdoors. Perhaps three hundred square feet. And would there be a pick or rake or something with which I might scrape the frozen ground? I was not, I explained to my puzzled audience, accustomed to demonstrations in subzero weather.

Stalin summoned Vlassik who took me into the garden. The

snow was thin and patchy. The earth was metallic with cold; it rang like a bell.

There was a depressed rectangular area which, Vlassik explained, had once been a swimming pool but was now filled in. With the suspicion of a smile he added that the leaders, when swilling pertsovka, occasionally pushed each other in; the security police worried about the effect of this amusement on Stalin's health. Along the edge, near the dacha's artificial heating, the ground seemed relatively soft.

Vlassik disappeared for a moment into what must have been a tool shed, and came back bearing a small mattock. "Will this do?" I nodded and sank its point into the loosely-packed earth. It yielded more easily than I had expected. "Are you cold?" he asked. It must have been far below zero Centigrade but I shook my head.

After five minutes I signalled I was ready. I returned indoors and found the three Soviet leaders all seated on one divan, tossing off small glasses of brandy.

"I am prepared, Excellencies," I said. "But may I respectfully suggest that this officer Vlassik, who has been most helpful, and other possible witnesses be requested to leave us alone. Our experiment is not to be shown to parties not directly concerned. Assuredly, as your electronic devices already have discerned, I bear no weapon. But naturally it might be better if someone were to search me first."

Beria, without embarrassment, proceeded to do just that. I noted, as he ran his white hands swiftly along my back, chest, sides, and legs, that he had learned more than the administrative techniques of his profession. When the police boss stood back, satisfied, he patted his own chest below the left arm, adding: "I, of course, am armed as always."

"Good," I replied, "then perhaps we will be able to dispense with the guards behind the house. I saw two boot tracks under the trees while I was preparing our little laboratory. Trees are not good camouflage in winter."

Stalin chuckled. He instructed Vlassik to go and, on his way, to tell the MGB guards from the Ninth Kremlin Detachment to withdraw from behind the dacha. "You may advise them that this order comes from Comrade Beria, who is responsible for our safety." Vlassik saluted and left.

"Two final things," I said. "First of all, may I point out it is bitter cold. Although there is no wind I counsel you to put on greatcoats. Secondly, Comrade Stalin, if you wish to personally sponsor the actual creation we are about to see, like pulling a nuclear switch, I caution you that what may seem an act of indiscipline might occur among my troops.

"Pay no heed. If Comrade Beria will merely throw this among the soldiers, they will devote their attentions only to themselves." I picked up the empty brandy bottle and handed it to the police boss. Then we went into the hall and donned overcoats and hats.

Stalin, still wearing his shawl, swung into a long military garment of double thickness which extended down to his ankles. He jammed a fur-lined pillbox hat with earmuffs on his head. Mikoyan put on the black paletot with black astrakhan collar, and the hat in which he had arrived. Beria wore similar garb, but in pearl gray. I had only the Tbilisi visored cap originally provided by the Birinci Buro and Rima's sheepskin.

Stalin led us into the night. Beria brought up the rear. I noticed he had acquired an electric torch. I stationed the silent trio at the brim of the former swimming pool. They were now making no secret of their intense curiosity. Then, saying "watch this with care," I reached into my jacket pocket, took out three scaly little grains, and handed them to Stalin.

As he cast them into the scrabble marks of my mattock, I prayed that although customary dank, warm, springlike sowing conditions did not obtain, the magic first encountered by Cadmus three thousand years ago would prevail as infallibly as in the past.

Indeed, almost immediately there was a tiny stirring in the snow, a faint glint of metal. Slowly, silently, two flat, ovoid spearheads and the crest of a bronze helmet, stiff with its purple horsehair, rose up into the night.

There was a gasp from the little audience beside me, a rustle of predawn wind through naked branches and a scarcely detectable sibilance of stiff earth crumbling and falling aside as the force protruded from beneath its surface.

"Holy mother of God," said Stalin quite unconscious of the inappropriate phrase; he stared at the moving clods like a mesmerized bird. Mikoyan crossed himself almost dolorously—in the Armenian, not the Orthodox fashion. Aha, I thought, still the old seminarians. Meanwhile, Beria's tight mouth sagged and fell open.

By chance—for it was impossible to foresee the destiny of each individual serpent's tooth—the first crested casque to emerge proved to be that of a royal chieftain who soon was thrusting upward: waist-high, hip-high, then shivering in purple tunic, knee-high; his shield uncovered, a short sword with crystal hilt clasped in his strong right hand, and his hairy legs shivering in greaves. An intense and ferocious expression gripped his shining, strigilated face as he prepared to lead his phalanx into battle against unknown foes.

Beside him appeared two hoplites in breastplates of infibulated metal plaques and metal casques, with round shields of double-thickness oxhide, wearing high, rough-leather sandal-boots, and carrying javelins. One of them had the device of an erogenous lapith drawn upon his buckler. The other's was plain leather, hairy side out, with a dried cistus stuck in the grip. The eyes of the spearmen, as they opened, were fixed on their royal commander, awaiting some order from his contorted lips.

The three Communist chiefs stood in silent amazement. For the first time in their combined existence they were embraced by a sense of numinous awe. "In truth," whispered Stalin with no attempt to conceal his astonishment; "in truth, this is a greater miracle than the atomic bomb." As for me, I suppose I had proven a new scientific theorem: dragon's teeth sprout in snow.

At this instant the ancient king contorted his eyes, screaming "Eleleu, eleleu." He pointed his stabbing sword at the Soviet dictator and waved on the two spearmen beside him as he turned to attack.

"Hurry," I shouted to Beria. "Hurry. For Heaven's sake throw the bottle at them."

But he seemed paralyzed; he did not move. I couldn't tell whether he was struck motionless by fear or whether he secretly favored the warriors' intention to slay their creator.

Suddenly aware of the threat, Stalin stood still, arms akimbo, absolutely and admirably unafraid. I reached down for the mattock and hurled it among the Greeks. Instantly they ceased their assault, and turned savagely against each other. Grunting, hacking, sobbing, they fought with a clashing, panting noise. Gore was soon spattered on the snow.

But as I looked at Stalin, a frenzied alarm began twisting the marble of his expression: one of the spearmen—the prince's sword thrust into his back—staggered forward and, falling, slammed his shield against the Soviet leader's head.

Stalin reached up as if to loosen the collar of his greatcoat; his eyes were blinking in a daze. He seemed intent on speaking, on saying something of utmost importance.

Again I hollered at Beria: "Shoot! For God's sake shoot!" He never moved. I had a strange feeling that he was contented with the desperate outcome of the exercise. Meanwhile Stalin, his eyes rolling up, slowly toppled forward, spumous froth on his lips.

"Vozhd, vozhd," shouted Mikoyan. Beria, with the well-filled shoulder holster, merely looked on. He watched while the prince coldly and efficiently finished cutting his spearmen down and then, wearily, with the suspicion of a groan, himself subsided in the snow. A javelin had pierced his chest from side to side. Blood spread in coagulating pools as the three men, so very recently born, died.

CHAPTER

X

"VLASSIK," screamed Beria. There was no immediate re-action. The command to remove all security forces from the garden area behind the dacha clearly had been efficiently and successfully carried out. Mikoyan signalled to me, and together we tried to lift Stalin.

His stubby shape was awkward and far heavier than I would have thought. Just as we were clumsily bearing him into the dacha Poskrebyshev ran out, followed by four uniformed MVD men, machine-pistols slung about their necks. "Doctors," ordered Beria. "Bring doctors right away."

"Has someone attacked the chief?" Poskrebyshev asked, looking with unmasked hostility at me. Beria shouted:

"No, you idiot. It is a stroke, Sasha. A heart attack. A seizure."

Poskrebyshev, puzzled, first stared at the gaudily attired Greek bodies sprawling in their own blood, then at the unconscious Stalin, with eyes turned upward into his head and a bruise begin-ning to swell on his cheek where the spearman's shield had struck him. The secretary rushed inside to telephone.

"Bury those bodies, and bury them instantly, secretly and deep," Beria ordered the MVD quartet. "And if a word of this ever escapes from any of you, you know what to expect." He looked at me. "As for you, Armenian, we will come to that later."

Before I had a chance to contemplate this threat, Dr. Lukomsky, Stalin's physician, arrived. Apparently he had accommodation somewhere on the property. He was clad in a military coat thrown over what seemed to be a kind of caftan. He was carrying an old-fashioned black kitbag.

We started laying the stricken leader on the divan where we had been sitting but Professor Lukomsky waved us on toward a low-ceilinged room with unusually small windows. As we passed through the bare, uncurtained door, I saw it had an automatic bolt, controlled by a switch at the bed-table. Clearly it was Stalin's bedroom.

We stretched him, as directed by the doctor, on an outsize sofa upon which the dictator apparently preferred to sleep. The physician loosened Stalin's tunic, undid the pants at the waist and, with Poskrebyshev, gently drew off the soft leather boots. At that instant Matryona Petrovna entered, sobbing into her kerchief and nervously fingering a little chaplet. Behind her I could see two more Chekists with tommyguns.

Lukomsky lifted each of Stalin's eyelids and peered beneath with a needle-like torch. He felt his pulse, his temples; with a stethoscope he listened to his heart. He spoke to him softly but received no answer. "No, no, no, he is not dead?" moaned Matryona.

Lukomsky then turned to the little group watching and said in a quiet voice: "He is not dead. But he is suffering from a cerebral hemorrhage. I do not know if it was caused by a blow or not," he added pointing to the increasingly dark contusion.

"It is obvious that he is totally paralyzed on the left side of his body and largely on the right. He is unconscious now and I doubt if he is even physically able to speak. I have already sent word to Kuperin to come."

"Principal Kremlin physician," Mikoyan whispered.

"At first examination," continued Lukomsky, "it would seem there is bleeding inside the brain. Perhaps also a clot that produces such quick paralysis. Very heavy. Very serious. Probably climacterical. I would not be certain he will recover consciousness."

He looked directly at Beria who, to my amazement, seemed to be smiling to himself. He had taken off his overcoat and was playing with the shoulder holster outlined beneath his arm. "Ech, ech, ech," he was muttering. "We shall see," he said in Georgian. "Soon we shall see indeed."

Then, abruptly, he roared at Lukomsky: "It is critical? He will die? That is certain?"

Lukomsky was frightened by the responsibility forced upon him. He answered only: "I cannot tell. Surely it is serious. Has Comrade Stalin been under sudden strain? Where did he get that bump on his head? It is all most unusual.

"You know, he is now seventy-three. I had cautioned him. Was he drinking? Was he drinking much? Was he very emotional? You must tell me. I have to take immediate precautions before the specialists arrive. I dare risk nothing drastic."

Beria was openly taking charge. "Yes, Comrade doctor," he said, "Josef Vissarionovich had been drinking. I tried to dissuade him but he wished to make himself amiable to these." He stared coldly at Mikoyan.

There was a flicker of movement on Stalin's face, a hint of awareness. Beria dropped his commanding attitude and fell to his knees beside the prostrate figure. Slowly Stalin opened his eyes, and wearily he closed them again. Matryona brought a glass of heavily-sugared tea, and the doctor tried to spoon it into Stalin's mouth. He failed. The warm liquid slopped over the dictator's uncollared tunic.

It was evident that he was barely able to breathe. What slight movement his chest gave was most irregular. Mikoyan whispered to me, his gaze subconsciously fixed on Beria, "Perhaps it is better we should go. Perhaps we should be out of the way. There is not much room. The specialists are coming." He took me by the arm and, as Beria, still apparently unsure if his boss would live, began kissing Stalin's motionless hand with his preternaturally moist lips, Mikoyan guided me out the door.

When we entered the hall I heard the fustian Lukomsky say: "We must have artificial respiration at the soonest moment.

"We must have heart massage."

We reached for our coats at the entrance. No one was there. Poskrebyshev and Matryona were still in the mortal bedroom. Mikoyan opened the door and, before we could leave, four men entered in baggy bell-bottomed trousers, one enormous in size and carrying a bulky case. They rushed past us.

"Kuperin," said Mikoyan. "Kuperin and his assistants." No one else spoke. The principal Kremlin physician was familiar with the way.

Mikoyan nodded to the sentries at the door and walked directly to his car. I couldn't figure out how he distinguished it from the other hulking, black ZIS's parked in a cluster beside the dark snow-covered trees. There was no one inside.

Waving me to the other door, Mikoyan, to my amazement, clambered into the front. He slid behind the chauffeur's wheel, stepped on the ignition, revolved the engine several times with practiced expertise, turned on the parking lights, and drove slowly toward the outer gate.

The Trade Minister explained: "Before Beria takes over the security forces and seeks new scapegoats—ourselves—I must get you away. Whether I wish to or not. It is bad enough that you are an Armenian, that I introduced you here, and that one of your abominable tooth-men probably murdered Comrade Stalin."

"You think he would dare to touch even you? Just because you are my congener?"

"Indeed," said Mikoyan. "He has been planning to do precisely that for a long, long time. He is working up plots against me, against Molotov, against Khrushchev. Beria needs no facts to support his cases. He manufactures them. But this time he must above all avoid the facts; this time the truth, not his fabrications, is unbelievable.

"He doesn't want anything but power. My head lies on the road to his goal. For this he certainly requires nobody's confession. This time he won't torture people to tell a truth that sounds like lies or lies that sound like truth. He will torture them to tell lies that sound like lies."

"People will be arrested?" I asked.

"Arrested? No, packed into the Lubyanka like sardines. You and I will be lucky not to be among them. They'll be heaving them in, ruffling their feathers; and if they complain to the new party leadership, 'you are persecuting us for being faithful chickens,' the new party leadership will reply, 'you should have been ducks.' The new party leadership will be Beria's men."

At the last gate, entrance to the dacha property, Mikoyan slowed up the car. He thrust out his face so that it could be well recognized by the guards who, peering from the boles of sentry boxes, hesitantly barred the way.

"This is an emergency," he said in a soft, deadly voice. "A crisis of unparalleled importance has arisen. You two wait here and make yourselves available to instructions from Comrade Beria. Mind you, from Comrade Beria in person. Later in the morning I shall give you additional information."

He enunciated with great clarity: "Open immediately. An impossible emergency has occurred." With no more ado, the car edged slowly but firmly, like a juggernaut, toward the grill. Mikoyan gave the colonel-in-charge few options: to open the gate, to see it smashed, or to order that a leading member of the Presidium be shot down. A clumsy steel pawl screeched; the barrier swung inward. We hurtled into the night.

For some reason it astonished me that Mikoyan could drive so well. His decisiveness was also surprising; he was capable of initiating action of a wholly original sort. He read my mind. As the tires spun down the sideroad toward the Pravitelstvyushchi Chaussée he said, talking out of the side of his mouth with his eyes focused on the white path of the headlights sweeping ahead:

"We are, I regret, inexchangeably linked together in this tragedy. You saw how Beria refused to do what you had told him he must do. It is clear he had no wish to save the Vozhd. Now a time of troubles is upon us. I can trust no one to do what I must do. But first you must disappear. And I mean just that. Disappear."

For a moment I thought he meant this in the Stalin-Beria sense. Then I realized that, were this the case, it might have been far easier for Mikoyan to leave me at the Nearby Dacha. He sensed my thoughts. He glanced for an instant at me and said:

"It is not that Armenian blood is thicker than water. But if Stalin dies, a dangerous period lies ahead. I can take no chances. I do not know just how Beria plans to distort tonight's events to take advantage of them. But clearly he has one sacrificial lamb available. That is me. A second is my brother. It is a question of Beria or the Mikoyans. No one can doubt what choice that white-assed devil will make."

"But I had thought Beria was your friend?"

"Anybody with Beria for a friend," said Anastas Ivanovich, "doesn't need an enemy."

I regarded his profile as we rumbled down the avenue into Moscow's outskirts. Against the powerful street lights, his little prognathous jaw looked grimly set. His nose arched down like a beak above his sad, drooping mustache.

"What do you plan to do?" I inquired.

"I am going to get you as far from Beria as possible before the news of Stalin gets around. And the man who will help me is the only one in Moscow whom I trust. He knows that Beria's agents can make you admit to anything—including an assassination plot, in which both I and any of his rivals would be named. If I can get you and your dreadful teeth away from here, no one will dare mention what really happened. It is too ridiculous, too impossible. Even Beria's executioners would laugh at him."

I agreed. I repeated that it was strange Beria had failed to shoot the writhing Greek warriors when I warned him. Did he really hope something would happen to his chief? Or was he too perplexed by the sheer impossibility of what he saw?

Mikoyan quoted the line of King Arshak that all Armenian children learn: "When I return home I shall take cruel vengeance for everything." There was an intercalary knock to the strained motor.

The dawn police patrol obviously saw nothing peculiar in a huge black ZIS with top priority plates whizzing along the empty streets, splattering muddy snow on the first shift of workers going to their jobs. They must have taken Mikoyan for a regular chauffeur and me for a special guard. The lavender curtains covering the back windows hid the fact that we were alone in the swaying car.

Slowing down enough to minimize any danger of accident, we turned by the Kremlin's Borovitsky gate, headed over the dirty Moskva river tossing riven floes of ice, and swung in the direction of the Lenin Hills. It was still dark. Lights were starting to appear in windows of flats in the enormous castellated luxury apartment blocks recently erected for the favored new class.

"I dare not use a telephone," Mikoyan murmured, as we drew before one of the lesser, outmoded cubes. "Come with me." He left the car behind a row of ZIS's and TAIGAs lined along the curb. I followed him through a hallway scarcely in use for more than a year, but already redolent of cabbage and black bread, to an elevator which rose shakily to his push.

We got out on one of the upper floors. He rang the bell outside a somber door. Suddenly I realized this must be the back entrance to his brother's apartment. "It is Anastas," he called softly when the first shuffling sounded within. I understood that, regardless of his importance, whoever answered would welcome reassurance that his callers were not the usual MVD nighthawks.

The door opened ajar. Artem's unshaven face, strikingly similar to his brother's, appeared. There was a sleepy mutter and we were drawn across the threshold. The Minister signalled me to an armchair. "Take a pee, if you want." But I nodded negatively. Fright had induced anuria. "Say nothing. Do nothing. And make no sound if anyone comes." Then he disappeared up the hallway with his brother.

Armenian blood may not always be thicker than water but family ties are certainly tight. These two, the best known team of brothers in the Soviet Union, were also of that great clan of living Armenians; Anastas and Artem Mikoyan, William Saroyan and Khatchatourian the composer all belonged to the select band. Yes, and Charles de Gaulle, who, as they liked to boast in Erivan, was born at the Alaverde copper mine where his father supposedly was an engineer for dirty French capitalists.

Although it was still well before sunrise I felt I had been there for hours when the pair emerged. Artem made tea in a handsome Tula samovar and Anastas talked. I would be driven in the aircraft designer's car to the new Red Army field near Vnukhovo, where Artem was testing his MIG model 17. The trainer version had twin seats for experimental purposes.

I would be presented as an aerodynamics engineer taking part in the flight program. The necessary coveralls, parachute, and other equipment would be given to me and I would be dropped either near Sochi, where Artem Ivanovich first saw me, or at any other point I wished to designate in the general vicinity. Anastas did not care to know where. Indeed, the less he knew, the better.

I would be on my own from the moment I left the plane. Fortunately, no one would believe any story I might tell about dragon's teeth, or Kuntsevo. That was the magic of magic.

If I were captured by police in the area, they would have little difficulty proving I was a spy. But there would be no embarrassing Moscow link.

I gulped my steaming tea and said nothing. I was wondering how it felt to parachute. Anastas shook my hand perfunctorily and then left, making no secret of his haste. I saw the profound oubliette of his mind reflected in his sad, dark face.

Moments later, Artem Ivanovich beckoned; we descended in the growling front lift. His car, chauffeured by a sergeant in uniform with airforce markings, drove up. I was introduced summarily, with a nod and no explanations, as Comrade Engineer Popov, hardly an uncommon name. We rode eastward out of Moscow, toward a dull red sun struggling to fight through the boreal rime.

Our car avoided the administrative buildings and what seemed to be a small factory, and drove along the airstrip to a shed. There the designer quietly, and in a most ordinary voice, requested our flying suits and two tested parachutes to be brought. He also ordered his personal MIG-17 trainer. This was wheeled out forthwith by a small tractor with a bar that coupled to the tricycle landing gear. Making routine inquiries about weather along the southward route to the Black Sea, Mikoyan quickly drew up a flight plan for Rostov, on the lower Don, and for Sochi, where so many leaders had holiday dachas.

Without more ado he signalled me to follow. We climbed on the wing, I aping his every movement, and in a minute we were jammed tandem, almost piggyback, into a cockpit overloaded with instrument dials and levers. I wedged tighter in behind as the plexiglass canopy slammed shut with a grind and a hum. I could feel the entire body of the tiny plane shake with the force of its powerful engine.

My famous pilot turned us away from the uncoupled tractor, headed slowly and deliberately to the lane giving on to an astonishly long runway, and then muttered a few words into the transmitter attached below his mouth. Through the earphones of my flying helmet, I heard the clearance being granted. By leaning forward from behind, I could see Artem push two levers and pull back slowly on the controls. Then, with astonishing silence and very little sense of speed, we shot upward through the low-lying morning mist.

"Look for Rostov, on the larger map," Mikoyan growled into the intercom. "We will refuel there. Meantime you had better start considering your program. You understand that after Rostov our separation will be abrupt.

"You also understand that I have never heard of you or seen you before. David, quite fortunately, is a frequent Armenian name. And you have a typical physiognomy except perhaps for your size. This is good. When I remember your appearance, I shall remember a hundred others."

It was the first time I had ever been in a jet, much less a fighter that approached the speed of sound. My stomach zoomed from the back of my eyes to the bottom of my feet as we soared up, through a fluffy mass of cumulonimbus clouds, and thrust suddenly into brilliant sunlight.

The plane flew in utter silence, a splendid mechanical swallow. It gave me puzzled pleasure to think that somewhere behind and below us echoed a frightful whine. Wild, gloomy times are roaring toward us, I thought, and our speed increased at an exponential rate.

I was jammed tight behind the great engineer. The flight suit loaned to me was excessively constricting. It had been fitted for a far smaller man. Fortunately, my smelly coat was left behind; Mikoyan's chauffeur had orders to burn it.

I hunched deeper into the uncomfortable seat, staring through the plastic carapace at the magnificent clarity of the sky. "Are you all right?" Artem Ivanovich muttered over the intercom—and then shut it off. It occurred to me there was something remarkable about a rascally Armenian spy being hurtled through space by an Armenian Hero of the Soviet Union.

West of Rostov, as I could judge both by the map clutched in my lap and by the Russian conversation Mikoyan had struck up with ground control, we landed at an airforce base. Although it was a Sunday, the place was humming with activity. At Artem Ivanovich's instruction I remained in the cockpit studying diagrams with what, I hoped, seemed professional concentration.

After an exceptionally short time, the aeronaut climbed aboard again. The cover slid shut above our heads, we taxied with a roar to the end of the strip, then with a spasm of whining which we soon left behind, we shot up again. From the compass and also from the position of the sun, which was now quite free of cloud cover, I could tell we were heading southward, toward the Caucasus coast.

Well out over the Black Sea, Mikoyan guided us down to wave-top level, explaining: "Here we are below all radar screens." Then he pointed on a course for Sochi, and told me I had better speak up if I preferred any other destination, because we were traveling at immense speed. I leaned forward to designate the region south of Sukhumi on his map. "Anywhere there," I said to the intercom. "If you think you can drop me without being spotted."

Soon we were flying along the dull, greasy rollers under a low cloud cover. The sea was naked: no ships, no trawlers, not even a porpoise. "Better get set," Mikoyan murmured. Suddenly he pulled back hard and the MIG shot upward into the clouds. He swung into a sharp turn, angling hard on the starboard wing and then he pressed a button. The canopy slid backward as he brought the plane almost to a stall.

"Emergency procedure. Out you go. Good luck," he said. I felt my seat shoot into space. Breathless, gasping too hard to think, I pulled the handle of my parachute and found myself gently drifting down in the soft, foggy air.

I plummeted through a cloud-hole perhaps five hundred feet above the earth and saw, below, a strip of coastal plain running into the quiet sea. I could detect a few pygmy cattle in the distance, rows of fence, and lots of scrubby, green bushes which looked like tea plants.

I wondered how I could possibly escape detection by some sky-gazer in this populated if rural landscape. With the instinctive desire to create a diversion, I fumbled through the fastening of my coveralls, untied my handkerchief, then, at brief intervals, cast my remaining dragon's teeth downward, to the fertile flatland.

I reckoned they would land miles apart, thus obviating the danger that the murderous crop of soldiers would promptly kill itself off after sprouting from the dank soil. Surely their unusual attire and incomprehensible tongue would occupy local authorities. This would give me time to assemble my flustered self, and prepare an escape route.

Moreover, I calculated, there was truly a poetic justice in this diversionary effort. If my map reading had been even remotely accurate, the ruins of Dioscuria, so long the temporary abode of my tooth-men, lay off the cape below, basking beneath the waves.

My parachute dangled through the spindrift and, swinging on its pendulum, I fell into the sea. The water was warm and slightly muddy. I disengaged from the harness and, lying on my back, edged shoreward, dragging my equipment behind. In minutes I was able to plough up through the muddy beach.

I gathered together my flying suit and parachute, and then, using a well-weathered piece of driftwood, I dug a deep hole in the mud just where it met the sea. I sank my bundle into this and filled it up; soon the ripples had removed all remaining traces. Exhausted, I crawled under a bush at the border of the flats. Pulling the visor of my cap down over my eyes to shield them against the setting sun, I succumbed to sleep.

When I awoke it was very late. The sliver of a first-quarter moon was descending from the star-foam into Turkey, and a cool breeze from the south blew through the subtropical night. My clothes were dry and not much worse off than that day so long ago when I had first received them.

I was hungry and thirsty but felt strangely resolute. Good fortune already had buoyed up my threatened lot; there seemed little reason to expect greater dangers than those I had already surmounted. I took out my compass, checked it against the North Star and then began to trudge carefully up the coast in the general direction of Sukhumi.

It was a difficult walk. Trundling over and under rail and wire fences and making my way through the tangle of occasional tea plantations, I did my best to avoid houses, going far out of my way to skirt them as I discerned their shadows in the sequined predawn grayness. Whenever dogs barked I lay motionless on the soft, grassy loam. At last, working inland in gingerly fashion, I came to a dirt road and decided to sit there, waiting for sunrise and destiny.

Pretty soon a battered truck came bouncing up the ruts and

the driver stopped for me. He was an unusually handsome young Russian, far more involved with his own appearance than with his unexpected passenger. In the almost springless vehicle, bumping, shaking, swaying along the uneven road, he kept glancing into the rear-view mirror and taking a comb from his breast pocket, straightening his long, curly locks and rearranging them along his forehead.

Through laconic exchanges I gathered he worked for a tea collective, and was going to Sukhumi to pick up drying machinery. He hadn't the slightest interest in my origins or destination.

As the morning blossomed we passed by the ruins of an old bridge, then the remnants of an ancient fortification, and finally headed through the trading quarter and down to the waterfront jetties and ramshackle sheds where, I suppose, his equipment awaited him. I didn't ask. He let me off near one of the piers and I walked away through a sentimental little garden of palm trees and rose bushes, not yet in bloom.

Already the municipal loudspeakers blared. I noticed that few people were moving; instead they stood riveted, listening with keen attention, an expression of shock on their gaping faces. The radio was saying, first in Russian, then in Georgian, that Comrade J. V. Stalin had suffered a brain hemorrhage Sunday night and since then had never regained consciousness. It was Tuesday, March 4.

Stalin's right hand and leg were paralyzed and he seemed to have lost the power of speech in a heavy illness affecting important areas of the brain. His heart and breathing were impaired. His pulse had mounted to 120 beats a minute, his blood pressure was 220 over 120 and his temperature was 38.2 degrees centigrade.

The bulletin was issued on behalf of the government and of the Central Committee of the Communist Party of the Soviet Union. It was signed by the Minister of Health and ten physicians. I noted the names of Kuperin and Lukomsky among them. I also noticed that the bulletin said the leader had been stricken in his Kremlin apartment. History, I considered, is nothing but a pack of tricks we play upon the dead.

I cannot say I was stunned but evidently all other listeners were. Their inner emotions, however, were not mirrored in their faces. They stared at the loudspeakers as if hypnotized, as if expecting the horns to break off from their crude attachments above street intersections and to leap into some kind of mournful dance. And they murmured to each other in hushed undertones as if paying personal respect to the dying tyrant—and also as if to take special pains to avoid being overheard.

I strolled along the waterfront promenade wondering how I could possibly re-establish contact with Rima. The hatchery was a good forty miles away, and without telephone. There was no means of ascertaining if—or when—either she or Shamyl might come to Sukhumi, although on Tuesday, the customary market day, there was a chance they might show up.

As I walked down the harbor street lined with low buildings, unshaven stevedores and sailors shuffled by. Some were gabbling in animated undertones, others waving their hands, or nervously fingering beads. I noticed the splendid-looking "Gruzia," moored once again at the jetty.

There was a current of electric alarm in the air. The radio, between interludes of sad, muffled music, kept transmitting medical communiqués. Stalin, it said, had full aritmy, whatever that may be. The way it was announced gave an especially fatal implication. There was inadequacy of oxygen. The degree of disturbance in brain functions had increased. Therapeutic measures were being applied.

The loudspeaker said: "The state of J. V. Stalin continues to remain grave. The patient is in a state of deep unconsciousness . . . Medical measures taken during March 4 consisted of introducing oxygen, introduction of camphor compounds, caffein and glucose . . . For the second time leeches were used to draw blood . . . penicillin therapy was intensified."

I found it almost impossible to juxtapose these lugubrious technical words, the placid atmosphere of the rundown seaport, and the tranquil but obviously worried crowd—with the strange scene two nights ago in a wooden dacha outside Moscow amid a forest of birch and fir trees, decked with wet snow. Brain hemorrhage and leeches; indeed a startling counterpoint to the kilted, buskined hoplites introduced by sorcery into the sullen forests of the slavic north.

Finally, I decided to make my own way toward the Mtchishta. I walked back to the main street, turned inland from the wharves and headed through the main plaza and the government buildings of the Autonomous Republic.

A sleazy looking bus was accepting passengers while the driver nibbled pumpkin seeds and exchanged gossip with idlers under a plane tree. A chalk sign on a slate said the bus was bound for Novi Aphen, so I bought a ticket.

When we started off with the usual shaking lurch, I regarded the little crone beside me, her visage largely covered with a black cotton shawl. She was clearly Abkhazian or Adzharian; at least she had been reared in Islam and the tradition of the veil.

She turned her withered face, eyes glittering above a birdlike, narrow beak-nose, and moaned: "Ah, the great man. The poor leader." Then she whispered in sibilant confidence: "As always the Turks knew, the Turks know. There are Turks in the hills right now. Ready to exploit our troubles."

"Turks?" I said. "What can you mean?"

"They say five hundred Turkish troops in feathered helmets and white skirts have been discovered in the hills. Fighting troops. They must have come from airplanes. There were strange airplanes roaring through the silent night. Ah, this is what they say. But they don't tell us. They don't tell us little people when the great Comrade lies dead."

"Dead?" I asked.

"Dead, of course," she whispered. "Otherwise the Turks would never have dared to come."

Five hundred Turks, I wondered? And then it came to me in a flash: the last few seeds of Hellenic warriordom dropped so haphazardly this morning from the upper air. Their diversionary talents exceeded my fondest hopes.

At the edge of Sukhumi a roadblock had been erected and militiamen were verifying the documents of all people travelling in and out. With them were two MGB agents. Like nuns elsewhere, MGB agents always appear in pairs. I was not worried about the validity of my Milli Emniyet papers or about my connection with the recent horrendous events, since nobody would believe or even mention them. But I was indeed worried that I might be swept up by an unthinking police net and subjected to embarrassing questions on my past and future movements.

I could not escape this first routine surveillance. But I was warned. As soon as we resumed our journey and rounded a series of curves along the Novi Aphen road, I asked the driver to let me off, mumbling incomprehensible excuses about having forgotten a parcel for my mother.

I found, when I stood in the dust, that chance had deposited me across the way from an old-fashioned Abkhazian restaurant. Famished and conscious of a very dry throat, I wandered down rough-hewn steps and into an open bower with tables of chunky, flat, tree stumps. There, in a roofed shed with one missing wall, the cooking was done.

Dirty slabs of meat and smoked cheeses hung from the rafters. With a gourd scoop, the boss was ladling red wine out of huge tuns sunk into the dirt floor while his wife cooked shashlik and cornmeal mush in two pots strung over a little fire of pyramided sticks. I ordered mush, cheese (which proved to be astonishingly salty), and an earthenware jug containing two calabashes of heavy red wine. I carried my meal to a corner stump-table and sat quietly munching. Dipping the cheese in steaming cornmeal, I watched the birds enjoy the early spring warmth by skittering among unfolding vineyards overhead.

I looked up, and started. The lovely Rima was entering, accompanied by Shamyl. With his high cheekbones, almost triangular eyes, and red-brown hair, he really looked far more like a follower of the famous Avar prophet-warrior than the stench-ridden, bibulous operator of a state fish-hatchery. It was easier to imagine him as a dashing Caucasian delikan, riding in goat's-hair bourka cloak and high lambskin hat, the severed hands of enemies dangling from his saddle-bow, than shifting fingerlings from pan to pan—or lying paralyzed amid his vomit.

I felt uneasy. I remembered how the kindjal swords of the mountain-men were traditionally inlaid with bloody mottoes: "I am slow to take offense and quick to avenge it"; and Chakobsa, the mysterious Hunting Language in which these desperadoes secretly discussed their sanguinary plots. Then I recalled that Shamyl knew nothing about my love for his passionate wife.

This was a harmless alcoholic—and yet he descended from the

tribesmen of the white-peaked Adai-Khokh and Elbruz, marked by the blond Khevsour strain of armed fighting men, said to have been Crusaders' offspring. They had already left one genetic memory before, long ago, the Czar's armies arrived, subdued the wild clans, auctioned off the village-women and drove ramrods through their prisoners' ears.

Rima's husband did indeed come of fierce stock who venerated murderers and robbers. Surely among his tribal forebears was Kholchar who shouted as they burned him at the stake: "Look your last. You will not forget me. I have kissed the white breast of each of you, my doxies, even as I have stolen the pantaloons of the Khan's favorite wife. Be silent, ye children of whores: I made you so."

What a come-down; the cuckolded village drunk.

Rima was carrying a round loaf of bread and Shamyl purchased cheese and wine. They turned downward toward the little out-door eating place. Rima spotted me immediately. The color of her cheeks heightened; her eyes and lips seemed to open slightly in an incandescent smile. She headed straight for my broad, flat stump, pulled out two three-legged, low stools and, in Russian, said: "We meet again on a sad day, Comrade kinsman." Only then did she turn to Shamyl, murmuring a few phrases in Abkhazian. She wanted some dried peppers. He nodded and went back to the cooking place.

"Thank God you are alive," she whispered quickly. She crossed herself furtively and backwards, in the Greek style. "Shamyl will drink a great deal. We are coming back from Suk-humi. Let us do this right and you can return in the truck with us."

When Shamyl came with the peppers we all ate in silence, slaking the salt-thirst of the cheese with excellent, fresh wine. Shamyl became increasingly talkative. "Although you are a kins-man of Rima's mother," he said, "you claim to be Armenian. I do not understand. But (alcoholically) you Armenians were princes of this area before the Russians came. The Argutinskys and the Batonishvilis who possessed David's harp and the sling that slew Goliath. Let us drink to Armenians, Rima," and he drank, throwing back his head and clutching his jug in both hands as if it were one of the ancient Caucasian drinking horns we had seen at the museum.

The wine took increasing effect. "Hah, we of Abkhazia and you of Armenia share Russian rule," he said. "And they are poisonous as the snakes of the southern flatlands whence the Persians came and where they were driven back. We may be small peoples, we Abkhazians and you Armenians. But we are not made for the yoke."

I murmured that for an Armenian there was no choice when it was a matter of Slav or Turk. They amounted to the same thing. "Ah yes, you Armenians are Christian," he burbled happily. "And Armenian Socialists are the most Christian of all." He looked at Rima through his narrow eyes. "The Christian teaches to turn the cheek. But we Abkhazians are the cavalry of God."

I quoted from the Bible: "Their horses are swifter than leopards and are more fierce than the evening wolves. And their horsemen shall come from afar; they shall fly as the eagle that hasteth to eat." This delighted Shamyl.

"The Armenian cousin has earned himself a drink," he said, and strode light-footed, but unsteady, back to the sunken tuns for a fresh jug. When he returned we set to work, quaffing its excellent contents, glass by glass. Rima saw to it that her husband had the lion's share. I looked at her, soft, warm, and smiling. As she leaned forward to pour more wine, I could smell the fragrance in the aureole of her hair, in the milk of her breath, and I could feel the pressure of her soft leg beside me.

A fat, dark man, his buttoned sweater stained all down the front, came bursting into the placid restaurant. In Russian, he shouted: "Comrades. Terrible news, Comrades. Stalin is dead. Comrade Josef Vissarionovich is dead." Our reverie was shattered.

There was stillness at all tables. Somehow the sweet wine and the cordial sun had made us forget the tense day. The intruder took a large sheet of typescript from his pocket and began to read what was clearly an official announcement:

"Dear comrades and friends: The Central Committee of the Communist Party . . . with profound sorrow . . . the heart of the comrade and inspired continuer of Lenin's will, the wise leader and teacher of the Communist Party and the Soviet people, has stopped beating . . . The immortal name of Stalin will live forever in the hearts of the Soviet people and all progressive mankind. Long live the great and all-conquering teachings of Marx, Engels, Lenin, and Stalin . . ."

The silence was thunderous. Nobody dared look at anyone else. Then there was a scraping of stools and a shuffling of feet. One by one, each stump-table was abandoned. The lunchers, almost all men, quietly filed up the stairs and into a life that, for the first time in years, quite suddenly was uncertain.

"Where are you going, Comrade?" Shamyl asked as he stepped, like a sick and wobbly fox, out into the street. I told him my eventual goal was Gagra. "That is where we Abkhazians fought the Turks—before we fought the Russians," he said with pride. "That is where the only Soviet olive grove exists. I will take you in my truck."

He pointed to the dented tank-truck, so much like those used to fill the petrol pumps of state farms and tractor stations. "Fish," he said. "I am bringing back fish from Sukhumi. Fingerlings for the hatchery at the Mtchishta. Mtchishta means black. An Abkhazian word."

He started to climb to the driver's seat when Rima said: "Perhaps it is too late to drive Comrade David all the way. We will take him as far as the river. From there he can find the bus. Or maybe, if he wishes, he can spend the night. We have beds in the anglers' dormitory. And there is much to eat. Trout."

"Very well," I said, muffling my enthusiasm. "I shall spend the night with joy. This is a poor evening to pass alone."

Rima climbed aboard the truck from the righthand side and I followed, squeezing hard against her pleasant thigh. Shamyl, abruptly turning and returning, drove off unsteadily amid a brittle grinding of gears. It was evident he needed sleep far more than motion, and Rima suggested that I take the wheel.

We shifted her napping husband to my place, resting his head against the window-jamb. He snored, agape. Looking at him, I thought: a closed mouth catches no flies. Slowly and gently, I headed northward and she leaned restfully against my shoulder. In each village, groups of men stood gathered, in agitated conversation, while their womenfolk maintained respectful silence among the children.

CHAPTER

XI

BELOW the solemn peak of Bzoum-Ya-Khuapè, the fish pans silently reflected the cobalt blue sky. Crocuses were sprouting haphazardly in the grass. As the truck rattled up to the main house hungry trout swirled expectantly along the surfaces. "It is feeding time," said Rima. "Take him inside while I look after them."

I opened the tinny door and pulled Shamyl out. He was unconscious, slobbering and breathing heavily. I laid him across my shoulders and bore him into the house. I placed him on the unmade bed, loosened his collar and belt, removed his shoes, and left him to sleep it off. Rima cooked supper. Afterward the two of us walked to the anglers' platform, where we could look down on the rippling Mtchishta and talk without being overheard.

Very briefly I explained that I must go, without telling her precisely why: merely that I was in trouble with the authorities. There was no point in sharing any of the burden which Beria's feral torturers were so capable of extracting. But, I said, I intended to leave with her and also with the serpent's teeth.

"It is as a dream," she murmured. "Poor Shamyl. What a terrible mistake. I lived in one room with my parents; he looked so very romantic, and I wanted so to get away. And yet, the wife of an Abkhazian does not leave him. Her leaving is a sign that he is not a man."

"Well, is he?" Rima did not reply. Instead she asked: "How

can you possibly quit the Soviet Union with a quarter of a ton of teeth? Why, how would even you alone be able to depart?

"We need documents in our society. We need permits. Surely you are aware of that. Even Shamyl, who is preparing to ship a tank of fingerlings to Bulgaria for their tourist industry, had the devil of a time securing proper papers. Papers for himself. Papers for the fish."

"Wonderful," I interrupted. "That is the best news yet. When is the shipment due to leave?"

"In two days," Rima replied, looking puzzled.

"And he has his passport? His travel documents? His bill of lading for the fish?"

"Of course. That is what he picked up today in Sukhumi."

"Very well. We have no problem."

Then I elucidated. With me I had sufficient equipment to alter Shamyl's passport by duplicating the ink and adding adequate stamps and embossments. I would substitute her picture and descriptive details. Moreover, I would amend the letter accompanying the trout consignment. She would be authorized to oversee the shipment as far as Burgas, Bulgaria.

When Rima inquired, "And how about you?", I quizzed her for details about the portable tank in which the fingerlings would travel. She told me it was precisely the same size as the regular tank clamped to the truck chassis. They were, in fact, interchangeable.

I told Rima that, if she would keep Shamyl out of the way all the following day, I was certain I could weld a waterproof section in the tank for myself and the sacks. I had seen a primitive blowtorch and welding equipment in the truck shed. Then, I added, she could smuggle me and the Cadmean cuspids aboard the ship.

"Are the fish to be shipped on the 'Gruzia'?" I asked, recalling that this handsome vessel normally made the Black Sea circuit—Sochi, Sukhumi, Istanbul, Burgas, Varna, Constanța, Odessa, Sochi.

"Yes. How could you know?"

"Because this morning I spotted her alongside the wharf."

"It is true," said Rima. "And the captain is an old acquaintance. He is head of all merchant marine in the Republic of Georgia," she added. "He is very flirtatious. He has a reputation as a dandy."

"So much the better. If anything unexpected occurs you will have to use your head on him. Not what's inside your head, but what's outside will be more important."

Next day Rima effectively took care of Shamyl. She added brandy to his glass of morning tea and encouraged him to drink away his hangover. She also gave him fortified wine outside in the sunlight. Soon again he was stretched out snoring on the mattress.

I, meanwhile, unscrewed the regular tank from the back of the truck, hauled it off by a rope slung to a bollard, and then loosely attached the one for shipping fish. I put the tools and welding metal into the truck and drove a kilometer down the road so the racket wouldn't awaken the Abkhazian from his stupor.

All morning I worked in a bosk beside the path. It was a comparatively easy job. The transport tank had a large hinged opening set into its rounded upper surface. This was employed to insert or remove fish, and also to feed them. Atop was a spigot, to which was affixed a thermometer.

I crawled inside carrying the torch and sections of the regular tank. I cut these into required shapes and welded them, making a false bottom over all but the tap-end. I drilled a line of airholes below this. Then I tested it for water-proofing. It was perfect.

The space underneath the false bottom was more than adequate for myself and the rustling sacks. And it now had two entry points: a trap door I had inserted in the main tank wall, plus one at the other end. Both I had lined with thick rubber rims extracted from old tire tubes.

When I had finished, I hid the remnants of the permanent tank under a pile of fertilizer, screwed the transport tank on firmly, and drove back to the hatchery. I spent the rest of the afternoon and evening wearily climbing up to the warrens of the Bird Rock cave and then—each time with a 250-pound-sack—struggling down again and stowing them carefully under the false bottom.

Rima signalled me Shamyl was still asleep. I crawled inside the new tank and confirmed there was plenty of room for me to make the trip to Istanbul, and to store beside me the necessary food and water.

That night I went to the anglers' dormitory. With my inkpad and other Milli Emniyet equipment, I worked by kerosene lamp until dawn. I affixed a picture of Rima into Shamyl's passport and modified both that document and the consignee's bill of lading. My papers were of scant value but I duly stamped them. If I were caught, nothing could save me. I left behind my suitcase with its modest contents. My final preparation was to unwrap my charger from the *Pravda* sheet and to clean it before restoring it to its prescribed safety position, ready for emergency use.

The next morning, when we were scheduled to depart, I told Rima that alcohol alone might not keep Shamyl out of harm's way long enough. Should we be delayed and should he recover sufficient sobriety to remember the trout shipment, disaster could occur.

So, while he was half asleep, I carefully knocked him out, then tied him neatly and firmly in a clothesline. I bound a gag into his mouth with Rima's scarf. And I bore him to the anglers' dormitory where I stuffed him in the solitary cupboard. I drilled four breathing holes into its sidewalls so he wouldn't suffocate, shut and locked its door, and threw the key into a fish pan.

Then I drove the truck beside the pan from which the fingerlings were to be loaded. Together Rima and I carefully ladled hundreds of fish and many buckets of water into the tank until it was quite full. She measured the temperature, explaining to me that on a long trip the coolness should remain constant.

She would have to feed the wriggling cargo each day and inject fresh water to liven up the oxygen pumped in occasionally through the tap. The captain had already received aboard the "Gruzia" several barrels of chemically suitable water furnished by the Abkhazian fisheries trust.

I told Rima to take with her only the exact amount of clothing that would seem logical for a Black Sea tour without long stopovers. Then we went through her larder and assembled food for me: flat Abkhazian bread, tins of sprats, a large bottle of pickled tomatoes, and a one gallon water canteen which Shamyl customarily filled with wine for anglers' picnics.

She tucked her passport and papers in a worn silk purse with a clasp. Then we climbed in and she drove carefully, nervously, silently toward Sukhumi. She never once looked back toward the Mtchishta, not even through the rear-view mirror.

"The wife of an Abkhazian does not leave him," I remembered.

"Maybe I'm doing a terrible thing," Rima said suddenly, staring at the road ahead. "We've been here, my family, since before time began. And now I'm running away. Running from both the present and the past. What a dreadful influence you have. But then I really am a slut. I like being a slut. I like adventure; and I have a weakness for David."

"Call me Kevork," I said. "That is my real name."

"Just who are you? You have so much to tell."

"Yes. But do not worry about severing bonds, either to the present or the past. Shamyl is no fit husband for you. Nobody knows that better than yourself. As for the past, you are both Greek and Circassian by blood and they are the greatest wanderers in the world—save Armenians and Jews."

"But think of the history to which I am rooted. Think of the burden you bring from Dioscuria."

"I bring only one burden: war, the means of making war. And war will bring us our own kind of peace."

She drove silently for a while. Then she said: "It's not right, my disappearing from this spot."

"You are not the first to disappear, Rima, my lark, my exaltation of larks. Whole peoples have disappeared before you. Where are the Avars? Where are the Pechenegs? Where are the Chechens and the Ingushi? Where are the Scyths and the Huns? All that is left of the Scyths is hammered gold jewelry in the Hermitage. And the Huns? They are not even a memory. Only one word has lasted from the Hunnish language and that was preserved by Roman historians. The word is Strava. It means funeral."

"Which describes what's ahead of us?" she said.

"No," I said. "We are escaping to life. Yours shall be a magnificent life. The road to it is paved with the corpses of unborn warriors."

When we could see the hamlet in which the Abkhazian restaurant was situated I asked Rima to halt. We pulled the truck off the road into a small dell where tiny cows were grazing. There was no herder.

I removed the covering and cushions behind our seat, exposing the circular hole I had cut into the beaverboard partition with a fretsaw. The partition came out easily, unblocking the forward entrance to the compartment I had manufactured below the fish tank.

I lifted this up on its hinge. With a pocket torch, I showed the interior to Rima. Disapprovingly, she peered into the darkness to see a compartment approximately two feet high, four feet wide, and ten feet long, totally dry despite the swishing, trout-filled water above. At the far end, jammed awkwardly together, were the sacks of teeth.

I shoved in the parcels of food and water. I put the flashlight in my mouth. Then, feet foremost, I inched in until all but my head had disappeared. I took the torch from my lips and laid it beside me. Then I said to Rima:

"It is best to do this now. It is just remotely possible that a description of my appearance has been circulated. This way, we won't have trouble even if we come across more roadblocks. We must take precautions.

"Now drive carefully ahead. When we reach the wharf and are ready for loading, find your friend the captain. Tell him to be sure his ship's crane is firmly attached; it should hoist us slowly aboard. Say that the water balance in a full tank changes easily, and that the fish are delicate.

"You must have him guarantee you space in a forward hold because the engine and propeller shaft are less noisy there. Also, the tank must be solidly lashed, and kept in an area adequately supplied with air. Finally, it must be accessible to you. Explain that you must take the temperature, revive the water supply, feed the fish, and inject oxygen from time to time.

"This is briefly outlined on the shipping papers. But you would be wise to speak to the captain directly, and insure that all details are properly carried out. I don't know where you will sleep. Obviously some arrangement has been made.

"You notice the bill of lading does not specify who will accompany the trout to oversee them: merely an expert from the Mtchishta hatchery. No doubt the captain will be overjoyed to see the expert—in the flesh."

Rima nodded sourly. She took my protruding head prisoner in her soft arms, held it with tender gentleness, and gave me a passionate kiss.

"My hero," she murmured. "My Kevork. What a funny thing to change names like that. I shall never get used to you. But I shall never cease trying. Farewell sweet Armenian."

I pulled in my head, and worked shut the pawl that closed the entrance from inside. Then the truck began to move, awkwardly turning in a series of maneuvers, until I could feel the firm, pocked surface of the main road once again.

Now, in the darkness, with scarcely any springs and no soft cushion to shield me beneath, I felt like a boulder rattling down a mountain slope.

The noise I heard was a strange mixture. The thundering bumps and screaming groans of wheels and truck body were accompanied by contrapuntal swishings of water, as the fingerlings swayed and swung immediately over me, journeying to their Bulgarian fate. The slurp, slurp, slurp above my eardrums made me thirsty. I took a gulp from the canteen.

All this made me think suddenly of another Armenian, that droll skipper from Istanbul who was charged by a Turkish court with scuttling his caique in the Sea of Marmora. His defense was simple. Addressing the judge, he said:

"Your worship I had a cargo of salty cheese. And mine was an old ship. And there were many rats aboard. And they kept on eating cheese until they got to the bottom of my cargo. By that time they were dying of thirst.

"They heard the water rushing by below, slurp, slurp, slurp, so they ate through the bottom of my caique in order to get a drink. And the boat sank, your worship. That is all."

I heard the trout-filled water sloshing from side to side only a few inches above me, and it began to drive me mad. But my sentient musings were interrupted, for we jolted to a stop. Then, through the air holes, I listened as militiamen questioned Rima.

There were eristic mutters. Then the lid must have been swung open on the tank above, for I could almost feel a stick fumbling like a dowser around the water-filled metal partition overhead. Suddenly we started off again.

Time passes slowly in a dark, restricted confinement and discomfort increases by geometrical progression. I comforted myself this time by quoting from the admirable epics of my people: "Ah, man of little faith, why this fear?" And again: "Lose not heart! Spur me on! You shall not be parted from me."

Alone with the fingerlings I lived a private microcosmic, macrocosmic life apart from all reality. I wondered if Rima could feel the invisible beam of my intense and walled-off gaze.

For a long, long while we waited at what I judged to be the entrance to the pier alongside which the "Gruzia" was moored. At last I heard workmen's hands unbolting the tank from the truck chassis, and girding with scratchy chains the world I shared with frenetic troutlings. Then, slowly, I felt a soft and mollifying lift, a swing, a lowering, until I judged we had landed in the "Gruzia's" bowels.

"Aye, aye, it is good to visit here," I quoted nervously to myself from Mher.

I had allowed my watch to run down; my last contact with the finite was broken. I dozed, dreamed, forced myself to repeat lines of poetry and translate them successively into different languages. I even invented gymnastic exercises for each of my four limbs, exercises that were capable of producing a satisfactory strain in the cramped available field of action. When I thought of time, it was unending; so I ceased, by discipline, to think.

Eventually I heard a scratching on my private entry-lid, followed by a knocked dot, dot, dot, dash. Rima surprisingly had both the rudiments of Morse and an inkling of either Beethoven or the BBC. I eased the pawl backward and, pushing the slab of metal against its upper hinge, peered out.

She was stooping beside the tank, swaying slightly with the motion of the ship; the light from a rectangular storm lantern in her hand showed an anxious look furrowed on her lovely features. "Thank God," she said. "I still can't believe it worked."

"Why are you wearing a nightgown?" I asked.

"Nothing in life is free," she said, giving me a flensed and untrusting look. I was relentlessly myself. "The captain?" I inquired.

"Naturally. I do not spend myself on useless gnats."

Although her eyes were shaded, I could tell from the blurred reflection that the expression on my face was far from pleasant.

"He made me sleep with him. He swore otherwise he'd flush the trout overboard."

"I don't swim that well," I said. "So, is he any good? Did you like it?"

"Don't worry. He isn't David Avetikyan."

"Neither am I. I'm called Kevork, remember?" I muttered, stiffly crawling through the constricted porthole and trying to stand. "I thought Soviet women were supposed to be so prudish."

"They're Russians and Communists. Whereas I am not either," she answered coyly. Then, after a moment's hesitation, she added: "I really am somewhat loose, you know."

"I know. Possibly that is why I love you, although I never fancied I'd emulate a rutting donkey. I knew, Rima, you were not so innocent as you sometimes talk."

She took me by the hand and guided me up a tightly circular iron stairway to the square-shaped opening above the hold. There was no hatch cover, and I could see the starlit night.

"Walk softly," she murmured. "But don't worry. I told the captain I had to inspect the trout, and he gave orders to the watch. Only one sailor is on lookout in the forward section, one in the stern, and two on the bridge. Now follow me. We can slip directly under the bridge and no one will see us. I have the run of the ship. And you could easily be taken for a passenger—there are four Turks and many Bulgarians and Rumanians aboard."

"If that's the case, I prefer to be taken for a Rumanian."

She led me to a lifeboat. I helped her up over the rail and then climbed beside her on the outer tarpaulin. The central ridge of canvas shielded us from anyone who might walk the deck. It was calm. Clasping each other, we peered into the sea below. The edges of the "Gruzia's" wake gleamed phosphorescent in the darkness. We made love until the first tinge of gray started up in the East.

"Look to the left," I murmured into Rima's ear. "That must be the coast near Trabzon and Samsun. Armenia. Our ancient kingdom. Look long and well. Then you had better take me down to my little nest before your captain gets suspicious."

"Don't call him my captain," she said. Together we descended and I groped inside my metal cave, fumbling about for the sack of my belongings. From it, I extracted my Turkish and Soviet passports. "Here," I said, handing her the latter, "my Turkish papers will suit me well. Throw the other overboard."

All next day, which I spent inside my dark and clangorous container, I could feel the "Gruzia" making way southward, and then westward along the coast of Trabzon, of whose fame my mother had told me so much. How apt, I considered from the musty blackness: there was a city where Armenian and Greek had contended almost since time began.

Perhaps the Argonauts, first bearing my precious crop of teeth through these waters, had sailed past even before the ancestors of Mher wandered down; but when Xenophon fought his way northward here to the sea, it was Armenian flesh through which his soldiers cut their way.

There, I mused, the brutal Mossynoici lived, trading in fat tattooed boys, bloated on marrons, for lewd or hungry purchasers. And the alcoholic honey of Trabzon, distilled by bees rendered drunk on the Pontic azalea, was renowned for its devastating effect.

One of my English colleagues at Robert College had told me the great Lord Curzon first saw Trabzon through a hole in the green silk quilt which sheltered him against the cold. Not even a chink in my quilt of iron, I reflected, as we lumbered past.

Was I never, I mused, to view Trabzon, glorious under the baldricked Lascaris rulers before the coming of the Seljuk and the Ottoman, site of the Panaghia Chrysocephalos, where my forefathers exported bales of nuts and creaking piles of timber, making their Mongol clients pay in silver aspers? Where the Strategikotatos, Grand General of the Comneni, planned his battles long before the heathen Turks converted our Armenian abbey church of Kaimakli into a shed for cows? Here was I, heir to all this splendor, rattling blindly by like a sprat in a neglected can.

The following day I squirmed about, preparing for our departure from the ship. I removed the charger from its protesting haven, and eased my swollen gut for the first time since I had quit the Bird Rock coven. I counted out my thirty gold pieces and tied them in the corners of a handkerchief. Then I thrust the passport, in an oilskin envelope, into my jacket pocket. I could not sleep for restlessness and discomfort. My bones ached and my mind was preoccupied.

I could feel a new motion, which told me we had passed Cape Carambis and had swung sharply into the Bosphorus. The sudden current seizing the hull hurtled us furiously southward. Some hours later I felt the engines slow down and then churn into reverse. I knew we were sliding toward Galata Rihtim, where the Black Sea ships tie up on the Rumeli wharf of Istanbul.

There was a grinding along the pier-side; as always, the Turks had allowed the knotted rope cushions, designed for gentling the shock, to rot away like everything else in their corrupted land. I imagined the noise of gangways being run ashore far above me to let the police and customs men aboard.

The search was cursory; perhaps Rima's flirtatious captain, being a Georgian, had not allowed Marxist lore to erase from his memory the art of greasing Turkish palms. In any case, there were no footsteps in my silent hold. Late again that night, I heard the familiar scratching and rapping signal.

Rima looked distrustful when I told her she must replace me inside the tank while I went ashore for aid. But I convinced her there was no other place in which she could disappear. It was better, I said, for the captain to imagine that she had given him the slip at the instant of arrival.

She crawled in, and I clambered up the cramped, volute stairway to the forward hatch coaming, where, slipping among the deck shadows between crates battened down under tarpaulins, I lowered myself from a knotted towline made fast to a port side cleat, away from the jetty. Once in the swirling current, I allowed myself to drift past two large white vessels from Bulgaria and Rumania to the wharf where trans-Bosphorus ferries regularly swing in from Asia.

It was nothing to clamber up a slimy support-pole by grasping the huge, rusted nails driven like hand-holds into its side. I lay beneath the mole, holding tight above the spray, until my clothes were dry and a storm cloud from Anatolia had obscured the moon.

Then, extracting my passport from its oilcloth pouch, I hauled myself up on the walk. Bending over crab-like to give the impression of a porter who, his earnings squandered on drink, had been overcome, I began tottering along the mole toward the Galata exit. An old man was sweeping the pavement with a twig besom. At the foot of the Rihtim steps, the guard paid no attention; he was asleep.

Stooped and stumbling, I headed toward the Galata bridge which leads to the old imperial city. Behind me lay the row of ships silent at their moorings, and the locked gate by the Customs House, fastening an iron picket fence that was supposed to hem in foreigners until their papers had been examined.

To my left, small motorboats and caiques were still sliding along the swift current where the Bosphorus eddied into the placid Marmora Sea. To my right, wagons with ungreased axles squealed behind little underfed horses, rattling along beneath arched harness rigs. I realized it must be after midnight and that they were hurrying to get across the Golden Horn before the central section of the bridge was lifted, blocking street traffic for the two-hour period when ships swung in and out of the bustling Horn.

The bridge appeared, and I straightened up. When I arrived at the subterranean bypass below the Pera side, I began to walk rapidly into the tunnel so I wouldn't be caught when the span was hoisted. I hurried along, and the entire passageway was still redolent with cooking-food from the row of small restaurants, now silent, where people come to dine on fish, kebab, and enormous shrimps from the south.

At the right turn, under the bridge itself, two old men chatted quietly before a kiosk and bookstore with its windows shut. And on the other side I could see, as I angled along the sloped passageway leading upward to the bridge, shopstalls littered with remnants of the day's sales: rotten peaches, crushed walnuts, hazelnuts, cherries, a grumous slime of broken melons and grapes. When I reached the level of the bridge itself, I noticed a cluster of bobbing row-boats tied beside the traverse. The moon slid out of its protective cover and the Galata Tower stared ominously down from the sudden halation.

I had never before crossed at this hour; the amount of people scrambling to get over before the span lifted surprised me. Handcarts were being trundled beside donkey carts drawn by tiny patient asses, and gnarled porters were tottering under bales and heavy boxes slung from shoulder yokes. Both at the outer entrance to the Golden Horn and in that famous bay itself, freighters, with steam up, idled, waiting to start their passage in or out.

Trying to look nonchalant, I ambled along past sleepy bridge guards, and around midnight I reached Unkapani Caddesi. Unkapani runs along the southern shore of the Horn, where part of the ancient wall of Constantinople stood.

There I turned right, past a few stunted runnels, and walked as far as Rustem Paşa mosque. Just after a grilled gate, I turned right again. The former Ottoman prison, now a kind of tenement, had laundry flapping on lines between the old tiers of cells.

I pushed into the network of alleys and shuttered shops until I reached 35 Zindankapi Abacilar Caddesi. Number 35 is a modest little house and one of the finest restaurants this side of Moslem Paradise. Pandeli Cobanoglu, a rascally Greek friend of mine, runs it. A light shone from the back of the ground floor; surprising, because Pandeli serves only lunch. The door was ajar.

I entered. Pandeli was sitting with two stodgy men in shiny black suits. A tric-trac board was laid out between them. A bottle of Metaxa brandy stood half empty beside it. They were drinking and shouting. Pandeli threw the dice. I coughed. The three looked up.

"My child," Pandeli hollered. "My little bird. Where have you been these last months, Georgios? What foul prison do you come from now?" He rose to his full height, which just came to my shoulder. He clasped me to him with his surprisingly strong, simian arms.

As always, he was just a bit drunk. Sometimes he spoke like a dizzard, but I had never seen him entirely discountenanced nor entirely sober. He tottered energetically back to look at me, and sought to speak faster than his tongue could manage, so that spittle formed at the corners of his mouth. Looking at him, I thought his sour breath would make the leaves of an orange tree wilt; but his heart was good.

His hair and mustache had grayed during the past year, yet there was immense and gusty vigor in his stumpy, tumescent body. His droll features competed to assert themselves: long nose, enormous ears, thick, humorous mouth. There was a cunning look in his eyes as he regarded me. "It is something you have come to ask me for." This was not an inquiry.

He turned to his companions before I could answer and said with his customary brusque rudeness: "Until tomorrow, then.

It is long since I have seen this friend." They nodded, pushed back their chairs, smiled and departed. Pandeli reached for another glass in the cupboard at the rear. "Pour," he ordered. He locked the door with a heavy key.

I quoted: "David said: 'Where have we a cask of wine?'"

Pandeli looked puzzled. "Armenian," I explained. "David of Sasoun. Our hero."

The story I told was brief, incomplete, but not an entire lie. I needed a small, oared barge, and a boatman of absolute reliability and discretion. If possible, I would employ him this very night, slipping out of the Horn at the time of maximum traffic and confusion. I would pay the boatman well.

I also needed a large, substantially built caique capable of long voyages, for example to Samsun, to Izmir, to Piraeus or to Cyprus. It would be preferable if the captain were a Greek. For these things I was prepared to pay handsomely—in gold.

Pandeli had been examining me with mounting interest. When the word "gold" was spoken, he could not keep a flash of greed from the depths behind his brilliant eyes. He reflected a moment, poured himself another glass of dark brown brandy, and drank it slowly but steadily, as if it were goat's milk. Then he said: "I know you well, Georgios, well enough to understand that none of this is intended for the authorities of this blessed Republic, especially those bashibazooks of the law with whom you have had so much experience.

"But I can do it. This I can do for you, child."

He clapped his hands and shouted: "My little bird! Send Yanni." At the head of the staircase in the rear I heard a woman's whisper, and then a young man came down. Pandeli didn't introduce him, but I assumed this was the son, his great pride, who was supposed to study medicine.

"Go and find the Gimp," he said gruffly. "Send him here as fast as he can manage. It is urgent. When the Gimp is on his way, you can look for Michali—Michali Pantelis who has that big sponge-fishing caique. Look near the fisherman's wharf behind Abacilar jail. He usually moors there."

When the boy had slipped out and Pandeli again had locked the door, I continued my requests. "I have with me a woman."

"What is unusual about that?"

"This is a special woman. She is special to me, and she is also of special interest to the police. She has no valid entry permit."

"What is her nationality?"

"She is Greek—a Greek from Russia."

"That is no problem," said Pandeli. "It is my privilege to help."

"Very well, when I return—and if your friend the Gimp shows up in time, I hope to be back by midday—I shall bring her along. Can you see to it that Yusuf lunches here? I would discuss this with him. He knows his way around. And I have confidence in Yusuf.

"One more thing. I shall wish to store here two sacks of grain. It is a special kind of grain. It is bird seed for fighting partridges. I have discovered a seed that gives even the smallest chukar the illusion that he is an ostrich with iron spurs. I intend to sell this shipment to a friend who is a fancier of this sport. He has much money. That is why I need the caique."

Pandeli didn't even pretend to believe me. He merely said: "Don't bother to go on. Everything shall be as you wish it to be. Yusuf will come for lunch. And there will be no bashibazooks. Not even the Birinci Buro. Or the Milli Emniyet." He studied me astutely. I returned an impassive stare.

"You know," he continued, "that heathen Naci Perkel would never deign to lunch in this humble tavern. Each day he joins the Vali at Taksim's casino. They keep it open at midday only for the Vali and his friends. Lobster and caviar. One says this alone costs our noble Republic more than five million lira every year. Now drink. I have known you to drink, Georgaki."

I drank. He drank. We finished the Metaxa. He produced another bottle. Seven stars. "Pay no attention to the stars," he counseled, following my eyes. "This is my personal reserve. I simply refill it and cork it up again from time to time." His tongue was thick and the dribble splattered as he spoke, but there was neither sag in his energy nor diminishment in his alertness. The brandy was warm, soft, strong.

It seemed but a few minutes before Yanni returned. After his discreet knock, he was admitted together with a hideous Albanian whose baggy trousers had a seat broad enough to contain the Prophet himself when he should decide to be reborn to man. His left leg was bowed, and he walked with a pronounced limp. I reached into my pocket, worked one gold piece out of the knotted handkerchief, and held it forth for him to see. "How is that, my eagle-man?" I asked. "Do you think you can help me out? And now?"

The Gimp took the old rial, turned it slowly round in his thick fingers, then bit it carefully. His rebarbative face scowled. He grunted. "It will do. When do we go?"

"Now," I said. "Come with me." And, as Pandeli once again unlocked the door, I added: "With any kind of luck there will be two of us for lunch tomorrow. And fodder for fighting cocks in your upstairs larder. Do you think if Michali comes you can keep him here until I am back? It will be worth his while."

"Michali does what I tell him. He has special interest in doing so."

I followed the shuffling Albanian into the night, and I thought to myself how wrong Finlay had been. Finlay was one of my colleagues at Robert College, and it was he who had tattled on me for those small peccadilloes which produced my first encounter with prim authority. And Finlay used to quote from an ancestor who had written of Byzance: "In concluding the history of this Greek state, we inquire in vain for any benefit it conferred on the human race." In vain? Pah. Pandeli alone was a monument.

Down at the fish pier, where iron grills leaned against the walls of tiny cooking booths, three young men were knotting up holes in nets. I rolled up my jacket, tucking it under my arm, and asked the Gimp to give me his cap. When he handed me that dreadful object with its sagging visor, I noticed he wore beneath it the white skullcap of the proud Albanian mountain Ghegs. My respect for him increased.

His boat was tied to the last post. We climbed in, and he fitted the round oar pulls by short rope nooses to bollards on either side. Then, with efficient strokes, he spun us out into the current. One of the young men gave a weird shout that seemed to originate right behind his navel. "Hey, Topal," he called, looking up from his nets, "where are you off so early?" The Gimp said nothing. Topal, in Turkish, means the lame one.

It is not a long distance, going under Galata bridge and over to the Rihtim. Topal followed in the wake of a Marmora steamer swinging beneath the raised center span. He brought us swiftly and quietly past the ferry-port, and then, pulling hard against the drive of the Bosphorus current, he took us in toward the Rihtim, and along the silent line of Black Sea vessels.

"Gruzia" showed no sign of life, not even the shadow of a watchman. I noticed my bowline was still hanging where I had left it, the end drifting idly in the garbage-filled water. I signalled the Gimp to make fast, whispered that I would rush my business to complete it before dawn, and then I wriggled up the knotted rope.

I heard a stirring inside the trout tank when I scratched and rapped upon the lid. Soon Rima emerged, stiff and dishevelled. She wanted to talk, but I placed my hand on her mouth, murmured "There isn't time," and scrambled inside myself.

Using her torch and pulling their clumsy dead weight, I eventually worked the two sacks through the awkward aperture and lumped them side by side at the bottom of the hold. "Stay here," I instructed Rima, and again I clambered over the stairway baffle and spiralled up to the deck.

Reckoning that with my filthy Turkish cap and the secret of my presence on the voyage, no one would take me for other than a local seaman, I decided to risk direct action for the sake of speed. Threading the rope through a grommet, I swung a handhoist over the hold, lowered its cargo tray, scuffled down the circular stair again, and heaved the sacks upon it, balancing them against each other.

Then I took Rima by the hand and led her to the deck. I showed her Topal and his boat, coached her on how to slide down the bumpy line, and instructed her to stay quiet, doing nothing, saying nothing once she got there. As soon as she was aboard, I signalled the Gimp and swung the creaking hoist over the port side.

The Albanian pulled the sacks aboard his protesting little boat, and I speedily hauled at the pulleys, bringing the hoist back and coiling the rope shipshape and Bristol fashion. I had closed the lid of the fish tank, which was clearly marked for shipment to Burgas in Bulgaria. There was no sign that anyone had occupied the hold.

The only thing the captain would find amiss aboard "Gruzia" was the disappearance of his girl friend, presumably down the knotted rope which I now descended.

The Galata bridge span was in place again as we sped back with the current so I knew it was after five o'clock. Gray and pink pastel layers of dawn were unfolding across Anatolia. I took the Gimp's cap and jammed it on Rima's head, tucking inside it the soft tendrils of her golden hair. I warned her to huddle next to the sacks and to look as old, forlorn, and dilapidated as she possibly could. In this fashion we returned to our mooring at the fisherman's wharf.

We left Topal testing the Persian rial between his rotting teeth. Several yokes the hamals used in daytime to carry loads of fish were in a shed toward the center of the pier. I took one, swung a precious sack to each end, and then, with straining back, lifted upward and lurched along Unkapani to Zindankapi Abacilar 35.

Pandeli, wide awake, reeking of cognac, his mustachios wet with saliva, opened the door. He bundled us in and led me, staggering, up the back stairs to deposit my sacks one by one in his kitchen larder on the third floor. Then he took a long, approving look at Rima, and embraced her. "Chrisomou," he said. "Now I know what they really mean by Golden One."

We were all too nervous to sleep. Pandeli kept drinking. My mind was abustle with plans; and Rima brimmed with such curiosity that her eyes were unable to remain still. After dawn, Pandeli's son brought us tea and scrambled eggs with onions. Then, since I had been told the caique-master was not expected before eleven, I borrowed a black shawl from the hook where the cook's wife had hung it, wrapped its copious camouflage around Rima and over her gleaming hair, and announced we could risk a stroll at this bustling early hour.

We walked by stalls where ears of corn roasted on metal sheets spread above charcoal. Vendors were selling small grilled fish for thirty kuruş each. Hocas with canes and skullcaps tapped between donkeycarts and wheezing, elderly buses. Glistening merides, sinagrida, and barbounia were laid out on stalls at the entrances to the seafood restaurants. Caiques were loading huge tuns of oil and wine.

In the narrow alleys off the waterfront, porters padded across the cobbles with woven slings across their bent backs, straining beneath their loads. Peddlers pushed handcarts of peaches and apricots. Enormous sausages dangled from hooks in tiny shops whose entrances were crammed with displays of walnuts, hazelnuts, pistachios, canned goods, and tins of olive oil. There was tapping in the cordwainers, and hard-handed sailors fingered the ropes, shovels, pitchforks, and nets laid out in the booths of harbor-suppliers.

When we stood at the edge of Unkapani Caddesi, gazing northward over the Golden Horn, I told Rima how the last Emperor Constantine had stretched a heavy chain across its entrance to block off the fleet of Sultan Mehmet during the famous siege, but how that brilliant young conqueror assembled droves of oxen and had his ships, with crews aboard rowing in the air, dragged by bullocks, slaves, soldiers, and seamen from the Bosphorus across Pera into the Horn itself. The outflanked emperor, with his cohorts, gazed helplessly from crenellated walls.

I told her about Byzantium and Greek greatness: about the imperial escopetters, sebastocrators, and diadochs; about the Great or Proto Spatharios, the Grand Skevophylax, the Protovestiarios, and the Grand Logothete; about dekarchs, kentarchs, and turmarchs; and about the army of the Palaeologus crown, the mailed cataphracts with their clattering quadrigas, their mangonels, arbalesters and arquebusiers, and the engineering drungars who mobilized the sleepy and resentful oppidans. I told her all this. And then I told her how, when the capital in the end did fall, a song was written, a lament my mother in her soft, Armenian-accented Greek would sing to us as children:

> "A bird, a beautiful bird, flew out from the City.
> It shook one wing, and then it was covered with
>   blood;
> It shook the other wing, and there was paper
>   with writing beneath:
> 'Woe unto us, woe unto us.
> The ramparts are lost. The Imperial Throne is
>   destroyed.' "

Rima's eyes gleamed with pride as she saw spread before her the panoply of this brave old world, this ostentation of peacocks that represented another Greece, less ancient than her own.

When we got back to Pandeli's, the ship-captain was already there. The two of them were sipping little cups of syrupy coffee. Pandeli introduced us and then, leaving Rima, I took Michali to the second floor where the waiter ceased laying crockery on the tables and left us alone to talk. Michali told me he was "interested" when I showed him one gold piece and said twenty-eight more would follow if we could arrange convenient terms.

He looked reflectively at the rial, fingered its weight, laboriously calculated its worth in terms of paper lira. Then he asked if my journey would in any way prevent his normal commercial efforts along the route. Quite the contrary, I replied. And the destination? So far as I was concerned, I told him, Cyprus. After that, it was entirely up to him.

Again he reflected. "They need large pots in Famagusta," he observed, "large pots for their wine; I have a cargo of enormous earthenware from Samsun. Yes, I can make a deal.

"You wish to start when? This very night? Well, so be it. I can load. And your own papers? You handle those affairs? And the woman? She is not coming with us? No, of course I shall not tell her. But that is a task I do not envy you."

I handed the sponge-skipper four more gold pieces and asked him to take me to his caique and confirm what he had told me of its size, sea-worthiness, the condition of its sail and Swedish engine. He introduced me as Georgios to his crew of three. One of them was a deaf-mute. I thought: so much the better, a smaller percentage of potential blabbers. I told Michali I would come aboard at sundown—with only two large sacks as baggage. He asked no questions.

By the time we finished our arrangements and returned to the restaurant, it had started to fill. All the clients were men. Pandeli was in the middle, waving his shirt-sleeved arms, wiping his hands from time to time on a dirty apron. The mustachioed little Greek was an absolute tyrant; he immediately ordered each client to his place. The favored guests, friends, were seated below, along lengthy tables set parallel to the white walls of the small room.

Those for whom he had no special regard were shepherded up-stairs by a waiter.

Pandeli—called Cobanoglu only by the police—was equally despotic with the meal. You ate what you were given. You dared not even ask for salt or pepper. It was assumed that every dish was perfectly seasoned. Pandeli supervised as the courses were ladled out—vine leaves stuffed with rice and raisins, baby fried squid, cold octopus, döner and şiş kebab, tomato and onion salad, fruit, cheese, a ceaseless flow of wine. All the time our host, gulping huge quantities of wine himself and wiping it with a flourish from his mustache, moved about pounding people on the back and keeping up a running chatter.

Rima was astonished but, when she whispered questions, I merely nodded. I was waiting for Yusuf. Finally, sweating and in a hurry, he arrived. Pandeli pushed an extra place beside me at the table, and Yusuf heaved himself into it with a greeting, a mumbled apology, a nervous smile and a shrewd glance at Rima.

Yusuf owned a shop in the heart of the bazaar, only a few minutes' walk away. He was a tall, heavy-set, bird-featured Jew from Bokhara, with Solomonic stars in his eyes. His cousins at Tabriz and other cities in Iran and Afghanistan kept him supplied with jewels, rugs, Persian lacquer, and occasional items of contra-band: to these he added stocks of local antiques and of opulent imitations. He displayed in his windows just enough of an alluring assortment to attract wealthy tourists. Once they had entered Yusuf's two small, dark rooms and had been enticed to his coffee or minted tea, they were hopelessly hooked.

Yusuf frequently protested about the hardness of his fate and about how often he had been wiped out by disaster. He went on and on about the Varlik Vergisi, that law, enacted when Hitler was winning in World War II, which penalized Turkey's non-Moslem minorities; about the famous bazaar fire, which he considered his special martyrdom; about occasional riots and police bribes, which, apparently, happened only to him. His way of life, however, seemed marked by increasing signs of prosperity; he was a member of the yacht club.

There was no chance for conversation during lunch. Pandeli hovered over us and forced even the abstemious Yusuf to drink a scantling of retsina. But, when we finished eating, I committed Rima to the charge of Pandeli's son and took the Bokharan for a stroll along the waterfront.

As soon as we got outside, I explained very tersely that I was involved in a dangerous undertaking, that I had genuine affection for Rima and might some day marry her, that she was here with a Soviet passport and no Turkish visa, that I had more or less valid papers, and that I was personally in difficulty with the police.

Would Yusuf help?

I knew the answer in advance. "Of course," he said with a gnostic look. "I will even get her another passport. Would Argentina do? You say she is Greek? Her accent is most curious. But there are many Greeks in Argentina. And she can come live with us until you are back. It will be nice for my wife and for my daughter. And my son is far too young to worry you. I notice your Rima is not hard to look at."

Yusuf rendered me one further service. I had said I needed a hand-gun to protect me in forthcoming adventures. He took me by the arm and led me to his needlessly modest store in the bazaar. Ignoring both the clutch of potential, inquisitive customers and his own eager assistants, he guided me through to the inner sanctum where his most precious possessions were kept in an old-fashioned safe. Pulling shut the curtain to close off the little room, he spun the knob of a combination lock, reached in, and extracted a 32 caliber Webley Scott revolver.

"Here," he said, "this is just what you want. It is useful and cheap. Not a military weapon, a murder weapon. After perhaps a dozen shots, the steel begins to bend. It is a present."

"You mean?"

"It was sent by my cousin in Afghanistan. He bought it from Pathan tribesmen on the Kohat Pass. You might not believe it, but they make the butts from stolen truck tires and the barrels from the steel of railway ties.

"We do some business with the Pakistan army. They don't like to pay much and we produce at cut-rate prices. In fact, our fabricators make all small arms from tommyguns to automatics. British. Russian. French. Belgian.

"Look at this. Webley Scott. But they stippled the name in

wrong. It says 'Webley Scott, Birminoam and Londo.' Not 'London, England.' They even make errors with Kalashnikov. But you shouldn't care. I guarantee this pistol will fire accurately at least twelve times. That is enough. For protection or for piece-rate killing. Precisely what you might need."

When we returned co Pandeli's, it was late afternoon. Only the scullery staff, Pandeli, his son, and Rima were there. Rima was learning the craft of tric-trac. She showed no talent. "Lucky in love," I said, "as the English say." She was completely puzzled.

I patted her arm, took her hand and led her to the empty second floor. When I told her that I was leaving shortly and she would stay behind, she stared at me with horror and then burst into tears. It was the first time I had ever seen her weep. I clasped her to my chest.

"It is only for a week or two," I assured her. "I must make our fortune if we are to live the happy life I intend you shall now begin. But what I have to do is not only dangerous. I know you are more than brave enough to face danger. But you would be in the way and make it more difficult for me to accomplish my purpose.

"Tonight I must go off with the treasure whose fate you confided to me. I have an idea that can make us rich very soon. So do not worry. I shall take care. But it is far easier to take care of myself and my mission all alone.

"Yusuf is a good man. He will look out for you. You will live with his family and you must do what he says. He may appear evil, but he is a true friend. He is wise and cautious. Do not disobey him.

"Now," and I lifted her face for a clinging farewell kiss, "control yourself as you know how to do; let me dry off your tears. When we descend, Yusuf will lead you off and guard your life and happiness as if he were your father. Both he and Pandeli know where I can be reached."

Rima took my hand and scanned the palm for cheiromancy. "Bad. Bad. Bad," she protested. "What happiness? First you stole me from Shamyl with your carp-slippery words. Now you leave me helpless and alone in a wicked city where even you are menaced with arrest."

In a fury she turned, gave me a defiantly lubricous look, ran down the stairs, pecked the astonished Pandeli on the cheek, grabbed Yusuf's arm, and pulled him through the door. They disappeared into the jostling hurlpool. "She is more Diana than Aphrodite," observed our host in a parodic undertone.

I asked Pandeli to send a hamal to carry my sacks to Michali's caique. Then I told him I would endeavor to find ways to keep in touch from time to time. For a start, I was certain he could reach me, if need be, care of my cousin, Sahag Sasounian, in Famagusta, Cyprus. That was sufficient address; I had never met him but I knew that cousin Sahag was the town's leading Armenian citizen.

It took Pandeli's son a long, long while to come back with the hamal. Dusk was already lowering when the porter swung the sacks on to his yoke, and by the time we thrust through the rabble to Unkapani, turned left opposite Rüstem Paşa Cami and worked our way to the fish wharf, it was nearly night.

A sailor lifted a seamy arm to what once had been a smart checked cap and instantly inquired in a hoarse voice if we were looking for Captain Pantelis. I nodded. He led us along the friable edge of the seafront to a squat, powerful caique. "Niki, Samsun," was painted on her orange bows.

Michali, busy with his cargo of tuns, vats, and earthenware, paid no attention. The sailor swung the derrick toward us, and the hamal roped my sacks to the hook. They were heaved aboard, and I helped place them carefully below decks, covering them with canvas. I had no way of knowing what power even a dash of spray might release inside those nubby grains.

All night I sat drinking raki in the stern with Michali until in the dark morning the usual star chased a horned moon across the Turkish sky, and we put out, swung behind a tramp steamer into Marmora, and set sail for Cyprus.

XII

ICHALI, my Ulysses, was a little, swarthy man. His cheeks were pinched, his nose sharp, and through one cock eye he surveyed the world with a vulpine expression. He always wore a raffish, sweat-stained Basque beret, and a baggy, homespun suit with tieless, buttoned collar. But I was soon to discover that he was subtle, audacious, entirely competent, and he even had his own kind of hubris.

He told me his original home was Euboea. When the Nazis seized Greece in 1941, he rented his ship to a fleeing American newspaperman and took him to Çesme in Turkey, where they were both arrested because their papers were not in order. But when the martial Turks discovered in their clothing an assortment of hunting knives, revolvers, and copious ammunition, to their astonishment they were released with friendly smiles. Pantelis decided to stay there until the war was over.

"At that time," he said, "my ambition was to make my fortune by harvesting and selling sponges. But Italy attacked Greece, and my favorite fishing grounds off the Libyan coast were banned."

He told me that, notwithstanding, he had always reckoned on an allied triumph. "I even renamed my caique 'Niki,' or 'Victory,' for it," he said.

He had assumed the Greeks would be awarded Libya with its wealth in sponges as payment for their suffering. "But," he went on, "Athens received the Dodecanese Islands instead, so I remained in Turkey."

He added that he had developed a brisk trade. I suspected he carried heroin between Anatolia and Thrace.

The "Niki" was well found. Her crew knew its job; the caique skewed steadily through the long, low Marmora swells. All the first day dolphins leaped about us, gulls, scanning us with wicked eyes, drifted lazily overhead, and combers beat rhythmically upon the Asiatic and European shores until, in the narrow Dardanelles, these drew suddenly together.

It was fair, smooth weather. At dusk, a round, orange moon hung swollen like some pustular fruit in the unclouded evening sky.

At eventide we were already in the straits. Once there, we lowered sail and chugged along through the night, our Swedish diesel at half speed. The deaf-mute, his knotty hands seeming to doubt the existence of objects, gave Michali and myself chunks of bread, salami, cheese, and olives, and a large, wicker-bound jug of retsina.

One man, with languid eyes, stood watch in the bow, and the third guided the huge tiller, clasping it affectionately in his arms.

The mettlesome little captain, although alert to every possible problem, sat back and began whittling a spillikin. Nothing was required of him on this efficient ship, save to entertain his guest.

I asked which, of all his voyages, had been of greatest importance. For a while he thought, then looked at me through his cock eye: "Surely the most important one was with the American. It was as a result of this trip that I came to live in Turkey. Maybe some day you will meet him, if he is still alive.

"They say he is influential, well connected even if stupid. His name was Sulzberger. See, I have his card." He pulled out a grimy wallet and produced a well-thumbed, yellowed card: "C. L. Sulzberger, The New York Times": the fustian, a particle of the past. I had heard of *The New York Times*. It was America's *Cumhuriyet*.

"But the most interesting trip," Michali continued, "was when I was very young, a child, and my father took me along on a saint-smuggling expedition."

"Saint-smuggling. That is strange contraband."

"Yes," said Michali with a stir of callow humor. "But the people in our village included many refugees from Izmir. They had been settled there after the war with Turkey, and they all worshipped Saint John of Cappadocia. We had an humble church, and we had his icon. But we didn't have the saint himself. The Turks had him.

"You see, our Saint John had been born in Russia. That was a long time ago. He was taken prisoner by the Tartars. They sold him to an Ottoman officer as a slave. The officer lived in Prokopion, Cappadocia. Prokopion is also the name of our village in Euboea. That is why the refugees were settled there.

"The Turk tried to make Saint John accept his faith. But he refused. So the Turk, who was a good man, let him alone. Turks aren't bad if you stand up to them," said he sourly, as if even the Turk were entitled to more than his scruple of wormwood.

"One day, the officer decided to make the pilgrimage to Mecca. He took along his most pious servants and slaves. Except, of course, John, the Christian.

"Not long after they had ridden off on their long journey, the Hanum gave a large party for her husband's relations so the entire family might eat together and pray for his safe return. When John served the pilaf, she said with a sigh: 'My husband's favorite dish. If only he were here to partake of it.'

" 'It shall be done,' said Saint John. 'Just hand me his plate.'

"Everybody laughed and sneered. They said: 'The slave is hungry and wants food.' But John went to the stable where he was quartered, and he prayed: 'Oh, you who once in Babylon, answering the prayers of the prophet Abbakum, brought invisible food to Daniel in the lion's den, please answer my prayer too, and send this food to my master in Mecca.' "

Michali recounted all these archaisms and his superstitions in the homely vernacular of the Euboeans.

"Many weeks later," he continued, "the master returned and asked who it was who had brought his own decorated copper plate to him in Mecca, full of delicious pilaf and still warm. They answered: 'It was your slave.'

"Now those who had laughed at Saint John believed and honored him. They saw that he was holy. The officer set him free to go where he wished. But John was modest. He had no vanity. He remained in the stable.

"It must be more than two hundred years since he died, but everyone in our village knows the story. Many true-believing Greeks then lived in Cappadocia, and they were aware that John was a saint. They exhumed his corpse long after it had been buried. It was found to be still uncorrupted, and it had a special, sweet fragrance like roses.

"The body was placed in the Prokopion church. However, the soldiers of Haci Neceroglu Osman burned it down when they were marching against the apostate king of Egypt. Yet Saint John's remains survived the fire intact. Soon it became known for its ability to work miracles.

"On Mount Athos, the Russian monks of Saint Panteleimon the Healer became envious of this trait. They regarded John as one of their own since he had been born a Russian, and they demanded his body. But the Greeks of Cappadocia are famous for their cleverness. They can see a flea wink. They can forge a shoe for a gnat. They are even cleverer than Armenians.

"So they negotiated with the Russians. In the end, they sold only Saint John's brittle right hand. And the Russians had to pay a great price before they could cut it off and take it to their monastery. Prokopion kept the rest; and it continued to make miracles.

"When the war came all Greeks were forced out of Cappadocia. They had to leave in such a hurry there was no time to bring along the Saint. Many from Anatolian Prokopion were moved to our Prokopion in Euboea. And there it was determined that John must be reunited with our people.

"So the mayor formed a special crew to man the largest caique we could find. My father, who was a famous fisherman and smuggler, was named captain. He agreed to everything on one condition—that I be allowed to come. That was 1924. I was fourteen.

"We sailed off on a sheep-selling expedition. You know the people in that area are great shepherds."

"Do I know!" I interrupted. "That is my country. Cappadocia is Armenia. Hassan Dagh is a sacred mountain."

[155

"At any rate," said Pantelis, "we took great pains. We idled along the coast. In one village, we bought a lot of brown coal. We herded the sheep and the turkeys together. Yes, we had turkeys, too. We shoved them together and put great sacks of coal all over the forward deck. Both the sheep and the turkeys had their legs tied, and you never heard such baaing and whistling. Did you know that turkeys whistle? They whistle through their ears. And their wattles change color when they're angry. They were very angry.

"Finally, we got to the tiny harbor lying nearest to Prokopion. We had the correct papers. And we offered such a good price that soon we had sold all our animals. The Turks were very pleased.

"We then explained that we came from a Greek village also called Prokopion, and we would like to go up and look at the church in their Prokopion because several of our crew had once come from there.

"The Turks didn't mind. We all went up together, drinking ouzo on the way. They like our ouzo better than their raki. You know, the real mastic taste. From Chios. By the time we got to Prokopion, they were drunk. I've been told their Koran forbids spirits, but, believe me, there are few people who drink as much as a thirsty Turk.

"So we poked around the ruined church. Sure enough, there was the smashed altar and, under a pile of rubble, the coffin of Saint John. We pretended to pay no attention. But we marked it well.

"When darkness came and the Turks were lurching and belching and clapping us on the back as we stumbled to our ship, two of our company stayed behind. They carried the coffin to the caique and quickly covered it with coal. The rest of us took a long time to delay the Turkish procession.

"That's all. Nobody suspected anything. We have put John in a silver casket, covered with glass. Now you can see him any time in our new church. It is splendid."

"What does he look like?"

"Well, it is not for me to say that he is the worse for wear. Naturally, his hand is still at Athos with those Russians. As for the rest of him, his features are not intact. His skin is like boot leather. But he is home with us. And he is very holy."

"A fine story," I remarked. "A splendid voyage. Worthy of the Argos." I thought suddenly of our cargo, of my teeth.

Late next day, as we glided gently toward Cape Helles, Pantelis mentioned the need for clearance with the port authorities from Kum Kale, where a police boat checked manifests of craft that might be leaving Turkish waters, even if, in fact, they were merely planning to swing east and south to Izmir and the Hatay. It seemed far too much trouble to attempt to forge new stamps into my Turkish passport, especially since I feared the Birinci might have been instructed to set customs on the lookout for me. I mentioned to Michali that there was a problem.

With courtesy and craft, he proposed stowing me together with my sacks in what he called "the special place." The "special place" turned out to be a secret compartment, set beneath the lavatory in the after section of the hold. One merely swung the toilet bowl up on a hinge and it exposed a good-sized space with adequate entry for the stowage of contraband cargo.

The toilet itself was never employed; only the sea. What Michali usually put underneath it was beyond me; heroin requires little room. Nevertheless, I worked my sacks sternward with the help of the two vocal crewmembers, laid them gently inside, and then familiarized myself with the workings of the hinge. When we saw the little police boat's red light winking around a cove in the distance, I clambered down.

"Did you sleep well on your birdseed?" Michali inquired in the morning when I awakened, almost stifled, to the motion of long combers swinging across the Aegean. "Did you dream of sharp-pricked chukars heeling each other to death? Or was it the plump-breasted variety that enticed your attention?"

"That's not what I'm paying you for, Captain," I said with asperity. "Anyway, it seems you cleared the harbor master with amazing speed. I heard no sounds of inspection down in my little stateroom. How much does it cost to bribe a Turkish harbor master nowadays?"

"Twenty lira," was the answer. "Twenty lira if you know the right man and have done him favors in the past."

For the next two days we swung from wave-top to wave-top, the "Niki's" pudgy bow plunging and rising, rolling and twisting in what seemed a needlessly awkward and exaggerated way. I am not a maritime creature, and I lay amidships, nestled between two rows of barrels, occasionally staggering in agony to the low wooden rail. Nobody paid the least attention.

This was the season of the great Aegean winds, the Levante and the wild Meltemi. They beat upon us separately, spinning "Niki" in their vortex. Overhead at night we could hear the first birds coming down upon the storms, the doves in V-shaped eche-lons, each led by their lonely little crane, and the lascivious quails, small sacred birds of Artemis. Our caique scudded along the waves, burdened with its groaning eathenware, like the old trakonderi, the sluggish meen, the triremes, skaphai and carracks of the Knights of Rhodes, the sakturia and travaccola that had roared through these windy waters since time began.

At dawn, a monstrous black squall suddenly hit us at full pelt. Michali, who sacrificed to older gods in time of stress, cast a panni-kin of wine on the heaving waters, and shouted: "Mermaid, Alex-ander the Great still lives and reigns."

Strangely enough, these heathen rites worked. Great Poseidon was as effectively pacified as if he had been approached through the holy iconodules of our Armenian mother church. The curvet-ting sea lay down in a green sheet; "Niki" gave up her loutish wallowing; our short sail puffed out to catch the following breeze, and we chugged calmly southeastward toward Cyprus.

"How are you going to avoid the British?" I asked Michali when, once again master of my emotions, I had resumed my place beside him near the stern. "I have heard they keep gunboats on patrol, looking for arms smugglers to the guerrillas. And they must be helped by planes."

"Don't worry," he answered. "I have my ways. The only thing dumber than a dumb Turk is a bright Englishman." He spat over the rail.

"What I should like to ask," he continued, "is why you take your birdseed to Cyprus, of all places. These people are poor. They have no fighting birds. And there are no Arab sheikhs among them who might fancy the sport. I have taken you at your word on everything, including the extra gold you will give me when you leave us. But I want your assurance there is no military equipment in those sacks. I must always take special precautions to unload."

"No explosives. I swear this by the holy eyes of Saint Rhipsime, by my own dead mother's eyes. And the reason why? Maybe I'll just store my consignment in Cyprus for a while, until things calm down."

"Very well. Now I shall let you know my plan. You will again conceal yourself shortly before sun-up tomorrow. By then we will be in range of the radar plane. But I have no worry; I have made this run before, carrying other things than birdseed. And the British are not imaginative when they search; pots and barrels are normal cargo for Famagusta.

"Once the Royal Navy authorities have cleared us at sea, I can get your sacks easily ashore. Here again, I have a friend—the harbor master who works pants-and-behind with EOKA, the guerrillas, and who specially likes it when I bring arms.

"But have you any place to go? Do you know anyone? Will you have money after you have paid me? Will you obtain papers to avoid arrest? These lime-juicers have riddled the place with spies. They put out roadblocks everywhere."

"Don't worry about me," I said. "When I have no more gold, imagination is my money. And there is a cousin of my father who will help me. We are no deracinated exiles. Among us Armenians, blood runs in thick rivers. My kinsman will see that I am cared for."

Everything came to pass as Michali had forecast. From my nook beneath the toilet, I heard crates and barrels being moved around, the mumble of voices, then nothing. We resumed our passage, and I felt the pulse of the propeller as it pushed toward Famagusta. Finally we hove to and I listened as the anchor chain rattled through the bow scuppers. Footsteps echoed above my head, and then the ugly camouflage was disturbed. The hinge swung up and Michali, with an evil grin, beckoned and said: "Your time has come."

I scrambled out and stretched my stiffened limbs. The three crew members reached in and, with evident strain, hoisted my sacks and heaved them to the deck. There was no effort at secrecy. Michali himself climbed into the rowboat we had lowered and helped swing my precious cargo over the starboard side and deposit it in the heavy dinghy.

We were lying about thirty meters off a jetty on our lee, in a shallow basin filled with fishing boats and small coastal benziners. The city stretched behind, hot and placid, the ruins of churches and fortresses sticking out at places amid the tops of palm trees. The atmosphere was tranquil and remote as regret.

When we reached the pier, Michali blandly signalled to a porter with a pushcart. Together we lifted the sacks aboard. "Now," he said, "our last little matter of business."

I reached into my pocket, undid the corners of my handkerchief, and put all the remaining coins in his outstretched, scarified hands. He looked straight at me as his fingers tallied their number, then nodded, said: "Charity, my friend. Now I must be off about my pots. I shall take on English cloth here and English cigarettes. Then we are on our way to Beirut, where I have a special little job."

The lid of his left eye descended slowly, like that of a blinking tortoise. I took this for a wink. Michali, in excellent fettle, turned, climbed into his boat and rowed rapidly away with determined strokes. I told my porter to take me to the main bazaar, where I had no doubt I should be able to find the whereabouts of my cousin, another of the clan of the great David of Sasoun. I had been told since childhood he was a generous and loving man.

In the market place a sign immediately caught my eye. It read: "Curios. Fine Wine. Ladies & Gents Furnishment. Ivory Articles from Old Yndia. Propr. P. Mardikhian." I told the porter to wait and entered Mr. Mardikhian's emporium. A round little man was standing by the cash register. In Armenian I inquired: "Surely you know my cousin, Sahag Sasounian?"

The man looked up. Suddenly he waved his arms and shouted: "Sahag's cousin? A cousin of Sahag? Do I know Sahag? Hah! You shall come with me." He yanked off his gray apron, threw it to a young woman with plaited black hair, grabbed my arm and bustled me into the street. Without being instructed, the porter trudged along behind his rattling cart.

We walked for ten minutes. Mr. Mardikhian kept shouting questions in a high fever of excitement, never allowing me time to answer, clutching my arm, holding the biceps tight. "Aha, my young hero," he cried. "The blood of the Sasounians still runs fierce and purple, I can see." When we reached a stone and plaster house with a doorway framed in mimosa, he hollered: "If Sahag Sasounian is home, I have for him the most welcome of surprises." A handsome, stern, gray-thatched, furrowed face peered in from a doorway to the right: "And that is?"

"Your cousin. Kevork Sasounian, my friend."

Cousin Sahag, last leader of our eupatrid tribe, looked at me doubtfully. I explained about myself, my father, the sad disappearance of my family and how I had heard of him all my youth. I added that both my parents had admired him immensely, that all through my childhood he had been held up as an example of courage, and that his march across Anatolia while Ottoman soldiers massacred our countrymen was one of my childhood legends.

"Yes," he said with sorrow. "And now I see the resemblance in your features. Your father was a highly cultivated man. A true scholar. To think that an Armenian gentleman of noble family should end in so desolate a way. And your mother. Your mother was a brave, brave woman. She suffered much. I hope you were good to her. The rest?"

"Only two sisters," I said. "Also dead—I confirmed this in Istanbul."

Mr. Mardikhian, who had been standing, rubbing his white hands together, sensed the moment for departure had come. He told me to call if I needed him, but Cousin Sahag rumbled: "No Sasounian requires the help of any man while yet another Sasounian remains alive."

Cousin Sahag took me to a garden behind the house. A rope hammock was slung between two eucalyptus trees, and a circle of chairs had been placed around a wicker table. "Araxie," he called out, clapping. "Araxie, we have a guest. Bring us wine. Bring us much good wine."

A girl came out bearing a tray. She was beautiful. She had black hair, dark eyes of diaphanous clarity, a smooth forehead, perfectly arched eyebrows, a thin, straight nose with fragile nostrils. When she spoke or smiled, her gently lipped mouth revealed the loveliest set of tiny, white teeth. For the first time I saw the famous teeth like pomegranate seeds that feature in Persian poetry. But Araxie had something else as well: a slender, tall figure, straight as a poplar, with the tenderest of curves.

She set the tray down, enjoying my admiring glance, and her father introduced us: "You are cousins. Kevork Sasounian, whose father you never knew, but you have heard me tell of him. And Araxie. My only daughter. My peach. My melon. She is all that I have left. Now, girl, pour the wine. Am I a sparrow to pour water on myself? Am I a camel to drink from a spoon? We shall have a great cup, a cup as big as a basin."

Araxie offered me a large, earthenware mug, and looking from her deep eyes to the red pool of wine, I lifted it to her father and quoted: "They gave David to drink from that cup. David was drunk and became gay."

Cousin Sahag grinned. He continued: "Drunkenness took David and carried him off. David was drunk, he hung his head on his breast."

He took a huge drink and so did I.

At that moment, Araxie returned and said: "A porter is at the door with two great sacks in a cart. He says he is from my cousin." She was too timid to mention my name.

"True," I replied. "May I store them here a while, cousin?" I asked Sahag. "It is a curiously valuable consignment of seed grain that I have been charged to protect and eventually transport. By the Royal Horticultural Society. Kew Gardens. London. England."

Sahag told Araxie to have the sacks deposited with the wine jars in the coolest, driest part of the cellar, and to pay the porter. If the porter needed help, they were to call Oram. The handyman, I inferred. Then Sahag turned to me, and pouring more wine he murmured in a deep-throated voice: "My son, how can I help you? My son, how can I help you?"

I told him only parts of my story: that I had been framed by the Turkish police and forced to go for them to Russia on a disagreeable mission. That the threat of blackmail had only ended with my family's death. That I was now employed on a special botanical job. That I really had no ordered future before me. That I hoped soon to find a more suitable career, as I had need of money. I had special need of money. There was a Greek girl. I might marry her.

"Good. Good. Good," said Cousin Sahag. "I am glad she is

Greek. The Greeks are fine people. They have a splendid heritage, and they believe in the true faith even if they practice it in a somewhat different way. They are intelligent; they are loyal; and I am pleased. We will find you a career; you shall not lack. Tell me, young man, do you need funds now?"

I acknowledged that this was the case. He reached into his shirt, extracted a billfold, and handed me twenty notes, each for five English pounds: a fortune. Silencing my gratitude, he added: "And if you will permit me, your clothes are travel-worn. I shall have Mardikhian measure you tomorrow. For everything. New suits. Shirts. Shoes. You are a large falcon to adorn."

All afternoon and evening we drank, and I told him about Soviet Armenia, about Erivan and Ararat, about our famous Sevan lake. He was nodding, his eyes were half shut; he was remembering his terrible past, his vanished dreams.

After Araxie had served us a ragout of mutton and slabs of lavash bread, and after we had drunk two demijohns of magnificent, heavy wine, Sahag suddenly leaned forward to clasp me about the back and put his head beside mine, like a conspirator.

"Tell me, Kevork," he whispered, "you have had much adventure. Have you ever murdered? Have you ever killed a man?"

I acknowledged that I had, although this had nothing to do with my Turkish police troubles. "Naturally," he conceded. "An Armenian is too discreet for that. And too clever. But do you know much about killing?"

"I have killed with the gun. I have killed with the knife. And I have killed with my fingers. I have strong fingers." I made the twist that causes a cracking neck to go limp.

"To all in Sasoun he was a pattern of strength," chanted Sahag. "With bearing like his father's, his eyes brightly shining, his face like an eagle's, his cheeks noble, his curls like a flame, his stance and his arms of steel—beware, do not touch."

Then he peered directly into my eyes. "You have been sent by our Holy Mother in Heaven. You have been sent by Rhipsime. I will help you, Kevork. But you too shall help me."

He explained in a heavy whisper that Araxie had been seduced by a young Famagusta Turk named Turgut, a worthless fellow whose reputation was so bad that even his own race disliked him.

Turgut had given Araxie gonorrhea. Sahag was determined the Turk should pay for this insult. He wanted him dead. Plainly I had been dispatched by the Almighty to do the job.

I said only: "My forefathers left me a testament. Whenever you meet an enemy, delay not to fight with him."

"You shall do me this service and honor our family pride. And I shall make you rich, Kevork."

I bowed my head, feeling sad for that fine man, my cousin, and bewildered for my cousin, Araxie. "I shall take cruel vengeance for everything," I thought.

Sahag murmured in a strangely tender voice: "Meanwhile, you stay here with Araxie and myself. Our house is yours as your blood is ours. We will talk quietly another day about the service I have asked."

I moved into a pleasant corner room overlooking the garden. From Araxie, who seemed unbelievably modest and intact to have suffered so sordid a fate, I soon learned that Sahag was a lawyer and chief citizen of the Famagusta Armenian community. He had excellent relations with the Greeks, including the secret EOKA and the church, she told me, and he pretended excellent relations with the British. But, she added, he could never treat any Turk with the consideration he would give a dog.

Although I was delighted to meet my remaining family, the real reason I had chosen Cyprus to try and market my teeth was that it was the area most accessible to me where fighting was taking place, even if that was only on the scale of a limited EOKA insurrection. I fancied that once I contacted those secret guerrillas, I could easily persuade their leadership that a select group of hardy professional warriors, most of whom I had no doubt would speak a form of Greek, would be a welcome increment in EOKA's struggle against the British.

Thousands of British soldiers and armed police were combing the island every day. Surely the prospect of what could at the very least be a puzzling diversion might be welcome to the insurgents. I knew the engagement was so miniature that I had no hope of disposing of even the major share of my crop, yet I was anxious to obtain cash assets from limited sales before entering broader realms of business.

Several things occurred before I managed to put my plan in action. First, I met a Jew who called himself Avrahm. He ran a small tourist office in Famagusta and handled many Israeli clients. He was slight and wiry, with tan hair and haunted blue eyes. He had a frigid but not uncivil exterior. Sahag often invited him to dine. From our initial meeting, Avrahm displayed inordinate curiosity about me. He seemed to suspect I had something to do with a military enterprise. According to bazaar gossip, Sahag told me, he worked for an organization named Shin Bet, the highly secret intelligence service of Israel.

Secondly, I took to screwing Araxie and found this exceedingly enjoyable, although well aware of the medical chance involved. But it was hardly diplomatic to inquire of her health before proceeding under her dress. Whatever the risk, it was well worthwhile.

Her lithe body and flashing eyes, glittering like shiny black olives, proved better guides to her true self than the demure manner she maintained in her father's presence. Every man is aware of the special smell of his woman, sometimes like musk, sometimes like amber, sometimes like mist, sometimes like dawn, sometimes like evening. Araxie smelled like the fouli flowers in a Mediterranean fig orchard.

Moreover, she was instinctively cautious and discreet, moving into my bed like a cat at night, biting off into sibilant whispers the sounds of her pleasure, and slipping away on noiseless feet long before the morning star began to rise.

Thirdly, I killed Turgut. This was neither a difficult nor, as time proved, an unpopular achievement. Indeed, the Turkish community made only a minor fuss when the newspapers, printing this latest EOKA murder story, stated that Turgut had been an agent of the British.

I was not entirely surprised by the story, since I had torn the word "EOKA" from a *Cyprus Mail* and had taped it to the dead Turgut's forehead with adhesive. The fact that the British were provoked into new searches, restrictions, and reinforcements around Famagusta was not seriously discommoding, at least not to Sahag; and the fact that the Greek majority used the occasion to beat up members of the Turkish minority inspired delight in our Armenian household.

By the chance of misfortune my vengeance on Turgut for

sullying the honor of our noble family was seasoned with a particular savor of vindictiveness when, a few days before my plan had reached the stage of fruition, I received from Istanbul a letter sent by Pandeli Cobanoglu and delivered by an unknown messenger in the care of cousin Sahag.

"Bad news, My Little George," this letter said. "The Turks are suspicious once again. Something curiously strange has happened and I am not certain what it means. But these Turks are interested both in you and Rima and in a most obsessive way.

"Now I am a brave man, My Little George, but I am not made of wood. They asked. They insisted. They put me to the question. My feet still hurt.

"I fear I told them where your golden girl is. And I fear the worst if they should find her. But I have managed to alert Yusuf, in time I hope. Those Turks. Only we Greeks and you Armenians truly understand them.

"First I received an invitation from Lotfi Kirdar, the Vali, to attend him at his luncheon in that vile place Taksim's. The invitation was rendered urgent by two attendants from the Birinci Buro. So I went, even though it was our own lunch time and we serve our guests food, not rat droppings such as fancied by the Vali.

"Lotfi Kirdar was sitting there at a table with your great friend, that heathen Naci Perkel. I was made to stand beside them while they ate and some of these fat thuggee-masters of the Milli Emniyet stood around sneering.

"Finally Lotfi Bey looked at me as if I had just arrived and said: 'I hear you are serving poison once again, despite my warnings. Now listen, Greek, I will let you off with a threat instead of closing your restaurant for violating the sanitary statutes. But you shall tell my friend here something in return.'

"Then Naci Bey—and he is a smooth type, that one—smiled sweetly and inquired: 'I know we share the acquaintance of the admirable Gentleman George, Kevork Sasounian as some know him. You must tell me where he is. And his lovely girl-friend also. This is necessary for reasons of state.'

"Well, My Little George, you must know I am not easily bandied with. I told him you had gone abroad, although I knew not where. And I swore by the Pantocrator that I knew nothing of a lady-friend; none in particular, that is to say. It is then that they questioned me. Imagine, in the dressing rooms below the Taksim dance floor, where those Hungarian whores take off their clothes!

"All I can tell you is that so far they have not much to go on. Yes, I did admit to knowing a girl named Rima. But I could not tell them where she was. Nor you.

"It seems that Rima left a husband in that awful Bolshevik Russia. He appears to have some official connection. The interrogators kept asking about police and agents. And something called the KGB. What is that KGB? Is it like the NKVD which caused such harm to the Crimean Greeks?

"Do not reply, Georgakimou. And above all, do not attempt to come here yet. It is dangerous. Dangerous for all of us. I have warned Yusuf and through him Rima. Now it is best we should all lay low, as so often in the past. Do not communicate. But leave an address, should you depart, and tell your cousin Sahag where you may be reached. Your faithful and courageous Greek friend, Pandeli."

Thwarted of my natural instincts for direct action because of these cautionary words, I confined my initial anguish to meticulous planning for the downfall of Turgut. He was not a bad-looking young man, except for viperine eyes and the unusually large ears so often awarded by Allah to Turks. A bit shorter than I, with thick neck, thick chest, thick waist, sinewy arms and a thick head, he nevertheless had a handsome bearing, red hair, and an air of intelligence unusual for his breed. His manner was hearty, and he was given to enunciating proverbs whenever the occasion permitted.

As far as I could gather, there were two reasons for his undoubted unpopularity even with other Turks: First, he had deceived several husbands, brutally beating them when they protested and subsequently dropping their disheartened wives; second, he had extorted small sums of money from many tradesmen by threatening them with accidents if they did not pay.

For a man of my experience, the operation had been very easy. I took pains to avoid being seen with Turgut, so that my name could never be associated with his. But I sent word to him that I needed a valiant partner on an audacious if highly prosperous undertaking. He accepted the bait. So, soon we took to lazing after lunchtime on the deserted beach below the Norman cathedral when every Greek, Turk, and Armenian in Famagusta was enjoying a siesta.

When I had entirely won his trust, I gave him twenty English pounds, instructed him to hire a donkey, and made an assignation to meet me at a lonely rock spit, further down the coast. I confided to him that a heroin shipment was to be delivered to me there, for sale to a pusher who had contacts among the British forces.

The project appealed to Turgut. It was impossible for him to contemplate doublecrossing me, since I had not told him the name of my pusher and had warned him special identification procedures were necessary prior to delivery. Nevertheless, I said he would be required during one entire night when we would receive the goods. I needed him as a bodyguard and to handle the donkey on which we would transport a camouflaged bale. Turgut was to bring no firearms. One must avoid suspicion in any accidental encounter with authority.

I had chosen the night before the new moon. Turgut rode up mounted on his ass, tethered the beast to a bush and joined me quietly by the lapping waves. "Where is the boat?" he muttered hoarsely.

"Who told you it was by boat?"

Before he had a chance to look puzzled, much less to draw the knife he had dashingly tucked into his sash, I thought of Araxie and thrust my knee hard in his groin. Then I thought of Rima and hammered the back of his neck with my twinned hands as he fell forward on the rocks. I made quite sure he was not yet dead, so that, just for the pleasure, I could kick him hard and painfully several more times. Murmuring "Turk, damned Turk," I pummelled him in the liver, ribs, throat, glottal cartilage, in fact, everywhere except the face. There was to be no problem of identification.

I had to shoot him. This was the EOKA way, although I preferred my hands alone. I took my Webley Scott, which was similar to those often employed by Greek officers and, therefore, presumably EOKA—although its markings would be unidentifiable to ballistics experts. I then shot him very carefully in the back of the head, taped my newspaper clipping to his brow, and put the gun back under my belt. Afterward, I carried his body to the munching donkey.

I slung him on his belly across the saddle. Then I undid the bridle and, with it, strapped his hands and feet underneath. I kicked the animal and beat him with a stick until he clambered up the slope and started to trot down the road toward the city and his master. Turgut had been just tall enough for his fingers to trail in the dust.

When Sahag returned for lunch next day, news had already spread through town that the guerrillas had struck down an informer in their resolute war against the British. "Another abominable crime," he proclaimed with loud disgust as Araxie brought us wine and mutton.

"Typically foul EOKA work," he added. "They are cowards. They shoot in the back. I hope the British catch the rascals who did this. I understand they are already holding several suspects. The British are proud, just people. They belong here. It is not good to tweak the lion's tail."

But when Araxie disappeared into the kitchen to help Oram wash up, my host gripped my arm with wiry fingers, looked sharply into my eyes and said: "You delayed not to fight with him."

Then he added: "A father's thanks, my boy. I say no more. This afternoon you shall come to my office, where your money awaits you in the strong box. I have always had faith."

That night, when she came, Araxie said nothing of the incident. But she bit my lip and raked me in her ecstasy. Despite myself I thought of Rima. "Again, my sullied hummingbird," I murmured with deliberately inciting passion; "again."

CHAPTER

XIII

O NE evening Sahag invited me to come with him to visit the home of Loizides, a Greek friend. I wore the darker of my two new Mardikhian suits of excellent English material and less excellent American cut; Mardikhian had been born in California.

Loizides, a pleasant, small man, introduced us to the others in his party: Lawrence Durrell, an English writer who worked in some capacity for the administration in Nicosia, George Seferiadis, a Greek ambassador in the Middle East who was visiting Cyprus on holiday and, rather to my surprise, Avrahm.

We sat under carob, fig, and lemon trees and among the last, torn blossoms of jasmine, fouli, and begonia, and we were served heavy, scented black wine.

When I commented on the wine, Seferiadis told me: "Well you might like it. This is the Commanderia the Crusaders drank on their way to the Holy Land. It used to be made by the Knights of Saint John in their Commanderie here. The art has been brought down through the ages. It is of sweet grapes, matured in enormous casks, which are opened only every twenty-five years to be partially refilled and re-aged."

Suddenly he lowered his head in thought, half shut his eyes, and his long, sallow, high-domed face assumed the appearance of an unhappy lemon. He began to recite in a surprisingly tuneful voice:

"I moored alone and brought this fairy story,
    If it is true that it is a fairy story,

If it is true that man will not set in motion once more
The old deceit of the gods."

"He is Seferis," Loizides whispered to me. "Seferis, our greatest poet since Cavafy. Let us encourage him to more."

But there was no more; Seferiadis sat in gloomy silence, holding
his head in both hands, his elbows on his knees. Sahag quietly
drank and Loizides kept pouring dark streams of wine from a
gigantic pitcher. Durrell, a stocky young fellow with broad,
agreeable features, blond hair and a hearty, bluff manner,
shouted abruptly: "Come on, George. Give us 'The Lustful
Elpenor.'" Seferiadis remained moodily still.

Durrell was a man of great gusto, a kind of juvenescent genius.
He drank large amounts of wine and kept seizing handfuls of
gleaming olives from a bowl on the table, plopping them into his
mouth, spitting out the pits, and constating with admiration:
"Hah, surely the best food. Older than meat, older than wine." His
conversational style was distinct and rich.

The talk shifted to religion. I noticed that Durrell shared the
Greek delight in argument and speculative thought. With a glint
of mischief in his eyes, he asked Loizides: "Tell me, did the
schism really come over the fight on Filioque? Or was it a difference of protocol on Systatic Letters? You know what I think? I
think it was because you Greeks always looked down on the barbarian Romans. You thought they ate the flesh of wolves and bap-
tized infants with saliva.

"How about Armenians?" he asked Sahag. "Are you Mono-
thelete or Monophysite? I have never quite figured out."

Sahag grunted. I felt in him a stir of callow resistance.

Seferiadis looked up. "The answer to your question," he said
in a soft voice, "is that the Armenians, being better pagans than
we were, sacrificed animals at Lent, ate strangled meat, and ab-
stained from singing alleluia after Septuagesima. Also, they used
unleavened bread for the sacrament."

"Why not?" my cousin gruffly asked. "What could be better
than lavash? If it was good enough for our Lord, it is more than
good enough for those who worship him."

"How do you know Christ ate lavash?" Durrell interrupted.

[171

With that, he began to sing with a bawdy expression: "Roll me o-ver, roll me o-ver, roll me over, stick it in and do it again."

"You know, Christianity is an untidy religion," Seferiadis said somberly. "It requires more naivete, more faith, than belief in an earth goddess or the sun. Surely Socrates knew more of the real meaning of religion than that advertising man, Saint Paul."

"Yes," said Loizides, who had studied law in England. "To be a true Christian needs greater effort than to believe in voodoo. Imagine dreaming up virgin birth! Or arguing about whether a holy spirit can be represented by a pigeon, and if it speaks for a Father or a Son who are one and the same thing! Artificial insemination by a pigeon! Or making cannibalistic symbols into sacramental rites!"

"Only lawyers and poets can be successful priests of such a faith," Durrell shouted, reaching for more olives. "Or mystics. Or good simple folk who believe in legends like dragon's teeth."

I found myself in a corner with Avrahm. He whispered insidiously: "Has it ever occurred to you how curious it is to see an English official in this house so often, when everyone knows Loizides is high up in EOKA?"

"I have never been here before. But indeed it would be strange."

"They say Durrell is a writer," he suggested with insinuating implications. "A very well known one."

"Maybe he's looking for a theme."

When the others had gone and Sahag took me gently by the elbow, Loizides said: "Why don't you leave your cousin for another drink. A man that size gets very thirsty, eh, Kevork?"

Sahag agreed. He walked out of the garden while I sat, waiting for our host to make the first move. Another murder? I speculated. Lives were easily dispatched on Cyprus. Clearly, something more than a fresh gallon of Commanderia was coming.

We sipped from our mugs and eyed each other. "It has come to my ears that you believe you may be able to help my friends," Loizides said.

"Are the EOKA your friends?"

"They are the friends of every Greek. Make no mistake."

"Well, in that case, perhaps I can do something for them. Something extremely practical. And valuable?"

"What is your price?"

"It is subject to negotiation. Quantity as well as quality is involved."

The night was still, the humid air like mud—the kind of night that precedes a tramontana. In the distance I heard crepitant noises like shots.

"I don't know what your weapons are," said Loizides. "But I have been authorized to inform you that a demonstration would be welcomed."

"By whom?"

"By the proper authorities. I can set up your contacts. If you are sure that you have something of real value. And if you are ready to run certain risks."

"As to value, tell your friends I know how to put teeth into their operations. Teeth that will bite the British. As for your second condition, I am accustomed to risks."

"Very well. You will be standing under the street lamp two blocks down from Sahag's house tomorrow at ten P.M. You are to keep your equipment samples at minimal size. We want nothing so bulky that the operation can be messed up."

He handed me a slip of paper with a number written on it. "Memorize it. A car with this number plate will drive up, stop thirty seconds, then drive on. One minute later another car will come. Its front door will swing open. You will quickly slip in beside the driver. That is all I know. Understood?"

"Small samples," I replied. "Ten P.M. Second car. Thanks for a pleasant evening. Good night, Mr. Loizides."

EOKA, as everyone in the Levant knew, stood for Ethniki Organosis Kypriakou Agonos, or National Organization of the Cypriot Struggle. It was the underground army fighting against Britain with the aim of joining Cyprus to Greece. Nobody could guess its size or whether it truly represented the island's Greek-speaking majority.

There was no doubt, however, that it was murderous. It seemed to prefer killing antipathetic Greeks or suspected agents rather than engaging directly with the sizable British forces stationed there. It moved in mystery; mere mention of its name produced an uneasy atmosphere.

Everything went well the following evening. There was no one else near the street lamp; the first car stopped, drove on; the second car picked me up. The driver, a nondescript heavy man with a two-day growth of beard, greeted me pleasantly and promptly warned me not to look behind. I had already glimpsed two figures by the headlights of a passing car, noticed they were wearing dark glasses, and that they had hidden their faces behind briefcases.

"I don't see your samples," said the driver. "Have you got them?"

"I have my samples. Your leader will be satisfied."

There was no further conversation. Whenever headlights loomed ahead, I could feel the two behind lifting briefcases to their faces. I was surprised there were no roadblocks or police halts and was impressed by this hint of EOKA's efficient network of informants.

Some miles out, after climbing slightly from the Famagusta plain, we turned off the narrow highway and down a still more narrow dirt road. This soon led to our destination, a quiet white house on the edge of an olive grove.

At one corner was a square tower, a kind of machicolated keep. A chunky farmer in white shirt and homespun pantaloons opened my door and led me from the car into a small room decorated with icons and pictures of archbishops. Then he left and the light went out.

There was no moon. The stars gave little illumination through the curtained windows. Among the olives I could hear nervous sheep bleating a nocturnal eclogue.

After several minutes, another door opened, and I was summoned, stumbling, into an even darker room. I assumed the shutters had been drawn tight; and I could not see the wooden chair onto which I was pushed.

When my eyes became accustomed to this new degree of blackness, I could discern several figures seated in a semicircle. At one moment a torch must have moved on the other side of the door, for my sensitive eyes caught a gleam from its reflection under the crack. I managed to see that even here, in utter night, my interlocutors were wearing tinted sunglasses. There was a peculiar dead odor, like agaric fungus.

A man started talking to me in English with a strong Oxford accent. I immediately reproved him, saying it was obvious from the excellence of their intelligence, as previously displayed, that they knew I spoke fluent Greek.

Another voice interrupted. It was mild, calm, but betrayed the habit of command. Aha, I thought. An officer.

The voice explained: "We have invited you here because you are said to possess something which could be of use to us, and that you are willing to sell this at a profit. If you satisfy us, we are prepared to come to an arrangement.

"You must excuse the precautions but they are necessary. Security is essential to our operations. Whether or not we make a deal, you will have to forget this evening. Forget that we exist. I warn you that if you do not wholly forget everything, you will find we are ruthless. And you are being watched.

"There is nothing personal about this. Remember, we are at war. We are at war with Britain. We have nothing against the British as a nation. Therefore we have not killed any English. As yet, at least.

"This is a war, a savage war, and if you can help us, we are prepared to pay. Our program has been to frighten the British but not to kill them. We wish to demonstrate their folly in trying to hold Cyprus against the will of the Cypriot people. We kill only Cypriot traitors; and informants. But soon, we fear, we will have to kill the British, too.

"Now tell us what you think you can do to favor our cause."

I must keep my manner matter-of-fact, I thought to myself, for they could easily think me insane and shoot me on the spot. Quietly, painstakingly, I began recounting the secret of my wares.

"I can guarantee, if you are prepared for a fair price, to provide a force of hard, professional soldiery. They may be behind in weapons training but are surely adept. War is their only profession. They are Greeks, although of strange provenance; not Cypriots, but they can easily be indoctrinated in your cause.

"Moreover, an enormous reserve force can be hidden for an indeterminate period of time and in the smallest conceivable space, awaiting your command to strike. Nor need this reserve be fed or watered during the weeks or months of waiting."

Quickly, before I could be interrupted by rude remarks, I said

[175

that I had brought with me three samples which could demonstrate the truth of my astonishing claims. The rest, I added, were well hidden. I had left in safe hands a letter instructing the recipient to lead the police to my trove should I not reappear within twenty-four hours.

I continued: "In a moment, you gentlemen will see you are not dealing with a madman. You may soon consider your own selves mad when you see what you will see."

There was a silence.

"You doubt me, gentlemen? Very well, give me a chance to demonstrate which among us is the fool. Merely tell me if I am correct in supposing what your organization may require. I am certain that I can adjust my wares to fit your needs."

In the darkness, the quiet, authoritative voice explained tersely. EOKA's central committee, Kendriki Epitropi, controlled a series of groups and subgroups, each of which was called an Omas, or team. Each Omas was headed by an Omadarch, or group leader. No one knew anybody outside his own Omas except the group leader. Therefore, if one Omas were discovered, its members could not betray other groups, even under British torture. Any recruits or hirelings must accept blind obedience.

"And the commander?" I inquired.

"He is Dighenis," said the voice. I knew that nom de guerre. Dighenis was a hero of Byzantine poems known to all Greeks of Istanbul and therefore to all Christians, even us, the Armenians. Rumor suggested this new Dighenis was really a certain Colonel Grivas, a right-wing Greek officer who had been born in Cyprus. He was reported to have landed secretly near Tisouri, in the West, a few weeks earlier.

"Very well. I am ready," I continued. "But I regret that some of you will have to take a minimal gamble on exposure. Surely you are not poltroons. I can give no convincing demonstration in the darkness, although, as you soon will see, what I have to show is no mere prestidigitation and can be accomplished either visibly or invisibly.

"Please," I said, looking in the direction of the unknown commanding voice, "won't you arrange for me to be taken to a cleared space of ground? At least twenty feet square. Designate as many of your company as you wish to come and watch. Then judge the validity of my claims."

There was a moment of whispering. I was conducted to the first room where I had waited. The white-shirted farmer stood beside me, easily visible by the light of a solitary candle. In a corner, a grizzled old man with a machine-pistol was stretched out on a palliasse, one eye open. A few minutes went by and I was taken through another door to an open courtyard at the edge of a fig orchard appearing silvery in the faint starlight.

Standing in a cluster were six dim figures. Five had scarves or handkerchiefs tied about the lower part of their faces, bearing ghostly-looking sunglasses on their eyes. Hats or caps were pulled low over their foreheads. They wore ordinary town suits, three in jackets, and two with rolled-up shirtsleeves, in vests.

The sixth figure, which I rapidly identified with the soft voice in the blacked-out room, belonged to an unmasked man, whose unusually large dark spectacles gave his face a scaly glitter. He was very small, both short and thin, and dressed in what seemed to be an outmoded uniform, some kind of puttees, and a Sam Browne belt. An outsized revolver was strapped to his hip.

His face was so pale that even in the half-light it contrasted with the shadow of a luxuriant upturned mustache. He looked very much like Groucho Marx, the American film comedian. But there was nothing comic about him; he emitted an air of controlled, feral strength. Obviously, this was Dighenis. I could only assume the others were members of the Kendriki Epitropi.

"We are ready," said the mustachioed boss tersely. "You may begin."

I marched four paces from the group, scratched two holes into the ground, and thrust in a pencil to make them deep enough. Then I reached carefully into the inner compartment of my wallet, extracted two of the nubby teeth, shut my billfold, and tucked it back into my buttoned shirt pocket. I stuffed the sharp little grains into the earth, patting dirt on top of them. I calculated two would be enough to underscore my experiment.

There was no sound, save the distant whir of doves and the occasional hoot of an owl. Stepping back, I stared down while the watchers regarded me in doubtful silence. Suddenly there was a visible stirring. In the astral haze, two shadows appeared and inexorably began to grow.

Above one towered the outline of a long ashen spear. Its bronze head probably had originated in a Cypriot copper mine, before being forged in some Minoan settlement along the Argolic gulf. The spear was followed by a tufted face, a glittering apotropaic neck charm, a round leather shield, chiton, and thonged-leg bindings. The other outline with bronze sword, helmet, and breastplate, looked of superior rank, a polemarch. His expression seemed harsh and bellicose.

Silence prevailed except for the gentle crumbling of dry clods as they fell aside from the rising thrusts. Dighenis and his leaders seemed to cease breathing. But one of them could bear the strain no longer. He exhaled, with a deep sigh and, incredulous, murmured, "Blessed Pantocrator, save us from what we think we see."

Dighenis spoke. "Do these creatures understand Greek?" he asked with unnatural calm. Evidently they did not comprehend him. They simply turned toward his voice, their faces showing no reaction. "A classicist," said the unperturbed Dighenis, collectively addressing the masked men, "say something in the ancient Attic."

One of the Epitropi shouted with a loudness evidently designed to reinforce his waning courage: "Soldier, ground your weapon and stand at ease." He said this in archaic but mellifluous accents. The second of the tooth-men, plainly understanding the command, repeated in some muttered dialect an order to the spearman. Promptly he slammed his weapon's butt to the ground and pulled his shield across his chest. The polemarch himself drew his sword and held it beside him.

"And now, by all that is sacred to Greece and to our cause, what can we do with these strange recruits?" Dighenis muttered in bewilderment.

"Hold on, sir," I interjected. "They are not yet recruits. Not until we have made a deal. First we must arrive at a commercial understanding. Then it is your privilege to do with them as you like. Meanwhile, I suggest your aide, the interpreter over there, should instruct them to await further commands. They can be dangerous. But they know the meaning of discipline if it is properly imposed."

The classicist hastily conveyed this idea, without awaiting word from Dighenis. Then, in the half-light, the EOKA leaders clustered about the strange pair, examining them, eying their armament, touching their clothes, at last mustering the courage to pat their flesh and adjudge if it was real.

"Incredible," said one. "They aren't even cold. I feel a pulse."

The tooth-men stood still, rigidly awaiting orders.

"All good soldiers are the same," I remarked. "The first thing they learn is not to think. The second thing they learn is to handle the weapons they are given. The third thing they learn is how to kill. These are good soldiers. They are suited to your purposes."

"I am forced to believe all you have told us," said Dighenis. If he was astonished, he muffled it successfully. "How many could you provide if I should desire to make an arrangement?"

I, noticing he said "I," not "we," replied, "That depends upon the price. I can offer you up to half a million. But it is obvious even to an innocent like me that this would transcend your purpose.

"With half a million, you might wish to conquer Turkey, not simply chase the British from your island.

"And do not forget that these are Greeks. Some, perhaps the very stock that smote those proto-Turks, the Trojans, and ravaged their monstrous city of Troy. Surely, if you were to lead them, Dighenis, they thirst to do the same again. Those Trojans were Turks even before Turks were Turks and now the Turks are the Trojans of this era. They are there only to be destroyed.

"But there is a price, Your Excellency. For anything over one hundred thousand men it would cost you two hundred pounds sterling a head. For anything under, the price is double. For less than a hundred, it comes to five hundred pounds a man."

These words produced stunned amazement. Before the flurried guerrillas could compare ideas, I added: "Do not think I have with me the wherewithal to manufacture an instant army this very night. The rest, I repeat, are hidden in a safe, safe place. Far away from here. And you would be in no position to find them, hard as you might look.

"Remember, moreover, that should I not return in time, a sealed letter awaits with a trusted friend who will automatically turn over to the British what I already know of your security arrangements and contacts in Famagusta. That same friend—and make no mistake, he is no Armenian kinsman to be bullied—would also know how to dispose of my treasure—in a manner least suited to convenience you."

With this series of misstatements, calculated to reassure my delicate personal position, I folded my arms akimbo and looked Dighenis full into the dark glasses. My pair of ancient bodyguards stood quietly. The noise of their breathing was heavy, as if for a long time they had been incarcerated in an airless chamber.

"Omadarch Ypsilon," said Dighenis to the interpreter. "You will remain with these—these creatures, while we deliberate. As for you, Armenian, you may return with your guardian for the present."

I was again taken to the white-shirted farmer and the iconed room. The lazing guard had gone. The candle sputtered, and I noticed that Makarios, last of the archbishop-ethnarchs, now a British prisoner in the Seychelles, was at the far right of the line of clerical pictures. A metal cross encrusted with blue beads hung from the frame. I assumed the beads were to fend off the evil eye. I wondered if my tooth-men came under that malevolent category.

An hour later I was summoned outside to receive Dighenis' answer. We stood together in the courtyard, alone save for Ypsilon and the tooth-men. "I am a villager," Dighenis said. "I was brought up in Trikono before I went to Officers Academy in Athens; my philosophy comes from my village. The village atmosphere of honesty and family life is what still governs my thoughts. All my life I have taken care of myself and lived according to the strictest discipline. Why, I never even visited a coffeehouse until I married at the age of forty.

"I'm telling you this because what you have shown me here is not comprehensible to a simple village mind. But then it is not comprehensible either to a more worldly mind; for I also have fought in Turkey and I have studied in Paris. Were my village school teacher here, I would heed his advice, but he is long dead. Nor can I consult a priest, because I have no truck with priests, although I am a faithful son of the church.

"I can understand that what you have to offer might actually present us with certain opportunities. Each country must develop its own particular guerrilla system, and it is possible that we could make something of this weird event.

"But I have concluded for practical reasons that for us flexibility is the most vital weapon. The British have forty thousand troops here, yet we with but a handful have made them afraid of us already, for the people are behind us. What you offer would handicap our flexibility.

"Perhaps, as you say, these things are human. It is even possible that they are Greeks, which makes them in essential ways acceptable. It is evident also from their behavior that they are soldiers.

"Nor do I doubt that among our Omas units we would be able to find sufficient men of education who could communicate with your creatures, help rearm and train them. Above all for sacrificial missions. It would be good to spend the blood of those who are not born of woman in order to achieve our goals.

"I can even see the potential value of secreting pockets of armed men, equipped only with primitive weapons, in tiny hiding places where their presence could never be suspected. In each instance, we might leave in charge one Omadarch, specially designated for his classical knowledge. At a given signal, he could create large new units and lead them on suicide charges to overwhelm the enemy.

"These things I have considered. But I have also considered the consequences. What would we do later with the poor devils who survive?"

"Kill them," I suggested.

Dighenis paid no attention. "As it is," he continued, "things can get out of hand. Someone seems, for example, to have murdered a Turk in Famagusta with the sole purpose of embroiling us.

"And there is something else. We do not need men. We require only a handful. But they must all know what they are after and be sworn to our cause. How can we swear to our cause objects that do not understand any cause?

"What you have demonstrated is a great miracle. No one can explain or even contemplate what dire arrangement you first reached with the devil" (here he crossed himself) "to produce this awful crop.

"But it is not for us. I have decided. For moral reasons above all.

"Finally, money. Armenian, your price is absurd."

"I am prepared to bargain," I suggested.

"The EOKA does not bargain. The EOKA commands. Yet, since you came in good faith, we simply command you to depart."

"And what will you do with my men?" I asked, nodding at the silent spearman and polemarch.

"I shall pay you forty pounds for the two of them, since you have gone to the trouble of visiting us. That is a price not subject to discussion. And I shall keep them for what purposes I decide. Here is the money."

He handed me forty single pound notes which I didn't bother to count. "Now go." He turned his back and said something to Omadarch Ypsilon, who murmured a phrase to the tooth-men.

I felt a knife-point in my ribs and, irritated and discomfited, I was led through the icon-chamber to the automobile that had brought me. The driver was sprawled behind the wheel. He straightened up and grinned when I arrived.

There was nobody on the rear seat. As we drove off, he patted a holster slung beneath his left shoulder. "Just so you don't get strange ideas," he said, switching on the parking lights and turning up the dirt road.

It was almost dawn. An occasional truck rattled toward Famagusta, and there was more movement of military transport than I had seen before. "A sweep," my companion commented drily. "They are looking for the gang that bumped the Turk off. Hah. Good job, that."

We were stopped by a roadblock made of up-ended petrol barrels, but the search was cursory and we were not asked for papers. I was impressed by the driver's bored air of disdain. When we drove on into Famagusta's network of narrow streets, I heard the crump of rifle grenades and saw several Cyprus police, wearing steel hats and carrying shields to fend off stones and Coca Cola bottles, gingerly closing in around a square. The air smelled of tear gas.

As we headed to the original pick-up point, the driver abruptly said: "I hear the demonstration didn't go too well."

"What demonstration?" I asked with pretended innocence.

"Come off it," he said. "I am not as pumpkin-headed as I look. Maybe I can help you." He pulled the car in at a curb, switched off the motor, and inquired: "You know Avrahm, I believe?"

"Yes, I know him. I am surprised that you do."

"Of course I do. You see, we fought the British side by side before."

"You and Avrahm? Where? How?"

"In Palestine. Before it was Israel. We were in the Irgun together."

"But how come that you . . ."

"I too am a Jew. I am from Salonika. We fled to Palestine through Turkey in 1941 when the Nazis came. I joined the organization there. But when the Israeli government was formed, they were not very tender with us. At least not all of us. Not those of us who had shed their blood. So I came here."

"Why are you fighting the British again, then? After all, they tried to save your people in Salonika."

"Oh, I don't know. I like to fight. Or rather, I like to kill. And if not the British, who else? The Nazis are no longer around. One must make the best of what one has. And I can't keep fighting Jews. Also, I find I can assist Avrahm from time to time. This will be a good way back for me, should I ever decide to return to Haifa."

"How can I trust you?" I inquired. "It is already evident you are a double agent. Maybe you're a double-double agent. Maybe you want to set me up for your present employers."

"That's your problem," he said. "Kif-kif. I am also exposing myself more than is good, as you can see. I suggest you call Avrahm. Just say Mario sent you. Mario is not my name. Avrahm has a message for you. I suggest it is important. Most important."

He ignited the engine, accelerated, whizzed to the lamp post near Sahag's house, dropped me and spun away, handling the car with speed and grace.

By the time I arranged a rendezvous two days later with Avrahm, the miniature battle of Famagusta had intensified. Although newspapers gave the event little coverage, word filtered through the bazaar that two EOKA agents in garish costume had assaulted a picnicking British lieutenant and his lady companion. The Englishman, after being severely hacked with edged tools or weapons, shot them dead. My men, I thought. My hoplites. Then I thought: There goes forty pounds.

Avrahm received me at his tourist agency, locked the door and took me to a back room where there was a desk, a coffee table, four chairs, a filing cabinet and a wall safe. There was also a radio which he turned on loud; against eavesdroppers, I assumed. An announcer was speaking in Greek of "would-be assassins disguised as peaceful mountain shepherds . . . British tolerance but firm respect for the law . . . no violence can be permitted . . ." Avrahm signalled me to a chair. He said:

"It is good that you came, that you heeded Mario. I think you can be of help to us. I know we can be of help to you. No. Don't interrupt.

"We have received a report from Istanbul. Our people there know Yusuf. After all, he is a Jew. We are told strange things by him. It seems you had a Russian mistress hiding in his house. No, I repeat, you must not interrupt. Well, Georgian if you wish. Or Greek. It doesn't really matter.

"It also seems her husband is some kind of minor bureaucrat. He complained to the authorities. Not even a Soviet tchinovnik likes to have horns pinned on him by an Armenian. But it would surely be of little interest to Moscow that one of its functionaries was cuckolded. It would certainly be of insufficient interest to attract the attentions of their counterintelligence. No. I insist. You must hear me out to the end.

"We decided to investigate Yusuf's incoherent tale. He babbled about Milli Emniyet. About Soviet security. Even about some fable of a secret weapon. Things he heard from the girl. So we decided to investigate. Yes, we have men in Russia too.

"We have not learned a great deal. But enough, I may add. Enough to convince us you really had some dealings on a military project, that you fell out, that you skipped, and that they are furious. They are hunting you down. High names are mentioned. Some of them, it seems, still hold power, despite Stalin's death. Like Serov."

"Serov?" I asked. "Now head of the KGB," Avrahm replied.

"Do you know Mikoyan?" he inquired with a snap.

I was appalled by the question and the indication of what was already known and what the Communists were perhaps intending to do, now that the bibulous idiot, Shamyl, had complained.

"I regret," Avrahm continued, "that your lady has been taken off somewhere by the Milli Emniyet. We do not know where or just exactly why. On the other hand, it is not hard to guess. Perkel detests the Russians. But, being a good bazaar man, he is not above a trade. I doubt if he feels in debt to you, an Armenian who tricked him.

"Now you have seen how the Turks will doublecross you. And we know through Mario that you yourself have learned Grivas will doublecross you in the end. You can only trust the Jews. Therefore, I make you a proposal.

"You will come to Israel with me. You will make a demonstration of what you fancy might interest us. If you can be of help, we are prepared to do a deal. We will pay you. More than that, we will use our influence on Perkel to obtain your lady's release —in Yusuf's custody. You trust him? Yes? How is that? Is this fair?"

I nodded.

"Very well. Prepare what you consider necessary, including your passport. You will need no visa. Dress normally. But limit your baggage. You must bring the necessary samples along. I shall drop by at Sahag's in two hours. You may tell him I have invited you to Troodos so we can benefit from the mountain air."

The opportunity to save Rima while also repairing my fortunes was as welcome as it was unexpected. I found that Sahag was out but Araxie greeted me eargerly and asked where I had been.

"My little dove," I said, "I cannot tell you now. Yet it is of no importance. I have a sudden, an excellent business opportunity that may keep me away for several days. First I am going to Troodos with a friend. Then I may be forced to fly to Greece.

"Do not worry. I shall write. Tell your father I will certainly be back. I rely upon his cousinly care in seeing to my possessions. Above all, my sacks. Let me warn you, my pigeon, you know nothing at all about them. Even that they exist."

As I embraced her, inhaling the lovely pomander of her hair, I whispered into her ear. "Seductress, why did your father tell me you were sick? Was that his strange manner of seeking to protect your vanished maidenhead? You are not sick. Who knows better than I, Kevork?"

She thrust me away and, holding my shoulders in each hand, stared mischievously into my eyes. "So," she babbled happily, "he told you. It was you, then, who avenged me."

I was bewildered and embarrassed. She continued: "I pretended Turgut gave me clap." I was surprised she used this word. It is ugly in Armenian.

"That much I know. But why?"

"Because Turgut betrayed me. For another. One cannot do that to an Armenian girl. No vile Turk can do that and expect to live. I knew my father would arrange to have him killed. Now we each possess the other's secret. Go. Go now and come back, my eagle."

CHAPTER

XIV

AVRAHM's little Renault wound carefully and skillfully toward the edge of town, avoiding main streets, and slowing to a crawl each time a police or military sentry loomed in the canicular night. We passed close to the funest shadow of that renowned Venetian castle known as Othello's Tower.

"Othello wasn't a Moor at all," Avrahm said to me with earnest pedantry. "The Venetians would no more send a Negro than a Jew to govern one of their provinces. He was a Greek named Mavro. When he married a local Miss Cordato, he added her name to his. Mavro means black. There is still a Mavrocordato family."

I digested this useless information without comment. But, I thought, no matter what his color, Othello's murderous tradition was being honored.

Like myself, the Shin Bet agent had no baggage. He read my mind and said: "True, we are not going to Troodos together. I am dropping you off on the way with a colleague who has made the needed arrangements. And I am confident, my slippery friend, that you have secreted on your person those things which interest us. If that's not so, it would not go well for you."

Automatically I felt for my billfold, where, wrapped in a sheet of toilet paper, lay twenty more of my precious granulated teeth.

We were heading along the thoroughfare to Nicosia, but outside the capital we swung right, in the direction of the coastal mountains. Avrahm told me I would be spending the night in Kyrenia. He would turn me over to his associate, Reuven.

In the meantime, he regretfully required my passport. This was needed both to register my presence at distant Troodos, in case of police inquiries, and as a talisman to insure my return—no matter what the outcome of discussions with his superiors. I handed him the document, and he informed me: "Reuven will have whatever else you need."

Kyrenia proved to be a pleasant, seaside village set among Gothic ruins beneath a towering peak. We drew up before a rambling yellow building that extended aimlessly along the shore. "Here is your hotel," Avrahm said. "And if I am not mistaken, there is Reuven."

A squat, muscular man arose from a cane armchair and approached us with a malign smile. He was bald, sun-tanned, and a jagged scar ran along his face from forehead down to jawbone. He wore a half-sleeved shirt, loose khaki pants, and the kind of sandals Central Europeans sport on beach holidays.

"Shalom," said Reuven. "You have no luggage? Well, let me take you to your room. We leave early in the morning. Goodbye," he added to Avrahm. "Until the next time." Avrahm drove off with a wave.

Inside, Reuven took over the task of registering my presence, introducing me in English to a stocky man at the counter: "Mr. Simon, this is Mr. Catsellis. The owner's son. He studied hotel-management at the famous Cornell University."

I gathered I was Mr. Simon. Gravely I shook hands with the hotelier. He smiled as if this baggageless phony, who didn't even sign his own name to the entry form, and who was accompanied by a man so sinister in appearance that he almost advertised his clandestine trade, were merely a harmless civil servant come to bathe.

Reuven led me up the stairs to a box-like, calcined room with one bed, one chair, one bureau and one coat-hanger in the closet. "You may use my bathroom," he said. "I am next door."

I declined the plumbing, remarking that it was easy to pee from the balcony outside my window. Then, without a by-your-leave, Reuven retired and locked my door. I was nonplussed by this precaution.

It was still dark when the key turned and the light flashed on. Reuven signalled for me to hurry up. In a few minutes we descended. Three other men were standing at the entrance beside a heap of knapsacks and briefcases. A 1500-weight British truck drove up, and Reuven helped us and our baggage in over the tailboard. Next to the Cypriot driver, two obvious Englishmen were seated.

No one seemed inclined to chat. We drove in silence along the Nicosia road, swinging wide on the narrow, hairpin turns, eventually emerging on a sere plateau dotted with Turkish villages. Men in black, baggy trousers were already stirring, taking sparse flocks of goats into the stubble fields, leading donkeys to the local well, or gleaning straw.

We passed the main airfield on which were parked many military and civilian planes, and then turned off through a slight gap in the wire fence, a gap that must have been deliberately prepared; it was not guarded. In the slowly graying predawn light, I could see a small, mottled de Havilland biplane of a type already outmoded before World War II. "That's us," Reuven said gutturally. I stared with trepidation.

The moment our truck came to a halt, the two Englishmen jumped from the front door and soon were busying themselves with this travesty of an aircraft. Painted in luxuriously spaced letters along its fuselage were the words "Hornton Airways."

"Who are Hornton Airways?" I inquired as we began to stack baggage inside the cramped cabin. One of the Englishmen, shoving parcels under seats and in the rear, looked up with a grin and said: "Us. My brother and me. Hornton. He's air crew. I'm ground crew. Some day, if we make enough money, we hope to be the owners. Right now it's in hock. Wizard hock."

"You mean you two and one plane. That's all?"

"That's all."

I scarcely felt reassured. Nevertheless, I wedged into the forward seat of the five in the passenger compartment, calculating that my weight should be ahead of the center of gravity if we were to get off the ground. On aircraft, like women, the center of gravity is forward.

Reuven and the other three, who had not yet identified themselves, jammed behind. The plane was filled to bursting when

Hornton No. 2 pulled the door tight, twisted the catch, then wormed his way forward to join Hornton No. 1, who was having trouble getting the portside engine to cease sputtering.

There was no shilly-shallying with officials. Again I took this as a tribute to Reuven's organizing and bribing abilities. The de Havilland bumped forward, creaking and whining, the motors protested loudly, and suddenly we were airborne. We flew directly at the tomato-red sun.

I looked out the window. It seemed to me the wings were trying to flap like those of an aged crow. The low mountains east of Nicosia loomed like Himalayas and, since we failed to gain any perceptible altitude, I feared we were bound to crash; but the pilot evidently knew his terrain. He guided us through by following a winding dirt road until we emerged over the coastal plain, and suddenly the green sea itself.

There was no mention of breakfast as we chugged through the lower air. A voice behind me murmured, "Want a drink, mate?" I craned my head around, saw a wicked, humorous Celtic face, and grabbed the bottle. It was Keo brandy, bad enough at any time, but horrible at sunrise.

Nevertheless, it contained its quota of false courage for a poltroon like myself, and I took a large draught before passing it across the aisle. Everyone except Reuven drank, even the two Hornton brothers who sat just ahead in the cabin. They were intent on cajoling the engines into greater efforts and occasionally tapped messages on a radio that looked like Marconi's original model.

The brandy eased the atmosphere and inspired a nervous palaver. My three co-passengers identified themselves: a red-haired, brachycephalic American Flying Fortress pilot, probably a Polish Jew; a bovine English engineer, his face unclouded by thought; and the owner of the Keo, a wiry Scotsman named MacDonald who described himself as a demolitions expert and said he had been hired on a piece-rate basis, whatever that meant. It was obvious that all of us were on missions having to do with one or another form of monkeyshines and that Reuven was experienced in conducting such unorthodox tourist parties.

The flight, which takes little more than an hour in transport planes even two decades old, endured for a clattering three. We drank two and a half bottles between us, the Horntons partaking heavily. Reuven made no comment. He sat back in his seat, which held his stolid body in a firm grip, and pretended to doze with nonchalant disinterest. Yet I am sure he heard every word and understood our thoughts by extrasensory perception.

We crossed the Israeli coast, with Hornton No. 2 feverishly tapping messages and both brothers straining to listen through earphones that apparently gave poor reception. We flew over a long beach, skirted a city, passed a large airfield and finally came to rest in rising spumes of dust on a small dirt landing ground.

As we drew to a halt, two vehicles drove up, a jeep bearing several military-looking men in khaki pants, shirts and sweaters, and an old Humber sedan which still retained the dun color from its days as a wartime British staff car. We were helped down the plane's single step, limping in cramped positions.

My three companions with their baggage were piled into the Humber with all but one of the party of greeters. Nobody asked for our papers or even addressed a single word to us; there was a flurry of conversation with Reuven. I never again saw the Horntons or the trio of destructive technicians.

With some difficulty, because of his short, heavy legs, Reuven climbed into the jeep's back seat, and our driver summoned me beside him in front. He jammed a motorcyclist's casque on his sandy, close-cut hair, and pulled on dark-tinted, anti-dust goggles. He and Reuven seemed to have an excited debate about something, but, despite my linguistic talents, I could understand no Hebrew. Then we drove off. I had had nothing to dilute the Cyprus brandy, but there was still no talk of breakfast. We seemed in a frenetic hurry.

"Your plane was late," the driver said gruffly, as if it had been my fault.

"Where are we going?" I inquired.

"You will see," the driver said. Reuven ignored him: "Sde-Boker," he said.

Sde-Boker meant nothing to me. Reuven explained: It was the Negev kibbutz where Ben Gurion, until recently Prime Minister of Israel, had retired. This puzzled me. Why take me to a former politician?

The driver, obviously an officer of importance but a carper, evidently told Reuven to shut up. Blandly sure of his own authority, Reuven ignored him and added: "Ben Gurion was also Defense Minister, you know."

The trip was tedious. We followed a tarmac road for a short span of time and then turned southward through barren countryside, circumventing and avoiding whatever settlements or installations existed in the region. This required us to shift into four-wheel drive where traces of road just vanished.

The sky glowered. Winter clouds lumbered overhead. A few heavy raindrops splattered down but no one offered me a coat or thought of stopping to raise the canvas top. We saw few automobiles and, apart from occasional farms or agricultural settlements, the only life seemed to be herds of goats, scrabbling on the hard ground behind their wethers' brittle bells, and two Bedouin caravans moving silently across the desert on hideous, nodding camels.

Finally we arrived at a deserted spot where three jeeps were assembled. Several uniformed sentries with machine-pistols and rifles patrolled the vicinity. Beside the jeeps stood a group of men chatting. Inside one vehicle sat a stumpy little figure with wings of white hair jutting out to either side of his forehead, almost like fluffy horns. We drew up and descended.

Reuven took me by the elbow and led me to the short man in the jeep, saying: "Here he is. The Armenian. Kevork. From now on, the problem is no longer mine." As an afterthought he added, turning to me: "This is Mr. Ben Gurion."

"I am honored. Your Excellency," I said in English. The former Prime Minister examined me with a shrewd glint and made a remark in Turkish. Later he showed knowledge of Russian and Greek. But he insistently conversed with the others in Hebrew, when he wished me to be excluded, or in English, when he wanted me to understand.

"Well," he said, with an East European accent, "I am told by Reuven that you have something of enormous importance which might be of great use to us. He says you are prepared to make an arrangement if we are satisfied with your demonstration.

"You must know we are open-minded people. We, more than others, are disposed to believe in miracles. The fact that we are in our own country after two thousand years is miracle enough.

"But we are not easy to convince. I have been informed you are a confident young man. If it is in your own interest, trustworthy. Well, that's reasonable. We can insure your trustworthiness. I impugn no deceit. But I wish you to be aware. We Jews are ruthless when required. People who dream great dreams must be ruthless—if ever their dreams are to come true. I dream of joining the future and the past. And you?

"Now I have said enough. These men, who will observe your experiment with me, are probably known to you from their faces. Their photographs are often in the press. In any case, this is Lavon. This is Peres. This is Dayan. As for Reuven, you already are acquainted."

The old man pulled himself uncomfortably out of the jeep, refusing Reuven's assistance. He was of ugly but efficient build, like an aged, gnarled squash. I already knew from the *Jerusalem Post* which I had skimmed on the flight from Cyprus that Pinhas Lavon was Israel's Defense Minister, that Shimon Peres was a principal aide, and that Moshe Dayan was one of the foremost army leaders.

Lavon, who seemed about 50, was well groomed with silvery hair parted at the side, warm twinkling eyes, and an informal manner. He was small, about five feet eight, trim, narrow shouldered. He wore a tweed jacket and gray trousers, a sports shirt with—unlike the others—a tie. He smoked constantly and, I noticed, occasionally popped hard candies into his mouth instead of cigarettes. I also remarked that he spoke in a melodious baritone voice.

Peres was a compact, dark man whose speech was crisp and forceful. He had a plainly Russian accent in English. Dayan seemed more flamboyant than the others. He was strongly made although not at all tall, especially according to my standards. He had a protruding, hard-centered black patch tied over one eye and was attired in khaki sweater and pants with brown suede desert boots.

Acting as master of ceremonies, Reuven explained to me that, for security reasons, I would have to give my demonstration at least twelve feet distant from the audience. He warned that nothing untoward would be permitted. The two guards had been specifically commanded to shoot me—"or anything," if need be.

I looked behind and saw a pair of hard-muscled youngsters staring at us. One carried a twelve-gauge shotgun, with shortened barrel, and the other a stubby machine-pistol of an unfamiliar type.

Finally Reuven said that I must hold myself in readiness to answer questions. No decision could be given until the meeting after the test. Should the final response be negative, I would eventually be conducted back to Cyprus, where Avrahm would return my passport. In that event, I should remember, for my own safety, that nothing of these occurrences could ever be revealed. To anyone.

With a grim look, accentuated by his scar, Reuven explained that world Jewry was a more scattered and influential body than the Armenian international. Israel had agents everywhere, prepared to obey even the most brutal orders. With the caricature of a wink, Reuven lifted a spatulate finger to his mouth as a sign of silence, then, muttering "or else," drew the same finger horizontally across his throat.

At this point, it was evident the moment for action had arrived. Ben Gurion, Lavon, Peres, Dayan, and Reuven drew together in a cluster where they were joined by five other khaki-clad men in forage caps or berets, all evidently officers although they wore no pips. I thought it strange that, for an assembly of such vital importance, a retired politician should be so obviously in charge.

I turned my back and walked carefully to the prescribed distance, warily followed by my guards. Then I poked a single hole in the earth. Having learned by experience there was no use beginning with a display of more than an initial sample, I drew one little tooth from my billfold and held it between thumb and forefinger so my audience could see its small outline in the dull light. I dropped it in the hole and patted dirt back on top like a child putting the finishing touches to a sand castle. The watchers looked on with silent interest.

By now I had complete self-confidence in my numenous wares. I didn't even keep my eyes on the burgeoning sand but concentrated on the alarmed expressions spreading across the gaping faces of the Israelis. Ben Gurion looked amazed and grimly delighted. He half lifted his pudgy hands, covered with the spots of keratosis, and stood like some small demiurge conjuring elemental forces from the earth. He kept repeating Hebrew words which I took to be a prayer.

Next to him, Lavon stared with pale visage and eyes like poached eggs. Dayan's single orb almost popped with ferocious concentration. The others started to gesticulate and muttered various abracadabras in several languages at once.

My creature grew rapidly into what I took to be a hoplite, wearing the traditional purple tunic designed to keep blood stains from showing. He had long hair which had been recently dressed, indicating he was prepared for battle. His buckler was round, and he bore the full panoply of weapons and defensive armor. This included a hemispheric metal headpiece lined with felt and topped by a small crest, jointed cheek plates, a nasal visor and neck-guard. The thorax covering his chest and back was of two slabs of bronze, joined by buckles and engraved to imitate the thoracic muscles in front.

He wore a leather jerkin. Brazen greaves protected his shinbones. His wooden-shafted spear was only six feet long, fitted with a leaf-shaped metal point, the grip bound in leather to produce a surer grasp. A two-foot sword was swung in a baldric from his left shoulder. He was a very small man, about five and a quarter feet tall, exceedingly well made, trim and powerful. He stood straight but relaxed, his eyes blinking with interest as they focused on the astonished audience facing him.

"Have you anyone here who speaks classical Greek?" I asked Ben Gurion.

The tough little statesman shook his white maned head as if coming out of a trance. "Why, I do," he replied. "Do you think he will talk to me?" He began a burble of phrases bearing some resemblance to the ancient Greek taught nowadays in the tradition of Erasmus, but uttered in a markedly Russian accent. The hoplite clearly didn't comprehend a word.

"Forgive me, B.G., if I try," suggested a slender, dark officer with tanned, elongated face and neatly trimmed mustaches. Within a few moments, carefully adjusting his phraseology to suit the replies he managed to elicit, he had established a workable channel of communication.

"That I should ever live to see this day," said Ben Gurion,

rubbing his chin and glowing with pleasure. "It is almost as if I had a chance to talk directly with Isaiah. The Greeks were the first philosophers. Our prophets were not thinkers of their caliber.

"The Greeks asked questions about the nature of things. Our Bible said God created everything, even the bad things; that God embodied everything. Therefore we Jews didn't have to create a science like the Greeks. We were not always in search of an answer.

"But how can this warrior be fitted into our tradition? How does he embody God in any way? Is he a good thing or a bad thing? This is a miracle I could never even have imagined as a child. What do we do with it, now that it has come my way?"

At this point Reuven whispered something to Ben Gurion, who then consulted Lavon and Dayan. "How many more of these could you deliver, and when?" the one-eyed man asked.

"The figure is not precise. Approximately half a million. And, with efficient cooperation from your people, in forty-eight hours at the most."

"They are all trained soldiers, even if their weapons are obsolete?"

"Yes. I vouch for this."

"And their motivation?"

"That I cannot answer. They are disciplined and accustomed to obeying orders from their officers. They have no anxiety about death. They believe in their own gods. And, I suppose, in destiny."

Ben Gurion interrupted. He was staring fiercely at the hoplite, a hard quality in his stare. Continuing to regard him, he spoke in a solemn way:

"Our people cannot understand destiny. They believe in freedom of human choice. Human beings can make their own fate. All history proves this, and most recently and especially the history of Israel: because the Jews survived for two thousand years even without Israel. That was due to our book, the Bible. There is no abstract destiny involved. We don't believe in fate."

"But surely, B.G.," Lavon interrupted. "It is fate that brought this opportunity to us. This is no event that can be traced to Biblical prophecies."

Dayan asked: "On the basis of your experience, Kevork, how

long does it take to familiarize your troops with modern arms? To learn a few contemporary phrases of command? To accept some fundamental concepts of our time."

"To tell you the truth, sir, I do not know the answer. But they are intelligent, they are experienced, they are inured to combat. And they have not even the slightest fear of dying."

"Nevertheless, they are not Jews," Ben Gurion interrupted.

"I cannot dispute that point," I said, "although I don't know just how you would define a Jew."

"A Jew is someone whose mother was Jewish and who considers himself a Jew."

"In that case, none of these men are Jews," I replied, looking at the bewildered hoplite as if he were already surrounded by 500,000 peers. They had no mothers.

"Also, I am neither historian nor theologian, but it is possible that some of them were born before such a thing as Jews existed. Certainly before Moses received the holy tablet from the Lord Almighty."

"It is hard to imagine Israel depending upon a striking force of heathen non-Jews to defeat the Arab enemy," said an obviously puzzled Ben Gurion. "How does this agree with the concepts of Zahal, our army?"

Lavon was not through with his line of speculation. "Surely your men could be led in small groups by proper cadres, specially trained in languages and primitive psychology?" he wondered.

"Yes, I am certain of that. And I am certain that your own army, more than any other, might find the intellectual cadres suited to such an attempt."

"Nonsense," Dayan interjected. "I could never adjust strategic or tactical doctrine to such soldiers. Even with half a million. And think of the cost of arming them."

"There are always the Americans," Ben Gurion said. "They are generous with their contributions when they think it helps them . . . or their politicians." Then he stopped, halfway along a new line of thought, and added: "Yet I can see it is impossible to expect a non-Jewish force to play a significant role in maintaining Israel's security."

"They are not indoctrinated," said Dayan grimly. "I cannot use such men."

"Perhaps you could convert them," I proposed.

This brought a roar from Peres. "Convert them? First teach them our language? Then teach them our faith? Then move them thirty centuries forward into time? What nonsense. They would all be dead before they were of the slightest use."

Ben Gurion added: "One must also consider the economic factor. Reuven says you told him the package would cost five hundred million dollars, my Armenian friend. That is much money. A great deal of money. Even for Rothschilds.

"I suspect there are more efficient ways to spend that amount for defense. You know," he intimated in a way the others comprehended, "there are new weapons abroad in this world. Weapons that take no account of masses. Weapons that allow even a small David to destroy a great Goliath."

He nodded his head, turning slightly around and pointing his obstinate chin westward. I could not tell if he meant to designate Goliath's home town of Gath, which supposedly lay along the coast near here, or the mysterious new nuclear plant the Turkish press said Israel was building at Dimona in the Negev. We were standing on Negev soil.

"Very well, B.G.," Lavon continued obstinately. "But there are lesser uses we might make of this windfall. You all stress the obvious disadvantages of such mercenaries. But in terms of special tactics, I can see certain advantages. Not expensive in terms of price or quantity. And astonishingly helpful. I suggest we talk."

They had an agitated confabulation in Hebrew of which I understood nothing. Finally it was decided our entire group would drive off together. I asked what should be done with the toothman. "Bring him too," said Dayan.

The mustachioed officer with the El Greco face and dolichocephalic skull went up to the little hoplite, soothingly talked to him, took him by the elbow, and led him to a jeep. When the motor started, he almost leapt out with terror. He screamed loud incantations in a frenzied voice. But we restrained him and followed the motorcade through the scrub desert until we reached a cluster of low houses.

"This is Sde-Boker," Dayan said when we halted before a bungalow patrolled by armed guards. "Whatever you do, keep him quiet. Here, throw my coat over him and be sure his helmet stays covered. Lay his spear athwart the seats. That's it. I shall see if they can find a tranquillizer shot in the kibbutz clinic. Now," he said to me, "come along."

I was instructed to sit on a camp stool on the porch of the building in which Ben Gurion lived. Apparently I was to be available for immediate consultation if difficult points arose. A sentry with a tommygun and bandolier of cartridges stood with his back to the door, facing the stern desert landscape.

Inside I could hear an impassioned debate. As the voices rose, odd words of Hebrew were shouted again and again in argument: Aman, Mosad, Zahal. I understood nothing. The sentry, who evidently heard, remained bleakly impassive.

At one point the door burst open with a bang, almost pitching the soldier on his nose, and a dumpy little potato-shaped woman with short gray hair bustled out carrying a tray. "Here you are, my poor boy," she said to me with a Germanic intonation.

"Coffee and cookies. You can't sit here forever waiting for those fools to make up their minds. Schlemiels, that's what they are. Power-grabbers. Everybody in that room is looking for the power my husband gave up. Everybody wants power. They wouldn't know what to do with it if they had it. If you gave them Aladdin's lamp, they would be afraid to rub it and tell the genii what to do."

"I have given them Aladdin's lamp," I said. "That's what the argument is about."

"Paula. Paula!" came a gruff voice. It was Ben Gurion summoning his wife. She turned and angrily headed back inside. That is an interesting woman, I thought. A formidable woman. I should not like to be married to her.

The day passed slowly. There was no abatement of the tense discussion. At one point I was beckoned into the room by Lavon. It was a plain, homely study with simple desk, several chairs, a sofa and bookshelves crammed with ill-assorted volumes. Books and magazines were stacked about the floor. Ben Gurion sat behind the desk, obvious master of the conversation. Everyone else seemed to be circling warily, gesticulating at each other. Lavon asked:

"It is true, is it not, that I understand you correctly when you say anyone, not you alone, can bring this force to life when and as desired? There is no special hocus pocus or secret energy possessed by you alone?"

"That is right, sir."

"And it is also true the force can be held indefinitely in reserve and brought to life, brought into action, at any convenient moment?"

"It is true, sir."

"And a properly trained linguist and soldier could bring such a force into being at any place provided only there is sufficient earth available to nourish each man?"

"Yes, that is correct. I need only add that the teeth must be kept carefully in a safe, dry place. I could not be responsible for the effects of moisture. Or contamination."

"Finally, what do you estimate as the requisite time to bring each to life, ready for action?"

"Sir, it has been my experience that three minutes is ample. Three minutes per man. Should the entire force be sowed simultaneously by enough sowers and on a sufficient territory, all could be combat-ready within that time."

"Thank you," interjected Ben Gurion. "You may go back to the porch."

As early evening set in, Reuven emerged. "You are to come with me," he said. "There will be no answer tonight. Possibly not for days. I shall look after you."

"What about my man?" I asked, nodding toward the hoplite, who was now dozing after having been given two pills, a glass of wine, and an injection. "Don't worry. He will be all right. But we cannot take him with us. It is better he should not be seen."

I seemed doubtful; Reuven understood. "No matter what else happens," he added, "you will be paid at least for him; in any case."

He led me to one of the jeeps, climbed behind the wheel, said a few quiet words to the guard where the vehicles were parked, and drove off. It was a dusty, uncomfortable ride. A bone-chilling wind whirled out of the beclouded night.

When we finally reached the tarmac, Reuven glanced at me. He asked: "Have you ever been to Tel Aviv? That is where I am taking you."

"Once," I said. "I spent the night in a whorehouse."

Reuven was shocked and astonished. "How is that possible?" he inquired, "a whorehouse?"

"Well, it was by accident. I was a military driver for the British. Syria and the Lebanon. After they took those countries in 1941. They were short on trusted people so Armenians were much in demand. Everyone trusted Armenians.

"Something was going on in the Lebanon. I forgot what it was. But I and another driver, a Tommy, had to take a party of newspapermen from Cairo to Beirut. There were eight war correspondents and two British officers.

"It was a disorganized affair. The officer in charge was inexperienced and stupid. I think he had been seriously wounded, so he was put in this job to convalesce. At any rate, we left Cairo late and we had a long, long journey.

"After we traversed the canal at Qantara, we had to drive all night. Across the eastern desert. We kept having flat tires. There weren't any spares. So we had to take out the interior tubes and patch them together while the correspondents stood around us cursing. The other officer made tea over petrol fires.

"We got to Tel Aviv the following evening, and everyone was fatigued, worn out. But the officer in charge had done nothing about providing our group with billets. There was no place at all in which to sleep. He said we must go on. We refused—the other driver, I, the correspondents. One of the Americans, a huge, fat fellow with red hair and an impressively bloated face, said he knew of a whorehouse where there might be room.

"So we drove around in the dark. There was a blackout then. Although Tel Aviv was still a pretty small metropolis, it was hard to find our way according to the fat reporter's directions. But finally we got there, and, sure enough, they decided to let us enter. Business, it seemed, was disappointingly bad. We could have three rooms, the twelve of us, and if anyone wanted one of the available girls, he could spend the night in her room at the regular price. That was part of their allied war effort.

"I had some money, so I took one of the girls. Not that I needed her, in truth; I simply liked privacy. Nice girl, a very impressively nice girl at that. She told me her name was Hannah Glickstein. After she got used to me, she confessed that this wasn't really her name at all. Her real name was Heneineh Arslan. She was a Druse. But she said it was a better business name to be called Glickstein. Jewish women have the reputation for being very, very hot."

"Glickstein, Mickstein," said Reuven. "Tel Aviv is now a big modern city. And you will see there are no bordellos around today. That was a symptom of British rule. And the Arabs," he added with a touch of a sneer.

"Maybe I'll see, maybe I won't. Depends how long it takes for your friends to make up their minds. It would be nice to find out what has happened to Heneineh."

"There are many Druses in Israel today," said Reuven. "They are loyal and proper citizens."

"Heneineh was very loyal and very proper." Silence.

"What were you doing in the war?" I asked, after a period of silence during which we rolled up to the main thoroughfare.

"I was in intelligence," he answered. "For the British, in theory, but actually for us. The Jewish Agency. First I worked in Cairo, then in Beirut and Baghdad. You see, I know Arabic very well. And in those days I did not have this face," he added, grinning and fingering his scar.

"There used to be a Nazi party in Cairo. The British broke it up, putting fifty of its members in a school they turned into a concentration camp in the heart of the city. Theoretically, this was run by the Egyptian police—under Russell Pasha and Fitzpatrick Bey.

"But there were constant security leaks and I was assigned to trace them. I found that a rabid Nazi from the Swedish Legation, which represented German interests, kept visiting the prisoners and bringing money. A grocer named Adams, Egyptian despite his name, smuggled in cash with food. The Nazis used this money to bribe their guards to take out letters and even to occasionally let them free at night.

"Otto Lehmann, the Nazi leader in the school, used secretly to visit a White Russian doctor who was the go-between with Axis agents. I broke that up.

"Then they sent me to Beirut. Under a new alias and with different papers. I had a wig and a mustache. I had to smash the remnants of a big German operation. This started when the Vichy French still held Lebanon and Syria. It was begun by Roland Eilender, a German born in Beirut. He was helped by Rudolf Roser, representative of the Voigtländer optical firm.

"Roser was joined by Fräulein Paula Koch and Sister Marie-Rose of St. Charles Boromée convent. Then, for special assignments, Major von Prat and Lieutenant von Lettow-Vorbeck, son of the African hero in World War I. They had a large network of Arab agents and another priestly spy, Brother Christopher of the Marist order.

"You may not believe me, but I broke this up too.

"Then I was sent to Baghdad. I operated underground until the Rashid Ali government was overthrown. My job was to expose the Grand Mufti of Jerusalem, who had fled there in 1939. I was unable to capture him. But I broke his ring.

"At one time, he was getting 1,000 dinars a month from Axis secret service funds plus two percent of the salary of every Iraqi government official. He got money from the Italians. And the Germans. And the Red Crescent. I was able to give precise information to Colonel Teague of the British Intelligence. So they cut off gold being shipped in by Italian diplomatic pouch.

"I learned a lot about our enemies in Baghdad. There was Taha Pasha al-Hashimi whose mistress was the sister of Dr. Amin Ruwaiha, Germany's number one agent. He was an arms supplier to Fawzi al-Qaoukji and his Palestine Arab bands. The ones we smashed later. Taha Pasha was famous for his greed. He was the link with the Golden Square, the officers who put Rashid Ali in for the Axis.

"When I was through with that gang, I was proud. Do you know what I helped accomplish? Mahmud al-Shaikh Ali, former Minister of Justice—in jail. And General Amin Zaki Sulaiman, once acting chief of staff. The Minister of Economics, Yunis as-Sab'awi and Colonel Salah ud-din al-Sabbagh, head of the Golden Square—sentenced to death in absentia after they escaped.

"Yes, that is what I did. That was my war. The British war. Before we fought the British. Before we fought the Arabs."

Reuven's eyes gleamed. He thrust his jaw forward like a bulldog.

The jeep was by then rolling rapidly through Tel Aviv along a street that seemed to run at right angles to the nearby sea. He jerked to an abrupt halt, hopped out on his side, waved me along, and led the way up the stairs of a modest yellow stucco building with drawn shades.

"This is our safe house," he said. "You will stay here until the decision has been reached."

"Safe house. Shin-Bet?" I ventured.

"Aman, Military Intelligence," Reuven replied.

He rang the doorbell like the s.o. of a Morse code signal. In a moment it was opened by a broad-beamed woman in early middle age. She had a violet shawl around her shoulders and was carrying a tapestry cartoon, wool, and her needle. Her plump, happy face looked vaguely familiar.

"Kevork!" she said. "After all these years. And what are you doing in a house like this?"

"The last house I saw you in was more respectable, Miss Glickstein."

CHAPTER

XV

REUVEN was the complete spy but he didn't know what went on under his own prudish nose. It was clear to me that he had a good mind until he made it up. During the days that followed I told him more than once: "You are Intelligence, Reuven, and that itself is a contradiction. But when you say Military Intelligence you expose an internal fallacy." He may have had his little joke when I first mentioned Hannah Glickstein and he seemed never before to have heard the name. My joke was more agreeable.

Heneineh came to me that very first night. It was pleasurable to renew acquaintance with her plump shape, satin skin, and enthusiastic, gyratory body. She was not perhaps a beauty in the conventional sense but had mysterious abilities of her own. Moreover, as I made a point of telling her, this time I was truly a guest of the house and her hospitality was free.

I soon learned that Heneineh, a member of the redoubtable Arslan clan, had been rewarded for that Druse family's valuable services both to Britain and, before Israel existed, to the Jewish Haganah. Her people in the Hauran and the Shuf and Metn districts of the Lebanon had been of more than a little use in operations against the Axis, and especially in Reuven's, when he was tracking down Nazi agents. Her own tribal branch resided in the northern hills above Israeli Mount Carmel. It was now loyal to the new state. At one time she had served Aman as a "swallow" girl luring Arab spies to her bed.

Heneineh told me: "My father used to say when the French were driven out of Syria and the Lebanon, and the British and the Arabs were driven out of Palestine: 'There are three things no man can do—be born twice, die twice, or live the same moment twice.' Therefore he swore allegiance to Israel. I suppose I was part of the deal."

"And you kept the working name Glickstein?"

"Yes. It is easier for this profession too."

Reuven assured me she was a discreet, loyal, and economic housekeeper in this hide-away for spooks. We were well protected; I soon observed that we were constantly guarded from a house next door and from another across the way.

Apart from Heneineh's cordial and libidinous entertainment, the days and nights dragged. I was given no news whatsoever concerning my prospective deal. I listened to the radio broadcasts of the British, Americans, and Turks; I read newspapers and magazines, fuming away the empty hours. And, always carefully supervised by Reuven, I was permitted to tour the city and lunch or dine from time to time in restaurants. The latter was a questionable privilege.

Reuven introduced me to a friend of his whom I knew only as Eliahu, a stolid man with round head, regular strong features and a slightly wall eye. Eliahu, who was agreeable but exceedingly earnest, appeared to be a diplomat with extensive experience. I assumed he was home on leave. He was clearly not an Intelligence agent; he was far too open, frank, and indiscreet by nature. Nevertheless, he and Reuven were obviously intimate. I learned they had served together in Turkey at one time during the war.

Eliahu talked interestingly about religion in which he displayed a curiously detached interest. His passion for the Zionist movement and Israel arose from reactions to persecution in Russia, where he had been born. The Bible, for him, was more a political constitution than a sacred revelation. Indeed, his considerable learning was tinged with mistrust for God.

He argued: "I understand man's thirst for God but I have learned that one must live without ever slaking that thirst. God is an expensive and futile hypothesis. Nothing would be changed if He did not exist. It may surprise you, a Christian, to hear in a Jewish state the belief that man can only be free without God because, to be free, he must be wholly responsible and answerable for what he does."

One evening, when Reuven took the two of us to a seaside restaurant in the former Arab quarter of Jaffa, Eliahu discoursed on this favorite topic. "Ours is not a religious ingathering but a racial return," he announced.

"Our religion is borrowed from others, all of them ethical codes embroidered by myth. Even our holy Menorah candlestick comes from the seven planetary deities of Babylon and Egypt.

"Genesis is a stew of Ugaritic, Hittite, Hellenic, and Phoenician legends. We have just cleaned up and made a pap for children all that we have thus inherited. In our censored Bible, Ham doesn't castrate Noah as Zeus did Cronus. And we have conveniently forgotten that before the Creation Rahab rebelled against God and was kicked to death."

We were sitting at a corner table looking out across slow rollers beating on the wintry beach. A waitress with red cheeks, a thick mouth and what my linguistic expertise distinguished as a Brooklyn, U.S.A., accent came up and, looking at me, perhaps because I was the largest, said in English: "What's your trouble, Mister?"

"Crabs," I said scratching my lower belly and thinking of Heneineh. "What do you do for crabs?"

"But this is a kosher restaurant," Reuven protested. Eliahu considered the matter with serious interest. "I think they get them with small nets attached to the ends of poles," he said. "You find them along the supports of wharves. Also, children often look for them under rocks."

I kept scratching my crotch. "I was thinking of what they call the Prince's pear in Turkey." I continued unabashed, "maybe because their Princesses didn't wash. Oil of bergamot." The waitress blushed purple. Reuven kept protesting: "Crabs aren't kosher."

Eliahu was unperturbed. When we had ordered our meal he

continued: "It is a pity the best legends have been excised from biblical texts. There was a wild ox called the Reem in ancient days.

"One pair lived on earth and copulated every seventy years whereupon the cow bit the bull to death and produced two calves. There was also a bird called the Zis which taught sacerdocy."

"This is no Zis," I said, masticating a sinewy chicken. "The only Zis today is a Soviet motorcar."

"Do you know who the first woman really was?" asked Eliahu. "It was Lilith. She was made of ordure. And the next woman was Naamah.

"Lilith and Naamah became prostitutes and strangled babies, seduced sleeping men. Lilith's thousand children were called Lilim. The censored Book of Numbers says: 'The Lord bless thee in all thy doings and preserve thee from the Lilim.' "

"That is very interesting," protested Reuven, "but we are not scholars. We are not mystics but new men devoted to making the desert bloom. We are not sacred people from a bigoted past but pioneers from the cultured West. It is the West, through us, that has driven the desert back. Our ancestors, who passed down their fairy tales"—"edited fairy tales," interjected Eliahu—"came to Palestine as tribesmen from the East. We return as the spearhead of the West."

"Perhaps an avenging West," said Eliahu. "We bring our anti-Semitism with us."

One evening Reuven was visited by Ygael, the man I had met at Sde-Boker and in whose charge the hoplite had been left. For a long time I heard their low voices talking in the parlor beneath my room. Then Heneineh summoned me downstairs. Ygael was courteous and composed; Reuven seemed strangely truculent.

"Well," he said. "At last we have the word. A decision has been taken."

"And what is that?"

"We will buy ten of the teeth. As they are," said Ygael. "We will do our own planting. And we will keep the soldier you produced for us in your test. He has already learned much. We can find uses for him. I doubt, my friend, if you would even recognize him now."

"And the price for this arrangement?" I inquired.

Reuven blurted out: "Five thousand dollars for the lot. Dollars. American. Cash."

"That is not enough," I said. "Why, I was offering a wholesale price of a thousand dollars a man for a half million. Eleven men will cost you fifty thousand dollars retail. I am not stupid my friends. Do not forget the law of the Middle East. An Armenian is always smarter than a Jew."

"Not smarter than a Jew with a pistol," answered Reuven with a crooked smile and producing a snub-nosed Beretta from his pocket.

" 'Hey, father,' said David," I said. " 'I could knock down the door with my foot; your door and you yourself would fall to the ground. But how can I come to your help, father, if you are deceived by a whore?' "

Reuven looked bewildered. "What do you mean?" he asked.

"Nothing. Nothing. Just quoting. This is not the first time an Armenian has been buggered Turkish-fashion."

I went upstairs. Ygael followed me with quiet deference. I got my wallet and counted out ten of the smallest bicuspids, hoping they might sow a withered and unsatisfactory crop. With Ygael still tagging behind, I returned to the shabby parlor, held forth my hand beneath the glow of a hideous rosy-shaded lamp and said to Reuven: "Count. Then give me my money and arrange for my return."

With calm dignity Reuven accepted the teeth, placed them in a wooden box and handed them to Ygael. He then licked his stubby right forefinger and flicked out fifty one-hundred dollar bills. He gave these to me and, as I was inserting them in my billfold, added: "I am afraid, my friend, there is another bit of bad news. You would be ill-advised to go to Cyprus at this time. Here is your passport. I will help you to proceed anywhere else in reason."

As I took the document, which was obviously the same one I had left in Avrahm's care, he anticipated my questions and continued: "Avrahm himself has had to leave Famagusta. There has been a serious violation of security and the British are clamping down. In your own interest we advise you to postpone your return and in our interest we forbid it. Apparently there has been a link established between you and our organization. We do not intend to risk that you might be put to the question."

"Well, then, what do you expect me to do?"

"You can stay here. Or, if you prefer, we are prepared to get you to Turkey, Greece, or even the Lebanon if need be.

"I would not counsel you to go to Turkey," Reuven said. "They are looking hard for you and your lady is the bait in the trap. Your lady and Yusuf. You would be wiser to stay away and leave the rest to us."

"You mean I should trust you to fulfil at least part of our bargain?" I sneered. "Well, I will give you this. There is nothing but trouble in Turkey. And no money in other places. However, I suppose Beirut will do. How can you get me to Beirut? I thought the border was closed. Israel is at war with all the Arabs."

Reuven smiled sardonically. "The Lebanese are also a commercial people," he said. "And they are not Arabs. They are Phoenicians. They are last in war and would like to be first in peace. If that is where you wish to go, your wish is our command. But I cannot think the commodity you offer is of interest to the Lebanese."

"Very well," I said. "And" (looking at the quiet, sensitive Ygael), "I hope that hoplite cuts your throats one gloomy night."

When Heneineh joined me later in my bed, smelling astringently of the Pear's Soap to which I had introduced her, she whispered: "What is wrong? They keep muttering to each other. They forget I'm there and they also forget that I speak Hebrew. Anyway, they don't care. Everybody trusts a Druse. There aren't enough of us to distrust."

"Well, what are you getting at, my partridge?"

"It is simply this. The Jews won't tell you. But I heard Yusuf has given up your girl."

"The Yids, the filthy Yids," I moaned.

"Why do you use this word?"

"You forget I spent my childhood in Germany. Or perhaps I never told you. A Yid is a Jew when you don't like him or when you owe him money. That's what the Germans taught me. They are very learned, very cultivated, the Germans."

"But what are you going to do now that you know?"

"I'll sell my secret to the Arabs. That's how I'll get my revenge."

"I heard you were going to Beirut," Heneineh whispered. "I know much that they do not know. My cousin comes tomorrow to lead you on the first lap. He is part of Reuven's network. We of the Arslanis are loyal to Israel—for our fee."

The cousin showed up after breakfast, driving a battered taxi. Reuven gave him the fibre suitcase which, after my unexpected stopover, he had bought on my behalf and fitted out with a minimum wardrobe. "No bad feelings," he suggested as I said goodbye. I disdained to answer but gave Heneineh a healthy buss instead, something which astonished the spymaster. Then I climbed in the front seat of the cab and off we drove.

Heneineh's cousin was a young man named Kamal Mansour who spoke Hebrew and good English besides his native Arabic. He told me he came from the Druse village of Isfiya on the crest of Mount Carmel, and that this would be our first stop. A dark, good-looking fellow with an air of natural elegance, Kamal already had a job on a Jewish newspaper and was hoping to enter the Israeli diplomatic service.

To while away time we talked about his people. There were only a few tens of thousand Druses in the world, he informed me, 17,000 in Israel and 90,000 in the Lebanon. The religious center was Al Bayadeh in the Lebanon with its theological seminary.

"We are the Unitarians of Islam," he said, "the Muwahhidin. Our idea of God is tolerant and modern. For us He is indefinable, incomprehensible, ineffable, passionless. So we see no reason to argue with those who disagree, much less kill them. For us no war is holy, only occasionally necessary.

"We are so few that we are like the sheep of Panurge. Whichever way we are pushed, we will go. So some of us are loyal to the Jews. Some of us are loyal to the Arabs. But in fact we are true only to ourselves.

"The sixth Fatimite caliph, Hakim, is regarded by us as an incarnation of God. He will reappear on earth and render his creed supreme and place all holy cities from Mecca and Jerusalem to Lhasa and Rome under his blessing. Only at that time will Universal Intelligence in the person of Hamza, Hakim's vizier, reign."

This was all Kamal would tell me. The Druses preserve sworn secrecy concerning their beliefs. Their white-turbaned Aqils, equivalent to a clergy, are known for the infinite capacity of their discretion and ability to conceal.

When we reached Haifa, Mansour turned right and the taxi chugged with difficulty up the winding Carmel road. He explained that the car belonged to the village community, which used it to transport people and commodities to and from the port.

At Isfiya, a dusty hamlet with a splendid view of the Lebanese massif to the north, we drew up before a plain building that housed the clan chief who was also the community's mayor. An oblate man with a furuncle on his cheek, he received us with affectionate gravity and, as if he were introducing great lords, presented one by one his peers, the other Aqils. Then with equal dignity he led me to the adjoining room where we all squatted on hassocks around a large copper tray heaped with delicious pilaf dotted in Turkish style with raisins.

I remarked in English to Kamal that a near-sighted dinner guest in a Turkish household, a man who already knew both the joys of iç pilaf and how well raisins go with buttered rice, was surprised to discover after having devoured several mouthfuls of food, that the taste seemed bland and that the raisins were moving on the rice. These turned out to be flies, and not even fruit flies at that. Mansour roared with laughter and, before I could stop him, repeated the tale in local dialect.

The old mayor patted his white turban and said in mellifluous Arabic: "The word Druse which comes from Darazi who founded our sect, also, as you know, means bug. Nevertheless I can assure you there are no bugs in our pilaf."

After our excellent repast he called for coffee. Two pleasant looking girls, unveiled and with frank, open countenances, brought in little cups and a brass ewer from which they poured the bitter cardamon-flavored desert variety. Then, waving away everyone but Kamal and another youngster, the mayor told me:

"I have received word from Reuven that you have reason to go to the Lebanon, not in the usual way from Nicosia or another airport, but directly. Very well, that is no problem. We often make this journey to see our kinsmen. Our friend here, Hassan, will escort you over tonight. Now I suggest a rest. Much travel lies ahead."

By the time I awakened from my siesta the winter sun had set. Mewling gusts of cold wind were walking up the hillsides like centipedes. I saw a girl peeping at me as I opened my eyes and a moment later Hassan had entered the room where I was stretched out on a Kurdish rug.

"It is time?" I asked.

"Yes, it is time. The distance is not great. But there is much climbing."

I bade farewell to Kamal, the mayor and the Aqils. I found that Hassan had tied several lengths of heavy cord around my suitcase and placed it on the rear seat of the taxi. I squeezed into the front beside him and we drove off with celerity down a singularly rutted road heading northward toward the Lebanon. Swallows scissored through the gathering dusk.

Our progress was slow. After a while Hassan switched off the headlights, managing with exceptional skill to guide us along the winding path by the intermittent light of a moon all too frequently hidden by scudding storm clouds. Finally we came to a hut. Beside it stood a man entirely covered with a cloak and beside him were tethered two horses.

Hassan shut off the motor, descended, handed the car keys to the cloaked man, opened the rear door, extracted my suitcase, told me to hold it behind me by the handle, and meticulously bound it to my back with the cord. Then we mounted our horses and with little taps echoing off the rocky hillside, trotted in the direction of the massive Hauran arete which is the fastness of the Lebanese Druses.

There was no sign of a frontier or of any patrol on either side. Hassan explained in a low voice that the Israelis were aware of frequent border crossings in the region of Isfiya. They had full confidence in the loyalty of the Druse community which always reported any hostile or suspicious penetrations from the Lebanese side.

"They trust us fully," he said, "and they have reason to. We are neither a political movement like the Sunnis nor a time-serving religion like the Yezidis. The Yezidis worship the devil on the theory that this will give them a favored position if he wins his struggle with God. They reckon that, if God triumphs, He is bound to be merciful; so they have nothing to lose. We sneer at such cynicism.

"We are Druses because we believe in the truth of our revealed faith. In the end there will be ecumenical and universal tolerance. As for now, we accommodate to the governments that rule us, so long as they do not interfere with our rights. We have proven that we are worthy of trust—on both sides. We are mistrusted by everyone, which makes us the most trustworthy of all."

The reverse of Heneineh's logic, I thought. But the same conclusion. If you know where you want to go, you arrive.

In the occasional dim flashes of moonlight I could see that my horse was a pretty little bay with arched neck and Hassan's was a dish-faced gray. They picked their way among the rolling pebbles and brush with dainty accuracy and soon I reckoned that we must be well into the Lebanon. Hassan spoke in less muffled tones and I noticed that occasionally he interspersed his Arabic with French phrases, a habit I took pains to emulate.

By sunrise, which was late because of the season and because of the high mountains to the East, we had come to a little hamlet where everyone already stirring seemed to know Hassan and to accept his presence as routine. These included two gendarmes and some soldiers who were sitting at a cafe sipping tea and playing tric-trac.

My companion waved cheerfully to them and said to me, "Don't worry about your passport, visas, or other formalities. We are familiars here. People are used to us. And to our smugglers. There are many things we can send from Israel."

At the next village, around a bend in the road, Hassan informed me he would be taking his leave and returning to Isfiya. He introduced me to a merry, fat Maronite Christian named Pierre, a man who wore a fez despite his religion, who had a pleasant and continually amused expression on his face, and who, upon the receipt of two British pound notes, was ready to accept any instruction from my guide. Hassan told him to drive me to the

castle of Kamal Junblatt at Mokhtara. From there I would be
taken to Beirut.

He turned to me and added: "Now you must fend for yourself.
My instructions were only to take you this far and see that you
were set properly on the way. Goodbye. Good luck. May Hamza
protect you."

Descending from his Arab gray to water it at the village pump,
he shook my hand heartily, and watched me climb aboard the
Maronite's truck.

Then, leaving his horse with reins dragging beside the watering
trough, he sat down beside the unshaven soldiers and tried his
luck with the dice.

The winding road led past purling brooks, terraced vineyards,
and coppices of leafy trees, a testimonial to the hard work of the
Druse people who dominated the area. We passed a cluster of fruit
orchards and drew up before a large stone mansion where the
Maronite halted and gestured me in. I got off, untied my suitcase,
and looked. With some astonishment I saw a massive structure
of limestone blocks, conceived in the Arab-Gothic style of a hundred and fifty years ago when the Turks were running this part
of the world. Arches of banded color and stained-glass windows
lay before me, all set upon heavy rock foundations that must have
been built much earlier. It was indeed a splendid manor house.

A servant with a band tied about his brow and a scapular
cloak greeted me at the foot of a steep stairway leading up to the
main part of the residence. He took my suitcase, and touching
his brow to make the gesture of hospitality, he led me through a
series of barely furnished but enormous rooms whose walls were
hung with weapons and photographs. I looked at the handwritten
labels and saw my host, Junblatt, pictured beside his father on a
white steed and dressed in flowing Arab robes, and another with
Adel Arslan, chieftain of the rival Druse clan, often an active
enemy.

Finally we entered a stone courtyard. In the center was a dim-
pling fountain. A kitten lapped the cool water with fastidious dain-
tiness. Potted plants were standing in disarray. Over the low courtyard wall lay the mountains, gorges, fig and olive orchards of the
Druse farmers, and in the distance rose the great border range of

Syria. When I peered over one side I could see that a rushing stream of brilliantly clear water had been channeled directly under the castle.

Junblatt was standing, an agate gaze thoughtfully focused on the horizon, when he noticed my appearance. He did not seem surprised to see me. No doubt some kind of message had been sent from Isfiya because it was clear my host intended to lunch with me himself, and not to send me to the large common dining room beside his kitchen. There, as the Maronite had explained, all wayfarers were fed by his largesse, no matter whence or where they were going.

The Druse lord was a tall, thin, intense man with long nose, weary eyes, a mustache, brown hair, and surprisingly pale skin. He looked fatigued and care-worn. He was wearing the well-cut country clothes of an English gentleman. With great elegance, a mere exchange of introductions, he waved me to a sofa and offered me a drink while explaining with matter-of-fact courtesy that his own beliefs forbade him both alcohol and nicotine "not because of doctrinal matters but as part of the religion of everyday life."

Accepting a fruit juice, I waited for him to enlarge the conversational horizon. It soon became clear that he was exceptionally cultivated, and that his feudal inheritance had not prevented an endorsement and practice of considerable socialist dogma. His politics, he explained, in no way interfered with his Druse faith which was not Islamic but embraced gnostic wisdom and worshipped all holy men from Pythagoras to Vishnu. He extended his long skinny arms from west to east to embrace the entire world.

As we talked, a procession of servants began bringing us lunch in the courtyard which, despite the frigid season, was warmed by the midday sun. The plain wooden table carried in was soon covered with dishes of humus, flat Arab bread, tomatoes, and pomegranates. Then separate courses were produced: tabouli, a chopped mixed salad with leaves of lettuce; roast chicken; roast beef with mashed potatoes; a meat pie stuffed with piñon nuts; apples, bananas; syrupy Turkish coffee. Cats came from everywhere. They played under the table as we ate, brushing against our legs.

Junblatt pointedly asked if I had been in Israel. I said yes; and that I wanted his help to go on to Egypt. He would be more than happy, he told me. The Palestine war was idiotic. Some day it would be settled by negotiation. Nasser required a small victory first in order to salvage his pride. What ultimately must come was a binational state of Arabs and Jews. Like Moslems and Christians in the Lebanon. At this point Junblatt expounded upon his vision of the future.

After explaining that he was hereditary chieftain of two-thirds of the Lebanese Druses (Heneineh's kinsman Arslan, apparently, led only one third) he said this feudal authority gave him a great advantage. He could impose his own socialist theories from above. He continued:

"There is a general family of socialism. Don't you agree Mr. Sasounian? It seeks to integrate the individual into society. But here in the Middle East there are variations, as for example my own. Nasser, as a nationalist, goes back to Hegel. I am naturally a Marxist. Who cannot be?

"The first book of Marx was on Heraclitus and his theory that everything in this world is generated by antagonisms, like protons and electrons. Even Socrates was a Marxist; he used the science of dialectics. And Jesus, too, was a Marxist in that sense.

"This unity of tradition has its impact on everyone and everything, including religion. We are coming to a new epoch, even the Druses. Our own society is being transformed as society is being transformed everywhere. It is the young people who are doing this."

I had difficulty in stemming the flow of Junblatt's logic. There was no remote possibility of interrupting the torrent of his verbiage as it flowed across the paved courtyard precisely as the mountain stream flowed under it. At last, when he halted to sip his coffee, by then cold, I reminded him of my desire to visit Egypt. I recalled the kindness of the Isfiya Druses (though they were clansmen of Arslan) and inquired:

"To whom could you recommend me in Beirut, sir? Someone who might be able to place me in contact with the Egyptian security people? Their Intelligence, of whom one speaks so much? I believe I have knowledge that might interest them."

"Surely," said Junblatt, "you are not planning to sell espionage information resulting from your Israeli visit? I could never be party to such a sordid enterprise."

"No, sir. I assure you, as an Armenian gentleman and scholar, that is not the case. I deal in two-legged sheep: useful, if well-equipped and well-instructed. My knowledge antedates my Israeli trip. You are acquainted with everyone in Beirut—as a politician."

Junblatt regarded me with disdain. "I know you are Armenian," he said, making no mention of my gentlemanly antecedents or scholastic competence. For a moment he reflected, scratching his long chin. "There would be no harm," he murmured, "if you were to see Braidy, concierge at the St. Georges Hotel. He is informed on everything. In many respects you have much in common with him."

"Brady?" I wondered. "An Irishman? In a Lebanese hotel?"

"No, not Irish. Mansour Braidy. Levantine, shall we say. But I can see you are eager to move on. Do not let me detain you further. My servant will take you to the station wagon. I am sending it to the city for a consignment of improved seeds. You will be deposited where you wish. I suggest you see Braidy."

He dismissed me with a courtly nod and no shake of the hand.

I felt diffident about entering the St. Georges Hotel with my tattering suitcase which was immediately seized by a bellboy. "Don't take it anywhere," I cautioned him. "I am not staying here." I looked around the comfortable lobby, bustling with tourists, travelling oil men, and wealthy desert Sheikhs, here to spend a portion of their petroleum revenue on Beirut's famous night life.

Then, standing behind the porter's desk, I spotted Braidy. It had to be Braidy: he had a happily wicked gleam in his shifty eyes and a ceaselessly changing expression on his raddled, mobile face. At the instant I first glimpsed him he was simultaneously talking in English to one client, with his right hand writing instructions in French on a sheet of paper, and with a pencil stub held in his left hand scribbling in Arabic.

I stood in front of him until he had finished these transactions and then quietly slid an open envelope across the counter. "Braidy?" I inquired in French. "Please count the contents." There were ten pounds sterling inside.

"Yes?" he speculated, lifting his brows a full inch without remotely changing the suspicious expression of his eyes beneath.

"That is for you. I have been advised to speak to you about a problem. By Monsieur Junblatt," I added.

Immediately a reassured look smoothed the lines of his face. He asked: "What can I do for you? I am at your disposal, sir. You have only to ask and it is yours."

I looked about me furtively. No one but Braidy's assistant was within earshot. "Send him," I nodded at the latter, "to the boy who has my bag. Over there. The beaten up cardboard bag. Tell him to arrange for a suitable replacement. Not too expensive. But of solid fibre. Or leather." Braidy did this, and the man departed.

"Now," I continued. "I wish to make contact with some trustworthy representative of the Egyptians. Not the ambassador, you understand. Some person who deals with affairs the ambassador may not know about. You know just what I mean, Braidy. Monsieur Junblatt told me so. The kind of people who dope enemy agents and ship them home in wardrobe trunks."

Braidy looked frightened. "Please do not say such things," he pleaded. Again his eyes flicked over the expanse of lobby. Then he added: "Here, take this. Go there. But if you say I sent you I'll deny it." He gave me a slip of paper, torn from his concierge's pad, on which he had scribbled a name and address in French as we were talking.

"I'll return for my new suitcase. You can tell your man to put my belongings in it and throw the other one away. There's nothing valuable. Don't worry. It isn't locked."

The name Braidy gave me was Sharif, not particularly identifiable in this part of the world, and the address was near the entrance to the commercial bazaar. I took a taxi and was delivered to a low building with a radio and repair shop on the ground floor. I climbed the creaking stairway and found an office identified with the sign, in both Arabic and English: "North-South Communications Company."

That, I thought, is a dead give-away; but clever at that. No one could believe a spymaster would advertise his trade. I knocked at the door and entered.

"Mr. Sharif?" I inquired in English. The plump, swarthy man

with flocculent ears looked up from behind the rolltop desk. I continued in Arabic, noticing a poster of the youthful Colonel Nasser tacked to the wall behind him. I did not tell him who had sent me nor did he seem to expect me to. Possibly Braidy had telephoned while I was on the way.

Instead, succinctly but with an air of urgency, I assured him I was in a position to sell to his government a secret of profound importance. It could almost immediately alter the balance of power in the Middle East. I was not, I added, prejudiced for or against any of the countries involved. I was a businessman and prepared to come to terms for money.

Sharif listened and fiddled with a box of twelve-gauge shotgun shells.

I asked for nothing in advance save a visa to his country, if required; transportation there, for which I was prepared to pay; and assurance of an appointment with officials high-ranking enough to decide promptly whether or not the regime was interested in my offer.

If the reply was affirmative I promised delivery of certain vital material within a week at the utmost. If the reply was negative, I asked only for my expenses and an exit visa. Clearly, I concluded, my offer must be an honest one: the terms were so precise, and my demands, in case his government professed no interest, were ridiculously modest.

Sharif was intelligent. He hooded his eyes to camouflage any hint of reaction and asked in a palatal voice if I would like a drink. "Yes," I answered, wondering what a good Egyptian Moslem might offer. He went to a tiny icebox in the corner, under the stack of calendars displaying the Sphinx and Pyramids, and extracted a bottle of beer, a bottle of Schweppes tonic water, and a can of tomato juice. He opened the beer and poured out a glass for me.

"I do not drink alcohol," he said apologetically, and I watched with fascination as he filled his own glass half full of tomato juice and then covered this with Schweppes. The mixture boiled, foamed and rose until it had bubbled all over his dust-speckled desk. This did not seem to bother him. "Chin-chin," he said, raising the red-dripping glass in a toast. I stared in silence.

"It is a good thing you have come to me," he continued. "I am a cavalry officer and therefore a man of decision. You might not be aware of the fact that in my part of Egypt, Beni Mor, we produce the finest Arab steeds. This is the same region from which President Nasser comes." I did not see any connection.

"I have been with the Revolution since before it started. I am therefore in a position to give categorical answers. I am an officer and used to command. Therefore I can give you a categorical answer even now. Categorically, I shall command that what is to be done shall be done."

Sharif arose and began strutting about the room with the swagger of a horseless hussar. He pulled his round belly in and moved it up to his chest. Suddenly he looked at his wristwatch and turned toward me:

"There is a Misr flight in precisely seventy-two minutes. You will be on it. Necessary arrangements shall be arranged while you are in the air."

I had no special fondness for Misr, the Egyptian airline, which has a pronounced accident rate, and a talent for losing its way in sandstorms. Nevertheless, I figured, a man who could survive Hornton Airways could perspire this one out.

"How about my baggage?" I asked, explaining about the valise. "And do I need a visa?"

"All shall be taken care of," said Sharif imperiously. "The necessary instructions shall be given." He pushed a button beside his old-fashioned telephone and a timid secretary entered with a pad.

"Get Mr. Kevorkian's bag at the St. Georges," he told her. "Pay what is required. Meet us at the airport by the Misr counter. At fourteen fifteen o'clock. The usual flight."

Turning toward me: "At least you have a passport?"

"Yes, Turkish."

"Very good. In matters such as this it is necessary to be punctilious. Now you will meet me back here in twenty-three minutes. I have things to do."

Sharif himself drove me out in a Mercedes past a long stand of pines that surely would be emulated in the paradise of any sainted dog. The secretary, beside a handsome leather suitcase, was already at the counter holding my ticket in her hand. At any rate, I reflected, this adventure had secured for me the luggage of a gentleman.

The cavalryman personally conducted me to the aircraft, installed me in a first class seat that I supposed was reserved for government free-loaders, whispered something to the stewardess and then shook my hand with all the firmness his pudgy fingers could muster.

"Good luck," he said. "We are grateful for any help. I have already told Cairo this may be an interesting encounter. You will be met."

"Inshallah," said I.

CHAPTER

XVI

A big TWA liner had just come in when we bounced to a halt in Cairo and our cargo of ill-assorted Arab merchants and politicians followed a bevy of American tourists into the airport: fat men with cameras slung around their necks and unlit cigars in their mouths, earnest women with bobbed, curled gray hair and steel-rimmed spectacles, and long-legged girls chewing gum and chattering to each other in nasal tones.

As I queued up in the foreigners' line a captain in uniform and a brown-suited civilian with that malevolent look which marks most Arab secret policemen came up and inquired in halting English: "Mr. Kevorkian? From Mr. Sharif?" I answered affirmatively in Arabic. They took my passport, guided me to a VIP waiting room, and soon I had my visaed document and suitcase back.

It was early evening when we drove into the city in a chauffeured Chevrolet limousine. The captain told me this was at my disposal for the duration of my visit. He escorted me to the Semiramis Hotel beside the Nile, ordered the obsequious porter to treat me with care, asked if there was anything I wished, then informed me that the evening and the next day were at my disposal. However, he warned, I should be ready at nine P.M. tomorrow for an important appointment. He saluted, beamed, bowed, departed.

I opened my suitcase so the snoops would have no trouble with the brand new lock. Then I descended to the bar. Its tender, a Jew named Joe, recommended a drink of his own concoction called Suffering Bastard. It was more saporous than stimulating. I had four of them. Joe combined a friendly manner with a professional competence I had seen equalled among his Middle Eastern peers only by Baghdad's renowned Jesus who tended bar along the Tigris.

Indigestion and the Suffering Bastards inspired me to look around. As soon as I walked out the door I noted that I was being followed by a thin, slit-eyed man in a nattily pressed suit. He had a brisk stride and seemed ready for a long night's hike. A fat man was masquerading as the driver of a taxi the sofragi unsuccessfully tried to make me hire.

I shook the taxi after a long stroll to the souk, Cairo's famous bazaar. Then I shook the hiker by dodging through the crowds of peddlers, beggars, and peaceful hookah-smokers who dotted the narrow alleys. As I emerged past a coffee shop at the end of a long row of shoemakers I sniffed the honeyed reek of kef.

It was a splendid night. The stars glittered. The minarets groped delicately skyward. There was a rustle among the leaves and fronds edging a small park. I found myself beside the famous opera house where "Aida" had first been presented.

As I turned toward the heart of the city, one pimp after another emerged from the shadows, asking in sibilant English: "Anything you want, Meeester. Very nice shop. Very good souvenirs. Change your dollars. Girls? Ve-r-y pretty girls? Yesss?" I suppose it must have been Mardikhian's American-cut Cyprus suit that attracted their attention.

I was accelerating my pace when I felt a tug at my sleeve. I looked down, and saw a barefoot little fellow clad in dirty white gown and skullcap. "Fucky-fucky, five bucky," he chanted in a high-pitched voice. "Who?" I asked, "you or your sister?"

"My sister very pretty girl. Five bucky. Me and my sister, ten bucky."

I was bored and I felt perpendicular so I decided to go along. I hailed a cab, put the youngster in front with the driver, and drove off according to the lad's directions, looking behind to be sure we weren't followed. I had no intention of spoiling my commercial prospects with the reputedly puritanical Nasser.

Finally we stopped on the verge of a cluster of low structures built of dried mud. I paid the fare, waved off the cab, and followed my guide into a maze of crooked paths stinking of garbage. About four hundred yards in, we halted at a half-open door. The boy entered, reaching for my hand. A fat slut, skirt up to her hips, was lying on what looked like a heap of rags. I could see her lewd features by the light of a kerosene lamp set on a chair. Much as my antecedents encouraged me toward sharing this titillating Turkish delight, I was repelled by her chancrous leer.

"We fucky. We sucky. Very cheap, you lucky," she intoned with a salivated cackle.

"No thanks, ducky," I concluded the verse and fled, cured of any lascivious thoughts.

I stumbled over heaps of offal that filled the spaces between the dreadful hovels along the way, many tenanted by other whores beckoning from the paneless windows. My God, I thought, this makes Abanoz Street look like the nacreous avenues of heaven.

My evening of esthetically imposed abstinence produced a dreamless slumber from which I was awakened by a series of raps. "Wait a minute," I shouted successively in English, French, and Arabic and then, wrapping myself in a bath towel, went to the door where a pretty black-haired girl was standing, carrying a handbag and what seemed to be two pads and a cluster of pencils. She had a bright smile and copious breasts.

"I am Kadissa," she said in a soft, caressive voice. "Your secretary. May I come in?"

"Come in by all means. But I didn't need a secretary. Are you sure there isn't some mistake."

"No mistake," she replied in excellent French. "My ministry instructed me to come at nine o'clock and place myself at your disposal. Dictation. Tourist guidance. Information. Or anything else you might want." She stressed the word "anything."

"Kadissa, a Coptic name, means saint," she continued. "But they call me Issa."

"Are you a saint?" I asked.

"I am very good, they tell me."

"Well, I am more interested in the anything than I am in the rest," I concluded.

"That is quite all right. I am accustomed. Do you wish me to lock?"

She didn't wait for an answer. Putting down her handbag, pad, and pencils, she went to the door, hung on the knob outside a "Do Not Disturb" sign, shut it, turned the key, then looked at me inquiringly.

"I am unused to such gentle hospitality," I said.

"Oh are you?" She seemed surprised. "My ministry advised me that you were to be accorded the respect and privileges of a delegate to the Arab League."

"That's great," I remarked. "I can easily imagine what that implies. What ministry is that, your ministry?"

"I am not at liberty to say. Can you show me where the bathroom is?"

I went back to bed. After a while, during which I heard water running for a long time, she joined me, smelling pure, fresh, and soapy. "Do you always take a bath before?" I asked.

"Oh yes. Before and afterward."

"You are very charming." She was. She approached her task with thorough concupiscence. The accomplishments of the co-operative Copt, I concluded after a time, are not to be comprehended in advance.

Gratefully recognizing that I had been wrong to impugn too rigid a morality to my hosts, I spent an agreeable morning. Afterwards I allowed Issa to escort me around the museum with its magnificent pharaonic collection, the old citadel, and the island gardens of the Nile. My Chevrolet was apparently well-known either by its number plate or by its driver. Wherever we went, saluting police whisked us on. Eventually, so that I might sign the tabs in the name of the Revolution, we returned for drinks in Joe's bar and luncheon on the hotel roof.

Issa was as lovely and versatile in conversation as she was in bed. A well-made girl in her early twenties, she had good taste in clothes, and a decorous way of making up her face which accentuated her flat cheeks, wide, sensual mouth, and marvelously smooth glabella. She spoke good French, English, and, of course, Arabic. It was evident she had been excellently brought up in bourgeois circumstances. Finally, I asked the obvious question:

"How in the name of Nefertari's eyes did you ever get into this kind of work?"

"Well," she said, "it isn't always disagreeable. Take today for example. And I must accept what I can get. My mother is dead. My father is in prison."

"What did he do?"

"He was rich. They sequestrated our house but took his money. They made him keep the servants. When he could no longer pay them he was arrested—for breaking the law. Our house was awarded to a sheikh from Oman. I had no place to go. So I work for the ministry."

Issa told me that, although the Copts are the purest Egyptians as well as one of the oldest Christian communities in the world, they were suffering today.

"Do you tell this to all government guests who give you dictation or other employ?" I inquired.

"No. You are different. Besides, I am soon getting married. My fiancé's relatives in Paris hope they can get us out. They have money. And they have apparently shared it with an influential member of our embassy there."

"But doesn't your fiancé object to the kind of work you are forced to do for the ministry?"

"Oh, he doesn't really know. I shall be a virgin when we marry. No Copt marries anyone but a virgin. If the bride is not a virgin the marriage is invalid."

"That is interesting but slightly hard to understand."

"There is nothing hard to understand," she said, regarding me with innocent limpidity. "I know at least one Coptic doctor who supports himself largely by sewing up the membranes of prospective brides."

"Rather painful price to pay for fun," I observed.

"My mother used to tell me it has been that way for centuries. Coptic girls are very highly sexed," she added with a daintily suggestive smile.

"I noticed that."

"One must participate," she said. "One hand does not clap. I think you have already understood just what I mean."

Issa went home at seven, taking her notebook and pencils but promising to bring them back tomorrow. She refused to be driven in my car; this would embarrass her with her friends.

At a quarter to nine, I was sitting in the lobby reading the *Egyptian Gazette* and occasionally looking up over its pages at the two snoops who had lost me the night before, when the captain appeared and asked for me at the porter's desk. I strode toward him and he again saluted respectfully, then led me to the Chevrolet.

"We are going to President Nasser's private house. This is a most important occasion. You will graciously permit me," he said, and, before I knew it, he was in swift and expert fashion frisking me for weapons. "Good. Now we may take off."

It was a pleasant drive in the direction of Heliopolis. We finally pulled up at a series of low white buildings; one seemed to be the entrance to the villa where the new chief of state had lived as an officer, and which he had caused to be enlarged for his more grandiose new station. Several bereted soldiers bearing submachine guns looked quizzically at us. An officer of the guard half opened the door, peered in and received reassuring word from my escort. He bade us wait, crossed the street to make a telephone check, and then waved us to follow.

A military aide led the way into a large square antechamber whose edges were surrounded with ornate, ugly gilt furniture but whose spacious center was empty save for a Persian carpet of commonplace design. A few inscribed photographs of foreign statesmen reposed on the mantel.

When we entered, a door to the left opened and two men came into the room; one was a short, trim, handsome young Egyptian with black hair and eyes, a sensitive mouth, and a habit of swift gestures; the other was a white-jacketed butler, bearing a tray of cold fruit juices. The good-looking man gestured me to the corner of a sofa and dismissed my escort with the hauteur of unconscious authority. He took a glass after I had accepted one and introduced himself.

"Mohammed Heikal," he said. "*Al Ahram.* I am a friend of the President. He has asked me to be present at your discussion. And also at the display we are told you will make for us. Have no alarm. Although I am a newspaper editor, I am considered very discreet. The President trusts me. With everything."

He had barely concluded when we heard the slight noise of another door opening. Heikal beckoned; rising, he said he would lead the way. I followed him into a comfortable office with desk, radio, telephones, and easy chairs. Nasser himself was standing just inside.

I was immediately struck by the fact that despite his pretensions to Arab leadership, Nasser didn't look at all like an Arab. He seemed a pure-blooded Egyptian of pre-Arabic stock. He had closely cut, slightly curly dark hair with a light dab of gray at the sides, a fierce, curved nose, fine eyes, a strong jaw, a mouth that was not camouflaged by the small mustache, and gleaming white teeth.

A big man, over six-feet tall, he was almost my size although perhaps less fit and more given to weight. His shoulders and chest were broad, his hips wide and massive, and thick legs showed beneath the tailored trousers of his gray flannel suit. Having been to the museum that very day, I was struck by his overpowering resemblance to those monolithic stone statues of Pharaoh Rameses II.

"We know you speak excellent Arabic as well as many other languages," he said to me in excellent Arabic while pointing to a seat before his desk. "As a matter of fact we know quite a bit about you."

"Our services," said Heikal, placing himself opposite my quaggy armchair, and speaking in a soft voice. "They are very good."

Nasser smiled with pleasure. He leaned forward to hand me a Turkish coffee and a choice of Craven-A or Filtra cigarettes. He said: "We seek to meet the needs of our people. But to do this we must rely upon ourselves. We have been informed that you are in a position to help us.

"We Arab countries have a population of about sixty million. We can have a big army. We feel we should defend our own area. The Arab people refuse to live under the threat of fear.

"You, as an Armenian, know the effect of fear. I do not want to see my children as refugees. With my own eyes I saw refugees in Palestine. You or your parents saw refugees in Turkey. I do not want to see Egyptian refugees packing their belongings off.

"Once I thought there could be peace. I said to my troops and

officers in Palestine that we must do our best to have peace.
They disagreed. They said Israel would not agree to peace. I
replied that I had guarantees from England and the United States.

"But after the bloody Gaza incident, when I saw the same
officers, I felt responsible for the deaths of those thirty-two men.
There had been no Egyptian troops at Gaza except for administrative units. They lived in their billets without defenses—
no barbed wire or trenches. They were killed in cold blood.

"I said I was wrong. I was responsible for the lives of those people. I said if you see any Jew, kill him. You are responsible for
yourself and for your land. We can no longer rely on guarantees.
Fear dominates the area."

Nasser fixed me with a predatory stare. It was evident that he
was imaginative, tricky, emotional. He would go far; he believed
everything he said.

"That is where we are today," Heikal added, without fear of
interrupting. "And the Israelis have done their best to poison
our relations with the West. They have intruded spies and sabo-
teurs. They have sought to blow up and burn down offices of the
United States in order that we should absorb the blame."

Nasser resumed his peroration. "Ben Gurion's policy is based
on forcing settlement. It does not matter when Ben Gurion goes
temporarily out of office. He always comes back." I thought
of the debate at Sde-Boker as Nasser added: "And he runs
things in between."

"But to force a peace also means war. You will begin by war
and try to defeat your opponent before you can reach peace. This,
to us, is also a threat. And we look to the Israeli danger with more
concern than ever. Every day we wait for news that Israel has
invaded Egypt. As long as Israel exists there is a danger.

"This is where you come in, Sasounian. We have made our
arrangements for new arms supplies. But I am a career officer, I
know that it will require years to train a sufficiently disciplined
and durable mass of soldiers—to accept the burden history lays
upon our backs.

"I have been told that you are in some manner able to produce
a large force. Professionals who would not be the usual mercenaries, people for whom I have contempt; that they could be

relied upon to endorse our views, follow our leadership, and die for our cause. I am not entirely clear on this.

"Nevertheless, I can inform you that Major Sharif is by no means our only source. Had his report alone been received we would have laughed. But we are proud of our security services. We have heard much about you. In Turkey. In Cyprus. Yes, even in Israel.

"There, I gather, things did not go well—which is a mark in your favor, perhaps. Indeed, even in the Soviet Union there have been rumors. So you see, you are a man of mystery. Also, it may be, a man of promise. Now you must convince us."

Quite a speech, I thought. I could not understand why he considered it so necessary as a prelude to a commercial deal or military bargain. Then I noticed his left hand moved, just a flick, as he tapped the ash from the cigarette in his right hand, exhaling forcefully. I realized the whole discourse had been recorded. Of course, I reflected, this will be something for history if it comes off. For history as it is to be written in Cairo.

"If you could switch off the recorder, sir," I said respectfully, "I can briefly summarize what I am prepared to sell and on what terms." I did; after he had flicked the switch.

Heikal stood back respectfully as Nasser arose and guided us through a hallway and a small, simple portico to a lawn whose unusual greenness was enhanced by bright electric lights. He walked heavily along it, around a corner of the villa, to an open space where four army officers in battledress were standing, one holding a machine-pistol and three gripping revolvers in their right hands. I judged from their shoulder insignes that all were of high rank.

Nasser neglected to introduce us. They did not salute but merely stared with curious suspicion. Apparently they had been briefed to expect a momentous and perhaps startling demonstration. They were clearly ready to slaughter me, with or without command, if they deemed it useful.

"There," said Nasser, pointing to the enclosure. "Sharif said this was all you needed. Earth.

"No one is here but us. There are no other guards than these. And these are the most trusted men I have. You are free to begin when and as you will. But I warn you, no tricks. We are in no mood for tricks. My officers are just men. But they can be ruthless. Their punishment is rapid."

His sharp-featured face bore its predatory look and it was with unaccustomed trepidation that I strode three paces forward and, having extracted two flaky nubbins from the recesses of my billfold, poked holes a yard apart in the soft, well-tended grass, dropped them in, and stepped away. I had not reckoned with the nutrition factor of a lavishly gardened, densely fertilized lawn in the lush Nile valley. Within seconds I could see the dull gleam of Thracian helmets thrusting through the verdure.

These were not spearmen but peltasts with wickerwork shields shaped like crescent moons, dirty linen tunics, swords, and slings. A crafty Asiatic cast showed on their flat faces as they brushed the damp loam from their untended beards and peered around.

"Impossible," muttered the dazed Nasser. "In the name of Allah, the merciful and the almighty, quite impossible."

With an overconfident smirk I looked at his blanched countenance and said: "Your Excellency, the word impossible is a crutch for the simple-minded." Perhaps this was my undoing.

With the obsequious and unctuous manner of a dishonest Armenian rug merchant, one of the officers slunk to Nasser's side and whispered a few words. Slowly the dazed look faded from the President's face. It was replaced by a grim and almost manic expression.

Cutting the air with his right hand, he said abruptly: "Arrest this man. And take those things, those creatures away. Do with them as you have done with their predecessors."

To say that I was appalled would be a conspicuous understatement. The cluster of officers encircled me, all thrusting their weapon-muzzles sharply into my flesh as if for fear they might otherwise miss if called upon to pull the trigger. Nasser glowered; Heikal stared with distaste, and I, nervously, splaying my fingers, kept arguing "Why? Why? Why?"

Somebody blew a screeching whistle. The courtyard filled with armed men. I could see the bewildered little Thracians being pummelled off by four huge Nubian gendarmes. Then one of the generals in our group, a lean, saturnine man with piercing voice, barked: "Take this Israeli spy away."

Dumbfounded and wholly addled, I felt myself being propelled through the garden and a back gate by numerous hands which cruelly twisted my arms behind. I was cast into an army truck where, having taken the precaution to first cuff my wrists and ankles, several soldiers apparently assigned to the task of guarding my transfer set upon me. Since I was forced to lie on my stomach as they thumped me, I could see nothing until we grunted to a halt, the tail board lowered, and my legs and arms were unfettered. I was roughly shoved through a dark stone entrance, a dark ante-chamber, a dark hallway, and finally into a dark cell whose heavy door clanked miserably shut.

So forcibly had I been cast into this dungeon that I was catapulted against a hard wall to collapse dazed and aching against its base. Many moments later I realized I was not alone. In the shadow created by courtyard lights penetrating this small, high, barred window, I saw a crippled figure crabwalk across the cell.

"Kevork," came a doleful voice, "You too!"

It was Avrahm. He had been severely tortured.

"So that is why they called me an Israeli spy," I muttered. "Somehow they knew we had been together. But what brought you here? And why are you in such shabby shape?"

In low tones and curious accents caused by the loss of several bicuspids and by what I took to be an injury to his tongue, Avrahm began to talk. When it was decided to purchase ten dragon's teeth from my collection, Avrahm had been designated by the intelligence division of Zahal to conduct a dangerous secret operation in Cairo. The mission had been conceived and organized by Lavon. I remembered how he had argued in the Negev desert: "It is fate that brought this opportunity to us."

Apparently, as Avrahm explained in labored phrases, the affair was placed in the hands of a certain Colonel Jibly of Aman, the army secret service. Jibly insisted Avrahm was the man for the job. Avrahm didn't like the idea from the start; Jibly had been involved in an espionage disaster in 1950 and had acquired an unsavory reputation. However, Avrahm had no choice.

On returning from Cyprus he had been given precise orders and an indoctrination course. His mission was to plant the ten teeth conveniently near to chosen American and British installations in Cairo. He was to assemble and ignite flammable material.

Then, the moment the soldiers materialized, he was to use his linguistic abilities and instruct them to set fire to designated buildings.

The idea was simple. It was easy for the Israelis to infiltrate Avrahm, one single Arab-speaking agent, through Egyptian security defenses. It was equally easy for Avrahm to hide the manpower for his projected operation in the corners of his handkerchief.

He made contact with an Israeli "dead drop" and with certain "illegals" who had been planted in Cairo by Aman and Ha-Mosad, the Chief of Intelligence and Espionage. With the help of the "illegals," he reconnoitered Cairo and made his arrangements, including assemblage of gasoline-soaked rags and torches.

Unfortunately, everything went wrong. The tooth-men, planted in Garden City near the targets, panicked at the flames in their hands. Avrahm was unable to control or discipline them. They were rounded up by the normal guard contingents stationed outside foreign buildings. Their controller was grabbed before he could escape, shouting desperate and useless commands in classical Attic.

"It was a fiasco," Avrahm said. "It was so obvious it could not succeed. I am not even sure that Lavon, brusque, impatient and insensitive as he is, could really have imagined this would work. I remember, at the time I was training, some of my friends involved in the preparations whispered rumors that the orders laying out the plan of operations must have been forged by an ignoramus or an enemy of Lavon.

"In any case, they got us all. And right away. At first they claimed the affair was a secret Israeli weapon, some preternatural and diabolical thing we had been manufacturing at Dimona in the Negev. They kept insisting on this. And the more they tortured me, the more I confessed. And the more I confessed, the more they were convinced.

"But then, even Egyptian intelligence began to admit it was unreasonable that we would use our great Jewish brains to manufacture men from teeth. They acknowledged Dimona might be better suited to nuclear experiments than demonology. Anyway the former could be seen as probably more effective in warfare than the latter.

"At this point in the interrogations, I gathered, they claimed that all your tooth-men were Egyptian Jews. Admittedly, even with my confessions, they could not certify either their origin or nationality. But they bridged this gap by claiming we communicated by a secret, coded language.

"I don't know for certain what has happened to the others. They say, here in the prison, that at least some of them have been hanged."

"And what has happened to you?" I asked. "What will they do with you?"

"You have seen what they have done to me already. What awaits me is the rope. Now we are in Cairo prison. This is near Saladin's Citadel. It is where they keep their serious offenders so long as they can hope to stay alive. Even here we are just across from the City of the Dead. Egyptians, like Chinese, honor but do not adore their dead—as do the Spaniards.

"After final trials we are moved to other prisons, to Tora or Maadi or Helwan. That is, if we are to live. Those who will be hanged go to Bab el-Khalk. On hanging days they dress you in red pants, shirt, and skullcap and then run up a black flag when you drop. My trial, if that is what you call it, was today. Tomorrow I go to Bab el-Khalk."

"Nothing is more annoying than to be obscurely hanged," I said. "There is no other way?"

"Yes, perhaps there is another way. And I shall try and discover how far it goes. This dismal building is four stories high. One cannot escape over the high stone wall with iron spikes at the top. But there is one inadequately protected stairwell."

Here Avrahm was whispering—in Greek—to insure against eavesdropping.

"If, as they lead me off to Bab el-Khalk, I am taken down by that stairway, I may be able to leap."

"And kill yourself?"

"And kill myself. You can see I am no longer what might be termed a man."

"Poor Avrahm," I said. "In our faith they speak of Hell and I suppose it is tenanted by Turks and unbaptized babies. And you . . ."

"For me there is no Hell," Avrahm insisted. "And certainly

there is a God. There is a God who controls everything and who creates and destroys at will. But He is cruel and mischievous and exceedingly haphazard. By now I am convinced He delights in the noises, sights, and contortions of misfortune. He made this earth because He was bored and needed a new toy. And we, the Jews, are His chosen people. God must have his joke.

"If I do not get away down that stairwell, at least the Egyptians hang one properly. They are not like your Turkish friends, who stand you on a chair on a table, put you in a hood that makes you look like a ghost, and stick a placard on your chest saying what a criminal you are. Then they kick the chair away and let you slowly strangle. Here in Egypt, at worst, God will only make me dance for Him."

Avrahm scuttled slowly toward the faint light showing through the unattainable window. I saw upon his poor, drawn face a possessed stare. Outside our cell I could hear the shuffling advance of heavy boots. The peephole in the door was uncovered for a moment. A single humorless eye reflected in the glare of an electric torch.

The lock turned and four men, led by a frightened looking young lieutenant, came in. Ignoring my presence, they silently seized Avrahm under the armpits and dragged him out with astonishing ease. I reflected that he must have lost a fourth of his weight since I had seen him in Famagusta; and even then he was thin.

An instant later I heard barked, gruff commands and a dull thud. "Well," I reflected, "he found the low road."

I spent three days in the dank and disagreeable hostelry by the Citadel. My bruises throbbed; my nerves jangled, and my cuts festered in the insalubrious and feverish atmosphere. To my surprise, nobody asked any questions.

The peephole slid open and shut at irregular moments of the day and night, which themselves were not glaringly distinguishable. From time to time buckets of slops were shoved through the briefly opened door. It was hard to tell whether their contents represented pre- or post-digested food.

The furnishment of my cell was limited to one small, low stool that might have been a wooden cobbler's bench. I contemplated many ways of brandishing this as a weapon in sudden and devious escape schemes. In the end, I decided its only means of employ, apart from that for which it was intended, was as a weight for thrusts, pushes, heaves, hauls, and other exercises to keep fit over an interminable period.

I said nothing. No one said anything to me. Occasionally, in nearby cells, I heard grunts, moans, thuds, and scrapes. But I never sought to establish contact with the residents. I deliberately practiced the self-hypnotic methods of the mesmerites, much recommended among Armenians of my father's generation, and thereby managed to approach a temporary state of what the Buddhists call Nirvana.

Indeed, by intensive concentration, I was able to induce within myself a condition that ignored thought, memory, expectation, ambition or sorrow. Even pain dulled into nothingness and the only acute reminder of my unfortunate Cairene purgatory was the penetrating smell of other people's shit.

Thus, in this suspended condition when by deliberate concentration both fear and regret were consigned to nonexistence, it came as a surprise, but with neither the pleasure of anticipation nor the fright of harm, that the heavy portal was flung open and, preceded by the same scared young lieutenant who had summoned Avrahm to eternity, a trim, small American with bow tie and a conventional U.S. cut suit barely visible in the quasi-light, entered.

"My name is Roosevelt," said the American in flat accents, extending his hand in a manner not suited to the surroundings. I shook it. "Most interesting," I remarked, blearily suspecting yet another Egyptian confusion or jailer's trick. "I thought you were dead."

"That was another Roosevelt," he replied. "Or, in fact, two of them. We are a large family."

"Oh. I see. And you?"

"I am Kermit Roosevelt. And I have come to release you."

XVII

To my astonished delight, Roosevelt conducted me down the steep stairway where Avrahm had slain himself, and then out through the antechamber and entrance, past respectfully saluting guards. A car with diplomatic plates was waiting at the gate. The driver whirled us off along a series of alleys and by that ominous cemetery on the Cairene hills known as the City of the Dead.

We arrived at an old-fashioned, gazeboed house on Zamalek island where, no longer surprised by anything, I was shown my suitcase, neatly packed with its little store of belongings. A white-gowned, tarbooshed servant guided me to the bathroom. I shaved and showered while my remaining suit was pressed. By the time I descended, calm, clean and cologned, with even my wealed and welted bruises disguised by dabs of talc, my usual self-assurance had returned.

"This is John Eichelberger," Roosevelt said, introducing me to my host. "He is attached to our embassy. I am visiting him in connection with official business. We were instructed to seek your release. You are going to Paris. But first we will take you to Ambassador Byroade's residence for dinner. He can do the talking. Now have a drink."

A few minutes later several other Americans joined us. The conversation became merry and banal. Among the confusion of names I thought I heard "Sulzberger" and fixed my gaze on a medium-sized man in his mid- or early forties. He had spectacles, graying hair, and all his features were a bit too big for him: large ears, large fleshy nose, large, thick-lipped mouth. He was heavily sun-tanned, had very light whiskers, and spoke with the overloud voice of deaf men.

Nobody was paying much attention to me, so I went up and asked: "Is it true your name is Sulzberger?"

"Yes. Why?"

"Are you a newspaperman?"

"Yes. Why?"

"Well, then, I am glad to meet you. I am Kevork Sasounian. Not so many months ago I sailed on the boat of your friend Michali Pantelis who said he took you out of Greece by caique in 1941."

"He sure did. But how on earth should he happen to mention that to you."

"The tale is too long and variegated to tell. But he spoke inordinately well of you. I think he associates you with his youth."

"Pantelis wasn't young even then. But, of course, I guess he was still young enough to dream. All of us thought of a different kind of world those days. Where is he now? Greece?"

"No, Turkey. He has made his home there ever since your intricate trip together. To Çesme, I believe? Now he lives in Istanbul. Or at least that is where he presently moors his modest boat, the 'Samsun,' most of the time, as far as I am aware."

"That so? I'm going to Istanbul from here. How can I reach him?"

"Through Pandeli's. The restaurant. Pandeli can find him. Certainly you cannot but know Pandeli. And, incidentally, may I ask of you a favor?"

Sulzberger examined me quizzically. I could feel his slightly pop blue eyes as they scrutinized my powdered bumps. "Ask me what it is first," he said. "I keep my word—if I give it. But I don't make blind promises."

"Well, if you know Istanbul sufficiently well enough to know about Pandeli's, you obviously also know about Yusuf. The one who runs the famous and remarkable bazaar stall. I have a friend who is staying with Yusuf. Or was. I do not now know. Yusuf was looking after her for me. Will you tell Yusuf that, one way or another, he should get her to Paris. If he can. I shall give you an envelope of money on her behalf."

Sulzberger whispered something to Eichelberger and took me to a dadoed study off an adjoining room. I extracted an envelope and piece of paper from the desk, wrote a brief note to Rima, tucked in four thousand dollars of Reuven's money (astonishingly left untouched by my Egyptian friends), and handed it to the journalist.

"Her name is Rima," I said. "That is in itself enough. From there onward Yusuf knows what to do and how. But, in case he should ask whatsoever question, I want Rima to join me in Paris as soon as she can transport herself to there. She is to call immediately at the Armenian Church on the Rue Jean Goujon. Will you please write that down? I'll leave a message with the esteemed and venerable head of the church, Arkebisgobos Manoukian, who is my kinsman.

"If by then I have not yet arrived, she must give him a letter for me with her address. And she should tell His Beatitude, the Archbishop, how to reach her. He will help. And with this money, she should manage to accommodate herself all right. Now, don't forget, my dear new friend, to tell Yusuf he must spare no effort or expense to get her out. Is it possible that I, a stranger, can count on you for this?"

"You may count on me," Sulzberger said and gave my large hand a wiry squeeze. "But are you sure you know what you are doing? I know nothing about you; but there are strange tales. And Kim there," he added, nodding his head at Roosevelt in the hall, "plays for keeps. Even if he doesn't look the part. I'd like to see you and to talk about Pantelis. Kim says you're leaving. I presume Paris is the final goal. But do you know where he's taking you en route? He can be devious, Kim."

"If you don't know where you're going, any road will get you there," I said sententiously.

The party broke up by the mere act of dissolution; suddenly everyone seemed to fade away. Roosevelt took me by the elbow and murmered, staring at my ear half a head above him: "I am taking you to the Ambassador's now. He will explain."

The American envoy proved to be a handsome, dark, trim man named Byroade, more youthful and athletic-looking than I would have been led to expect by what one says of diplomats. He was friendly and forthright, coming into the entrance hall as soon as he heard us enter, shaking hands informally with a "Glad t'meet ya, Mr. Sasounian" and with, nevertheless, a sharp glance that darted across my bruised complexion. "Come in and have a drink," he said.

I noticed that he served us himself. He remarked: "Now that Ramadan has let you in I have ordered all the servants to go. I want to talk easily. There will be no one but Kim and you and me. There is cold supper. My wife is upstairs.

"Oh, and furthermore. You don't need to worry about bugs."

Bugs, I thought, in the American Ambassador's house! I hadn't . . .

"Not that kind," said the envoy, shrewdly reading my mind. "It is an Americanism. For electronic snooping devices. To overhear conversations. To eavesdrop. Don't give it a thought. The place was debugged yesterday by our marines."

When, with tall glasses of whisky, we had eased ourselves into chairs, Byroade asked: "Well, what did you think of Gamal? Of Nasser?"

"He's a bit oppressive in his hospitality."

"I meant before that."

"Well, it is hard to say. I deduce that you know more than I would have suspected. You Americans must have friends in high circles here."

"No comment," grinned Roosevelt.

"I suppose he is an astute and clever politician," I continued. "Because I am told such is his widespread reputation. But, if I may suggest, the science of politics sometimes differs from the art of ruling. Politics means staying ahead of the mob, not leading it, and the mob only obeys the logic of its own passions."

"There is no Egyptian mob," said Roosevelt. "Only a flock."

"Well, if that's the case, perhaps Nasser is the shepherd they need. He talks persuasively. But I believe him to be a fool."

"Why a fool?" asked Byroade. "That is one thing I never should have called Gamal."

"He is a fool because he does not believe the evidence of his own eyes, what I showed him, what I know myself he saw. Is that not a fool?"

After an interlude for sandwiches and cold beer brought by the Ambassador from the next room on a tray, he said: "I suggest we now get down to bedrock. You have been very polite, Mr. Sasounian. You have successfully restrained your curiosity. Why, you must be asking yourself, am I here?"

"That indeed. And also, why and how did you get me out of that foul prison?"

"As for the how, we have our methods. Favors are not unknown in Egypt; nor is the taste of money. As for the why, that is a horse of a different flavor.

"I can tell you this much. Yesterday I received from the Supremo a TOP SECRET COSMIC NIAC."

"I don't know what you mean," I protested. "I speak seventeen languages but I do not comprehend you."

"The Ambassador used to be a general," said Roosevelt.

"It was NODIS EYES ONLY and NIAC I repeat," continued Byroade.

"What the Ambassador means," said Roosevelt, "is that it was a very urgent and most confidential message."

"And the burden of it," the diplomat rattled on, unruffled by interpellations, "was that we were to attempt every possible means of obtaining your release in our custody. It seems, as far as Kim here and Eichelberger have been told, that you may have the answer to something we need very, very badly."

"Eichelberger is the fellow at whose place we just had drinks," said Roosevelt. "He works for the CIA. And so do I. There's no harm telling you. The secrets you have at your disposal appear to transcend in importance these confidences. I would like you to feel you can trust us, have faith in us."

"I cherish faith in few people, Mr. Ambassador," I said ruefully, rubbing the raddled gouts on my cheekbone and jaw. "But it is perfectly obvious that someone told someone about my tooth-men. I assume your government is interested."

"That is approximately right. And we intend to fly you out of here tonight."

"To Paris?" I remarked. The Ambassador seemed astonished that I should know.

"Yes, I told him," said Roosevelt.

"In that case I must warn you it is folly to send me there directly. Certain material I require is in Cyprus. And if you expect to remain as seriously interested as you have already shown yourselves to be, you must fly me to Cyprus first."

"I can have that arranged," said Roosevelt, when Byroade looked at him inquiringly. "In the plane that brought me here. There is no need for accuracy in our departure clearance with the Egyptians. As for Nicosia, Eichelberger can fix that right away with his British colleague. Let me use your telephone a second, Hank. I'll arrange it in a way the tappers will never understand."

When he returned, Roosevelt suddenly turned to me and regarded me straight in the eye. "I should like you to know," he said, "that we have means of insuring that you play straight with us. So let us not deceive each other."

"Deceive," I repeated. "Why should I ever deceive? I am a trusting and trustworthy man."

"We would like that to be so," Roosevelt continued. "And for this reason we have persuaded our Turkish allies to release a certain friend of yours into our custody."

"Rima," I murmured. "You hold Rima? And would you get her out to Paris if I fulfil my bargain?"

"We will," he answered. "And Perkel has wisely recognized already that the reality of our help is worth more to him than the potential of any exchange of pawns with Serov."

"Serov," I said. "Again Serov. I am puzzled by the name."

"He is the new Beria," said Roosevelt. "I believe you've heard of him.

At two o'clock in the morning a Levantine Englishman in hound's-tooth checks was driving Roosevelt and myself inside a handsome Jaguar to the airport where I had arrived. We entered by an unfamiliar gate; the heavily armed sentries made no effort to halt us, and we proceeded directly to a twin-engined Dakota bearing the star of the United States Airforce. Both propellers were slowly revolving.

The hound's-tooth Levantine was handing up our modicum

of baggage to a shaven-headed civilian built either like an icebox or a sergeant. "This is probably different from the way you came," said Roosevelt with a grin.

"Different," I replied. "Everything changes. As we Armenians say, you cannot step into the same river twice."

The Dakota took off immediately, chugging northward over the desert. By the time we neared Cyprus the sky was turning faintly lavender over the dull, mauve Aegean.

A car was waiting at the airport as the British authorities dispensed with normal red tape, and a pleasant American named Courtney led us to it.

"I'm driving you fellows myself," he said. "And all I know is Famagusta. You must tell me where." Roosevelt and I climbed in behind.

Being good, industrious Armenians, frugal with their hours, Sahag's household was already stirring like an anthill by the time we drew up before the mimosa-framed doorway. Rugs were airing over the window-sills; laundry flapped on the line that temporarily replaced the hammock between the eucalyptus trees; there was a pleasant smell of lavash baking in the oven; and a tub of herbs was retting on the porch. Even the plump pigeons were preening and strutted on their octagonally shaped cote.

I told the others to stay in the car, knocked sharply on the door and flung it open, shouting "Sahag, Araxie. Your cousin is home from the wars."

In a trice Araxie was warmly throbbing in my arms and old Sahag, still buttoning his fly, came stomping down the stairs, suspiciously regarding the two of us from beneath pendulous brows.

"I am in enormous haste," I said. "There has never been a more enormous haste. Forgive me, cousins, but I have come to take my sacks and then to go right off with them. You see that motorcar in front? It is awaiting me. We drive immediately for an airplane on a most singular and beneficial mission. It is most urgent."

"No," sobbed Araxie petulantly, "No, no, no. You cannot come and go like that again. You cannot treat me—treat us, like that. What are you, a Turk? Tell us where you have been, where you go."

Sahag added: "Invite your friends in, my boy. Just to remove the dust and refresh your souls. At least invite them in for a coffee and a sweet my daughter will prepare."

"I cannot, Sahag. These are Americans and therefore they worship at the altar of the god of money. For them time is money. They are helping me. I cannot ask them to abuse their god."

"I insist," Araxie screamed, pounding my chest with her little fists as tendrils of black hair unwound over her brow. "That is the very least you owe me."

Sahag looked at her sadly. He recited to her: "If anyone vexes him, he darkens at once, like the summit Nemrut." Then he added: "Leave him alone, my girl. He knows best what he must do."

Araxie turned and fled weeping to the kitchen. I beckoned to Roosevelt and Courtney and they, together with Oram the handyman, followed me down into the wine cellar. There, while Sahag stood by frittering his gnarled hands, we four heaved and pushed the awkward sacks up the stairs and out into the car. As we stuffed them on the rear seat I wondered how I had ever managed to shift their bulk around alone.

Finally the task was accomplished. I shook hands with Oram and gave Sahag a silent hug. Araxie never reappeared. I murmured to Sahag something about writing and also suggested that I might be eventually reached, care of His Beatitude, Manoukian. Then I climbed in beside Courtney and Roosevelt and we sped toward Nicosia.

Roosevelt explained at this point: "I shall not be travelling on with you. Nor, I am afraid, will you be very comfortable on this next lap. There is an old B-25 bomber on the British military strip with an American general who likes to stooge around and get the flying time. You know, extra pay. He will deliver you in Paris to one of my colleagues. And he will make arrangements to lodge you carefully—you and those," he added gesturing back at my sacks with his thumb.

We turned through the wire peripheries of Nicosia airport, at what seemed to be the same section Hornton Airways used although my memory is not accurate on minutiae. An ugly, twin-engined, twin-tailed bomber stood at the end of one runway. Beside it was gathered a burly group of crewmen in fur-collared

leather and cloth flying jackets and a straight young man with
the kind of cap with imperceptibly bent visor I had learned from
wartime movies was fancied by combat pilots.

He turned out to be the general. After one brief look, he said:
"I guess we'll have to stow those sacks in the bomb bay. Don't
worry. It hasn't been used for years. Doubt if we could even get
the doors open. As for you, my friend, you're a little big but
you're going to have to make the best of it. You ride in the tail
gunner's turret. I need my crew up front. They have jobs to do."

As Roosevelt and Courtney waved goodbye, a sergeant helped
me climb into the tiny compartment at the extreme rear of the
aircraft. There, by some acutely uncomfortable contortions,
rendered even more painful by the bruises I had recently acquired,
I managed to squeeze my amyotrophied bulk on to a small seat
facing backward and controlling a heavy mount of machineguns
pointing uselessly to the sky. "Fasten your belt," shouted the
sergeant. "Put on the earphones in case of emergency and
abandon aircraft." With that optimistic note he slammed the door
and left me locked in queasy solitude.

I experimented with the intercommunication radio as we
turned and taxied to a take-off position. A clipped voice I took
to be the general's reassured me that all my precious cargo had
been safely stored aboard. Then, with an ill-assorted set of bumps,
we shunted down the runway, soared over Nicosia, the Kyrenia
mountains, the azure sea, and turned westward, leaving behind
us a heliced trail.

It was a strange experience to be so entirely alone, although it
was by no means unpleasant. This was the solitude of a spirit in
clean space, not of a sullen prisoner. If I clicked off my radio, I
was wholly removed from contact with any other human being,
and when we slid into a pleasant white cumulus formation I felt
as an angel might feel, a bodiless soul floating free without the
least encumbrance by sordid physical attachments. There was
a total absence of both meaning and fantasia.

I looked at my watch as we skimmed over Italy and southern
France, but realized it had been broken in Cairo during another
and less agreeable form of confinement. I was dozing in numb
accidie when, by the pressure on my ear drums, I could feel we

were beginning to descend. I clicked on the radio and heard the pilot exchanging information with officials on the ground. Within a few instants we were bouncing along a concrete lane.

There was a continued coming and going of large planes with the markings of various airlines. I noted that we headed for a remote corner of the enormous complex of runways before finally grunting to a halt before two long black sedans and a khaki military truck. The sergeant soon came around and let me out of my cage. The handsome general shook hands perfunctorily and disappeared into one of the sedans.

A large, pink-faced fellow sidled up waving what looked to be like some kind of telegraph form. "Jim Hunt," he said. "I am taking over from Kim Roosevelt. But I really don't think there's very much for me to do. First thing is to get your stuff—those sacks, I imagine—into the car with you. And then I take you out to SHAPE. That's where I hand over."

The sacks had already been gingerly unloaded by the plane crew and were now borne over to the automobile. The driver opened the lid of an ample luggage compartment and they were stowed inside. "Fine," said Hunt. "Shipshape. Off we go."

"You say SHAPE and you say shipshape," I said to him as we climbed into the comfortable car and Hunt instructed the chauffeur. "Can you explain just what it's all about. I know that someone wants to discuss negotiating with me a transaction but that is all I know.

"Since I first heard that the Supremo—whatever or whoever that is—was interested in what I had to offer, I have been given nothing but perpetual motion and a goulash of words of the sort that I think you Yankees call gobbledygook."

Hunt chuckled. "I can well understand," he said. "But you and your project are so secret that even I don't know what it's all about. SHAPE is headquarters of the NATO alliance's high command. It means Supreme Headquarters, Allied Powers, Europe. I suppose you know what NATO is?" I nodded.

"General Alfred M. Gruenther is the commander-in-chief of NATO in Europe and of SHAPE. I am supposed to deliver you to him. And the curious thing is that for reasons I don't understand, I am supposed to deliver you at his house. You are a very special, precious property. If you would care to look behind you'll see what I mean."

I looked. No less than four automobiles followed us in a carefully separated row. All were filled with men and it took little imagination to reckon they were armed.

"It is now fifteen eleven," said Hunt, looking at his wrist. "I am to have you there at fifteen forty-five. We should do it easily. And I believe that when we arrive I say farewell. I will turn you over to one of Gruenther's staff. He is an English brigadier named Fergusson."

Soon we drove through a village, slowed down abruptly, came to a gate rather ineffectually guarded by a uniformed French gendarme and a white-helmeted American military policeman, and then turned up a driveway. I noticed that our retinue of protective cars respectfully halted outside.

There seemed to be a total lack of security precautions as the car rolled along a gravelled drive and parking lot to a pleasant white country house set upon a rise beneath fine trees and overlooking a green lawn that sloped to a pond and flower garden. An officer wearing formal accouterments and a bird insignia on each of his shoulders opened the door as we drew to a halt. Hunt led the way out.

He introduced me, asked the colonel to have an M.P. detachment unload my sacks, then turned, shook my hand and said, "It's been a pleasure meeting you, Mr. Sasounian." He jumped back in, drove off. The colonel stood politely with me while six uniformed men with white helmet liners carried my sacks into the house. They remained beside them in the entrance hall, awaiting further orders.

Having neither hat nor coat, despite the brisk winter weather here in France, to deposit with the white-jacketed servant, I was directly taken into a large and frumpishly furnished room where a group of officers, some wearing braided fourragères, was assembled. At the sill stood a tall, and most strangely old-fashioned-looking Scotsman; I could tell this from the kilt hanging about his long legs and below his regular red-tabbed officer's jacket. His bright blue eyes were made even more prominent by the monocle affixed in one of them. He had rather curly hair, a guardsman's mustache, and a very upper-class English accent.

"Brigadier Fergusson," I was advised, "of General Gruenther's Intelligence section."

"Hello Sasounian," he said. "Or should I call you Gentleman George?"

Suddenly I realized: the accent and appearance were identical and the difference between kilted uniform and Edwardian mufti was not so striking as to camouflage the resemblance between Brigadier Fergusson and Mr. Smith, the man who, so long ago, had briefed me at the behest of Naci Perkel on Soviet espionage.

"Sovershennoe Sekretno, Gaspodin Smith," I answered with a slight bow.

"Good on you. How was Armenia? Not very interesting I suspect. But we have to encourage our Turkish allies." As I frowned, he continued: "And now let me introduce you to General Gruenther."

Before I could move, a spry, little man with sharp features, long ears and nose and thinning strands of brown hair took a slightly limping stride forward and extended his hand in the friendliest and most informal way. "It's nice to meet you, Mr. Sasounian," he said. "It was good of you to come around. You may have the answer to something that's been bothering a lot of people around here. We've been hearing things about you. And not only from the Brigadier," he added with a smile. "It seems you've met before."

I kept regarding Gruenther with a puzzlement I hope I managed to mask. He was ordinary looking; you knew he would wear a brown suit and blue tie in mufti. But where had I seen that intelligent face? Suddenly I remembered. As a youngster, studying in Germany, I had been shown a famous picture of Erasmus. Here he was again—in American uniform.

There were four other officers in the room; all greeted me with friendly curiosity. Then another came rushing across the threshold, the blond young general who had piloted me from Cyprus.

"This is General Norstad, our air commander," Gruenther said. "He drove your taxi here."

"That's why I'm late," said Norstad. "I had to come by Fontainebleau."

"Now," said Gruenther, "I suggest we all sit down and then

I can explain what we want to hear from you, Mr. Sasounian."
We sat in comfortable armchairs and I glanced around at a most
unmilitary looking salon containing several religious paintings and
relics, two bridge tables, and an expensive record-player.

"There is no need to tell you that what we are about to discuss
is highly classified. There is no need for the following three
reasons. First of all, you, Mr. Sasounian, know more about the
major subject of our talk than anyone else in this room. Secondly,
I do not intend to tell you things you couldn't find out by yourself just by reading a good newspaper, the kind of thing you
can read any day in *The New York Times* by my good friend
Cy Sulzberger. And thirdly, you may not realize it but, until we
have finished with this project, you are under the strictest surveillance." A minatory hint came into his voice.

"You will remain under surveillance until we are satisfied that,
one way or another, regardless of the decision we may take,
nothing detrimental can happen to our alliance cause. Now, is
that clearly understood?"

I nodded. The General continued in a flat, middle-western voice,
as if he were giving an informal lecture to a high school class:
"It has come to our attention from various sources that you have
some mysterious formula to create fully grown, professional soldiers. I hate to say these words; it sounds like black magic. And
black magic is something that I, as a good Roman Catholic, don't
believe in.

"But I am ready to look at and listen to everything that could
conceivably help NATO. It can't be any secret to you, if you
ever read a paper in any language, that our biggest problem right
now is manpower. We have weapons superiority, and the will
to defend our civilization. But we just don't have the men at hand
to fight the kind of conventional war we would prefer to fight if,
indeed, a war must come. At least that is the way I see it personally. And I've got influence around here.

"The last thing we want to do is defend our way of life by
blowing up the world. We have to deter the other fellow. So
you see, Mr. Sasounian, what we need most is not a new kind of
weapon but men—the men to use old kinds of weapons.

"Militarily speaking, we are in a peculiar era. In ultimate terms, we are ahead. Short-term problems are our foremost concern. We aren't thinking of ten years hence but two years hence. That is where you come in, my friend.

"Right now, and it's already past 1954, we have a serious short-fall: while our West German allies are rearming, we simply don't have enough troops for our commitments in the center of Europe. Our troop requirement is not to flesh out the pipedream of our plan as conceived in 1952 at the Lisbon NATO meeting. It is to flesh out the minimum reality on which we depend.

"Quite frankly—and again without indiscretion—we need approximately ten divisions in this critical sector. It comes, all told, to about half a million troops. We see no prospect of getting them. It sounds a little crazy in my own ears to hear me ask the question; but I might as well be blunt: can you help on anything like that scale, Mr. Sasounian?"

"It will be expensive," I said, "but I am able."

"Money is no problem; we are prepared to meet almost any price if we are satisfied with your offer," Gruenther replied. "We have more gold in Fort Knox, Kentucky, than we have combat-trained soldiers in the field."

"General," I replied. "I am confident that I could help you with the problem. The price would certainly be steep; I calculate it might well amount to about a quarter of a billion dollars for half a million men. These troops, it goes without saying, would be combat-trained although, I may add, they would require weapons refresher courses of extensive duration. They are not up to date in contemporary armament.

"There is also a question of language. You would have to deputize a considerable number of officers to handle this special problem. I should suggest the best linguistic faculty might be formed around experienced Greek commanders and perhaps classicists, officers with classical educations, from other national armies.

"Quite frankly, General, I envision my contribution as more than simply provision of a vital and large contingent to an alliance which even my native land, Turkey, admires, sponsors and belongs to."

Fergusson gave me a shrewd and suspicious look. I thought I detected a wink in his right eye but speedily I reasoned that it was impossible to wink an eye that held a monocle—without dropping it.

"I think," I went on with temerity, "that the kind of supranational or international contingent I am offering could serve as a test-tube project on which your entire alliance might some day seek to model itself. This force, while substantially Greek-speaking, would owe no more loyalty to Greece than to any other of your fifteen members. It would be truly a NATO force."

I spoke with so much earnest pertinacity and passion that I almost succeeded in convincing myself. Gruenther and the others were plainly fascinated. The General said:

"That is really an interesting idea. You know, the only precedent for NATO was an ancient Greek alliance, the Delian League. And the Delian League eventually dissolved because the other members, nationalistic city-states, didn't like to be dictated to by the requirements of Athenian nationalism. If we could develop what you call a supranational force, classical Greek as its command tongue might be very fitting."

At this point, with his thoughtful eyes glittering and his sharp nose seeming to sniff the possibilities of this dazzling thought, he looked more than ever like that great classicist, Erasmus.

"Is it possible to calculate what effect those troops would have on the other fellow?" Gruenther asked.

"Yes, sir," said the Brigadier. "Our computer could come up with the answer pretty quickly if we fed it the right questions. It would certainly require the Russians to mobilize on a heavy and perceptible basis before trying anything and we'd have plenty of advance warning—which we wouldn't necessarily get right now. The computer could work out how many men the Russians would have to call up and how long it would take."

"You mean," I asked, "a machine can answer questions like that? In such detail?"

"Certainly," Gruenther answered. "If you want to get the answer to a complicated question, give it to Brigadier Fergusson and we'll get the reply before you and I have finished talking."

"Give me a question," said Fergusson.

"All right," I said. "The leaders of the Kremlin—if you will pardon me—pretend that American civilization produces nothing but shit. I know this. They told me so. Very well. I'm thirty-eight years old. With luck I should live to be seventy. If I have a defecation every day until I die and use ordinary toilet paper in ordinary amounts, how many trees will be destroyed and how much ordure will I produce?"

"I'll have the answer for you in a few minutes," said Fergusson with some acerbity and a maleficent gleam in his eye. "Will that be all, General?" Gruenther nodded and the Brigadier left our party, presumably for a telephone.

"I think you've now got a good picture of our requirements," Gruenther resumed, unperturbed, "and I admit we are impressed by your seeming confidence in your ability to handle the problem. Do I speak for all of you gentlemen?"

Gruenther looked around. The officers seemed dazed, distrait. There was such an atmosphere of unreality that they appeared to feel they were going mad or were playing parts in some weird fairy tale. "How about it, Cort?" the General inquired, looking at a very tall, solemn officer. "How about you, yourself, for example?"

The tall officer spoke in a low, quiet voice: "If this thing we are talking about works out, Al, it will solve the biggest headache on my desk right now." There was a long period of silence.

At that moment Fergusson returned and coolly said: "Here is the information, General. Shall I read it? Yes? All right, the answers are: thirty-seven full grown blue spruces. It comes to only thirty-two and a half Norway pines. As for poundage of manure, the answer is three-and-a-half tons. You, Mr. Sasounian, are capable of producing three-and-a-half tons of shit. Is that all right, sir?"

Gruenther examined him bleakly. "Let's go," was all he said. "What are we waiting for? I suggest we adjourn this discussion and get down to brass tacks. Can you give us a demonstration right away, Mr. Sasounian? Do you require special facilities or conditions?"

"The answer is yes and no, General. Yes, I can give you your demonstration. No, there are no special facilities or conditions. I have on my person the requisite materials. I need only a small space of ordinary ground, preferably of adequately watered earth. The lawn I saw when I came in will do exceedingly well, General."

Gruenther nodded. He stumped out with the agility of a very

tough little hare. The others filed after him. Fergusson took my arm and guided me. We went through the front door and down to the turbid pool where I saw a few trout lying in a torpor along the sides.

"Will this be O.K.?" the general asked.

"Yes, it is fine."

"Very well. Fergusson, be sure and have the security boys check the entire area again for snoops."

"Already done, General," said Fergusson. "Not even an eagle-eyed midget with a telescope could get a look. It's getting along for dusk and you need infra-red to penetrate this winter mist."

"Good. Now, Mr. Sasounian, we will all stand here. You must excuse these two" (he referred to a brace of M.P.s with tommy-guns who materialized from the bushes). "But we are the victims of our own precautions. There must be safeguards against any kind of accident. Now again, have you any last suggestions or advice for us?"

"Only this, General. I shall give you a demonstration involving three combat soldiers. It would be dangerous if anyone, for any reason, should cast a pebble—or indeed anything else—among them. That is the one event that might make them nervous, unpredictable, and even uncontrollable. May I ask you to give me this assurance, even though I know it is not needed."

Looking suddenly stern, Gruenther said with the authority of a grand commander: "He that is without sin among you, let him cast the first stone."

His tone was harsh. His voice was abrasive. He meant it.

CHAPTER

XVIII

By this time I was so experienced a dental merchandiser that I carried off the whole affair with aplomb and dignity, taking care only to safeguard my interests by pretending to use magical phrases and the whirligig movements of a prestidigatator as I began my demonstration. My hands spun strange designs while I muttered: "Ashkharhi djagadagire siroun aghchignerou yev gadagaser hayherou tzerken e," meaning, in my native tongue: What is the fate of lovely girls and mad Armenians?

None of my audience could possibly comprehend these esoteric words or hope to emulate my addled gestures. I trusted, therefore, that my treasure stored in the entrance of General Gruenther's house would remain safe from seizure and at the same time that this oratorical precaution would protect my own person as an evidently necessary catalytic agent.

When I had finished intruding into the dank soil of the Ile de France a trio of hairy hoplites, the usual stunned silence ensued. There was a sough of wind. Then, the general called Cort, said: "Great jumping Jehosophat! If the West knew it relied for protection on magicians it would give up."

"It might impress the Russians," said Norstad. Fergusson uttered no sound. His mouth fell open and the monocle finally dropped from his popping eye.

Gruenther issued a series of crisp commands. Fergusson was to escort me back to the General's residence and to take along one of the guards. Schuyler (which proved to be Cort's name) was to have the three tooth-men summarily overpowered, stripped, bathed, shaved, shorn and locked up in safe isolation. A certain Colonel Wood was to burn their clothing and store their metal armor and weapons under lock and key. SHAPE medical authorities were to find competent psychiatrists to examine the unexpected visitors. And any members of the Greek military mission to headquarters who perchance had received a classical education were to be listed.

As I turned, firmly prodded by Fergusson, and followed by an American tommygunner, we headed back up to the house. Behind me a group of soldiers materialized in the growing darkness. I could hear them overpowering my hoplites amid much shouting, screaming, and occasional strident yells: "Aaaaiiieee! Otototoi!"

The Brigadier took me to a very large reception room where we sat in a corner saying nothing to each other. After the elapse of much time Gruenther stumped in. He remained impeccably polite but there was no vestige of his earlier informality.

"I have just talked to the President of the United States by scrambler telephone, the device which permits completely confidential exchanges. And I told him about this, this case. He wants me to bring you over. You know, the President was NATO's first commander. He has an intense personal interest in anything concerning our alliance.

"Your sacks are already being conveyed under guard to the airport. My aide has placed your suitcase in the car that will take you there. Colonel Wood will escort you. He is armed. You will need no papers although I have been informed you have a valid Turkish passport. So much the better.

"Now then, you will depart this house in eighteen minutes. Sandwiches and drinks will be brought for you and the Brigadier. Wood will advise when to leave. I shall see you aboard the plane, my plane. Have you any questions?"

One thing, I said. I needed to prepare myself for such a journey and required replacements for the teeth I had used up. Without explaining my recondite purpose, I asked Gruenther to permit me to be left alone in a room with my treasure for just a few minutes. I used the occasion to tie three granular nubs in my handkerchief corner reckoning that more might present the possibility of trouble, especially if I were tempted to repeat the performance that had had such deadly effect on Stalin.

When I had finished I returned to Fergusson and the guards again took over. I had no more questions concerning my uncertain future nor, I noted, did Fergusson favor conversation. As I ate and drank he simply regarded me sternly through the monocle that had been firmly restored to his glowering right eye.

When I had finished Wood came in, a pleasant-looking be-spectacled American officer. We were driven in a dark Chevrolet, a guard sitting beside the army chauffeur, from the small village of Marnes-la-Coquette to Orly, a massive cluster of airports. There, in the same far corner where Norstad's plane had landed, a large four-engined plane stood with propellers slowly turning. It also was marked with the U.S. star emblem.

The colonel led me directly to the boarding steps and I followed him into a luxuriously equipped fusilage. An unusually large crew cabin, and rows of comfortable seats, were cut off from a closed compartment where, I was informed, the General himself liked to travel. He could either work there with his aides or stretch himself out to sleep.

I sat in the front row, Wood beside me, and I noticed that a group of American sergeants, all visibly armed, filed in and sprawled behind us. They seemed poured out of the same heavenly mould: close cut hair, broad shoulders, thick bellies, and steatopygous behinds.

Hardly had we begun a long, slow winding climb through the heavy cirrus accumulation of the early night when the aircraft's crew chief tapped me on the shoulder and said the General wished to see me. Wood led the way back to the commander's comfortable stateroom. I found him thoughtfully pouring a heavy brown liquid onto slices of orange, ice, and what seemed to be cherries in three squat glasses.

"Come in, Mr. Sasounian," he said, without looking up and concentrating intensely on the concoctions before him. "I took the liberty of making you an Old Fashioned. An American drink, you know. Bourbon whisky. But we no longer get the right kind of cherries. Not since the Jugoslavs took Zara from Italy. The Maraschino distillery people fled.

"Ah," he said, with a self-satisfied smile. "Try that. That should do the job. Here Jack," to the colonel, "I know you won't object." Then he waved us to padded armchairs.

"Now, I know I can't force you, Mr. Sasounian, but I'd certainly appreciate it if you'd tell me something about how you acquired your astonishing secret."

"I was lucky in love," I said. Succinctly, leaving out details, names and places, I recounted a version of my story. I said the discovery was turned over to me by someone whose family had been charged with its safety all these centuries since Jason's dissident custodians fled northward along the Colchis shore.

I added: "The one thing I cannot reveal is the precise formula, including movements and words involved at the instant of plantation. It is something of the order of importance of the detonating factor in an atomic bomb. But I will assure you, General, I am in a position to promise without qualification that I possess the entire and multitudinous lot. There aren't any more on earth."

"Well, sir," said Gruenther, "it must be pretty obvious how impressed we are. Otherwise I wouldn't be flying you to see the President. But you are in possession of a secret that might mean the difference between war and peace in the next couple of decades, of a secret which is important to NATO's survival.

"The President is the only man with authority to deal with this matter. But before you expose its workings to him, I want you to understand its significance to us.

"You see, just to say that the United States has a nuclear deterrent won't keep NATO together. So we are trying to work out a forward strategy—right up to the Iron Curtain.

"So far, we cannot match the Russians in conventional weapons and conventional manpower. The only thing to do is to make war impossible, not to abolish one category of weapons as has been suggested for nuclear weapons."

"I agree, excellent sir" said I, assuming the pose of a strategist, like Sultan Mehmet.

"Yet we may be forced to reduce our living standards by trying to keep the requisite defensive force in being," Gruenther continued. "We would have to reduce our living standards even more by trying to match the Russians in conventional weapons and manpower than by keeping a force that relies on tactical atomic weapons."

"So you want to put teeth into your defenses?" I inquired, pleased with the pun. Gruenther paid no attention. He went on:

"Now I don't know if it would ever be possible to train men like yours in the use of nuclear arms although I suspect the problem would be easier than one might think. After all, if you are going to promote people suddenly from the bronze age to TNT and tanks, why not promote them an inch further into time?

"Moreover, I was intrigued by the idea you mentioned of an international or supranational contingent. NATO's great weakness is that no allied commander has the authority to reply immediately—and I mean immediately—to any Soviet action in Europe. He must first consult his governments, all fifteen of them. That is just too late for effective action. Yet no member of the Alliance is prepared to write a blank check in advance giving a commander such authority.

"But if we had at our disposal a critical shock force that owed allegiance to NATO as a whole and not to any member nation, the Alliance might be able to draft the necessary diplomatic agreements allowing for its immediate use.

"And I'll tell you another thing. We should be in the guerrilla and subversion field more than we are. This is a national problem rather than a NATO problem. Guerrilla action has been relegated to a second place consideration because it is regarded as a national problem.

"In other words, if any army began to occupy part of a country, guerrilla action in that occupied country would be the responsibility of the nation itself. It is very difficult to coordinate guerrilla planning and subversion planning during peacetime. This requires a high degree of centralized authority—as in Russia.

"Here again, however, it is possible to conceive of using a supranational force for guerrilla purposes—a specialized NATO reserve for use under given circumstances. This is the first time we have even been able to imagine thinking in such a way.

[259

"Therefore, you should now have a good idea of why you interest us so much. And also now, sir, I think you should go to bed. That is what I intend to do. See you in the morning."

I put down the drink, which was peculiar in taste and name, but clearly contained alcohol, and shook hands with the likable little general. Then Wood led me forward. We arranged two tiers of seats in such a way that, with blankets and pillows made available by the crew, we could stretch out comfortably. The last thing I noted before dozing off amid the canoe-like swaying motion of the plane was the row of stolid, short-cropped, overfed sergeants sitting in line behind us.

Rather to my astonishment, when we were awakened amid the unfurled darkness of the transatlantic dawn, the crew came down the aisle serving an immense breakfast including beefsteaks. I ate little. Behind me I could hear the munching of my burly guardians.

Military precision marked our arrival. Gruenther descended the ramp first, shook hands with whispering officers and disappeared into an enormous black car. Wood led me down, advising me not to worry about my cargo which was being unloaded by a security detail. He conducted me to a second car which whizzed off with a sticky noise in the direction where I imagined Washington to be.

It was still early when we drove up a short street between a massive square building on the right and the wing of what seemed to be a haphazard set of connected structures on the left. "This is the East Gate entrance," the colonel said. "It is more discreet. The press hangs out at the other end of the White House. They are very inquisitive about visitors. For your own good and our good we want to keep you out of harm's way."

Within the foyer, beside a paunchy policeman, stood a bald, mustachioed officer with sullen, scorbutic face. "General Schulz," said Wood. "I now turn you over to his care. Goodbye. I don't know if I'll be seeing you again."

"That sounds ominous," I replied, shaking hands with Schulz and following him inside. He said little in his corrosive, querulous voice, merely beckoning me along an intricate arrangement of corridors. "Wait here," he told me as we came to a glass door.

Through it I watched him go down a long, pleasant lawn. It was green and featured by several huge, graceful trees with crinkling leaves.

An instant later he returned. "The President is practicing golf shots," said Schulz. "General Gruenther is with him. You are wanted there." His manner had become that of a toady.

We stepped out into the pleasantly crisp air. A lukewarm, red sun had risen above the line of saffron and russet treetops. Schulz conducted me around a bunch of bushes to a nook obscured from both the grill fence bordering the lawn and from the presidential residence itself. There I saw Gruenther, now wearing civilian clothes—the brown suit and azure shirt I had expected—talking in modulated tones with a tall, blue-eyed man wearing a pince nez, and another extremely handsome white-haired man with well chiselled features.

They were watching while still another man in sweater and visored cap, whose rubicund face I immediately recognized from photographs, bent over a little white ball, holding a steel-headed metal stick in his two hands. He leaned, then stopped abruptly, strode to a worm wriggling across the grass and stomped it, saying: "I kill the bastards whenever I can. I got into the habit with caterpillars. They ruin the trees."

He returned to the little white ball and again bent down over it, his legs apart. "Lord, give me strength to hit it easy," he muttered. Then he dipped, swung the stick, and off went the ball on a high loop toward the trees.

"Now that's the way to hit an eight iron," said the President. "That ball went a country mile."

"Mr. President," said Gruenther, who took over the major domo functions from Schulz while waving the latter in dismissal, "this is the famous Mr. Sasounian."

"Well now," said Eisenhower. "I'm glad to meet you. Al here tells me very interesting things about you. Unbelievable, if you ask me."

"And these," said Gruenther, continuing his introductions, "are Mr. Dulles and General Snyder. Mr. Dulles is chief of our Central Intelligence Agency. General Snyder is the President's trusted

[261

friend and personal physician. We thought it might be well to have him here during your demonstration."

I felt as if I and my weirdly fissiparous secret were intruding into the bowels of America's locker-room civilization.

"Young fellow," said the President, regarding me with skeptical but wide blue, lucent eyes that so captured my attention I forgot the snub nose, unimpressive to a nobly featured Armenian, and the ridiculous appearance of his cap, "General Gruenther here has told me such a screwy tale about you that, had it been anyone else, I'd have known they were out of their mind.

"Now I've got a pretty good idea of what you're supposed to be able to do. That's why I've asked Mr. Dulles and General Snyder here. This is as discreet a place as I can think to conduct this crazy kind of experiment. The fewer who see it the better, whether it works or doesn't work.

"And the only Secret Service men around here are so close-mouthed and loyal that I don't have to worry about them leaking on that score. Nobody can see us here. Even from the White House itself," he added, pointing a semicircular arc with the metal stick in his hand. "We are cut off by the trees and bushes.

"I suppose there isn't any reason why you shouldn't go to work right now. We've all of us got lots to do and General Gruenther says this is exactly the kind of place you like to operate in. Last time, he says—yesterday—you did your job right out there on the lawn of my old house at Marnes.

"All right, get going. And Al," he added, turning to General Gruenther, with a sudden glint in his eyes, "if this thing doesn't work the way you say it does I'll have another job for you. I'll make you head of the Red Cross."

I noticed the faintest movement in a bush behind the President. Some discreet guard was doing his work. Then Mr. Dulles took me gently by the elbow and led me toward the center of the demilune copse, inquiring if a flat patch of grass, cleared of drifting leaves, would suit my purpose. I said yes, but I was curiously worried. My desire to perform had been strangely embraced with doubts and sunk to the merest velleity.

"Curses upon you, Mher, plotter of evil," I murmured to myself. "You are like Antichrist, you who grew on the earth."

Without more ado, I turned my back on the distinguished audience, poked my finger deep into the damp earth, whisked one grain from my handkerchief pocket, made cabalistic gestures, dropped it in, patted the dirt back, and again proclaimed loudly in my melodious language: "What is the fate of lovely girls and mad Armenians?"

The result was immutably foreordained. Within an agonizing moment of silence there thrust forward from the ground an Attic javelineer with all the gear of the akontistai, the two long horse-hair sphendoné cords, the leather pouch of stone and clay shots and the short akontion spear attached to its propulsive thong.

"Well, I'll be . . ." said the President, holding his jaw in one hand and relinquishing the metal stick. Mr. Dulles took off his pince nez and wiped them on his handkerchief as if to remove the image of what he had seen. The blood drained from his face. Snyder wasn't even looking at the javelin-thrower. He stared at Eisenhower with evident concern.

"Are you all right, Ike?" he asked, forgetting protocol in his worry. "Remember your heart." Gruenther's carefully composed face mirrored inner contentment. There was a noise in the bushes, a rustling and a thump. "My God, Joe's fainted," came a low voice, presumably from the Secret Service.

At last the ashen Dulles spoke. "If you've gulled us on this, Sasounian," he said, "it's the greatest conjuring trick since Aaron diddled Pharaoh."

Suddenly Gruenther barked an order. Two men with drawn pistols emerged from the shrubbery behind the dazed Greek, still blinking and brushing clods of dirt from his shaggy face. One smote him just below the ear, where his leather helmet gave no protection. The pistol butt promptly rendered him unconscious. The other injected him in the shoulder from a long syringe.

"It's a tranquilizer as you ordered, Al," said General Snyder. "I suggest you boys wrap him in your overcoats. Take him to my office. He'll be out of the way there. With his lack of resistance to modern drugs we should be able to quiet him under sedation for days, if need be. Arrange that nobody except myself is allowed in. Nobody."

"I guess you'd better all come in with me," the President ruminated. "Yes, that includes Sasounian. I don't suppose any chief of this state or commander of its armed forces has ever faced a problem like this. By golly, its implications are more fateful than Hiroshima."

Closely attended by Snyder, he led the way around the secluded low clump to a doorway, entered, swung left through an office where silent secretaries regarded us, and then took us into an almost round room with wall-to-wall carpet, comfortable chairs, a large desk, and the seal and personal banner of the American President.

"Sit down, gentlemen," he said. "This is going to be a son-of-a-bitch of a decision. No word of what we say is to get past this office. Apart from security, I don't want any of those damned politicians getting a hint of this.

"Anybody who reads the Federalist papers, as I have, will see that the people who wrote our Constitution thought it over for a long time and very carefully before they came to any decisions. But they never thought about anything like this. How could they? Not even I did until just now. Or yesterday, when Al called me on the scrambler.

"Now let's see what it means," he meandered on, leaning back in his desk chair as the rest of us, following Dulles's example, pulled our fauteuils closer to him.

"Everybody knows we're short on troops in NATO. We'll certainly be short at least until the Germans have rearmed. Maybe even after.

"But one task of our governments is to spread the moral principles of NATO: freedom, peace, self-defense. Each soldier must think about the Alliance, about his own country, and his cause.

"Sure we need troops. But it is going to be impossible to give them the same kind of morale if we make an army out of these . . . these . . . people. You may train them with weapons. But you can't train them with ideas. They'd die of old age first. And they're not Greeks; they belong to city states and rival tribes. Isn't that so, Mr. Sasounian? That's about the way General Gruenther has presented it to me."

I nodded assent.

"Okay then. What that leaves is something like the mercenary units which have so often fought in past wars. You know, one of my favorite books is 'The White Company.' There were all kinds of English and Swiss companies that sold their services in medieval and Renaissance Italy. But the problem presented now bears no comparison.

"I don't say your soldiers, Mr. Sasounian, wouldn't be very good soldiers. Good soldiers in fact might be found elsewhere. They might be found among emigrés in Europe, refugees from communism, or among adventurous-minded Germans. But they would have to be organized in some form of foreign legion.

"Anyway, I don't like this kind of approach. War is no longer a private effort of gentlemen commanding mercenary armies. It is a great and brutal effort on the part of entire nations.

"What I would like is to find some Peter the Hermit who could lead a crusade for our ideals and enlist the enthusiastic support of all democratic populations. But I don't see any Peter the Hermit types around. And mercenaries certainly aren't the answer.

"The biggest fundamental problem we face is morale and public opinion. Any alliance of democratic powers has to respond to the public opinion of each one of them. And this isn't an easy thing to resolve. So you can see that your answer, my Armenian friend, can't meet this difficulty either.

"You are not going to stir up public enthusiasm for a barbarian force of mercenaries, no matter how well we train them. And Lord knows how we'd explain their origin. Imagine our own Congress. Think what those goddamned Democrats and leftists would do with that one.

"And then there's another point, Mr. Sasounian. The trouble with your secret—your secret army—is that it is outmoded. It was a great advantage to have more trained manpower in the days of Cadmus, in the days of Jason, and right down to the days of Haig or Ludendorff or Foch. And I know Al Gruenther. Like every general since time began he wants more troops. But, even if we have a short-fall now on the NATO side, there are too many soldiers in the world. Troops aren't the real answer anymore.

"Until recently they were. Look at China. By golly, look at China. Or Russia. Marshal Zhukov told me he used to send infantry ahead of tanks through mine fields so the men could get blown up first, clearing a path for the armor.

"I'd like your army of tooth-men, Mr. Sasounian. On paper, it's the answer to a planner's dream. On paper, it's the one way we could swiftly plug the gap that busts our blueprints. But the real fact is, the long range fact, that we need cheaper and more efficient ways of destroying enemy soldiers, not of creating our own.

"When the enemy knows we can kill his soldiers off, he will stop making bigger armies. That is the deterrent! When he knows that! That is my goal, gentlemen, and I don't think we're going to find the solution in a crash training program for a half a million hoplites.

"And I would like to add one thing. You don't need men for fighting nowadays. You need machines. You don't need unmotivated men like yours. You need motivated machines. That's what my problem has become."

I could feel a tremendous psychological change in the President. He had made up his mind after thinking aloud, weighing the advantages and disadvantages of the problem. And once the moment of decision had been reached and surmounted, his personality altered.

He was not a large man, certainly not by my standards; nor did he seem impressive or dynamic with his button features, bald head and pink skin. But now he seemed to swell, like a genie in its bottle. The tint of his complexion darkened and became rubescent as blood suffused his face. He gave the impression of somehow growing and dominating the room.

"Do you agree, gentlemen?" he inquired. "Yes, Mr. President," said Dulles although there was an unmistakable hint of disappointment in this expression. "Yes, sir," said Gruenther in a brittle voice. Snyder nodded.

Eisenhower made a slight gesture and Dulles arose to escort me. The President thanked me courteously, much as if we had been discussing a minor business deal. He arose, came out from behind his desk and shook my hand.

Then I joined the C.I.A. chief and the physician, going out past the antechamber through which we had arrived and wandering down the hall where Snyder showed me a little room filled with stuffed, mounted salt water fish, and other angling trophies.

"President Roosevelt's," said Snyder. "He was quite a fisherman. Nobody ever knew where to put the results. So they just dumped them on me."

He regarded me through his kindly eyes. "Don't be too disappointed, young man," he said. "You'll live through it. So will we all. And there's no point ever thinking you can repeat the story, even years later. Everyone would believe you mad."

Gruenther had stayed behind in the oval presidential office. After a few minutes, he came walking springily down the uncarpeted hall, his clipclop stride detectable by the echo of his limp.

"Come along, young fellow," he said as if nothing had happened and taking me by the elbow. "You may not believe it but we're off again to Europe. I have a pretty heavy schedule." Then he added: "I am authorized to tell you that your girl is safe in Paris. Now, isn't that something?"

He said nothing about the recent conversation and events. But, when he saw the look of doubt on my face, he added: "Don't worry, pal. Orders have been given to put your hoard aboard." I know English well, as a linguistics expert, but I simply couldn't tell whether he meant "hoard" or "horde."

Just as we were about to depart through a different and perhaps even more discreet door, the professorial Mr. Dulles appeared abruptly. He took me aside, peered carefully at me through his gleaming pince nez and murmured: "It is only fair to tell you since you have been quite honest with us that we have received a very plain hint from Moscow that were we to make use of your secret—of which, I gather, they seem to know at least a bit—they would regard it as a hostile act. From Serov himself. Very, very unusual. I thought you should know, young man. It may help you to understand what happens." He regarded me impassively, nodded, and waved farewell with a gesture like a Roman salute.

When we arrived at the airport amid gathering swirls of fog our convoy of four automobiles drew up before a different plane. This time it was an enormous, high, monstrously cumbersome affair.

The same six sergeants were busily at work heaving up freight, including my precious sacks, shifting them from a fork-lift to a doorway in the bottom of the aircraft where helping hands and other mechanical devices seemed to have no difficulty moving everything inside. As I followed Gruenther and Wood, climbing through an entry port that forced me to stoop uncomfortably, I noticed the only resemblance to the carrier that had brought us across the Atlantic was the silver U.S. Air Force star and lettering on the side.

Within it was like a clumsy ferryboat. Gruenther beckoned me to a seat beside him on a kind of padded bench, a bunk where tired crew members slept on long flights. In front, the cockpit was filled with efficient looking flyers nattering into the communications equipment attached to their ears and throats. I don't know where Wood, the sergeants and our other companions vanished in that immense vehicle. But I imagined that by now the General trusted me entirely, since we sat together alone, strapped in by belts, regarding the highly professional activities of the flying crew.

There was no window on either side of us and, judging from our climb, first into the plane and then mounting the various steps, I reckoned we must be at least the height of a four story building. Yet I felt the great dinosaur slowly muster strength. There was a kind of gentle heave and soon, by looking at the clouds through the bemisted windshield, I knew the contraption was actually flying.

For a long time Gruenther said nothing, leaving me to my troubled ruminations. Then he suddenly looked askance at me and asked: "Tell me, Mr. Sasounian, is it a great advantage to be a linguist and an expert in linguistics? I have often wondered."

"Well, General," I replied. "It depends what you want to say and to whom. The Emperor Charles V, they say, recommended that Spanish should be spoken to the gods, French to men, Italian to ladies, German to soldiers, Hungarian to horses, Czech to the devil, and English to geese.

"Medieval scholars proved to their own satisfaction that Eve was seduced in Italian, Adam was misled in Czech, the Lord scolded both in German, and the Archangel Gabriel drove them out of Eden in Hungarian. The Persians claimed Gabriel spoke Turkish because they considered it the most menacing of tongues. Personally, I agree with the Persians."

Gruenther looked impressed. He scratched his chin and reflected. A man who seemed to be the flight engineer came back with coffee and sandwiches in waxed paper. We munched, sipped, and after a while I dozed. It had been a difficult if in-

268]

conclusive day. There was nothing I could do to ascertain the course of its dénouement until the General was ready to tell me.

I don't know how long I slept. I was in the middle of a dream that I was back again in that awful fishtank on the "Gruzia" and Rima, appearing alluringly meretricious, was rapping, rapping, rapping on the door. Then I felt someone punching my shoulder. It was Gruenther. "Well, fellow," he said, "No one would ever believe what we've just been through. And I know that's only a tiny part of the tale as far as you're concerned.

"Think what a newspaperman could do with this. You know, I was a newspaperman myself once. My father ran a weekly in Nebraska, the *Platte Center Signal*. I'd help out by setting type and writing articles. Once I wrote an editorial. It criticized appropriating funds for the military. What do you think of that?"

I didn't know what to say nor could I possibly understand the purpose of the conversation. But before I could think of an answer Colonel Wood emerged, tapped me on the shoulder, nodding to the General, and said: "It's all ready, sir. Come with me if you don't mind, Mr. Sasounian."

Gruenther looked at me curiously. He said: "We are over the Newfoundland Basin. It is one of the deepest troughs in the North Atlantic—three miles deep."

I followed Wood down an awkward stairway. Suddenly we were in a vast chamber, high, wide, and immensely long, occupying virtually the whole aircraft.

At the forward end I saw my sacks, attached to a series of steel barrels arranged on twin rollers that led, like a railway spur, to a broad rectangular gap which, from the noise and cold wind rushing through, evidently lay open to the winter night. The six sergeants still looking heavy, leaden-featured and identical as a sounder of swine, stood by the sacks and barrels examining a tangle of straps and ropes.

"Now," said Wood, regarding his wristwatch. "Now is the moment. This is an order from General Gruenther." And all of a sudden, as the pilot nosed the plane up to tilt the ramp toward its tail, the barrels began to roll. Heavily, noisily, they rumbled down to the rectangular gap, pulling my sacks along. Suddenly they disappeared into the darkness, whop, whop, whop.

I screamed. I think it is the only time I have ever screamed. I turned on Wood in a rage as he drew a pistol from beneath his jacket. Before he was provoked into using it, someone clubbed me sharply from behind. As I sank into unconsciousness, I knew from long experience in Turkey that it was a blackjack.

How much later I came to didn't matter because, far transcending the throb within my skull, was the sudden awareness that all the power and wealth I once possessed had suddenly left me, that again I was the poor Armenian, like all my race again deceived by friends. I was lying on the crew bunk. Gruenther, with a sad expression, was helping the flight engineer and Wood to pour brandy down my throat from a small metal cup.

"You are the greatest mass-murderer in history," I spat at the little general. "My siblings. My siblings. All alone, single-handed, you are responsible for the death of half a million men. You are another Hitler, worse than Genghis Khan."

Gruenther paid no attention. With intense solemnity he read softly aloud from a small blue book held so tightly in his two hands that the knuckles stood out white. "For Thou restrainest the wicked desires of men's souls," he read, "and settest them their bounds, how far they may be allowed to pass, that their waves may break one against another: and thus makest Thou it a sea."

He closed the book gently, looked at me and said: "St. Augustine. The Confessions."

"You talk of Saints," I grumbled. "You talk of God. If you killed God for my poor siblings, before they could even know Him, you killed God for all of us. How can God's own creatures, even if inanimate, be godless?" Suddenly I sprang at him, stretching out my arms and remembering how at fifteen Mher had strangled a lion with his own hands; but Wood and two of the sergeants held me back.

"Now calm down, Mr. Sasounian," said Gruenther. "I am obeying the orders of my commander-in-chief, the President of the United States. And you might be interested to know that, in extremis, I have full authority to send you over with your precious cargo.

"You might also be interested to know that I put up quite an argument for your case. I made an argument you never thought of. I said that, after all, if there ever was a nuclear holocaust, we could first have these teeth planted in slowly dissolving capsules.

"Thereby, after every vestige of mankind had been destroyed, seven years later, when the radiation vanished, we could thus be sure the earth was again inhabited by humans. But the President rightly pointed out that, as far as we know, you have no Amazons in your collection, only men. There could be no more than a single generation. That ended that.

"Now I am a Roman Catholic. As you may have heard, we consider artificial contraception and abortion immoral. A form of murder. It involves destruction of souls, even their destruction prior to actual birth. I admit it is hard to define precisely what a soul is. Our Catholic Encyclopedia defines it as the ultimate internal principle by which we think, feel and will and by which our bodies are animated."

"But you killed my men," I insisted. Although remembering a similar argument with Rima, so long ago in the Bird Rock cavern.

"I gave this matter an incredible amount of thought," said Gruenther. "As a Catholic, it was not an easy decision. But the most difficult decisions must sometimes be taken, I am sorry to say. And I decided these could not be considered humans in any sense endowed with souls.

"During the War, I was chief of staff in Italy. But it was as the only high-ranking Catholic officer that I was consulted on whether to bomb the Abbey of Monte Cassino when we learned the Germans were using it as an observation post.

"Well, I decided it was. That is one of the tragedies of war. This time again I was faced with a decision. The President specifically asked me for an opinion because he knows about my religion.

"I told the President that this was a subject of grave concern to Catholics. You, not being a Protestant, are perhaps unaware that we are much stricter than they are on the sanctity of any form of human life. It was Martin Luther, after all, who argued that a twelve-year-old idiot should be drowned because he was mere flesh, massa carnis, created by the devil since there was no soul within. No Catholic could ever endorse such bestial heresy.

[271

"I told the President he was right, after all: we could not use these mercenary tooth-men and we could never risk that they might fall in someone else's hands, some enemy's. I said teeth from a pagan era that apparently bore the capability of becoming barbarians with an apparently human form could not, if destroyed, be by any definition considered as souls affected by original sin.

"This is dogmatically sound. It cannot be doctrinally determined that such a people, your tooth people, were in any way visited by Christ."

"Nevertheless," I sputtered, "they were men. You murdered them by drowning them."

"Murder? Would they be drowned on their way to the bottom? Is an acorn the same as an oak?"

"But these were men, at least potentially. At least if given a chance. You saw yourself."

"It is theologically demonstrable that they cannot assume any form of life," Gruenther rejoined. "By the time they descend three miles among the seaweed—if there is any—they will arrive as lifeless teeth, the discarded, primeval teeth of a dragon that never existed. There will be no half-million skeletons drifting along the bottom of the Newfoundland Basin. Because the teeth had never first been touched by earth."

"What a disingenuous theology," I spat out with savage venom. "You true-believers who consider birth control a crime because it hampers the implantation of seed! And what are my teeth but seeds? If they are seeds of trouble and of war and death, does this in any way distinguish them from the seeds of other men, of sperm? Hah!"

Bitterly I reflected: once again, like so many Armenians before me on the verge of tasting the power and the glory, I was a little man who failed.

XIX

F ATE so often brings one to one's antecedents and now I am a maquereau with three girls running for me on the Rue Godot de Mauroy in Paris. Godot de Mauroy was a nineteenth century wood merchant. My merchandise is livelier but also produces heat. Anyway my girls say: "We aren't made of wood."

The métier is harder in Paris than in Istanbul but then I am a man of much experience. In 1946 the women's liberation movement forced through a law outlawing respectable lupanars like the Sphynx and the House of All Nations. Madame Marthe Richard got the system changed in the Chamber, despite the quiet opposition of the Church which, as Gruenther indicated, is wise in human matters and which also was said to have certain real estate investments likely to be damaged.

But if the big money suffered, the "loi Marthe Richard" gave new opportunities to the girls and to enterprising small businessmen like myself. We make out, my charges and I, in the neighborhood's little maisons de passe. Jacquie and Nicole are good workers and reliable.

There is a restaurant, L'Horizon, in the next street, and we all have lunch each day together before they start their trade. The proprietor is a fellow Armenian and serves good Levantine food although he is a timid man of thin spirits. Sometimes we share a raki and a gossip during the long afternoons.

In any case, as the girls go off laughing, arm in arm, I always sit a while over a Turkish coffee, unsweetened, the way Naci Perkel served it, dreaming of the past and what might have been.

Sometimes I go for long, morose walks and I think about the frail little French children with big eyes and small features furiously kicking rubber balls around the Tuileries. I remember my own dreams, and conjecture about theirs.

Then I fumble in my pocket and feel a slight totemic dent in my handkerchief. I had two precious teeth left over, after the disaster, but one of them got lost in a laundromat. I suppose its fate was precisely that of its brethren in the Newfoundland Basin.

But I have one yet and I cherish it, wrapping it carefully in its soft linen corner. And I wonder: will I ever use it? Will I demonstrate to unbelievers how once I had the world within my grasp? Will I prove the phantasmal incubus that was mine?

As I have earlier written, we Armenians have a poem which says: "From my soul I wish to wash off the dust" and I suppose it is this aching mood that has impelled me to recount my tale. It is a tale some fragments of which are obviously known by famous men still living as I write my notes in L'Horizon on idle afternoons.

Surely they will never comment; no statesman willingly subjects himself to ridicule. It is far easier to pretend ignorance behind the mummery of classified information and national security, to bask in the maze of distorted photographs, fingerprints, foibles, files, and rubber stamps in which the idiosyncrasies of our age are tucked away to lie undetected by time, like the glorious dust of departed pharaohs beneath their pyramids.

Stalin and Beria are dead and these events, like many other dreadful secrets, with them. Anastas Mikoyan, whose survival talents are the equal of my own, if on a higher plane, can be relied upon to be discreet.

Ben Gurion is not the man to willingly make himself out a fool. Before their deaths Nasser, the marvelous tightrope acrobat, had no desire to dig any pits to add to those already studding his Pan-Arab path, and Eisenhower clearly had enough troubles with his slowly declining health. Gruenther, justly or not, was after all named by Eisenhower to head the Red Cross. A brilliant and effective man, he is the acme of permanent tact; unlike me, he has not even written any memoirs. Kim Roosevelt left the spook business for public relations, a different form of human engineering, and Brigadier Fergusson went on to become Governor General of New Zealand before retiring to pleasant memories and the House of Lords.

As for the rest, there really is not much to say. They have changed the name of Abanoz Street in Istanbul to Halas. Abanoz means ebony and Halas means liberation which some have been eager to interpret in a moral sense. The new Halas Street connects Ball Street and Weeping Willow Street and is now a busy taxi passage, serving as a shortcut between more distinguished portions of the town. Sordid ghosts peer from the shabby houses that remain on either side.

Ahmed Emin's body was found floating in the Marmora Sea, in swollen, battered condition. Issa apparently got herself well sewed up by a competent surgeon because she is now married, fat, unhappy, and has six children by, I assume, the carpet-bagging Copt she wed.

Oh, and I almost forgot. Shamyl died of liver trouble. He was not one of those long-living Abkhazians to whom the drinking horn was like that of the rhinoceros, endowed with sustaining vigor. And Rima? Rima actually got away. The C.I.A. did help her out and she left word with Archbishop Manoukian. She is well and happy.

How do I know? She is the best of the three girls who run for me on the Rue Godot de Mauroy. She earns twice as much as the others.

This is a New York Times book.

I wish to acknowledge the editorial help of Kay Chernush, Susan Sevray, Isabel Bass and, above all, of my wife, Marina. Also the tolerant and helpful comments on the manuscript from Clem Wood, Irwin Shaw, Arthur Koestler, and James Jones.

Furthermore, thanks are due to Macmillan, London and Basingstoke, and to St. Martin's Press, New York, for permission to quote occasional lines from English language editions of "Heroic Poetry" by Sir Maurice Bowra.

C.L.S.